The
WILD ORCHID
Society

LAURIE MOORE

Thorndike Press • Waterville, Maine

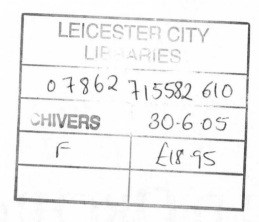
Copyright © 2004 by Laurie Moore

This novel is a work of fiction. Names, characters, places and incidents are either the product of the author's imagination, or, if real, used fictitiously.

Published in 2004 by arrangement with
Tekno Books and Ed Gorman.

Thorndike Press® Large Print Women's Fiction.

The tree indicium is a trademark of Thorndike Press.

The text of this Large Print edition is unabridged.
Other aspects of the book may vary from the original edition.

Set in 16 pt. Plantin.

Printed in the United States on permanent paper.

ISBN 0-7862-7155-8 (lg. print : hc : alk. paper)

For my daughter Laura —
my pride and joy, and my best work.

As the Founder/CEO of NAVH, the only national health agency solely devoted to those who, although not totally blind, have an eye disease which could lead to serious visual impairment, I am pleased to recognize Thorndike Press* as one of the leading publishers in the large print field.

Founded in 1954 in San Francisco to prepare large print textbooks for partially seeing children, NAVH became the pioneer and standard setting agency in the preparation of large type.

Today, those publishers who meet our standards carry the prestigious "Seal of Approval" indicating high quality large print. We are delighted that Thorndike Press is one of the publishers whose titles meet these standards. We are also pleased to recognize the significant contribution Thorndike Press is making in this important and growing field.

Lorraine H. Marchi, L.H.D.
Founder/CEO
NAVH

* Thorndike Press encompasses the following imprints: Thorndike, Wheeler, Walker and Large Print Press.

Acknowledgments

In memoriam: Griff Moore, E. G. and Lenore Frels, Grant Morrison and Wallace Hassell. Beloved family members who influenced my life in the most positive of ways.

And for making my world a more interesting place, many thanks to my family and friends; the two Jims; Judge Patrick Ferchill and Judge Steve M. King; Hazel Rumney and my editor, Mary Smith of Five Star; my agent, Peter Miller, of PMA Literary and Film Management, Inc.; and the authors and aspiring authors at DFWWW.

Finally, to the men and women of The Blue who have dedicated themselves to protect and serve the Panther City, you have my admiration.

Chapter One

Something went terribly wrong.

By the time homicide detective Cézanne Martin felt the sting of Deputy Chief Daniel J. Rosen's fingers digging into the small of her back, the chief's hatchet man had already pushed her into the cluster of microphones set up beneath the front portico of the Fort Worth Police Department. Directional lights from a half dozen TV mini-cams brightened the blue shroud of winter, and each flick of the switch spotlighted her.

She looked beyond the podium at the frenzy of reporters and vapor-locked. The media lusted after allegations of police misconduct, and this particular pack expected a juicy story to break.

In a ventriloquist's voice meant only for Cézanne, Rosen spoke through clenched teeth. "It's the old Chinese curse — you got what you wished for." His hand dropped away and his lips peeled back over his teeth to form a tight grin.

She glanced at the chief flanking her other side. The old man looked into the distance with the thousand-yard stare of a combat veteran and she suspected he was thinking about the Lady Godiva murder. Anyone in Tarrant County who wasn't dead or in a coma knew the Mayor and City Council were meeting in two weeks to decide his future. If the exposure of lurid details in the Carri Crane killing sent the PD reeling with a political black eye, the scandal caused the chief to politically hemorrhage. The man's job was hanging by a tourniquet.

Rosen inched over, snaked his arm around her shoulder, and gave her an avuncular squeeze. Reporters may have been taken in by his apparent show of camaraderie, but Cézanne understood. Knowing too much had made her a threat. He slid his hand down the back of her sleeve and dug in hard enough to make her hunch involuntarily.

With mock cheer, he said, "I give you the acting Captain of Homicide, Cézanne Martin," as if he'd just slit the Price-Waterhouse envelope and pulled out the card announcing Best Director. "For the past three years, our little homicide detective attended night school to get her law degree. Cézanne passed the bar and now she's a newly licensed attorney, so the City of Fort Worth will be in capable hands."

He clapped her shoulder hard enough to perform the Heimlich maneuver. His message: he wasn't proud of her, she infuriated him. That she possessed an arsenal of intimate details linking him to the cover-up of the Lady Godiva murder was enough for him to wish her a gory rendezvous with a high-speed bus.

"Yessirree." Rosen pressed the flat of his hand into her back until he positioned her directly in front of the mike cluster, "We thought for awhile we might lose her to a corporate law firm, but she's still here."

He's thinking, Damn the luck.

Freezing temperatures on top of a fifteen-mile-per-hour wind chill factor undermined her attempts to keep her legs from shaking. Locking her knees together did nothing; instead, they seemed to be made of melted wax. The viewing audience expected confidence from The Blue.

She forced a smile.

At the rear of the pack, a question pierced the din and Rosen fielded it. While he worked his charisma on a racehorse redhead with a seductive twinkle, Cézanne absently recalled a maxim of police work drilled into her by her old partner, the late Roby Tyson: Any cop with a camcorder trained on him has problems. Roby would know what to do.

A fresh swell of grief inflated her chest and she fought the knot forming in her throat. It still seemed unreal. He'd been

11

gone only four days. Searching the gloomy sky, she wondered if Roby could see her through the rolling boil of storm clouds. If he could, she decided, it would hail.

Rosen was glaring at her. He must have said something.

The unmuzzled media pushed forward with microphones extended as if awaiting an answer.

"Enjoy," he mouthed without sound. Then he abandoned her.

Her pulse quickened. She only agreed to accompany the brass because Rosen promised to do the talking. That, and the fact he threatened her with insubordination. Now they were all staring. With heart racing, she swallowed hard.

How bad could it be? The liberal press only picked clean the bones of Republicans running for President, right?

The heat on her forehead increased exponentially until she was certain the foundation on her carefully made-up face would slide down her neck.

Then all hell broke loose.

Reporters pelted questions at her with the vengeance of a Biblical stoning.

"You look like a child, how old are you?"

"What kind of street experience do you have?"

"Aren't you the officer accused of killing

the exotic dancer at Ali Baba's last week?"

"Do you have anything to say about Darlene Driskoll?"

Her mind reeled. They were only here to discuss her promotion, Rosen had said so. Nobody prepped her for the sticky stuff. She looked to him for support and caught him smirking.

He knew. Son of a bitch set me up.

Backing away, she stepped on the toe of the chief's boot.

"Get your ass back up there," he growled under his breath. "You're the only one who can help me. Don't let me down."

So it was true — he'd been told to pack his stuff. Not that the department couldn't use an overhaul, but the chief's natural successor was Deputy Chief Rosen. If the Council put Rosen in charge, she was a goner.

Rosen hissed in her other ear. "You wanted the limelight, now deal with it."

Reporters lobbed questions in rapid-fire succession. She tightened her face into a mask of self-assurance and swallowed the lump in her throat. She had no canned speech to fall back on. And the public expected The Blue to radiate confidence.

Rosen held up his hands for quiet and got it.

"Good morning." Inwardly, she winced at the tentative sound of her voice. "We're

13

here to announce a few changes in the Homicide Unit."

"What are your plans to make Fort Worth safer?" Blunt and to the point.

"We'll be implementing a variety of changes under my command." Bureaucratic rhetoric tumbled out of her mouth. Her mind rushed ahead with lightning speed to amass words she could use to form coherent sentences. "The Homicide Unit needs revamping. I want quality personnel —"

"Are you saying there are no good detectives in Homicide?"

"Do you attribute the rise in crime to the lack of good cops?"

"How long have the police been doing a lousy job?"

The lightheaded rush that began behind her eyeballs migrated past her ears and settled in her lungs. Breaths came in short, shallow bursts.

"One question at a time, please. Nobody said these weren't good officers. The personnel changes I'm making will enhance —"

"Is it true you had an affair with Darlene Driskoll's husband? Isn't he a detective currently working under you?"

"That's two questions." Nobody laughed, not even a chuckle. "You'll have to ask whoever started those rumors. I only started the one about me and Brad Pitt."

Stoney faces told her that her feeble

attempt at levity bombed. When she looked around for Rosen, she caught her reflection in the window glass of the front foyer and saw her pained features frozen into a speechless trance. Rosen had stepped off to one side where he apparently had lost his voice and turned to granite, disguising himself as a piece of statuary between two flagpoles.

She found herself lapsing into pre-rehearsed jargon.

"Deputy Chief Rosen's given me the authority to make whatever personnel changes are necessary to enhance productivity within the unit."

Another wave of accusations and Cézanne spotted one particular dorsal fin moving in for a grisly kill. The zinger that came from Channel Eighteen's greasy-haired Garlon Harrier made the rest of the man-eaters look like a tank full of guppies.

"How'd the affair between you and Driskoll start, and were either of you disciplined by Internal Affairs?"

"Gentlemen — and Lady — we're here to discuss the Homicide Unit."

Whitewater crashed between her ears. The cacophony of accusations thinned until she expected to pitch over, face first, into the thick of them. That she could touch the skirt of her violet houndstooth suit and finger the leather thigh holster

15

through the fabric reinforced a certain level of comfort.

Gradually, she became aware of pindrops of sleet pummeling the metal overhang. Fragmented verses of Don Henley's hit song "Dirty Laundry" played in her head.

Kick 'em when they're up, kick 'em when they're down.

Garlon Harrier's eyes gleamed. His lips moved and toxic waste continued to spew out of his mouth. "Is it true you were on duty when Darlene Driskoll caught you in a sex act with her husband?"

The redhead's eyes danced. "Were you in uniform? I hear that's a turn-on for some people." She cut her gaze to Rosen and the hint of a devilish smile played across her lips.

Cézanne's first impulse was to coil into a fetal position and wheeze into a paper bag. But somewhere, deep inside a locked vault in her head, the teachings of rookie school seeped out. She leaned into the mike and repeated a stock answer.

"Departmental policy prevents me from commenting on ongoing investigations."

Harrier elbowed his way to the front. "Assuming rumors are true, Captain, did you ever make it right between you and Darlene Driskoll?"

Just when she was certain the vibrations distorting her hearing would drown out the

16

next question, Rosen stepped back into the warm wash of light.

"I think you'll be pleased with our decision to name Zan Martin as the acting Captain at this critical time," he said, golden-throated and grinning. "And while it's true she's only thirty-two, what she lacks in age, know-how, and experience to run a sophisticated unit doesn't detract from the fact that she's a crackerjack detective —"

Her mind quickened. What in God's name was he pulling?

"— and we have great faith she'll be able to handle the newest innovation in Homicide —"

Huh?

She jerked her head in Rosen's direction.

"— which is another reason for inviting you here today. To announce the creation of a Cold Case Squad to investigate Fort Worth's unsolved homicides —"

A what? Keep smiling.

"— There's not a more capable investigator than Captain Martin —"

A bullet through the brain stem would put an end to this.

She closed her eyes momentarily and concentrated on reinflating her lungs.

"— and that's why we've entrusted her, personally, with the Upper Westside murder." He jolted her into the here-and-

17

now with a slap on the back that bordered on assault. "We need an ace investigator. One who won't let this city down."

Reporters went wild. It had been dubbed the Great Dane Murder and it had collected dust for eight years. In front of God and a viewing audience of several million people, Rosen assigned her the high-profile homicide that left the Department stinging with long-term embarrassment. In the amount of time it took him to take a breath, the blood swirling behind Cézanne's eyes plummeted five feet, eight inches, straight to her insteps.

So this is how it feels to slip into shock.

Rosen kept yammering. "This Administration has every confidence and every expectation that Captain Martin can and will solve this heinous crime. Thank you for your time."

A reporter shouted, "Didn't the lead investigator die investigating that case?"

"Thank you." Rosen waved off questions.

Circling for the kill, Harrier backed her into a corner with his eyes. "How will you do that? How will you solve the Great Dane Murder?"

Hell if I know.

Cézanne thought fast. "Scientific breakthroughs occur every day. DNA evidence is now being used in the penal system to overturn Death Row cases, and we're lucky

18

to have a Medical Examiner's Office that keeps abreast of — "

Yanked from the mike by Rosen, her voice faded away.

"Thanks, everyone." He flicked them a half-assed salute. "No more questions."

"How long will it take? Another eight years?" Harrier again, taking another cheap shot.

Just when she thought she landed in the clear, Rosen unhanded her long enough to trot back to the mike for an encore.

"That's a very good question." He reached out, latched onto her wrist, and reeled her back in. "Zan and I were discussing that very thing this morning over a cup of coffee, and she assured me she'd have it solved in under two weeks."

Her jaw dropped open.

"Which means our little ace needs to get the show on the road, and I've got a department to run. Thanks again for your interest."

At once, the skies opened up and all hail broke loose.

The flurry of reporters raised their arms defensively and sprinted for their vans.

Rosen took cover inside the double glass doors. Cézanne scampered in behind him. Out of the elements, he glimpsed himself in the reflection of the glass. He produced a comb from his back pocket and ran it through his salt and pepper hair. "I think it went pretty well, don't you? How'd I look?"

Cézanne pictured him — not in his dress blues with his hair raked neatly in place, baring his pearly teeth over his gums for a quick spinach check — but in a hammerlock with the snub nose of her .38 jammed against his gullet.

She locked him in a deadly glare. "You set me up."

He clasped his hand firmly around her elbow and tightened his grip. Once he steered her beyond the earshot of detectives drifting into the foyer, stomping snow off their boots, he addressed her in a low growl.

"Two days ago I gave you a chance to resign. To go be a lawyer. But no, you wanted to play hardball." His eyes pierced her with an electrical charge that numbed her clear down to her toes. "I'm willing to make you one last offer . . ."

She torqued her jaw.

". . . because we're family, you and I. Because no matter how fucked up she is, I love my sister — which is the only *forcocked* reason you got into the police academy in the first place — a lousy promise I made to your mother and live to regret daily."

She winced under his powerful squeeze.

"Your no-account father turned a perfectly

good woman into a basket case —" he moved so close she could feel a fine mist of spit against her ear "— and if it hadn't been necessary to keep you from spilling the beans about that night —"

She knew what he meant. By now, he'd cut off her circulation.

"— well, I'd venture to say you wouldn't be here at all. Am I making myself clear?" From his back pocket, he pulled a paper folded into quarters and shook it open. "Sign it."

Her resignation.

Her eyes drifted over the letter. Accepting a new job as a briefing attorney for Moses, Lonstein, Cohen, McElwell, and Kidd. She looked at Rosen, holding out a pen, and knew he figured he could still do damage control as long as she wasn't around to muck things up for him. A sense of indignation raged from deep within. It gave her great pleasure to rip the offer in half.

"Very well, Zan. It's your funeral."

With the stride of a pilot, Rosen sauntered to the elevator. As the doors sealed off his unsmiling face from view, he got in a parting shot.

"Remember, Captain. Today you're the windshield, tomorrow you're the bug."

Chapter Two

Diagonally across from police headquarters, next to the Tarrant County Justice Center, a multi-story, coral-brick building with verdigris accents, Cézanne regrouped in the only place she wasn't likely to run into anyone she knew: county jail. It took ten minutes in the ladies' restroom with her elbows propped against the lavatory before her knees steadied; it took splashing cold water on her face before the angry red blotches no longer looked as if firemen used a pitchfork to put out the blaze in her face.

Good publicity, my ass, she thought.

But Lady Godiva rocked the community's conscience. When transients found the nude body of a flaxen-haired beauty, face down on the floor of a flophouse on Hemphill Street three weeks before, the first radio reports stunned listeners. By nightfall, TV's breaking news identified the victim as the only child of veteran policeman Charles Crane — now the former Captain of FWPD's Homicide Unit. When the morning paper hit the stands and the shocking blue eyes of Carri Crane jumped off the front page, readers fell in love with the photo of the stunning police cadet, and Cowtown rippled with a cry for justice. As the seedy story unfolded, confidence in The Blue eroded. Now people demanded accountability.

Only Rosen pulled a fast one. Cut her throat and field dressed her in time for the local morning talk shows. If she got lucky, she'd be taken hostage in a jailbreak and shot dead on the Courthouse steps before the noon broadcast aired. With her mind still on autopilot, she ran a wet hand through the fringe of bangs to separate them, then decided they looked downright spooky honed into points and stuck her head under the hand dryer until her hair fluffed into dark wisps.

Stinking psycho made her the acting Captain so he could use the Great Dane Murder to drive her out. Nobody'd been able to solve it back when they had fresh evidence to work with. Just because she wasn't a member of the force when it happened didn't mean she hadn't heard about it. How it brought night terrors to everyone who worked it. The way it soured personalities. Wrecked marriages. Drove men into twelve-step programs.

Caused the lead officer to hang himself.

Well she wouldn't quit. Rosen didn't just misjudge her, the eff-ing bastard was flat-out wrong.

He wasn't dealing with a weakling.

She would solve the Great Dane Murder.

Maybe even, by God, do it in under two weeks.

Standing in the restroom with her career about to go down the toilet, she knew just the man who could fix this. A salty cuss from the old school. A Neanderthal who refused to change with the times. To adapt to the computer age and learn to operate the MDTs in patrol cars. A black sheep with military tattoos on his forearms whose own professional future with the PD hung on life support.

And it didn't hurt that Rosen despised him.

At the booking desk, with one arm propped on the chest-high Formica counter, Cézanne waited for Lt. Sid Klevenhagen. A man fitting his description came swaggering in from a restricted area, drying his hands with a paper towel. His hair stuck up like wires in a curry comb and he had the shrewd eyes of an old dog that had been kicked too many times to think he was about to get a pat on the head. He crossed the room and stood tall behind the counter before sliding onto a stool. With arms braced across his chest, he made a demand.

"Who took your bracelets off?"

"Pardon me?"

"Hooks. Handcuffs. Where's the officer brought you in?"

"You're mistaken. I'm not under arrest." She unhooked the waist button on her jacket to give him a peek at her new gold badge. "I'm —"

"Don't fucking move or I'll come over this counter and put you in a hammerlock. Assault on a Peace Officer," he said, grabbing a sheet of paper from the stack and letting his pen hover over it, "that's the first charge. What else are you guilty of?"

"What're you talking about?"

"I'm booking you for Assault on a PO. Aggravated. That's a felony rap, missy. Five to ninety-nine, or life, if convicted."

"Excuse me?"

"You are not excused. I'm the one talking and you're playing dumb as a mechanism to interrupt, which I will not tolerate. You wait until I'm finished asking questions, then I'll excuse you."

She glanced around, hoping somebody might recognize her and intervene on her behalf. In that no one fit the bill, she checked his nameplate in hopes she'd made a mistake.

S. KLEVENHAGEN.

No mistake.

He snarled, "Put your hands flat on the counter and do not remove them until I say so."

25

"*Do not remove them?* I'll have you know I happen to be —"

"That does it. I'm coming around to frisk you."

"Like hell."

Klevenhagen, sliding off his perch now. Halfway around the counter. Taller than he appeared when seated. With rawhide skin stretched tight over his bones, he looked like the kind of man the CIA would disavow any knowledge of — an operative who knew how to kill using an aluminum pull-tab from a cheap brew.

"You're under arrest, missy. Don't make me have to tack on Resisting, too."

"Have you lost your mind?"

Toe-to-toe, now. And her eyes level with his gold panther shield.

"You don't seem to get it. I gotcha for assaulting a PO." He cupped his hand over his mouth and spoke under his breath. "The moment I saw you, I was brutally struck by your natural beauty. I figure that leaves me three choices: I can book you, I can have my lawyer call yours, or we can head for my place and negotiate an out-of-court settlement on our own."

A burst of sniggers near the coffee and donuts sheared her attention. When her eyes fluttered back to Klevenhagen, he had a lupine grin on his face and an aura about

26

him that suggested he was ready to mate for life.

She peeled back the flap of jacket and exposed the gold badge. At the same time, she presented him with a business card with her phone number stricken and her new office number red-penned in its place.

"I'm Cézanne Martin. Acting Captain of Homicide."

"I watch the news." Unimpressed.

"Do you always revert to high school antics when dealing with a lady?"

"You're no lady." In a whisper that bordered on conspiracy, he rasped, "You're one of us."

CIA. And the blue fish swims upstream.

She half expected him to follow up with a secret handshake. "I think you should know if I actually had assaulted you, we'd be having this conversation with you doubled over."

He leaned close enough for her to whiff coffee on his breath.

"You look better in real life. 'Cept you could use those ten pounds the camera added. What can we do to you, for you, or in spite of you?"

"Now I know how you did it," she said, more to the air between them than to Klevenhagen directly, "how you got yourself three pending sexual harassment charges with IA."

"I'll be cleared."

"Save it. I've seen your file."

"I've got nothing to hide. Those charges were levied by frigid females who are not suited to po-lice work." He accented the first syllable of police like a patrolman from the Roby Tyson days — when the PD took anyone who could read and write, that had enough brawn to blackjack thugs into submission.

"You'll need to check that attitude if you plan to work up in Homicide with me."

Clearly, the news took him aback. She couldn't tell if he was annoyed, intrigued, or ate bad Mexican food for breakfast.

"Why me? We never worked together. Hell, we don't even know each other."

"I liked the idea you were one of only three people with a personnel file thicker than mine." She eased her purse down by the strap until it came to rest on the floor.

"You expect me to be the lightning rod." His eyes narrowed. "Mighty white of you."

"Look, Klevenhagen, I don't know you except by reputation — and a terrible one at that. But a motor jock from Traffic Division told me you hate the brass, and that counts as a recommendation."

"Lady, I don't know if you've looked at your Captain's bars lately, but we *are* the brass."

"Not me. I'm just finding ways to keep busy between movie deals."

28

The slam of his pen against the countertop rang in her ears.

"I don't know who's been running their mouth, but I ain't interested. I like it here just fine. So get along."

She stood with her feet bolted to the floor, unable to move, but the bite in his tone had the hair on her arms pushing up to meet her sleeves. Only a crazy person would turn down a position in Homicide to stay locked up with prisoners all day.

Still bristling, he consulted her business card. "This your number?"

"Think of it as the Batphone."

"Well thanks but no thanks." The look he gave the donut dunkers suggested he might be fixing to exact retribution. They scattered as if his eyes had the power to empty double-barrel birdshot into their backsides. "I'll keep your card, though, just in case I ever kill somebody — or need to have somebody killed."

That ripped it. She'd heard enough wise-cracks for one day. People getting in little digs at her expense about the unfortunate shootout at Ali Baba's.

"Sorry to bother you, Klevenhagen. Apparently the joke's on me. Guess I was misinformed. See you around." She strutted toward the exit without looking back, feeling him leering at the sway of her buttocks.

"If I had a golf swing like that —" Klevenhagen said, loud enough to make her uncomfortable "— they'd call me Tiger."

The Homicide Unit was alive with raucous banter and no one seemed to notice or care when Cézanne entered the room. The warehouse of partitioned cubicles occupied the northwest corner of the PD's fourth floor and overlooked the Trinity River and the panorama beyond, and she could tell from the loud exchange of a few men lucky enough to have desks next to the windows, they were doubling as meteorologists for those without a view.

But the box office draw seemed to center around a discussion escalating between Teddy Vaughn and Doug Driskoll.

"You think the videotape's too grainy to ID the shooter in that Arab convenience store robbery?" Teddy said.

"Why do you ask?" Driskoll cocked his head slightly back and to the side the way he always did when he wanted to look down the bridge of his nose at Vaughn.

"I went to a photography school last year. I can show you how to sharpen that face shot by incorporating image enhancement software —"

"If this is your roundabout way of saying I can't solve a raghead's murder without your input, forget it. I don't need any-body's help. Matter of fact, there's no job in the world too big for me to handle."

"Really? Maybe you should go straighten out the Middle East."

She didn't mean to laugh, but Driskoll had a gift for bringing out the most gos-samer thread of evil in an otherwise decent person. In typical fashion, he waited until Vaughn's back was turned to flip him the finger. No one seemed to notice when she unlocked the door to Captain Charles Crane's office, slipped inside, and made herself at home. She needed a box to pack up his stuff. And keys to the file cabinets.

Her file cabinets.

Beyond the tinted windowpanes, the skies continued to darken. Not as black as the one that spawned the violent tornado that almost destroyed Downtown Fort Worth, and would forever be Cowtown's barometer to measure bad weather, but an eerie charcoal gray that cast a depressing pall.

Abruptly, a crack of metal came down against the secretary's desk just outside Cézanne's door. She knew immediately that someone rapped their Streamlight loud enough to get the attention of everyone in the room. Horseplay came to a halt.

"Any of you guys seen Cézanne Martin?" Rosen.

"With or without clothes?" Doug Driskoll.

Driskoll said something else but the rest of his comment drowned in the guffaws of their colleagues. She rose to her feet, smoothed her purple houndstooth skirt and matching Chanel jacket with the flat of her palms. Convinced that Driskoll had an extra Y-chromosome common to criminals, she moved to the door and opened it. Laughter died in their throats.

Smiles sickened on some of the faces. On others, grins flat-out died. In her quickness to take inventory of those poking fun at her expense, only Teddy Vaughn seemed not to participate.

"You wanted to see me?" she said coolly.

"Get over here."

In two-inch pumps, she surpassed Rosen in height. Anyone paying close attention should've noticed similarities in their physical characteristics: the shapes of their faces, cheekbones, and eyes seemed to carry the same genetic bar code. But no one had ever remarked on it. Probably because their last names were different, and her facial features were softer. Admittedly, Rosen cut a snappy picture with his silvering hair and lean, tawny physique, but the most striking difference in facial features came down to the eye color — hers, an odd shade of blue-violet her mother called periwinkle; his, a perpetually tumultuous cobalt. It amazed her, even with twenty years' difference in their ages, no one figured it out — not even Roby. At least if he did, he never said so. And from the get-go, Rosen insisted they not disclose their connection.

Under normal circumstances, they might have been friends. Cézanne learned the hard way that people bound by tragedy either remain steadfastly loyal, or fragment. Even as a kid, she'd sensed a strain in the relationship. He seemed to perceive her as the weak link in the chain padlocking the family secret.

"Listen up." Rosen squared his shoulders. "Captain Crane's on Emergency Family Leave. Assuming he returns at all, it won't be to this unit."

Eyes bobbed in their sockets, checking out the reactions of those around them. If Rosen's announcement made them squirm, they would be writhing on hot coals in hell when they heard the rest.

"In case you missed this morning's press conference, I announced Crane's replacement. Men, it's only fair you hear it from me." He took a deep breath, as if to better insulate himself from the stink of his own words. A shot of air left his mouth in a punctured-tire hiss. "Detective Cézanne Martin has been promoted. She's the acting Captain of Homicide."

A low, tortured voice, indistinguishable

above the collective gasps, served as the group's unofficial spokesman. The disembodied response seemed to sum up their feelings with an unusually PG-13 rating.

"We're screwed."

The phone in her new office was on its third ring by the time Cézanne scurried in to answer it. She tugged off one amethyst earring, swiped the receiver from its cradle, and identified herself in a way that wouldn't come off so authoritative that she sounded like she drove a Harley, or so sensual that the caller grabbed a *Playboy* and kept her talking.

"Detect— Captain Martin, Homicide."

The voice at the other end sounded deep and muffled.

"Is this the Batphone?"

Klevenhagen. She let the silence speak for her.

"If this is the Batphone, does that mean you're Batman? 'Cause if you're looking for a Robin, I'm too old for flesh-colored tights. You there, missy?"

"Captain Martin to you, Klevenhagen. What do you want?"

"Couldn't talk." He wheezed into the receiver with such enthusiasm her mind questioned what he was doing with his free hand. "Bunch of assholes here. Can't have them thinking I want to bail. Might affect my promotion status. I'm sure you understand."

"From what I read, you'll be eligible for promotion about the time Cuba liberates itself."

"Let's make it snappy, I'm at a pay phone."

"Why're you using a pay phone? Don't you have a land line over there?"

"Recorded."

"You don't have a cellular?"

"Feds."

Jesus. Paranoid and a sex pervert to boot. Probably should've demanded a look at the police shrink's files before trotting over to see him. "What's on your mind, Klevenhagen?"

"I want the job."

"Then why give me a ration of shit?"

"Let me put it to you this way: I'd run Rosen down with my pickup if it wouldn't mess up the grillwork. Given the chance, he'd do me the same way. So how long you figure I'd last up there if he thought that's where I wanted to be?"

"You weren't up for an Oscar. You hurt my feelings, some of the stuff you said."

"Lady, I got unfinished business with IA. If you know what's good for you, you'll pretend you hate my guts whenever Rosen's people are around."

He might be worth hearing out.

"We're Rosen's people, Klevenhagen."

"Not me. I hate the cocksucker."

"What makes you think you can work under me?"

"I've been waiting my whole life to be under somebody like you."

"Under my command, Klevenhagen."

"That's what I said. What'd you think I meant?"

She checked her watch. "I've got some rat killing to do. If you want to be second in command of this sinking ship, be in my office at three this afternoon."

"Fine. But don't think you can throw me down and rip my clothes off just 'cause you're the boss. I want you to know, up front, I cannot do it five times a day, I don't care what that fat gal in Records says. If you only want me for a sex toy you're gonna be disappointed. Three's the limit."

In stunned silence, she stared at the blotter. She'd made a terrible mistake. Before she could rescind the offer, he said, "Who're the other two?"

"What other two?"

"You never named the people with personnel files thicker'n ours."

"Roby Tyson and Big Jim Kickingbird."

"Then I'm in excellent company."

Her shoulders instantly tingled and she knew immediately what caused it. Any feelings of doubt about Klevenhagen had been vanquished into the ether.

Chapter Three

At exactly one thirty-five that afternoon, while most of the detectives were flopped in their chairs listening to their food digest, the worm turned.

Seated at her desk, Cézanne opened her purse and pulled out a small spiral notebook. She thumbed through it until she reached her hit list. Out of eleven people assigned to the unit, six had to go. Immediately. She stared at the names.

Charles Crane. *Already gone. Nervous breakdown.*

That left Lt. Henry Binswanger. *He's history. Screwed me over with Internal Affairs.*

Doug Driskoll. *Big red X for Casanova. Game player. Lied about being married. Screwed me in his wife's bed. Damned near got me killed.*

Greta Carr. *Stabbed me in the back over Lady Godiva. Needs the axe.*

Drew Ingleside. *Burnout. Close to retirement. Gone soon enough.*

Benji Wardancer. *Personal problems out the wazzoo.* Benji got a question mark penciled next to his name.

Jock Featherston. *Gorgeous. Conceited.*

Sneaky. Kick-ass reports. Another question mark.

Teddy Vaughn. *Quiet. A watcher and listener. Mouthwateringly handsome.*

Walter Cochran and Ramiro Sifuentes. *Permanent night shift. Live and let live.*

Roby Tyson. Absentmindedly, she ran her finger across his name, smearing the ink. *Roby Tyson — irreplaceable.*

Cézanne Martin. *Acting head of Homicide. In charge of the Cold Case Squad.*

Leaving an opening for another detective.

Five of them she could live with. The rest, well . . .

When Lt. Henry Binswanger slinked past her door after a full lunch — judging by the taut belly overhanging his Sam Browne — she called out. Still suited in dress blues from the press conference, his narrow-hipped swagger did the uniform justice.

"Got a minute, Hank?" It gave her great pleasure to address him informally and get away with it.

"Sue-zanne."

"Call me Captain. Pull up a seat and let's visit."

Chair legs in departmental-issue, gunmetal gray, screeched against the floor. He dropped, without energy, onto the cushion. Dull brown eyes embedded in skin the color of rye bread, seemed to reflect his feelings.

"You're close to retirement, aren't you?"

She already knew the answer, and asked purely for sport. The personnel file Crane kept in the cabinet she jimmied open with a set of lock picks she unearthed from the desk said so.

"I'd like to put in a couple more years."

"And you should." She lazily thumbed through his history. It pleased her to watch him fidget. Rather reminded her of that unfortunate Internal Affairs investigation when he sat beside Captain Crane and they tried to get her fired on account of the misunderstanding with that lying Doug Driskoll. "You have quite a bit of experience, Hank." She leafed through his last evaluation. "I see you've worked in every division except two."

"That's correct."

"How come you never worked in the radio room or at the booking desk?"

"I have no interest in communications or the jail."

Who does?

"Which would you say you hate worse?" Sensing his reluctance to answer, she reminded herself to smile. "If you had to pick, Hank, which would you like least?"

"I don't think I'd much like being cooped up all day with lawbreakers."

She gave him a look of practiced fascination. "I suppose the only thing that could make such an assignment worse would be having to work permanent night shift," she said with great showmanship. "Do you enjoy Homicide?"

"Sure."

"I wouldn't think you'd want to stay with Crane out of the picture and me in charge."

"Why not?"

It pleased her to see him picking at his cuticles. Unmitigated fear shrouded his eyes. "Are you saying you wouldn't have a problem working with me, Hank?"

"Doesn't make any difference to me who runs the show, Sue-zanne."

"But you liked working for Crane." Demanding.

"Sure."

"You two had a mutual trust?"

"I reckon you could say so."

"What would you say, Hank?" Fear flickered behind his eyes. She could see the exact moment it turned to dread, when he realized where she was headed. "Would you say you backed each other on things such as IA investigations?" She liked that several of his fingers had started to bleed, and handed over a tissue. "I'm giving you a chance to round out your career, Hank. You may not understand right now but in time, you'll consider it an unintended favor."

She'd seen a look like the one on Binswanger's face, once before. A guy learned he'd been cuckolded and pressed a cocked shotgun to his chin.

"Lt. Klevenhagen's transferring in from the jail, so that leaves a vacant slot for a lateral move."

"I don't want to transfer. And Klevenhagen's insane. You can't put that nut in charge of this unit."

"That would be a first," she said without looking at him, "me being around crazy people." She planned to say, "You may go," but he'd already rocketed to his feet and stormed out before she finished thanking him for his years of dedicated service.

One head rolling, and others waiting to be chopped.

With rapier speed, she ink-slashed Binswanger's name with a flourish. She rummaged through her purse until she located her powder compact and checked her reflection in the mirror. After a touch-up of lip gloss, she engaged the intercom button on her phone and said to Greta with great sweetness, "Would you please tell Detective Driskoll to come into my office?"

While waiting for Driskoll, Cézanne looked out her fourth-floor window. In the parking lot below, two officers yin-yanged their blue-and-whites so close they could reach out and touch each other through their driver's windows.

That's how it started over a year ago, she thought, recalling the night Driskoll called her

41

on the radio to swap information on a leaving-the-scene involving his personal vehicle. She caught the bad guy in a foot chase, after he bailed when the cigarette he flicked out the window blew back inside the stolen Suburban. Even though the seat caught fire, Driskoll had been grateful to have it back.

Want to go for coffee, Rookie?
Aren't you married?
You kidding? Who wants a ball and chain? How 'bout you, Rookie, you involved?
No. And to further clarify his status, *Are you seeing anyone?*
Just you. I'm looking at you and I'm not seeing anyone else.

She was still silhouetted against the windows with her arms folded across her chest when Driskoll's reflection appeared in the glass. He rapped his knuckles against the entry and greeted her in a low voice.
"Hey, babydoll."
"Captain, to you."
"Hey, Captain Babydoll."
She uncharitably hoped he was experiencing a sexual drought, especially now that she'd found an oasis in Bobby Noah, Sheriff of Johnson County. But with Driskoll's taut muscles, his dark hair silvering at the temples, and the Nicole Miller tie she'd bought him the birthday

42

before she found out he lied about the existence of a Mrs. Driskoll, Doug Driskoll looked like a million in singles. And when he stepped inside and threw the bolt in a way that suggested he came to double his money, Cézanne reminded herself not to look evil squarely in the eye.

"Knock it off and take a seat. We need to take care of a little housekeeping."

"Look, Zan —" he tried to cast his spell with those fathomless green eyes "— now that the old ball and chain's living elsewhere, we could catch up at my place."

Blood raced up her neck so fast she thought her jugular veins would rupture. It was all she could do to restrain herself from picking up the Barbie-sized, bronze statue of Blind Justice next to the cuss kitty she brought in to personalize the place, and render him into a vegetable medley.

"Living elsewhere?"

"It's not like she'll barge in, unannounced —"

"She shot up the *forcocked* house, you imbecile."

"— besides, I make a mean breakfast. Pancakes, sausage, the works. You've never had omelets until you've tasted mine. So light and fluffy you'd think they'd float." He moved closer to her spot at the desk and spoke in a sexy growl. "So, baby, after a steamy night with Big Doug, how do you want your eggs?"

43

"Unfertilized." She shoved a transfer sheet in his face.

He snatched it away and held it at arm's length. "What's this?"

"Let's cut to the chase, Detective. As of this moment you're reassigned to the Auto Pound."

"Auto Pound?" Words reverberated off the wall, hanging between her ears like ground glass on a European paint job. "Are you PMS-ing?"

Of the people who brought out the absolute worst in her, Driskoll and Rosen were currently at a dead heat.

"Like I said, effective immediately."

"What the hell's wrong with you?" His voice climbed in octave and pitch. "Auto Pound? I'm not putting in time. I'm putting in dog years. You got me transferred to a place where every stinking year's like seven."

Better than being put to sleep.

She caressed the butt of her dead partner's Chief's Special through the wool of her skirt.

Imitating Binswanger, Driskoll didn't seem to be listening when she thanked him for his dedicated service, and he didn't need her to show him the door. He left on his own, slobbering a blue drool.

While Doug Driskoll and Henry

44

Binswanger wandered around like the children of Israel, the rest of the detectives were hydroplaning on their own sweat.

Thanks to thin walls, Cézanne managed to hear Greta put the word out: the new Captain planned to even an old score. But before the ink dried on Driskoll's transfer to the police Auto Pound and Binswanger's to the booking desk, Rosen's secretary distributed a copy of his newest policy. Greta acted almost giddy when she dropped it on the desk, and the unmistakable hint of laughter flickered in her hazel eyes.

Holding the page under the incandescent globe of the banker's lamp, Cézanne invented colorful new expletives as she read the departmental letterhead.

Lateral transfers shall be limited to three per unit within a one-year period.

Along with a bee-essy explanation about the cost of training new personnel, the effect of interrupting productivity, and other Rosenesque double-speak. Regardless of whether other supervisors received copies, the son of a bitch penned it for her.

She allowed the memorandum to drift to the blotter, then nestled her shoulders into the well-oiled leather of Crane's chair and calculated her options.

Down to the last transfer, she'd need to be judicious. Greta should've been the next to go, but with the latest policy revision, letting others remain in the unit could be worse.

Around two-thirty, Cézanne reached for her purse. She wondered if she should invite Aden Whitelark to join her for coffee. The police psychiatrist would have the low-down on every member of the department, starting from their MMPIs all the way down to the last person reporting to IA. Badgering him into giving her a peek at the bed-wetters and sociopaths could make weeding out the third person simple. She was halfway to her feet when Klevenhagen came swaggering in with his hair sticking up like weathered pickets impaled with shards of ice.

She motioned him to a chair, opened his personnel file to the most recent complaint, and looked him up and down with a keen eye. Every fold, a military crease; every piece of gear spit-polished enough to burn the retinas on a sunny day; every fingernail clean and manicured. And the fresh scent of deodorant soap still lingering around him, even after he completed an eight-hour shift at the booking desk.

"It says here you've got three sexual harassment investigations pending."

He seemed overjoyed having his secret out in the open.

"You know what I think?" she said. "I think you pulled that last stunt with those female guards hoping they'd toss you out of the jail on your keister."

"That so?"

"Yeah, that's so." She dropped into the chair and leaned back enough to check the tiny run in her hose while still keeping an eye on him. The steely twinkle made it easier to level with him. "By now you know Rosen dumped on me."

She pointed to three large boxes on the floor. They were covered in dust, except for fresh handprints on the sides when they were brought in from storage. The name DANE KISSEL, now faded with age, had been printed on all four sides in black marker.

Klevenhagen cocked his head to check out the cartons. "Yep, you got yourself a real bondage case."

"A what?"

"Bondage case. The kind of case that ties you up and fucks you over."

She didn't know whether to laugh or take Zoloft.

"You may not know this, missy," he went on, "but I was Kissel's training officer. Matter of fact, I'm the one who nicknamed him the Great Dane."

"Really." She nuzzled deeper into the chair back and absorbed his words. Muscles in her shoulder seemed to unknot and she started to think of the crass, spit-shined man sitting across from her as Sid, instead of Klevenhagen. As if they would be allies, maybe even friends.

"Nice guy. Real smart. Not your average cop," Sid said. "A bit like you."

"What do you mean?"

"Some of us belong in law enforcement. Some of us are born into it. Our fathers did it and their fathers did it, so we do it. Kissel didn't belong here and he knew it. Neither do you."

"Thanks a heap."

"Don't take it the wrong way. Kissel got Officer of the Year three years running. But he wanted to be a lawyer. Not just any lawyer — the best criminal lawyer Fort Worth ever saw. Only he had to learn how the rules worked before he took on the people who broke them. By the time he died, he was damned near the best in town."

"How long did you train him?"

"We rode together during his probationary status."

"You learn a lot from riding shotgun. Stuff nobody else knows." She gridlocked his eyes with her own. "What'd you learn, Sid?"

"That he was a regular Jake. Except he set his goals way high. Think of the world as a big fish tank, Captain. You got angelfish, silver dollars, goldfish, guppies, tetras — and they all perform different functions. Take, for instance, your guppies. Nice fish. That would be your secretaries and clerks.

Neon tetras are those flashy, shallow little gals you see out clubbing; and, like the real thing, the bullshit and the needle-nose gar high-heels don't last long. You got your silver dollars; that would be your bankers and stockbrokers. You got your betas. They're your serial killers. And so on.

"Now, to clean up all the crap in this aquarium, you got your snails. They scour the sides of the tank, wiping up the mess."

"You're saying we're snails." Wrinkling her nose, disgusted by Sid's imagery.

"No. Snails're uniforms. Your beat cop." Sid seemed to be evaluating her curiosity. When her eyes thinned into slits, he delivered a ready explanation. "The brass is your plecostomus. A true bottom-feeder. They clean up the crap the snails leave behind."

"So we're bottom-feeders?"

"I am. You're not — you and Dane Kissel."

Sid looked out the window and stared at a far-off place, invisible to the rest of the world. He let out a fraternal chuckle as if he and whoever listened at the other end shared a private joke. "Kissel would've been Gov'nor."

"You think Dane Kissel was that smart?"

"Intellect has nothing to do with it." Still staring into his private place, Sid answered with great softness. "That was his goal. He didn't just think about being Gov'nor, he had a plan. Everything he did, he charted an internal blueprint."

"I never heard that before, about him wanting to be Governor."

Sid's eyes broke their hold in space and returned to the business taking place in Crane's ex-office. "Far as I know, I'm the only one he told."

"How many people did you tell?"

"You. And Jock Featherston, back when he and Crane worked the case."

"Do me a favor. Don't tell anybody else."

On his way to the coffee pot, before he disappeared from her line of vision, Cézanne called him by his Christian name.

"What are we? Me and Dane Kissel? What kind of fish?"

"P-I-T-A fish."

Her brows knitted, and she matched Sid's calculating eyes with intensity.

"Short for 'Pain in the Ass.' You're a Discus, you and Kissel. He was one of those Hi-Fin Diamond Blues, but you —" he wagged his finger "— you're the wild, rare, Royal Parakari."

"You're saying I'm high maintenance?"

"I'm saying you and Kissel aren't like the rest of the fish. You're independent, you don't school well with others, and in order for you to be comfortable, the rest of us have to sweat."

Chapter Four

When Sid returned with two Styrofoam cups of coffee, and placed one on the blotter in front of her, Cézanne explained about the next interview. "You're welcome to stay, but these woodsheddings are my responsibility. Unless you think I pulled the pin on the grenade, I'd ask that you just sit here and keep quiet."

"Like a mouse peeing on cotton."

She flashed a grin. The old tough could drop kick her down Belknap Street if he wanted to, and everybody knew it. But the nice thing about men like Sid Klevenhagen was that as long as everybody knew it, they didn't need to.

Still fuming over Rosen's attempt to curb her authority, she popped up from her seat and stuck her head out the door. Teddy Vaughn sauntered by, headed toward the evidence locker with a handful of evidence bags.

She called out with great authority. "Theodore Vaughn. Come in when you finish, please."

He nodded affably. As she returned to her seat and pulled Teddy Vaughn's personnel file from the stack, she smiled inwardly at

51

how the detectives' heads, buried in work, popped up like clay pigeons at the sound of her voice. She hoped the mere invitation to visit made them clench their buttocks hard enough to crack walnuts.

Teddy craned his neck around the door facing. His lip curled up at one corner into a smile. "I was going for coffee but it looks like you already have some." He took in the picture of Sid, lounging in the chair closest to the window, and flinched. "Howdy, Lieutenant."

Sid jerked his chin in Teddy's direction but his eyes never left the dossier.

Cézanne said, "All right you little brown-noser, come in and shut the door." She pointed to a chair and when he perched uncomfortably on the edge of it, she said, "What're you working on?"

"Driskoll just dumped that convenience store shooting on my desk. I don't think I ever had a case with a thousand pieces of evidence."

Her gaze flickered to Sid. She could tell by the slitted eyes, he was sneaking glances at Teddy Vaughn, and from the tautness of his jaw, was pretending not to listen.

"Shooter dropped a bag of quarters on his way out," Teddy said. "Some had blood on them. The videotape shows he grabbed a handful on his way out the door. Some may have prints." He grinned like a

52

twelve-year-old at his first cotillion. "No rest for the wicked."

She pointed to the boxes. "I guess you heard."

Slow nod. "The Cold Case Squad. I don't envy you."

"I have a couple of questions for you."

"Fire away."

"Who's the best detective in Homicide?"

"No, you don't," he said through a grin. "I'm not going down that road."

Sid's nostrils flared, and from where he sat, she thought he might be trying to bite through the inside of his cheek.

"See that file?" She pointed in Sid's direction. "I've been reviewing your clearance rate."

"Okay."

"What type of case interests you most?"

"It's not the case, it's the process of solving it that fascinates me."

Rolling her pen between her fingers gave her something to do besides study what appeared to be a faded hickey on his neck. Admittedly, Teddy Vaughn still had a boyish charm about him; she figured in part, because of flashes of red in his sandy hair, and cinnamon sprinkles of freckles on his forearms. But the guy was tall, with a neck made for fangs. Funny, she never paid much attention before.

She banished the image and got back to

business. "You're thorough, consistent, and always busy. All good qualities."

"Somehow I don't think you called me in to pay compliments."

"You're right. I brought you in to get to the bottom of something." She pressed her feet hard against the floor. If he answered the question right, he got the job.

"Shoot."

"What would you do if you had to arrest your own mother?"

"Radio for backup."

Drawing in a deep breath kept her from a tempting glance at Sid. "Thank you for your service, Detective. Go clean off your desk."

When Teddy Vaughn was halfway through the door, with a hangdog expression on his face, she called out after him. Halting in place with his hands clasped loosely in front of him, he seemed to be waiting to be sent to the corner.

"Just so we understand each other, I'm redistributing your caseload. When you finish clearing your desk, come back for one of these boxes. It's you, me, and Sid on this. Welcome to the Cold Case Squad, partner. And hey . . . you can still call me Zan."

"He's gay as a goose." Sid downed the last of his coffee, and reached across the blotter for the next personnel file.

"He is not," said Cézanne. "He's sensitive, that's all."

"I'm telling you he's a meat hound."

"I'd be interested in how you'd know something like that."

"Gay-dar. I can sense it. You may've noticed him staring at me."

"For God's sake, you're a lieutenant. He was probably petrified."

"That's what I mean. I was wonderin' when you'd notice."

"Notice what?"

"Hard as a rock. You may have seen me trying to act like I wasn't interested."

"Ohmygod. You haven't already signed your transfer papers, have you? Because I'm starting to think you may be psychotic."

"Check it out, missy. Everything you need to know's in this file." He leaned in and shot Teddy's folder back across the desk. "That boy's almost forty. Never married. Got his ear pierced."

"An old maritime custom. He traveled below the equator."

"I'll say. Probably dropped anchor in a lot of ports, too." Sid spoke out of the side of his mouth. His hand slid down as if the buckle on his Sam Browne needed protecting. "Oh, sure, he was happy on the ship, but that's just because he was up to his tonsils in seamen."

"I was working here when he went to

Brazil," she said to the anointed king of the double entendre.

"That must've been a sight. Wonder if it was the same guy put the hickey on his neck?"

"You saw that, too?"

"Looked like he got sucked into a turbine."

"I don't care which side of the ocean he swims in, as long as he does his job, so let's drop it. I need you, but I'm not saving your bacon if you get another sexual harassment charge. We have one more person to see before I leave." She checked her watch and saw it had stopped cold. "Do you have the time?"

"Sure." He smiled like a gold-plated sin and got to his feet. "I'll lock the door. You clear the desk. And try not to call me God in mid-stroke. It breaks my concentration when gals can't remember my name."

Shortly before three o'clock, Cézanne pushed the intercom to Greta Carr's desk. The short, pixie-eared secretary bustled in with her formless checkered shirt blousing out over her hips. Rhinestone bifocals balanced on her oversized bosom, hung by their earpieces from a silk cord. With her eyes rimmed red and most of the color drained from her face, two circles of pink rouge dotting her cheeks gave her the appearance of a Pierot clown gone bad.

"You wanted to see me, Zan?" Her eyes flickered to Sid, where they seemed to retreat into her head.

Cézanne said, "You know Lt. Klevenhagen." They exchanged perfunctory nods. "Who's still here?"

Greta appeared to be reading names from the ceiling. "Featherston, Ingleside and Cochran, I think. Wardancer left after lunch. He blamed it on the green peppers, but I think it was a bad case of nerves."

"I'd like you to tell Jock Featherston to come in."

"Sure, Zan. Is that it?"

"For now."

Greta no longer made eye contact. She slinked out in the vapors of sweaty perfume.

Sid snaked a finger under the flap of his breast pocket and pulled out a cellophane pack of peanut butter crackers from the vending machine. Over a shared snack, he divined the low-down on what he'd seen so far. "That's your plan? To drive her crazy, wondering if she's next?"

"Who? Lucretia Borgia?" Cézanne said tartly. "I considered her a friend. Crane made her spy on me and she did it well. Now I don't trust her. End of story."

Sid popped the last cracker into his mouth as Jock Featherston came in, already changed from suit and tie to gray sweats with the PD logo on the chest.

Tall, muscular, perennially tan, with his hair full of suspicious highlights that went off nature's gold color chart, Jock Featherston could scare old people into giving up their seats with little more than a squint of the eyes. And when Doug Driskoll made her the target of his early-morning cheap shot, it was Featherston's donkey-bray laugh that sounded above the others.

"Yo, Zan," he said in his surfer-dude imitation. He lightly touched her shoulder but she twitched him off, pointed to the chair, and made brusque introductions.

"You know Lt. Klevenhagen."

Sid dusted off cracker crumbs, and the two men shook hands.

Cézanne opened Featherston's file and scanned the bio sheet. Thirty-eight, a full six feet. One marriage in his twenties that soured after three years. Paid child support on two kids living in Oklahoma.

She said, "I never knew your name was Joe-Brock."

"I had a baby brother who couldn't pronounce it."

"How nice. What do you remember about the Great Dane Murder?"

He spread his fingers and raked them through his bleach-tipped buzz-cut. "A stalker was after the wife."

"What's the wife's name?"

"Tell ya the truth, I don't recall. We worked it hard the first few months. Me and Captain Crane teamed up after Joey Wehmeyer died. But we never could ID the stalker even though the neighbors reported seeing a guy prowling around a couple of days before the murder. Eventually, we went on to other cases, and Kissel's took a back seat. You know how it goes, Zan, if you don't catch them in the first twenty-four hours, the clearance rate drops dramatically."

He turned to Sid. "I haven't looked at it in a couple of years but it shouldn't take me more than a day or two to buff up. Matter of fact, I'm honored you called on me. Shows confidence."

Cézanne closed Featherston's file. She caught him staring at the boxes as if opening them might release certain evils.

"Did y'all ever focus on anyone in particular?"

"The stalker did it. We just couldn't get a make on him."

"What about the wife?"

"The wife? Naw, we pretty much cleared Mrs. K. About a couple hundred people saw her at the Trail Drivers Ball that night. Ingleside even ran down a photo, taken at the ball with a bunch of her cronies. Should be in the file." His face lit up eagerly.

Without guile, she said, "You're off the case, Jock. You didn't crack it. Nothing

59

personal, but I need a fresh perspective."

Featherston's eyes fragmented into knife-like points of reflected light.

"It's because of this morning, isn't it? We were just clowning around, Captain, like we always do. You've done it yourself. Nobody meant anything by it."

"Let's put this in the most favorable light, shall we? At least I didn't call you in to transfer you. But if you have any other information about this case, I want it coughed up, now."

"Anything that's not in those boxes died with the case." He rose to his feet and dried his hands against the thighs of his sweats.

"You're free to go."

"Don't you think you should let me help long enough to get you started?" His eyes, pleading.

"Thank you for your service."

Without warning, Sid sat up rigid. "I think you're making a mistake, Captain. There's no way you can take on this case all by yourself —"

Something about the glower Sid shot her made her think twice about telling him he had no right to interfere in her decision to cut Featherston's ropes.

"— There's enough to go around. Especially for Featherston. He's already got the jump." His eyes danced. "You're being punitive and retaliatory."

Her jaw unhinged, hanging in disbelief. Beneath the taffeta lining of her suit, her skin burned.

"This is exactly the kind of reason I didn't want to come work for you, Zan —"

Her mouth engaged and she could feel her eyes ignite like a couple of Sure Fire blowtorches.

"Ever since I came in, you've acted petty and mean-spirited." His head wagged from side to side. "No, ma'am, we ain't gonna see eye-to-eye on this deal, at all."

Finished, he flopped against his chair back.

"You may go," she told Featherston.

The door snapped shut.

"Whatever you do, don't say nothin' yet," Sid said harshly. He rose from his chair and put his back to the door's glass pane, then faced her, ashen-faced and anxious. "I'm sixty-three years old. Be sixty-four in March. I remember the names of everyone I ever interviewed, my first big case. You'd think he'd remember the name of a knock-out like Cissy Price Kissel, wouldn't you? I do, and the only thing I ever did was read about it in the paper."

"Don't ever speak to me that way again in front of a subordinate," she said, seething and through her teeth.

"You're gettin' way ahead of yourself, missy."

She ejected from her seat, ready to light

into him, but the urgency in his eyes stopped her.

"Simmer down, Captain. Don't be gulled. Stick around as long as I have, you learn to smell a rat. I think Rosen got to him."

She didn't quite get it and her face must have told him so.

"I've got problems with IA. You've got problems with Rosen. I've put some thought into what Rosen might do if we became pals. I put myself in his itty-bitty spats and here's what I came up with —"

She realized in her fury she'd been holding her breath, and she allowed it to flow out in a rush.

"— The best thing Rosen can do to make your life a living hell is to offer me a deal: unfound the charges pending in IA, in exchange for me spying on you the way Greta reported your goings-on to Crane. Why do you think that shooting at Ali Baba's went south? I'm telling ya — everybody but you knew what you were walking into. Doesn't it bother you nobody warned you?"

Her skin prickled into pyramids of gooseflesh.

"I knew what I was doing, coming here. But what Rosen doesn't figure is, I can be your friend and beat those charges. So here's my advice: we have an occasional public flare-up so the people that tattle will have tales to tell. Featherston's a start. That rat fink told three lies in three minutes."

She gave Sid a slow nod.

"Lie number one: he knew her name.

"Lie number two: he knows exactly what went on in this case because murders like this leave an acid burn on the psyche of the people who work them. But that's not all. Check out those dusty boxes. Notice anything unusual?" He didn't give her a chance to answer. "Two sets of fresh handprints. A little set, and a big set. Spray ninhydrin on the cardboard and I bet the big ones turn out to be his."

Her chest ached. Sid hit the nail. "What's lie number three?"

"A lie by omission."

She nodded, trying to ignore the chill bumps racing across her arms. "He didn't tell me about Kissel wanting to be Governor."

"Maybe he didn't remember." Sid, playing devil's advocate.

"He remembered."

Sid gave her a big smile and said cheerily, "Well, missy, I don't know about you but it's not every day I earn a Get-Out-of-Jail-Free card. Whaddaya say we head over to the Ancient Mariner and slam down a couple?"

"Thanks, but I have a date."

"Anyone I know?"

"Car salesman." When Sid's cheer turned to disappointment, she said, "Yes, I'm a cliché. I got promoted and for the first time in my life, I'll be driving my dream car."

"Run along, then. I'll deal with Teddy."

"What's to deal with?" She slung the purse strap over one shoulder and fumbled for her keys.

"You told him to come get one of these boxes. If he's still here, I'm gonna tell him you lost your mind and decided to pilot this bird yourself. I'll be open and notorious about it. Once everybody's gone for the day, I'm backing my pickup truck flush with the loading dock, and stacking these boxes inside. If I have to stay gone all night, I'll burn us copies . . . one for me, one for the meat hound, and the other for you to work on at your house."

"Greta can copy them tomorrow."

"You said you don't trust her."

"Then Teddy can do it."

"If I'm hearing you right, you've got two weeks. You're gonna waste a man making copies?"

He was talking about violating Departmental policy, removing originals from HQ. In a high-profile case with no shortage of media snoops, if they got caught, they'd be fired.

"You're putting our jobs on the line, Sid."

"You may not know it, but your job went on the skids the minute you found Lady Godiva dead."

Chapter Five

The Mercedes Kompressor in the Auto-Erotica showroom gleamed like luscious red lips wanting a slathering of kisses, and Cézanne fell madly, passionately in love the moment she laid eyes on it.

Hello, Ruby, my precious gem. You're the reason I took a two-year vow of poverty.

As soon as she stepped through the double glass doors, several salesmen made a beeline to greet her. But it was the lumbering, swarthy man in the turquoise Mexican wedding shirt, with the gold nugget rings, and triple-strand chains around his neck, that edged them out and beat them to the sale.

"Welcome to Auto-Erotica, home of the sexiest cars in Cowtown." He pushed his thick wire-rims back up the bridge of his oil-dotted nose. "Sleek, isn't she? This baby goes from zero to sixty in two seconds and that's not all."

The way he left a smudge trail running his hand along Ruby's curves made Cézanne's stomach wrench, and her ears deaf to his spiel. He had no right to man-handle her, certainly not to caress her rear end in a way that should have landed a man of his caliber in jail. Cézanne had no choice but to rescue her so no one could ever violate her perfect body again. And when Viktor — according to his nametag — put his unclean hands on Ruby's handle and popped open her door in a misguided attempt to slide onto the skin of her baby soft seats, she attempted to intervene.

"Stop. Isn't that where I should be sitting?"

Several hundred pounds of bulk plopped into the bucket, testing Ruby's coils and Cézanne's patience. She didn't like his Mister-T Starter Set and found the way he wore his shirt unbuttoned down to the third button — not to mention the pelt on his chest springing out over the flimsy material like the crest on a cockatoo — revolting.

Cézanne admonished him sharply. "Get out of my car." She figured he hadn't heard right, in that he continued grazing his chunky gold ring across Ruby's beautiful complexion. "Stop. You'll scratch her."

"Come again?"

She felt her temper climb. "If you want me to buy her, get out of my seat and start the paperwork. And I want a rag — a clean one — to wipe off the fingerprints."

Heads turned, eyes stared. Men who placed second, third, and fourth, jockeying for position in the footrace to serve her,

66

now laughed contentedly behind their desks.

The car molester swallowed hard enough to bypass his double chin. "And how does Fraulein wish to pay?"

"I have a cashier's check for half. My trade-in's out in the parking lot. And a letter of credit from my bank for the rest."

"I'll need your name."

She lowered her eyes to his hand, now resting on the driver's mirror. He jerked away as if scorched. She rattled her documents in his face, complete with vital statistics and a copy of her driver's license.

"What make is your trade?"

"BMW."

He seemed so pleased she decided not to tell him to look for a rusted-out, entry-level, one-eyed Beemer with a groove down one side that showed up contemporaneously with the shootout in Doug Driskoll's kitchen. She knew Darlene keyed the paint, but who in their right mind would stop to inventory fresh vehicle damage with lead blazing past her head? It was enough to escape without Darlene creasing a permanent part into her hair.

"I'll need your keys so the garage can check her out and get a value assigned to her."

She dropped them into his sweaty palm from far enough away so as not to exchange germs.

"If you'll follow me to my office, we can get started."

"You run on ahead and get me the key. I'll find you after the test drive."

"I'll have to go along." Huffy. Dangling the key.

"No, you don't." She opened her purse.

"Sorry to disappoint you, but I do. We don't normally do spot sales, and you wouldn't believe the number of times we've had to call the police —"

Her badge case slipped down to the bottom of the bag, and she dug for it. The Chief's Special got in the way, so she pulled it out.

"Oh, God." Viktor sucked air. Jumped back. Grabbed the pelt on his chest. "Just take it. Oh, sweet Jesus, Mary, mother of God."

"What?" Cézanne's eyes darted over the showroom, then settled on her piece. "You mean this?"

But Viktor was praying. With the color drained out of his face, and his eyes rolled halfway up into his head, he itemized a long string of sins. She decided to let him purge his conscience before telling him she was The Heat.

Carefully, she set the gun on the passenger seat and rummaged, once more, for her badge case.

"This ought to do it." She flipped it

open, but Viktor wasn't looking. He'd scrunched his eyes so tight a tear rolled out. His face turned beet red, making him look like a man who needed to eat more roughage. "Viktor?"

". . . And, Holy Father, I promise if You spare me I'll never bother the dog again . . ."

"Viktor!"

His eyes opened, and he sucked air.

"I am the police." Her new gold Captain's shield caught the light, and he stopped short of incriminating himself. "The key, please?"

"You're a cop?"

A nod.

He wiped his clammy hands on the thighs of his pants. Barked out a laugh. "What I said about the dog, you didn't really think —"

"Just gimme the damned keys before I call the SPCA."

Viktor dropped them into her hand, then hurried off toward the men's room, taking quick little geisha steps.

With the salesman out of earshot, Cézanne circled the Benz and stroked its hood. Then she searched her purse for a tube of lipstick the same color, and applied it, using Ruby's chrome for a mirror. When her reflection pleased her, she dropped to one knee and whispered into the grillwork.

"Hello, Ruby. Wanna go topless?"

An hour later, woman to woman, Cézanne drove Ruby out for good. The night had a curious electricity in the air and the streets still wore the sheen of that afternoon's rain. But it was the headlight beacons bouncing out of the alley behind Auto-Erotica, and framing themselves neatly within the Kompressor's rearview mirror, that gave Cézanne a start.

Whoever was tailing her needed practice.

"Let's lose this guy," she said half aloud and shifting gears. The wind caught her hair and blew it back from her face. Raw air licked her cheeks until they burned.

Ruby showed her spirit, cutting through the chill until the headlights shrank to the size of fiery opals. The lonely wail of Fort Worth's locomotive, The Tarantula, filled the night, carrying holiday shoppers to the Stockyards. In the distance, steam billowed into the velvety sky, momentarily obscuring the rhinestone stars, and Cézanne thought of Christmas, three weeks away.

She liked the prospect of Hanukkah better, but Bobby Noah acted lukewarm on the idea when she confided her Jewish heritage. It was probably all those presents that had him baffled, one per day. Men she picked seemed to have an aversion to gift-giving. Her gaze flickered to the mirror.

70

Still behind her.

With light rain lacquering the asphalt, she flattened her foot against Ruby's accelerator. Using police pursuit driving skills acquired in rookie school, she let the car take her on a wild ride.

Ahead, railroad warning lights paid homage in flashes of red; Ruby knifed across the tracks in daredevil splendor. In her rearview mirror, red-striped crossing arms lowered, shielding them from harm. A night with Ruby was better than sex — and lasted longer, too. With her head thrown back, Cézanne interrupted the pleasurable sounds coming from Ruby's engine with a delighted laugh.

Then everything went to hell.

Emergency overheads flashed in her rearview mirror. Her stomach sank. For one brief, crazed moment, an inviting thought that seemed to originate with Ruby, flashed in her head —

Let's lose this guy.

— then vaporized.

Sneaky son of a bitch must have set up around the corner from the Top Dog Lounge, waiting for drunks. By the time she pulled to the curb, the patrol car's pushbars were practically giving Ruby an enema.

The dark outline of a Stetsoned lawdog strutted toward her with a Mag-lite outstretched and his fingers wrapped around a gun butt, still sheathed in its leather holster. Heart drumming, Cézanne waited with her hands atop Ruby's steering wheel.

"I clocked you flying through that crossing like you're headed for the hereafter, so you know what I'm here after," came the gruff Southern drawl. "Driver's license and insurance, leadfoot." The light beam hit her squarely in the face. And then, "Jiminy Christmas, it's you."

Cézanne hadn't seen Jinx Porter, Tarrant County Constable, since Roby Tyson's funeral two-and-a-half days before — hadn't wanted to, either. But if one of Driskoll's cronies had pulled her over, everyone tuned to the frequency would've heard the embarrassing radio transmission to the dispatcher.

She imagined the illumination from the mercury vapor lamp's blue-white glow, carving Ruby's shape out of the darkness, made a perfect outline for whomever waited on the other side of the tracks.

"What're you doing out this time of night, Porter? I thought you only worked days."

"I'm training a new man."

While the constable switched off the Mag-lite and tucked it into the waistband behind his belt, she glanced in her rearview mirror at the flicker of headlights through the slow-rolling train wheels. An accordion version of "Cielito Lindo" blared over the constable's handheld radio, and when he caught her staring at it, he offered a ready explanation.

"The dispatcher must either be asleep or dead. I've been treated to station K-OLÉ for the last five minutes. I finally decided that anybody stupid enough not to realize their mike's hung in the on position ought to be fired. Which reminds me — where's the fire?"

"New car. No excuse." She did a quick, over-the-shoulder survey. Had the railroad crossing arms not lifted, she would never have said, "I don't suppose you'd consider extending a little professional courtesy?"

"I might." His breath turned to steam. "I don't suppose you'd consider having dinner with me?"

In the distance, cars moved forward. One in particular bore down hard. Time to go.

Cézanne whipped out a new business card. "Call me."

As she pulled away in time to beat the yellow light, sleet sliced through the night as if settling an old score.

Worse, headlights reappeared in her rear-view mirror.

She floored Ruby. Less than ten blocks from home, they slid around the corner, with the tail car dogging her. It took some doing, but she managed to elude him by cutting the lights and doglegging through a series of residential streets.

But the victorious exhilaration coursing through her veins came to an abrupt halt at the final bend.

Black ice.

The Kompressor went into a skid. Losing traction, Cézanne steered into the turn. A mature pecan tree in the neighbor's yard jumped out and clipped Ruby's fender.

At the moment of impact, her cheek slammed against the window, knocking her silly.

And poor Ruby without major medical. In her zeal to leave the dealership, after hours, with the Kompressor, she hadn't notified the insurance company to bind the new car. She didn't need an internal adding machine to calculate the damage, just an arm and a leg.

And Ruby was going to have one hell of a doctor bill.

Chapter Six

In Cézanne's dream-filled slumber, the country church was standing room only with faceless guests, and it was Bobby's turn to exchange vows. But when the time came to slip the ring on her finger, a midget jester, bearing a striking resemblance to Greta, appeared out of the ether. With bells jingling on her green and pink satin hat, she tumbled down the aisle in tights and pointy-toed shoes. A diamond wedding band that had to be piloted to the front row in a wheelbarrow took three groomsmen to lift it, but when Greta tripped them with an oversized shoe, the gemstone crashed to the floor in a million pieces.

Crashed, and pounded.

Banged loud enough to awaken Tutankhamen and unravel his burial garb.

She sat bolt upright. Electric blue numbers on the digital clock pulsed out the time. Six forty-five. In the morning.

For God's sake, she'd overslept.

The caller hammered harder.

Probably Sid, stopping to drop off a box full of copies from the Great Dane. After limping Ruby in from the black ice fiasco, she'd found his card wedged between the screen and molding. Remembering, events crystallized inside her mushy brain. Her new car had a dent in it.

She flung back the covers. Threw out a leg.

Maybe the dent wasn't all that bad. Maybe it was just a scuff mark. Maybe in the daylight it wouldn't look as bad as the end-of-the-world feeling that went through her gut in the dark.

Stiff-necked, with a purple mouse puffing at the corner of her left eye, it took a Herculean effort to slip into her robe without shrieking from the catch in her back.

Son of a bitch kept his finger on the bell. The ringing went on, non-stop. She snatched the Chief's Special from its resting spot on the night stand and hobbled to the front door. Checking the peephole did no good. A huge, dark eye pressed close to the glass obscured her view.

"Back off." The eye zoomed out to reveal the distorted, ebony face of Leviticus Devilrow. "Oh, hell. What did I do to deserve this?"

She placed the .38 on a chair and yanked the glass knob so hard every nerve in her body seemed to awaken at once.

With a downturned mouth and a thick tongue, the handyman said, "I come for the other half o' my money."

"Jeez, Devilrow, you couldn't wait 'til I got home?"

"I waited. You home."

She was about to ask how much she owed him for slapping the last of the shingles on her roof — the roof that took him ten months from start to finish — the roof that looked like a zipper on the Jolly Green Giant's loin cloth because he had rows of shingles going along the top and bottom at the same time. Instead, ripping open the door to let him in out of the cold made her wince with pain, and she forgot all about how she'd like to pick the .38 up by its barrel and brain him with the butt.

"You don't look so good, Miz Zan. You takin' up drinkin'? Was you in a barroom brawl? I always figured you for a scrapper, even though you dress in them fine clothes."

"Not that it's any of your business, Devilrow. I wrecked my new Benz."

"Sho 'nuff." His eyes shifted to the Kompressor and back. He shoved his mammoth hands deep into his overalls where pockets should have been, and treated her to a view of him copping an itch. "Guess you'd be fixin' to call the insurance man."

Insurance. Aw, Jeez.

Her spinal cord tightened like a cello

string. In the mirror of the Victorian hall tree, she glimpsed her face contorting into a ghoulish mask.

"Miz Zan, about that money . . ."

She looked past him, at the passenger seat of his rust-caked vintage truck. A young girl, scantily dressed for winter, shivered beyond the dashboard. Her round, flat face appeared to grow out of a blanket scrunched tight under her chin. Devilrow caught her looking.

"That's my sister Thessalonia's oldest. She run off with her no-account boyfriend and left Duty for me to watch."

"Who?"

"Deuteronomy. Thessalonia's oldest. My sister, Thessalonia? Miz Zan, you ain't much of a listener."

She wasn't. Not when Thessalonia's oldest shot her the finger. Or threw a gang sign at her.

The cold breeze slipped under her robe. "Devilrow, I don't have your money here. I'll write a check and you can take it to my bank when it opens."

"Wouldn't want to do that." He spoke with a deliberate grimness. "I needs cash, now."

"I just told you I don't keep that kind of money here at the house." She thought of the three hundred she transferred from the cuss kitty to the cookie jar, but that wouldn't do. Devilrow's final draw ran close to a thousand dollars.

His gaze darted over the porch, settling on nothing. "I might could excuse it for now, Miz Zan, if we was to strike a deal."

Ten months of the handyman made her bridle-wise to his suggestions.

She narrowed her eyes in a villainous squint. "What kind of deal?"

"Well, see, I'm supposed to go to *Eeze* Texas," he said, as if referring to a town instead of a direction. "I'm to pick up my brother, Ezra, from the FCI — Ezra got his Pardon — but my old truck's about to play out . . ."

She spun her hand in front of her at high RPMs, encouraging him to hasten his explanation using the universal gesture of speed. Not to mention, it didn't surprise her at all to learn Devilrow had kin in a Federal Correctional Institution since she pretty much felt, all along, he belonged in one himself. But the idea of a Pardon threw her for a loop.

"What do you want, Devilrow? Just tell me what you want. I don't want to know where you're going or why, or what kind of fix you're in. I just want to know what you want."

"You axe me, you're havin' a little trouble modulatin'. Now if you was to maybe take Duty off my hands a week or so —"

"Why would I want to do that?"

"— If I was to pay you —"

"You wouldn't be trying to bleed me dry if you had any money."

"Well, you does owe me for the roof. So, if maybe you was to let Duty stay 'til I come back, she could keep house. Maybe help out while you recover?"

"I'm not hurt." *Lie.* She squinted. "Shouldn't she be in school?"

"Thessalonia's girl, she dropped out."

"How old is she?"

"Sixteen."

"You're asking me to harbor a truant?"

"That'd be nize." He smiled until his eyes sealed shut and the corners crinkled like Raisinettes stuck near the edge of a chocolate pie face.

"Get her up here."

Devilrow beckoned the girl with a meaty hand. She descended from the pickup in the wake of an eerie, rusty-hinge squeak, and as her feet crunched without enthusiasm across the brittle St. Augustine, gooseflesh popped out like grassburrs over her bare legs. With matted hair braided into corn rows and a set of flat, unblinking eyes that agreed with her face, the girl projected the presence and misery of a hundred-year-old lady.

She stepped onto the porch in shoes that had come apart at the soles.

Cézanne felt a twinge of guilt. "What's your name?"

"Deuteronomy."

"Did this man kidnap you?"

"He my unca."

She favored the girl with a nod. "He says you can help me around the house." No response. "I would pay you, of course. But if you work for me, we're giving you a polygraph before payday." Not a humorous bone in her scrawny body. "A lie detector test." Slow head bob of understanding. "Where are your clothes?"

The girl let go of the blanket. It hung over droopy shoulders like it had been draped across a bony clothes hanger. She clutched the hem of her threadbare cotton dress, and fanned it out on each side like the first blossom of spring. The sudden movement carried the scent of nutmeg to Cézanne's space, along with the pungent odor of freshly picked herbs.

"Have you had your rabies shots? Not that you have rabies. I have a dog that bites. Well, he's not really my dog, he's my friend's dog. I'm only taking care of him because my friend killed himself. Probably because of the dog. Or maybe the dog did it. He's actually pretty smart. The dog, not my friend. My friend was intelligent, too, but he's dead. So I'm talking about the dog. He could've done something like that

— killed my friend, I mean. He's certainly got it in for me. The dog, not my friend. My friend's dead."

Conversation degenerated to mindless prattle.

Devilrow's eyebrows peaked like a couple of hairy arrowheads. It occurred to her he must've thought she went on another bender. Just because he got the wrong impression the day he saw her guzzling Jack Black from a bottle — the day the results of the State Bar Exam came in the mail — didn't make her a sot. She tried to tell him it was Roby's whiskey; that Roby always kept a bottle at her house for when he visited since she only liked piña coladas, strawberry daiquiris, and concoctions Roby referred to as sissy drinks.

She attempted to set Devilrow's niece straight. "When I refer to him, I'm talking about the dog, okay? I don't have any reason to be talking to you about my friend."

The girl appeared suitably impressed. Or confused.

Cézanne turned to Devilrow. "This isn't going to work. First of all, I don't invite strangers into my house —"

"But Miz Zan, you gotta help."

"— second, we don't seem to be able to communicate. Third —"

"But Miz Zan, you the only one I trust."

"— I'm not running a day care. If you want to bring her around this weekend to do some light housekeeping, I'll put her to work for a few days — no more. And she can't stay overnight."

"But Miz Zan, I needs to be on my way. I needs you to take Duty now."

"This weekend, Devilrow. When I'm home. Where I can watch her. If you can't live with the deal, don't accept it."

Even as she closed the door in their faces, she was thinking, *No way this is going to work.*

The stiffness in Cézanne's neck cost her an extra forty minutes dressing. She downed the coffee pot dregs, rinsed the cup, and untoggled the throw bolt securing the front door. If she got lucky, she could release the terrier from hell and beat Butch the dog in a race to the door. If not, she'd have matching fang marks on her other ankle. Tiptoeing back to the spare bedroom, she listened for jingling tags and the click of toenails against the hardwoods — a sure sign she'd have to sprint.

A creaky hinge became her downfall.

With lightning speed, the Scottie drew himself up. Thanks to highly polished floors, he scrambled in place for traction, giving her a two-second handicap. When she flung open the front door and hurtled herself out onto the porch with the piercing rebuke of Butch the dog hanging between her ears, the last thing she expected to see was Deuteronomy Devilrow huddled under her thin blanket with her legs drawn up to her chest, and her frail arms, hugging them. A small duffle bag sat off to one side. Leviticus Devilrow's truck was nowhere in sight.

"What are you doing here?"

"My unca say he be back next week."

"Jesus."

"No, my unca named Leviticus. Jesa's the Mexican man who come to fix our toilet."

Well, hell. Now what? Cézanne sighed into the frosty air. "Come in out of the cold. And watch out for the dog."

With the girl barely past the threshold, Cézanne pulled an umbrella out of the hall tree, fended off the wheat-colored dog with a fencing maneuver until she found the catch and swooshed it open.

"It's bad luck to open umbrellas in the house." Devilrow's niece.

"Oh, really?" Facetious. "Well let me tell you, young lady, it doesn't get any worse than last week."

But Deuteronomy mumbled, "That's whatchoo think."

"What'd you say?"

"My granddaddy loved little sayin's."

84

She flicked the air with a little finger move, and made herself at home on the leather Chesterfield sofa. "He had a little sayin' I stitched into a sampler when I was twelve. Here's the sayin': From the moment yo' born, 'til the ride in the hearse, it's never so bad it can't get worse."

Cézanne stared, mute.

After shooing the dog down the hall, she closed him off in the study and wracked her brain for a solution. She returned to find Devilrow's niece affecting a zombie's pace, trudging over to graze her bony fingers across the inlaid wood on a drop-leaf writing desk purchased through Sotheby's.

"All this stuff, it's yours?"

"Don't get used to it." But the girl ignored her and reached for the set of Limoges eggs balanced precariously on delicate gilt stands. "And don't touch anything."

Deuteronomy Devilrow pulled back her hand and faced her with a flat stare.

Softening her tone, Cézanne outlined the predicament. "I see several problems here. One, you're sixteen. I could call Child Protective Services and tell them your uncle abandoned you."

"But he didn't. He left me with you." Dull eyed. In a monotone. With a hint of intelligence.

"I suppose that would be an argument in your favor." She continued to tick off reasons for not going along with Devilrow's hare-brained idea. "Two, I have no reason to turn over my house to someone I just met."

"You think I steal 'cause my unca Ezra did time in the pen."

Exactly.

Cézanne started to lie, then took a long, deep breath and held it. "Hey — it works both ways. You should be scared of me. I could be a child molester." The girl blinked. "Okay, forget it. I don't know whether you steal or not, and I don't have time to find out."

"Whatchoo want me to do?"

Cézanne reviewed her options. "Catch the bus up at the corner and go back to Devilrow's. Or I'll call child welfare to come get you."

No sleazy con man's gonna run my business.

With a flat, unblinking stare, the girl stayed put. "I'll go. It'll be fine."

"That'd be best. I'm sorry. It would be different if we knew each other."

"How much a bus ride cost?"

"I don't know."

"I got no money."

"Fine. I'll give you bus money."

"I'll use it for food. I'm awful hungry. I can put this blanket 'round my shoulders and walk."

The girl was trying to scam her. "Whatever you think."

"Say, could you tell me where's the bad parts of town? So I don't get jacked on account of I'm homeless."

Huh?

"And don'tchoo worry. If somebody kills me, no need to feel guilty."

"Guilty?"

"Yessum." Duty glanced around wistfully. "I just thank God we got to meet, 'cause I don't have no identification. And if they find me in a back alley with my throat slit —" she made a grisly face and drew a long, skinny finger across her neck "— even if flies lay eggs on me, you'll be able to recognize me and tell my family after I'm dead." The girl glanced at her hand. " 'Course I imagine my skin won't be this dark."

"Huh?"

"I once saw a picture on TV, on the Discovery Channel, where maggots got a girl about my age — she was a Colored girl like me — and they ate the top layer of skin off and turned her into a white girl. 'Bout as white as you. Only you lookin' a lot whiter right now." Devilrow's niece fish-hooked a finger into her mouth and stretched enough skin aside for Cézanne to see a mouthful of teeth and a gold cap on a back molar. "I got no dental records, but see my gold tooth? Look real close — it's got a star cut out of it. That was my idea."

She let go and her face snapped back in place. "Anyway, it's not yo' fault. But now you know how to tell it's me when they put the drawing in the newspaper."

Jesus.

Cézanne dug in her purse. "Here's a couple of bucks. Get food and take the bus."

Duty fisted the money, pulled at her neckline, and shoved it into her bra.

Whatever. There was a murder to solve. Taking on a strange kid was not on the agenda.

Thirty minutes later, Cézanne pulled the Kompressor into her reserved space at the PD. She let herself in through a rear door and walked the corridor to the elevators at the front of the building. Ignoring the swell of civilians roaming the foyer, she pressed the button.

"Hi, Miz Zan."

Cézanne snapped her head. The voice came from floor level, and off to one side.

Devilrow's niece sat huddled in the corner, sharing her blanket with an ancient wino. The elevator binged and the doors opened.

"What're you doing here?"

"Tryin' to get the cold outta my bones."

"I meant what're you doing in this building?"

"My gramma, Corinthia — she say if I ever get lost, I should go to the po-lice station."

The elevator doors slid shut. "You can't just come in here and make yourself at home."

"This a public building?"

"Well . . . yes."

"I'm the public."

"You can't stay here."

"I only came in to warm up. I'll be gone soon enough. This is Albert." She thumbed at the sot with the five o'clock shadow, a lupine grin, and an eye made for evil. "Albert say he know a place kids can stay."

The news was enough to prickle the stubble on Cézanne's legs. She strode over and hauled Devilrow's niece up by the wrist. The girl was as thin as a cadaver.

"You're coming with me." To Albert, she said, "Get your ass outta here before I run your name through the computer for warrants."

Duty grabbed her bag and blanket, while Albert took his scraggly self and clopped out the door with the speed of an old Maine trotter. He was halfway down the street before the elevator doors reopened.

Cézanne gave Devilrow's niece the once-over. "What's wrong with you? Why would you cozy up to a perfect stranger?"

"I'm in the big city. I don't know nobody. The one person I axed for help, she say I'm a thief and she can't keep me."

Well, hell.

"We're stuck with each other for now, but this isn't the end of it. Devilrow's not pawning you off on me. We'll see about this."

They stepped onto the elevator and Cézanne punched four.

"Where we goin'?"

"To my office."

"You a policeman?"

"Acting Captain."

"Like play-acting?"

"No. I'm the Captain until they post the position and fill it."

"You could put me in jail?"

"If you did something wrong."

"My daddy in prison."

"What about your granddaddy?"

"Got no granddaddy."

"Yes, you do. You said you made samplers out of pithy little aphorisms."

"Don't know whatchoo mean by that, but the only granddaddy I knew was a travelin' man. Traveled right outta my gramma's house and outta her life. Only other time I heard about him was when my gramma took a court paper down to the funeral parlor to stop 'em from buryin' him in the family plot. 'Cept it was too late. My granddaddy was already in the ground."

With a somber nod, Cézanne escorted

90

Deuteronomy to the fourth floor Homicide office with two concerns pervading her thoughts.

The first: *I should have found her something more appropriate to wear.*

The second: *What the hell is that smell?*

"Do you have a change of clothes? Because if you're going to stay here until I figure out what to do with you, you'll need better clothes. Clothes make the man. Remember that. Look sloppy and people'll think you're sloppy."

"This all I have." Palms up and helpless.

"What's in the bag?"

Instead of answering, Deuteronomy hugged it to her chest and avoided eye contact.

"All right, I'll drive you by Leviticus Devilrow's at lunch, and you can run inside and change."

"This all I have."

She couldn't remember when, or if, a sixteen-year-old ever cut her off at the knees. Not only did she need clothes, she looked like she could use a good meal. "I probably own a decent outfit you can fit into." And then, a lowly shake of the head, "You'll have to fix that hair."

But she was thinking about a box of clothes she'd stored in the attic for charity, and how she should unearth them for Deuteronomy Devilrow as a consolation prize.

Chapter Seven

Up in Homicide, three cardboard boxes awaited Cézanne's arrival. By the looks of them, Sid managed to get the Kissel files to an overnight copy service and the originals back in lock-down before anyone was the wiser. But when she discovered Sid had accomplished the unbelievable without a bloodbath — got the wiry old cynic from the photo lab to print copies of crime scene photos for each of them — she rested her hands on the chair arms in relaxed command.

Screw Rosen.

In less than thirteen days, she'd make an arrest and the Great Dane Murder would be exceptionally cleared. She stood at the window and tracked a plane as it lifted off the tarmac at Carswell Air Force Base. Most cops spent an entire career without ever getting their hands on a case as big as this. Solving it would take everything she had.

Clouds the color of steel wool hung low in the sky, but that didn't stop the latest cadet class from participating in their rigorous physical training schedule. On the other side of the Trinity River, a mile or so from police headquarters, they ran laps in sweats and parkas, without regard to the bitter wind, with discomfort reflected in their faces.

"Duty, if you like, you can come over by the window and watch the police recruits work out."

The girl obliged, but instead of taking a seat, she stood where the cold light shaded her face a deep blue. "I like to draw. I draw pretty fair."

"Let's see if we have something you can practice on."

Cézanne handed over a fresh legal pad and a pen, shooed the girl off to one corner of the credenza, and went to work on the dummy file. According to a sticky-note Teddy affixed to the glass shade on her banker's lamp, Cissy Kissel was the beneficiary on her husband's one-point-eight-million-dollar life insurance policy. Even now, Teddy was on his way to the probate clerk's office to nose into Dane Kissel's assets. And Sid, probably rewarding himself with an extra few hours sleep for tending to the files, should be along shortly.

After awhile, she got used to the odd smell that seemed to ooze from Deuteronomy's pores, and for the most part, Devilrow's niece blended into the furniture. She had little to say and her large, acorn-shaped eyes appeared to soak in the atmosphere of Sid's great, metaphorical fish tank like a sea sponge. The only time she left Cézanne's office, she made a quick trip to the ladies' room. When she returned, Jock Featherston and Benji Wardancer were over by the coffee pot, eyeing her with curiosity and sniggering like a couple of cartoon dogs.

Cézanne watched the girl walk brazenly close. She filled a Styrofoam cup with hot water and stirred in a packet of powdered cider. Featherston said something unintelligible, then laughed, but Duty's mumbled answer vanquished their hyena grins.

When she came back in, Cézanne said, "Were those guys bothering you?"

"Not so much."

"Ignore them. They don't have a lot of respect for women. Police work's a male-dominated field. You learn to put up with it." As soon as the words were out, she wondered whom she was trying to convince. "So what'd they say?"

"Just axed what was I doin' here?"

"What'd you tell them?"

Duty gave a one-shoulder shrug and slid into her chair.

Around ten, Sid strutted in looking downright handsome for a sixty-three-year-old man. In his meticulously tailored suit, and custom-made, ten-X beaver cowboy hat, he appeared so happy with his new lot that the move from the jail seemed to erase years of life's experiences from his face. Even Sid didn't notice Devilrow's niece, shrinking in the corner, until Cézanne gestured with an obvious cut of the eyes.

Adjusting the woven leather tails of his turquoise and sterling bolo tie, he said, "Who's this?"

"This is Deuteronomy. Duty, for short." Craning her neck across the blotter, Cézanne took steps to keep Sid's undeniable wit in check. "No wisecracks."

"Like what?"

"Like you're on duty," she whispered. "Or, ready for duty."

"Off duty?"

Cézanne issued a warning. "Don't say anything that's not G-rated. She's a minor."

Sid strolled over to the credenza where Devilrow's niece was shading her sketch. "Howdy, Duty. I'm Lt. Klevenhagen — Sid, to you — and it's my duty to warn you this place can be toxic to your mental health."

He stuck out his hand. With a faint smile stealing across her face, she took it.

"What're you under arrest for?"

Mute, Duty shook her head.

"I see," Sid said knowingly. "House arrest.

You're not actually going to the pokey. Well, maybe the warden'll let you out on furlough when we break for lunch."

For the first time that day, Deuteronomy perked up. Instantly, Sid picked up on it.

"Hungry?" Without awaiting an answer, he said, "Me, too. Let's me and you go scare up some breakfast while the Captain runs the show."

Duty's eyes rolled in Cézanne's direction.

"It's okay, he's a policeman."

"He gonna lock me up?"

Sid cut in. "Only if you can't eat more pancakes. I'll lock you up and force feed you. It's my duty."

With a wink and a nod, he led the way out. Devilrow's niece followed, lemminglike, on the heels of his spit-polished lizard wingtips. The scent of nutmeg and alfalfa clippings lingered in her wake.

With the office to herself, Cézanne thumbed through the Rolodex and found the number for CPS. When a duty officer answered, Cézanne asked for a caseworker.

Momentarily, the voice of a frazzled, overworked man vibrated through the phone. "Lady, lots of kids get abandoned. Your call's a priority three — the lowest. We concentrate on infants and toddlers. We're overworked, underpaid, and if you want to file a report, we can have somebody out there in about six weeks."

Cézanne pulled rank.

We'll see about getting the runaround. Get me a supervisor. Put an end to this nonsense.

The phone clicked over, a supervisor answered, and she retold the story. Instead of taking the girl off her hands, the supervisor asked if she'd like to become a foster mom.

Out of ideas, she hung up, plucked out a copy of the first-line officer's report on the Great Dane Murder, and studied it. What began as a routine Friday night call, ended up putting a tuck in the tail of the police department.

See the man.

Possible homicide.

Caucasian male victim, DOS.

The man to see was the Panther City's wealthy wildcatter, Worth Price, Dane Kissel's father-in-law. According to the report, upon her unescorted return from the Trail Drivers Ball, Price's daughter, Cissy Kissel, found the undisputed prince of criminal lawyers in bed with a gunshot wound to the chest. When Cissy announced her husband's death by crumpling to the floor in a snot-slinging, crystal-shattering heap, Old Man Price made the shaky nine-one-one call.

Cézanne stopped reading and pawed through a brown envelope stuffed full of eight-by-ten glossies. Beneath the incandes-

97

cent wash of the banker's lamp, she examined them, one by one, with a magnifying glass, waiting for something to spring out. Something Jock Featherston and Captain Crane missed. Something she would find, if dedicated and careful. Something obvious and out of sync — like the Frisbee-shaped, leathery pad of skin dangling from the butt of the purple-assed baboon.

After awhile, she set the magnifying glass on the blotter, flexed her hand, and relaxed in her chair. Her mind momentarily drifted. While considering whether to have the crime scene photos blown up in size, she scanned the room, settling on the large glass rectangle Crane mounted over the screen of his computer monitor to magnify the type. In two snaps, she removed and placed it over one of the black-and-whites.

Time seemed to suspend. Before she completed her investigation, she would know more about Dane Kissel than he had known about himself. How he lived. How he died. Whether he harbored any secrets that went unburied.

At the next photo, her breath quickened.

Dane Kissel, face up on the bed, his countenance permanently freeze-framed in a ghastly mix of surprise and indecision; a close-up of the Great Dane's hand, his finger loosely curled around the trigger; Kissel's open eyes, doll-like and pleading, with remnants of dark froth draining from one corner of his mouth. And off to one side of Cézanne's blotter, a picture of Dane Kissel in life, his keen aquamarine eyes staring up into the lamp's harsh filament, smart and determined in the dress blues of the FWPD.

Hi there. I'm Cézanne. You don't know me, but I'm the one who's going to make it right.

That his features reminded her of Bobby Noah, brought sharp pangs of longing for the Johnson County Sheriff. But along with a dread that Dane Kissel's mysterious death would become the whale that swallowed her whole, came a strengthened resolve to untangle the web surrounding his mysterious death.

A sharp rap brought her upright. Jock Featherston framed himself in the doorway.

"That black chick's weird, Capt'n."

"How so?"

He mocked Devilrow's niece with an exaggerated dialect. "Yo' puppy's in Heaven and he didn't suffer much."

"She said that to you?"

"To Wardancer. She told me not to go to St. Croix. I'm not going to St. Croix, I'm going to the Bahamas."

"Ignore it."

"The chick's whacked out. Just thought

you ought to know, some of the guys don't like her."

"Which guys?"

"All of us, Capt'n. She creeps us out."

She noticed him staring at the papers on her desk, and casually collected them into a protected bunch. "Go easy on her, Jock. She comes from a dysfunctional family. Tell the guys I said to suck it up and deal with it. It's temporary."

Seemingly placated, Featherston left.

Had it not been for the pervasive smell of a stout poultice surrounding Duty, Cézanne might not have noticed when Sid and the girl returned. The girl picked up her legal pad and pen, retreated to her corner, and began sketching, undisturbed.

Sid strutted in, peacock-pleased. "Presenting Miss Deuteronomy Devilrow. Descendant of the Shreveport Devereauxs."

Cézanne's eyes bulged. Duty had on a designer suit the color of melted chocolate, and a pair of flats a shade or two darker. A gold pin bunched her corn rows together at the nape of her neck and a thin film of lip gloss covered her mouth.

Startled into brutal honesty, Cézanne said, "What happened?"

"My daughter — Betsy — the lawyer. Too many clothes. But the girl takes a size nine shoe, so we stopped by the thrift store and damned if they didn't have something she liked."

Duty smiled like a jungle cat after a big feast.

"I tried to pay for the shoes, but the girl claimed she had the two bucks."

Bus money.

Cézanne's jaw torqued. She noticed a familiar logo on the gold belt buckle and said, "Come here. Let me see how nice you look." But what she really wanted was to inspect the maker's label.

Ferragamo.

Dumbstruck, she looked over at Sid.

"It won't hurt anybody, Captain."

Cézanne admonished Devilrow's niece with a warning, "Don't spill anything on those clothes."

Sid went back to reading the Kissel file. Duty returned to the credenza with the grace of an empress.

Cézanne examined more crime scene photos until Benji Wardancer's strident voice carried across the room. The six feet tall, one-quarter Native American, with a multisyllabic, unpronounceable tribal name that translated into "Gentle Bison" — but converted even better to Benji — could actually project his voice more than a mile when riled.

Cézanne looked up from a photograph. She cocked her head enough to glimpse him at his computer.

From the downturn in conversation, he must've been using the Faces software in an attempt to glean a computerized composite sketch from a witness. But sorting through prototypes of eyes, noses, lips, and head shapes didn't seem to be working. Gentle Bison was fast becoming Frustrated Bison, judging by his strident tone.

"These eyes? These big ones?"

A man answered, "More like those. Well, maybe not. No, that's not it, either. I'm sorry, they all look the same."

Cézanne mashed a hand against her ear to cut the distraction, and absorbed herself in the details of the remaining pictures.

Dane Kissel had it made. Opulent bedroom. Gorgeous bed nearly overpowered by ormolu decorations, probably Louis XV. With a nice, big zebra skin draped over the sides. A nice, black and white striped hide with a huge bloodstain pooling from the exit wound in the Great Dane's back.

While Sid stretched out his legs and crossed them at the ankles, Cézanne handed over the first-line officer's report and concentrated her efforts on the postmortem glossies. Beyond the door to her office, Frustrated Bison made the transition into Pissed-off Bison.

"You said he had a round face," Wardancer fumed. "That's a round face."

"Not that round. You could tell he had a chin. It had a dimple in it."

"A dimple? Dude, you never said he had a dimple."

"I'm saying it now."

"He had a cleft chin?"

"That's what I said." And then, "You still got the eyes wrong. I told you they tilted at the corners. He had cat eyes but they weren't green, they were dark."

Wardancer, infuriated now. "Then why did you pick the light-colored ones? You never said —"

"His mouth was smaller. He had lips like the lead singer from N-Sync. Those are Mick Jagger's lips."

Duty dragged her chair closer to the door. She tilted an ear like a watchdog on alert, and scratched her pen furiously across the page.

Eventually, Cézanne's curiosity got the best of her. She set aside the magnifying glass. "What are you working on?"

"Nothin'."

"Let's see."

The girl flipped the sheets back into place and passed the tablet across the desk. Cézanne gave it the once-over.

On top was an excellent likeness of Sid. On the next page, Greta, with a phone pressed to her ear and a sour pinch to her thin lips. Page three, a flattering likeness of herself. Quite nicely, the unlikely artist captured the weave of her sweater jacket with its intricate buttons and the matching plaid of her kelly green and cobalt blue skirt.

"These are really good. Where'd you learn to draw?"

A shrug, and a downward glance.

Cézanne studied the dull eyes and cross-hatched cheeks in the next drawing with great interest.

"Who's this?"

"Sometimes I see things."

"Vivid imagination?"

A headshake. "Things that happen."

"You mean you overhear things."

"If you say so." Duty's gaze strayed to the ceiling, stalled in the corner, and dropped on Sid, still perusing the report.

At once, the voice of Raging Maniac rose above the din.

"I think we should quit. Maybe have you come back in a couple of days when your vision's not so blurred."

In a strange flash of intuition, Cézanne excused herself. Still holding Duty's sketch pad, she walked into the common area where Bison in Need of Medication sat at the computer, with great circles of moisture ringing his shirt sleeves. A heavy-set man with ruddy skin and his head wrapped in gauze sat next to her detective, and she

104

flashed the witness a smile.

"No luck, Benj?"

"It's not the right shape face, Capt'n. And the eyes are all wrong. I suggested Mr. Fontenot come back tomorrow but he seems to think —"

"That's him." Wardancer's witness perched on the edge of his chair, his head oozing pink behind the sterile padding. With his nose inches from the legal pad and his fingertip barely touching the corner where Deuteronomy Devilrow initialed her drawing, he announced in the most incredulous voice, "That's the maggot who shot my brother."

While Happy Bison reproduced the composite sketch of the armed robbery suspect and worked up a Crimestopper blurb for the six o'clock newscast, Cézanne retreated to the confines of her office and pulled her chair up even with Devilrow's niece. With elbows propped on her knees and her chin resting in her hands, she leaned in close enough to trap Duty's strange fragrance in her nostrils.

"What do you mean, you see things?"

"My gramma Corinthia, she a voodoo mambo."

"Mambo?"

"Priestess."

"You're saying she sticks pins in dolls

105

made to look like real people?"

"Mostly she use chicken feet and po-tions." Duty Devilrow seemed to withdraw inside herself. "And spells."

Sid perked up. "I think we ought to give her a photo of Rosen and a hacksaw, maybe see what all she can do."

"Who Rosen?" Duty said dully.

"Never mind him." Cézanne waved Sid into silence. The last thing she needed was a psychic crackpot hanging around drawing more than just composite sketches. She began to think in terms of potential rela-tives she could pawn Devilrow's niece off on. "Where does your grandmother live?"

"In the bayou."

"You mean near the bayou." No re-sponse. "Is your grandma in East Texas?"

A slow shake of the head and a woeful, "Louisiana."

Before Cézanne could come up with an alternative plan, Jock Featherston stuck his shock of chemically bleached hair through the door opening. Duty withered beneath his scowl.

"How's it going, Lieutenant? Anything I can help with, Capt'n?"

"Whatcha need, Featherston?"

"That drive-by over in Stop Six? Well, the kid's mother went on Channel Eighteen this morning, and put up a reward. That new investigative reporter, Garlon Harrier?

He's the one covering the story. Said we weren't on top of things. The only reason I don't drive my unit over and cold-cock him is — maybe with the extra publicity — we'll get some Crimestopper tips." Featherston grinned into their silence.

She dismissed him with a curt nod and a "Keep up the good work," but Garlon Harrier's irresponsible comments worried her. If they slacked off on the Great Dane, they wouldn't make the deadline and the chief was counting on her. But if civilians thought the police didn't consider the death of an African-American child as important as a rich White guy, there would be more heat from the top and another way for Rosen to put the screws to her.

While Sid had Duty tickled over a picture of a turkey he converted from a quick outline of his left hand, Cézanne raked her fingers through the thin wisp of bangs drooping over her forehead. She wished for the return of happy hour, with triple shots. For Roby Tyson to pat her on the back and give advice.

She returned her attention to the crime scene pictures and engrossed herself in the next photo, a floor shot taken near the Kissel's eighteenth-century mansion bed. Except for the stray cocktail napkin, a matchbook, and a thousand pinpricks of blood on the carpet, it could have been a still for *Architectural Digest.*

She passed the picture to Sid. "What do you make of this?"

"Shot at close range." He traced his index finger lightly over the photo to illustrate the narration. "See how the carpet's covered in a fine mist? An indication of high velocity bloodstains."

"That's not what I'm talking about. Look at the matchbook."

"Kissel didn't smoke. Leastwise, not when I knew him." For a long time Sid studied the close-up, seemingly without breathing. "Can't read the fine print."

When he tried to give it back, she said, "Are there any Feds you're on good terms with?"

"OSHA. I used to call in violations from the pay phone at the jail, hoping they'd shut the place down. Anonymous, of course."

"I'm referring to the FBI."

With fire in his eyes and conviction in his tone, he said, "Hate the cocksuckers. Always trying to steal your collar, sons-a-bitches are glory hogs. I've spent my entire career watching the Bureau horn in on local busts." The veins in his neck plumped up and his face took on a pinkish cast. "It chaps me, no end, the way those insufferable pricks inflict themselves into a situation when it looks like the crime's solvable. But you never saw them turn tail so quick and head for the hills when it all turns to shit — candy asses."

She suspected his thoughts grew out of a five-year slew of child kidnappings that ended in murder. The FBI's MO was to barge in, take over, and take off after a month's worth of leads played out.

Sid finally wound down with, "That's what you get when you try to run a law enforcement outfit with shysters, accountants, and Spanish teachers."

Undaunted, Cézanne said, "They've got that new software that's supposed to enhance photographs. I think we should ask to borrow it."

"You should. And take knee pads."

"What's that supposed to mean?"

"Means open wide and say, 'Ahhhhhh.' Hate the bastards."

She flashed one of her beauty pageant smiles. "See there? We're in agreement. I knew we'd have something in common."

"We do. We both have a partner who's queer."

While Sid was enjoying a one-man hootenanny at Teddy's expense, Cézanne noticed Duty in the corner, flashing a couple of finger puppet shadows against the wall. When she remarked on it, the girl stuffed something bulky down the front of her blouse. Obviously, Sid noticed, too.

"What are you up to?" Cézanne demanded.

A slow, suspicious headshake.

"What's that under your shirt?"

Big shakes.

"If you don't show me right this minute, Sid's going to dangle you upside down by the ankles, and shake you 'til your teeth rattle."

Apparently, Duty believed her. She dipped a hand down the front of her shirt and dug out a small pouch, attached to a leather thong around her neck. A powerful odor engulfed their shared space.

"What's that?"

"Mojo."

Cézanne grimaced at the stench.

Several seconds went by before Sid took the reins. "What's inside?"

"Lock o' hair. Couple of shells. A little oil. Herbs. Special dirt."

Sid's eyebrow shot straight up. "Special dirt? You mean like potting soil? Horse manure? Dirt blessed by the Pope?"

"Cemetery."

After a long pause, Cézanne asked, "What's it for?"

"The loa." When they exchanged confused looks, she said, "Spirit."

"Is that what reeks?"

"It's probably the snake skin. It goes bad." Duty lifted the pouch and crinkled her nose. "Must be working."

"Would you excuse us a moment?" Cézanne said pleasantly. She grabbed Sid by the wrist and tugged him out of his chair. Outside, with the door pulled to, she started in. "What in the cathair am I supposed to do? I've got a dead-end case, a brand new car with a big fat gash in the right front quarter panel, no insurance, and a snake charmer in my office, eavesdropping on confidential information and drawing composite sketches from eyewitness accounts."

"I say put her on the payroll. She can't be any crazier than people we've already got working here."

"Doesn't it bother you she's in there stinking up the office?"

"Don't smell any worse than cheap pipe tobacco."

"You're taking her side."

"I like her. Besides, maybe she can stuff Rosen's gonads in a pasta maker. Or stick pins in him — I like that even better. Squish-kebob."

Cézanne's eyes drifted to the frosted glass pane in time to see a shadow about the size of Duty Devilrow, hunkered over the desk. She grabbed the doorknob and flung herself inside.

"What're you doing? Step away from those pictures."

Duty appeared not to hear. She was mumbling an incantation over a photo of Dane Kissel at autopsy, and rubbing the bag between her hands.

Between gritted teeth, Sid said, "Give the gal room. I think she's bringing him back."

"This is insane."

"No, Captain, it's religion."

"I want her gone."

"I think we should keep her," he said with a certain finality in his tone. "Leastwise, long enough to see if she can put the whammy on Rosen."

Chapter Eight

An hour before the FBI closed up shop, Cézanne left Duty in Sid's charge and drove Crane's assigned patrol car down to the Federal Building. Inside the Bureau's local office, it took a bit of doing, but she finally sweet-talked an agent named Longley into putting off an early dinner with his future in-laws. He was only too happy to demonstrate the FBI's image enhancement software.

"I'm one of only two guys in the whole world who knows how to work this," he bragged. "You're lucky I'm lukewarm on my fiancée's family."

"Don't think I don't appreciate it." She did a mental eye roll.

"We're always happy to help out people with inferior equipment."

She couldn't be certain whether his gaze flickered to her breasts, but a lack of confidence that began at age twelve, when her playmates had so much on top they almost toppled over, made her reflexively square her shoulders.

Inferior, my ass.

Still looking crisp in tan and tweed,

113

Special Agent Longley removed his jacket and draped it carefully over a wooden coat hanger hooked to a brass peg behind the door. In no time, he had the system up and humming.

She started small, handing him the group photo taken of Cissy Kissel and seven others at the Trail Drivers Ball. "Can you blow this up?"

"Piece of cake. Which desperado are we looking at?"

"The strawberry blonde in the white gown."

He programmed the picture into the computer. A close-up of Kissel's widow came on-screen, her cheeks rosy from too much alcohol and her smile strained.

"How big do you want it?"

"As big as possible without sacrificing the resolution. I want a closer look at that dress."

"What're you looking for? A designer label?"

"Bloodstains. Or wine."

"I see. You want to see if we can ferret out possible bloodstain evidence." As if restating the problem would make it happen. He leaned closer to the monitor and centered on cleavage. "Nice rack."

Cézanne ignored him. "One of the witnesses who alibied her said she wasn't out of his sight more than twenty minutes.

That the only time she left was to go to the powder room to clean a wine stain off her gown."

The amazing technological features of the digital imaging and enhancement software cemented Cézanne's opinion — the biggest kid on the block always got the best toys.

"No wine stain," Longley said. "Unless it spilled down the side not exposed to the camera. But the dress is an Emmannuel."

"You're making fun of me, aren't you?"

"I'm not. It's on the jacket."

He isolated an area of cloth with the mouse pointer and blew it up in size. "This woman has money. David and Elizabeth Emmannuel did Princess Diana's wedding gown."

"How do you know this stuff? Do they teach haute couture at Quantico?"

He grinned big and shook his head. "My fiancée wanted one. Then she checked out the price. It's way too much to spend on a dress that'll just be used once, so we did the next best thing and bought a D'Emanuel instead. A knock-off."

But Cissy Kissel could afford the original.

"So, how do you spell D'Emanuel? And where's the company?"

"Why? Are you getting married?" he teased.

"Don't worry, I won't have your fiancée's dress copied."

"Then I guess I can tell you. The guy's name is Herschel Escamilla and he runs a sweat shop in La Jitas."

In other words, no man's land.

"What about this picture?" She handed over the first in a series of crime scene shots.

With the help of a high-resolution scanner and a few well-placed clicks keyed to filter out the photo's graininess, Special Agent Longley sharpened the next image, razor-clear. While Cézanne watched in awe, he zoomed in on a hatbox on the floor of the Kissels' closet. Words on a paper protruding out of the dislodged top came into focus.

"It's a rule book," she mumbled.

Longley became lost in his work, zooming in, clicking on commands for maximized effect, filtering out background images.

"There — can you bring it closer? Doesn't that look like a brochure?"

Longley responded with another click. Over the blurring of the background, the resolution of the print sharpened dramatically.

"Stocks and Bonds," he read aloud.

She caught herself nodding. "My victim was a Wall Street type."

The Fed blinked. Blue eyes regarded her calmly behind rimless spectacles. What began as a pinched smile evolved into a humorless chuckle.

"What's so funny?"

"You don't have any idea what you've got here, do you? I suggest you talk with our sex crimes expert."

She found the way he talked down to her embarrassing. "Enlighten me as to why."

"Stocks and Bonds has nothing to do with a bull or bear market. Unless, perhaps, you're following the Nikei lashed to the bedposts with a rubber ball stuffed in your mouth."

She blinked.

"BDSM. Bondage. Dominance. Sadomasochism. The Metroplex is full of swingers' groups in search of alternative lifestyles." Longley tweaked the picture with a click of the mouse. A photo-quality printer spit out a computer-enhanced copy. "Go into any adult bookstore and ask around. You can pick up a local magazine full of kinky Personals."

For a moment, Cézanne thought her ears plugged up. "You think my guy was a swinger?"

"As opposed to a day trader?" Forced smile. "Sure looks that way."

She handed over the next photo, the one with the matchbook cover face up by the bed.

The Fed worked his magic. In under five minutes, they were staring at the results.

"Dungeon of Decadence," she read aloud. "Jeez. If you're right, this is really twisted."

He shrugged off her concern. "The Dungeon of Decadence is out of business. But Stocks and Bonds is still in print."

In her entire circle of contacts, Cézanne knew only one person who possessed the kind of information she needed. She'd have to wait until Deuteronomy Devilrow was gone to make contact. There were still places a sixteen-year-old shouldn't be exposed to, and a caliber of people she didn't need to meet. In this case, a stripper from Ali Baba's named Reno.

Since Number One Madrid Lane was only a two-mile detour from what amounted to a straight shot home from the PD, Cézanne headed straight for the murder house with Deuteronomy riding shotgun. She looked forward to seeing Worth Price's place up close. To get a feel for people who drove twin Rolls Royces and sunbathed beside his-and-hers swimming pools. But mainly she wanted to know if Cissy Kissel could have made it home from the Trail Drivers Ball in time to kill her husband and get back before anyone missed her.

With the Country Club only a few blocks away and her fitted dress hiked up to her hips, she could have done it without breaking a sweat.

Cézanne pulled up even with the curb, where the posh section of Rivercrest bordered the ultra-wealthy City of Westover Hills. Even from a high vantage point, the house reeked of more money than the coffers of some nations. And people with the good fortune to own either Rivercrest or Old Westover properties made up Fort Worth's three categories of wealth: old money, nouveau riche, and filthy rich.

Worth Price fell in the latter, and he built his sprawling compound where two one-block cul-de-sacs named Madrid and Majorca run parallel. After returning from the European Theatre to a hero's welcome in 1945, Price commissioned the inviting Mediterranean mansion from a renowned architect in exchange for five oil wells. He ordered paint the shade of a blinding sunrise mixed into the stucco and had the roof layered in red clay tiles. The house took three years to complete and had all the amenities, luxurious touches, and modern conveniences Fort Worth natives expected from an ace fighter pilot with more money than need. Surrounded by columned Georgian manors, French châteaus, and Tudors built of moss-covered stones, Price's mansion stood out like a whale; and in the same way its maverick owner defined the City, the unusual style and size of the great mansion dominated the neighborhood.

In the early days before Price updated his home with central air conditioning, European shutters the color of an Alpine forest were thrown open to let in the summer breeze while fans spun lazily against the ceiling. And when the town catch finally married Evangeline Harris on his fortieth birthday, he paraded her out onto one of the wrought iron balconies while a hundred of the richest people in Texas made handshake deals in the courtyard or danced to the orchestra on the terrace.

The front of Price's palace opened on the Madrid side; the back, with its circular drive for deliveries, on Majorca. With Evangeline's feminine touch and landscaping flair, the estate grew into a two-and-a-half-story architectural wonder that graced the covers of several magazines and swallowed the entire block.

Duty's eyes got big. She licked her chops like a vampire at a blood bank.

"Pretty ritzy, isn't it?" Cézanne pulled a pair of binoculars from her briefcase.

The girl snaked her arms around her chest. "Who this house belong to?"

"Believe it or not, a cop used to live here."

"He crooked?"

Cézanne chuckled. "He turned into a lawyer and made a lot of money."

"What kinda lawyer?"

"A good one."

"No. What kinda law he do?"

"Criminal."

"He crooked."

Cézanne peered through the glasses. Cement lions with their front paws outstretched awaited visitors with one guarded eye open. A forbidding wall with jagged glass jutting up from the top flanked an electrically charged gate with a tiny metal sign that read: DANGER — HIGH VOLTAGE. Majolica tiles in festive glazes provided a facing for terrazzo stairsteps that branched off in two different directions, encircled a tiered waterfall, and reconnected on a patio just shy of the massive front door.

"This yo' friends' house?"

"Not exactly."

The girl shuddered.

"Cold?" Cézanne stopped focusing the field glasses long enough to adjust the dial on Ruby's heater.

"This a bad house."

"What makes you say that?"

Duty stared dead ahead. "This a bad house."

Without bothering to disabuse her of the notion, Cézanne twisted the lenses until the razor sharp image of a uniformed housekeeper, polishing furniture, came into focus. A tilt of her head raised the binoculars. She sighted-in the second floor.

"Do we hafta go in?"

"Not hardly. We're just pulling a little surveillance."

"Good."

Cézanne studied the layout beyond each unshuttered window with great interest. Tufted leather furniture and the heads of big game trophies mounted on the walls dominated one wing of the house; at the end of the opposite wing, a gauzy canopy draped over the pillars of a four-poster bed. As a betting woman, she ventured that with the late Evangeline Price resting in a mausoleum since 'sixty-seven, the Kissels had lived in the wing with the frilly touches.

Unmoved by the comments of her young charge, Cézanne nevertheless mumbled words of encouragement. "I'm almost through. Gimme a couple more minutes."

"Mmm, mmm, mmm."

"Is something bothering you?"

"This a bad house." And then in a faraway voice, "The reason they cain't get that spot outta the rug is 'cause somebody died in that spot and their spirit's still there, roamin' around lost."

Duty had different thoughts about Cézanne's house on Western. This time,

Devilrow's niece made a brief walk-through. She paid particular attention to the winged cherubs and mythological figures carved out of the limestone fireplace, and ultimately pronounced it a good house. But the way she stared at the mitered corners of crown molding as if she noticed something Cézanne couldn't see was a bit unnerving.

The girl didn't seem to mind staying in the worst house in the best neighborhood west of Downtown. That the brick and rock bungalow had a certain old world charm, was actually made better after Leviticus Devilrow showed up one day in his beat-up pickup, and conned her into hiring him as her handyman.

Except for the roof.

Devilrow may have been a hell of an ironworker, as evidenced by the slitty-eyed gargoyles fashioned onto an intricate, wrought iron gate that closed off her driveway from the New Orleans courtyard in the back yard, but he didn't know squat about shingles.

It was close to seven before Duty finished watching a mindless sitcom on TV, and wandered into the kitchen. Without prompting, she located the silverware drawer and removed a couple of pieces of sterling and two vintage porcelain plates from Cézanne's corner cabinet.

"Is this real silver?"

"Yes."

"My mama work for a lady, she never used the silver 'cept when she had company."

"If it's good enough for guests, it's good enough for me."

"You can melt it down, too, like if you was to fall on hard times. I know people who go in houses, get the silver, and pawn it." Her eyelids fluttered in astonishment. "Not that I'd do somethin' like that. I don't steal."

Cézanne listened in stricken silence. Clearly, she needed to unload Devilrow's niece, and soon.

After Duty finished setting each place, she filled two glasses with ice cubes that crackled and popped under running water. Over a bucket of fried chicken, corn on the cob, mashed potatoes, and gravy, Cézanne did some gentle probing into Duty's background.

"That fellow down at the office with the big bandage wrapped around his head said you drew a pretty good likeness of the guy who shot his brother."

With her head lowered and without so much as a grunt of acknowledgment, Duty gnawed her drumstick.

"What do you do with that — what'd you call it — mojo?"

"Make it safe from loa."

Cézanne wracked her brain. *What was the word? Spirit.*

"Is somebody after you, Duty?"

Liquid, unblinking dark eyes, seemingly without pupils, stared back. Duty shook her head.

"Is somebody after your mother? Your uncle, Leviticus?" What Cézanne got in the way of a response was a headshake of the gloomiest kind. "I thought I heard you talking a few minutes ago. Were you using the telephone?" She held onto the strained hope that Duty had friends in Fort Worth.

"Frieda."

"Who's Frieda?"

"The lady whose room I'm sharin'."

"You're not staying here. I'm taking you to Leviticus Devilrow's after supper." Cézanne sat up straight. "Besides, I live alone."

But under her breath, Deuteronomy mumbled, "Oh, no you don't."

"What'd you say?"

Duty's voice faded to a whisper. "That's whatchoo think." She carried her plate to the sink and scraped the remnants of mashed potatoes into the wastebasket. But the chicken bones, she wrapped in a fresh paper towel and shoved deep into her pocket.

"You can't feed those to the dog."

"I won't."

"Look, if you're still hungry there's plenty —"

"I'm not."

"— of food." Cézanne tried again. "I'd like to try and help if you think there's something I can do to make this easier."

In all her misery, Deuteronomy Devilrow answered in a low, ominous voice. "Maybe just be extra careful."

Around eight o'clock that evening, Cézanne shut Roby's dog in the study and drove Duty to Leviticus Devilrow's Eastside house. She parked at the curb while the girl stood on the darkened porch, knocking loud enough to bruise her knuckles.

Nothing happened.

Duty returned to the car. Cézanne powered down the passenger window.

Duty leaned her head inside. "Nobody home."

"Do you have a key?"

"No, but there's a busted window around back."

"You're sixteen. You can stay by yourself, can't you?"

Duty nodded. "Drive-bys don't bother me. I just lay low and pretend it's popcorn poppin'."

Major guilt trip. Not falling for it. Can't do my job with a kid around.

"Here's ten dollars for food in case the refrigerator's empty."

Duty stuffed the money in her bra and

walked, forlornly, up to the clapboard house.

When the lights came on inside, Cézanne pulled away from the curb. It was for the best, she reasoned. A lot was riding on solving the Great Dane Murder and the next two weeks were critical.

Around ten-thirty that night, Teddy Vaughn phoned.

He said, "Wake you?"

"I have thoughts racing around in my head like it's Texas Motor Speedway. Falling asleep would be a minor miracle. Did Sid tell you about Marie Laveau?"

"Who?"

"Our little voodoo queen. It's a full moon. I'll be lucky if she doesn't start casting spells."

"Lieutenant said she draws a mean sketch."

"I don't care if she can recreate the Mona Lisa with a paintbrush clamped between her incisors, I don't want her hanging around. Can you imagine the damage that asshole Garlon Harrier could do, using a lead-in like this? I'd be the laughingstock of HQ. Hell, if this leaks out, we may as well drive over to Madame Epiphany's and deputize a couple of gypsy tarot card readers."

"Lieutenant said he'd slip her twenty bucks to put a hex on Rosen. Said he'd give her another fifty if she could figure out a way to grow a terrarium in his crotch."

Cézanne interrupted with a delighted laugh. When she finally banished the unsavory image from her mind, she said, "You're calling to tell me you found something in the tax records and probate files on Dane Kissel, aren't you?"

"Maybe I'm calling to hear your voice."

The voice he was calling to hear slipped back down her throat, where it refused to come out.

"You there, Captain?"

"Yes."

"I made a lot of headway but I still need the morning to finish my search. I was calling to say I wouldn't be in at the regular time. I've got an early appointment with Kissel's insurance agent. They paid off, you know. Cissy Kissel's father brought out their hired gun and sued the company."

"Who's the lawyer?"

"Lucky McElwell."

A rush of air left her mouth.

Lucky McElwell was a heavyweight with Moses, Lonstein, Cohen, McElwell, and Kidd. Big civil practice; criminal, too, if the case was high profile. Fancy parties. Threw a bone to the cops every once in a blue moon by donating to the Police Widows Fund, and sponsoring an annual Memorial Day barbeque he never personally attended. Had a reputation for being a boozer. No DWIs, thanks to a couple of good friends in the brass. In a courtroom, the guy got away with murder. Whatever, nobody pricked with him.

Before switching off the light, Cézanne rolled over and set the alarm for midnight. In the dark, the empty bed seemed lonelier than ever. And judging by Teddy's breathing, he had something to say.

"Anything else?"

"No." The detective had a maddening way with direct, economical language. "You?"

"After work tomorrow night, I want you, me, and Sid to meet for dinner so we can pool information. Things will be a lot more efficient if we divvy up the interviews."

"You might get Lucky," he said with just enough playfulness that she wasn't sure he was talking about Price's lawyer. And when he said, "Some people think impure thoughts whenever a full moon comes out," she knew the detective was right.

With the light switched off, and the warm rush of air from the central heat caressing her bare skin, she wished she'd made time during the day to call Bobby. But the most disruptive thought worrying her was not Teddy's sexy voice, or the imagined scent of his aftershave on the pillow next to her, but the words he left her to ponder.

"People lie. Crime scenes don't."

Chapter Nine

A few minutes after midnight, Cézanne swatted the snooze button and forced herself to climb out of bed. By twelve-thirty, she had her second wind and struck out for Ali Baba's. When she whipped Ruby into the parking lot shortly before one, and strategically placed her under the orange glow of the only sodium vapor streetlamp, eerie memories of the previous week raised the hair on her arms.

The heartbeat of Ali Baba's could be felt in the loud, drumming music that filtered out and vibrated the Kompressor's windows. A quick inventory of the building's rear exit played tricks on her mind. For a moment, she thought she saw Michelle Parker — Hollywood, to her clientele — standing in the dark in a see-through wrap, her thatches of platinum hair cropped short, and her enormous breasts giving her the outlandish proportions of a Barbie doll, come-to-life. The image vanished almost as soon as Cézanne conjured it up, and she forced herself to enter the club, the architect of a new plan.

Ali Baba's cavelike interior held a myriad

of visual assaults. For one thing, the regular bouncer, Tiny, continued his seedy sojourn on life support pending notification of next-of-kin. And the new-hire, wherever he was, apparently left the entrance unguarded since she found herself gliding, unmolested, toward the curtained-off area with the overhead sign that looped a warning in flashes of red.

DON'T TOUCH THE DANCERS . . . IT'S THE LAW.

At the end of the hall, Cézanne parted the curtains. She stood in the entryway to Reno's dressing room for several seconds before making her presence known — long enough to spy a hundred-dollar bill positioned on the vanity — and to watch Reno's tongue move enthusiastically behind the unbuttoned shirt of a customer with his eyes tightly closed. The man, who appeared to be of foreign extraction, reveled in Reno's talents. Strictly for appearances' sake, Cézanne jammed her fists against her hips and assumed a shocked expression, waiting for one of them to notice her shrouded in the tacky red velour of the drapes. Neither did, until Reno tugged at his belt buckle and hit herself in the face with the strap.

She sprang from her knees like a clay plate at a trap shoot. Her date, a man of few words, noticed the action had stopped and opened his eyes. One look at

Cézanne's gold panther shield, and he spun Reno into the wrought iron stool tucked beneath the vanity and made a break for it. When she refocused her attention on the exotic dancer, Cézanne caught Reno's eyes roaming her five-feet-eight-inch frame.

"Well, well, well," Reno said, putting delight and surprise in her voice. She swabbed her fleshy lips with a trademark lick. "Never expected to see you back here."

Tossing long, fiery red curls back over her shoulder, the stripper reached for a pack of skinny cigarettes. She appeared much taller, balanced precariously atop silver platform shoes, and Cézanne wondered, half-heartedly, whether she had any trappings of piercings underneath the slinky blue bathrobe.

Reno beckoned her inside with glittery talons. "You here to arrest me?"

"The Grand Jury issued a warrant when you didn't show up to testify last week."

Reno was now faced with a potential practical problem of putting on her clothes and going Downtown, or finishing her stint onstage.

"Now listen, Detective —"

"I made Captain."

"Lookie here, sweet pea," she said, using her forbidding blue eyes to will Cézanne's obedience, "It's all over. Your partner's finished, Sugar Cane's killer's locked up, and Hollywood'll never steal another one of your cop boyfriends. So whaddaya say we kiss and make up?"

"You never let up, do you?"

The exotic dancer grinned. "What do beautiful women like us need men for anyway? Men only complicate things. They make women jealous and unsure of ourselves and lower our self-esteem. Did you ever wonder why women in prison always end up in sexual relationships with other women? We need the touch of another person, no matter what gender." She seemed to have her argument in favor of same-sex relationships down pat.

Cézanne tried to call a halt to Reno's disclosures. "I'm here for information," she blurted out. "I'll pay."

"You don't have enough."

"I can match what your trick left."

"I can make that much doing a couple of table dances." Her eyes darted to the currency on the vanity, and back. With a ravenous look Cézanne had come to regard as normal for Reno, the dancer said, "What else you got, I might be interested in?"

"What if I could recall that warrant?"

"You think I give a hoot about jail?" Contemptuous. "I don't give a rat whether you make that paper disappear or not."

Reno took a long drag on her cigarette, and held the smoke deep inside, before finally releasing it in a series of rings. "Let me break it down for you, sweet pea. I sell sex. You don't want sex — not from me anyway. You didn't come here to arrest me, else I'd already be in the cage of your patrol car. You caught me about to exchange a good time for chump change; still, here I am." Large blue eyes thinned in suspicion. "So . . . what do I have that you want?"

Cézanne vacuumed in a shallow breath. Even closed her eyes to avoid seeing Reno's reaction.

"Tell me about the Dungeon of Decadence."

Chapter Ten

Killing off two pots of coffee at the all-night diner made Cézanne's stomach churn at the prospect of another refill. But somewhere around two o'clock Reno agreed to talk, and Cézanne found herself listening to the exotic dancer from Ali Baba's tell the most fascinating story.

She awarded each word with the rapt attention it deserved.

"I never went to the Dungeon," Reno said, bright-eyed. "For one thing, when I first learned about play parties I was too young to join The Lifestyle. After awhile, I had other stuff going on."

The "other stuff," Cézanne learned, concerned Hollywood and her entourage of roommates. Reno spoke of past affairs with the girls who eventually turned up dead, as well as her latest prize-winning relationship with a frizzy-haired blonde from Ali Baba's. That the stripper with the Monarch butterfly tattoo on one buttock happened to be married had remarkably little to do with the grand scheme of things. It was enough for Reno to have played a historical part in Butterfly's coming-out.

Keeping track of all the players took considerable effort.

According to Reno, the Dungeon of Decadence began inside an old shiplap rooming house with flaking paint, sagging porches, and square wooden columns, topped-off at the third story by cornices and dental moldings. The address was barely outside the Dallas city limits, yet, centrally located enough for couples interested in role-play to attend the freaky get-togethers. In time, most of the core members branched off into splinter groups with fetish interests, but the one Reno eventually joined was called Purgatory.

"What're these parties like?"

"They're called play parties. If you're gonna get into this, you gotta know the slang." Then in a voice bordering on wistful, Reno gazed into thin air with her eyes at half-mast. "Imagine ten to twenty angry men wearing capes, carrying stun guns, walking around in a chronic state of arousal."

She had to be joking.

"The way The Scene works, you pay at the door," Reno went on, smoothing her hand over a fake leopard coat tossed across the bench seat of the booth. "They make you sign a consent form —"

"Who does?"

"The people hosting the play party. They

make you sign a consent form just in case something happens —"

"Such as?"

"Like maybe they get too rough and gouge out an eye."

Cézanne wasn't certain Reno was kidding about the eye part, but judging by the wave of indrawn breaths, the stripper made a believer out of the people at the next table. They snatched up their silverware and carried their breakfasts to the far side of the café. Clearing a room seemed to be another of Reno's freshly discovered talents.

A grimace of frustration replaced Reno's wicked amusement. "You gonna let me tell it my way, or not?" A moment of silence that bordered on oppression followed. "You have to show ID to verify you're over eighteen. The rest is just mingling and scoping for partners."

"What do you know about Stocks and Bonds?"

A sly smile crossed her face. " 'Tis better to give than receive."

"You let people tie you up?"

"In the beginning I was nervous. Anyone would be. But somebody told me wearing a collar meant you belonged to someone. That way, if somebody liked me and wanted to play, they'd have to ask my owner's permission. So I wore a collar. A big, black dog collar with chrome spikes."

"You don't worry about AIDS?"

Laughter flickered behind her eyes. "You don't actually have sex at play parties. It's more like an exchange of power. Once, I met this dude called The Executioner, who wanted to role play with me, but he creeped me out."

"Role play?"

"Dominator-submissive. Only he got it all wrong. I'm more comfortable in the role of Dominatrix. I see you're confused. Just think of it as the spanker and the spankee. I get my jollies spanking. See, I think you'd grow more as a person if you surrendered some of that macho crap you picked up in the police academy. You really should let me spank you. It's invigorating."

"Not to me. I was raised on corporal punishment, so no thanks. And you make me very uncomfortable when you talk like that, so stop it. I don't even like to think about you thinking about me that way." Cézanne reached under the flap of her bag and felt for her spiral notepad.

"Put that away. Right now, we're just talking girl talk, okay? Later, when I school you, then do the homework."

"Tell me about The Executioner. What's his name?"

"What's wrong with you?" Reno had suddenly become an expert at avoiding direct questions. "You don't tell people your

138

name. Oh sure, you can give them your street name, but privacy's what it's all about. Everybody has a dark side to their personality — even you. And don't try to argue with me on that." Clearly Reno was enjoying the attention. "This is just a safe way for kinked-out people to get together with other kinked-out people who won't pass judgment."

"I want to know about The Executioner."

Gazing into her memories, Reno lit one of her skinny cigarettes and took a couple of puffs. Given their history, Reno's monkeying with her smokes usually meant a stall tactic, and Cézanne could tell by the way the stripper made a big production pulling the ashtray over — first inspecting it as the cigarette dangled from her lips, then reaching for a napkin to wipe it down — and the way she started honing the tip of the ashes into a point, she was mentally rehearsing the proper amount of information to divulge.

"He wore a black hood. The only part of his face I could see were his eyes. They looked dead. The thing about the BDSM scene is pleasure and pain are the same. Only not with this psycho. This maniac wanted to hurt people bad." A hint of real fear came into the exotic dancer's eyes.

The way Reno told it, her built-in excuse for not participating worked. And she didn't get involved with The Executioner, not after watching what he did to another sub.

"What's a sub?"

"That's the person who plays the submissive role."

"What happened to her?"

"Him. The Executioner secured the dude's hands and head in the stockade, and flogged him 'til he passed out."

Cézanne flinched inwardly. "Did the guy file charges?"

As if to illustrate a point, Reno picked up the soiled napkin and rattled it in front of her. "Consent form, remember?"

Cézanne ran through a mental checklist: pay to get roughed up, sign informed consent, choose Bachelor Number Three, short ambulance ride to hospital.

"And what does one wear to these soirées?"

"Costumes. Lingerie. Leather."

"Depends on the guests, right?"

"Some wear them, some don't."

Cézanne's lightning intellect zipped ahead and readily got the idea. "Are you talking about what I think you're talking about?"

"Grown people wearing diapers and talking baby-talk." Reno's head bobbed like a spring-loaded Chihuahua mounted on the back dash of a lowrider. "People with interests in infantilism have their own group. Too distracting for the rest of us, all that whining and crap."

A trickle of sweat rolled between Cézanne's breasts. She locked her knees together to keep from squirming. "Are you still a member of Purgatory?"

"It folded. Most of the members joined other groups."

"And The Executioner?"

Reno shook her head. "Never saw him again. But this might interest you . . ." She signaled a passing waitress with her empty cup. "Hit me again," she said, and got a splash of coffee.

Then Reno's voice dissolved to a whisper. "Word around The Scene was, he was one of the founders of the Dungeon of Decadence; that he was scoping out Purgatory's membership for fresh meat."

Cézanne snorted. "Fat lotta good that does."

"I thought you'd be tickled pink."

"Why? The Dungeon of Decadence is defunct."

"Who told you that?"

"The Feds."

Reno spoke in a birdlike voice. "The Dungeon of Decadence isn't defunct, it just went deeper underground."

Chills popped up on Cézanne's forearms and stayed there. "So all I have to do is find out when the meetings are?"

"Members only, sweet pea. Can't get in without an invite."

Cézanne dried her palms against her skirt. With her sleep-deprived patience slipping away, she dug out a five, tucked one edge beneath the sugar dispenser, and gathered her coat and bag. "I suppose that's it, then. Thanks anyway."

"Where ya goin'?"

"To get some rest."

"Gee, that's too bad." A taunting melody in Reno's words made Cézanne turn around. The stripper cupped a hand to her mouth. "I thought you wanted to infiltrate the Dungeon."

"You just told me it can't be done."

"It can't." Huge blue eyes sparkled with mischief. "Unless you have a membership or go as somebody's guest." Reno lounged against the booth, striking a pose that bore a remarkable resemblance to Norma Desmond's staircase descent in *Sunset Boulevard*. "Pansexual groups have turn-key arrangements with other similar-interest groups. Defunct or not, I'm a lifetime member of Purgatory."

"You're saying I can go?"

Reno's answer would keep her tossing the rest of the night.

"Be my guest."

Cézanne woke up in the midst of a

Technicolor dream to the jarring sound of someone leaning on the doorbell. She shook off the peephole image of Mrs. Pietrowski, the next door neighbor, standing on the porch in her overcoat, with pink sponge rollers in her processed apricot hair. The green facial mask spread over the woman's scowling face had dried and cracked, giving her the look of a seventeenth-century canvas in bad need of restoration.

"I know you're in there," yelled the rotund old crank. "I hear you. You better open up or I'm calling the police on you."

Cézanne set her .38 on an end table, slid the bolt back, and yanked open the door. Wind whipped around her, blowing the scent of Mrs. Pietrowski's face cream up her flared nostrils.

"What's wrong?" She caught a flicker of movement off to one side and riveted her head. Deuteronomy Devilrow stood next to a support column, shivering. "What's going on?"

Mrs. Pietrowski braced her arms across her bosom. "My dog Roscoe was carrying on so I let him out. He about went crazy. I thought it was a prowler until we found the hired help sleeping in your dog house. I oughta report you for child abuse."

Cézanne's mouth gaped. "I didn't do anything."

"You're a cruel, inhumane person. Probably a racist, to boot. I bet you hate Polish people, too. I won't forget you had a boyfriend who told Polack jokes — and you laughed . . ."

Doug Driskoll.

"Well, lemme tell you, Miss Prissypants, I have friends down at the PD, too. You know Hank Binswanger? He's my dead husband's cousin. You've got about ten seconds to explain why this child's not good enough to sleep inside your house."

"She doesn't live here."

"That's not what she said."

Cézanne whipped around. "What the hell are you doing here?"

"I got scared." She pronounced it *scairt.*

Ohmygod.

"How'd you get here?"

"Walked part way. Hitchhiked the rest."

Mrs. Pietrowski unfolded her arms and drilled her fists into her hips. "You could at least feed her more than scraps. All she's got is chicken bones, and they're picked clean. I can have a news crew out here like that —" she snapped her fingers. "Last time the cops found a kid locked in the closet, starving to death, they locked up the perps and threw away the key. Now what do you intend to do about this?"

Cézanne swallowed hard.

Considering it was three o'clock in the morning, she did the only thing she could.

Invited the apprentice mambo inside, loaned her a pair of pink pajamas, and got her tucked into the four-poster bed in the guest room.

Chapter Eleven

Early Wednesday morning, Cézanne waited until the coffeemaker gurgled before dashing into the frost in her purple bathrobe and fuzzy flip-flops. While snatching the newspaper up off the ground, she discovered a new crease in Ruby's rear end.

"Ohmygod." She flung the paper off to one side, crunched across the icy lawn, and slumped to her knees. "Jesus, Ruby, what have they done?"

She writhed against the Kompressor's bumper and let out a colorful string of profanity. Porch lights from neighboring houses flicked on in a domino effect, starting with Mrs. Pietrowski's. Slatted blinds separated and eyeballs peered out. She carried on with wounded animal noises until the latch clicked and Duty stood in the doorway, wiping sleep from her eyes.

The picture of calm, Duty said, "Did you know yo' car have a new dent?"

Cézanne tried to organize the homicidal thoughts rampaging through her head. But when her mouth opened, she could only sputter gibberish.

"Want me to dial nine-one-one? 'Cause

it look like you havin' a seizure."

"I am not having a seizure," Cézanne wailed, spitting froth, her arms flung protectively across Ruby's trunk.

"Oh. 'Cause if you not havin' a seizure, you may be possessed by loa."

"Some asshole ruined my car."

"That could also explain it."

Cézanne took deep breaths until they had a dizzying effect. "Yes, I know my Ruby has a groove up her ass. Do I look blind to you? No, I'm not having a stinking seizure. No, you don't need to call nine-one-one, and hell no, I'm not possessed."

"Just makin' a suggestion."

In the reflection of Ruby's sheen, Cézanne glimpsed her hair standing straight up.

"Ohmygod, ohmygodohmygod. I haven't called the insurance guy," she moaned, then mentally begged the car's forgiveness.

"If you like, I could scrape some paint off."

Cézanne draped herself over the dent like a madwoman. "Why in God's name would you do that?"

"Maybe pay back somethin' bad to that dude, what hit her."

Whimpering noises came out of her throat. "It was that shithead driving the dually and horse trailer, I just know it."

In her lathered-up state, thoughts of delegating mayhem through Deuteronomy Devilrow actually seemed rational. She might have acted on them, might've put stock in what Duty said, if a blue-and-white hadn't rounded the corner when it did.

"Well, kiss my ass. Mrs. Pietrowski called the cops."

"Mmm-hmm."

Cézanne scurried to the porch, muttering expletives. "Can't find a patrol car on this side of town when that friggin' dog Roscoe tunes up like the Mormon Tabernacle Choir, but let a person notice a gouge out of her car and they practically roll up Code-Three."

Duty turned around and shuffled inside with her hand groping the seat of her borrowed pajamas.

After the impromptu Neighborhood Watch Program cooled down — after Cézanne picked out a violet wool suit and dressed for work — she found Duty sitting yoga-style in front of the TV watching *I Love Lucy* reruns. Wrapped in beige terrycloth from the guest bathroom with a towel twisted, turban-like, over her hair and her scrubbed skin glowing with the sheen of a freshly iced brownie, Duty seemed right at home in her new digs.

"You're staying in today," Cézanne said, building on her irritation. "Since you're being paid to clean I expect you to dust the furniture. Whatever cleaning supplies you need are in the cabinet under the sink."

Duty blinked.

"And lock up the dog when you run the vacuum cleaner or you'll have puncture wounds in the hose."

Duty cut her eyes to Lucy and Ethel, up to no good.

"I noticed you removed a couple of beeswax tapers from the candelabra in the living room," Cézanne added. "Don't light them. No need to burn the house down." And finally, "Anything you need while I'm gone?"

Duty sat glued to the small screen, seemingly oblivious to her presence. But the last words out of her mouth, delivered in a monotone, gave Cézanne good reason to leave uneasy.

"Know where I might could get a owl feather, a crow beak, and a blue jay crest?"

At the office, over a cup of Kona-grind coffee Sid shared from a Thermos, Cézanne registered her complaints against Devilrow's niece with the vigor of a disgruntled customer demanding a refund.

"You should see what she did to the guest room."

The lieutenant's eyes narrowed into a squint.

"She squirreled away chicken bones from

last night's dinner. I thought she might still be hungry, but this morning —" she took a deep breath and huffed it out "— this morning, I found them on the bookcase, crossed like 'X's.' And the room smelled worse than a bucket of week-old fish guts."

Sid sized up the situation nicely. "Wonder if Rosen has jock itch yet?"

Before she could answer, in walked Teddy with a stack of documents. Looking buff in tight Wranglers and a rust-colored leather jacket that complemented his hair, he handed each of them a set and kept one for himself.

Cézanne stretched her neck where she could see out into the foyer, and called out to Greta. "Unless it's a bona fide emergency, don't put any calls through."

She motioned Teddy to close the door.

"You'll like this," he said, thumbing through the pages and looking damned fine. "By the time Dane Kissel left the PD he'd paid off his student loan and stockpiled about twenty thousand dollars. When he died he was worth close to five million — not counting the one-point-eight million the insurance company paid."

Cézanne's eyes drifted over the bank statements with great interest. "Who got the five million?"

"It went into a trust for his kid sister."

"Good enough for me," Cézanne said.

"The fact he didn't provide for his wife suggests they might have been on the outs. You ask me, she had motive. About six-point-eight million of them."

"I don't think so." Teddy looked to Sid for encouragement. "I don't think she killed him. When you analyze the expiratory bloodstain patterns on the floor, you'll realize it's more consistent with suicide. We may not be working a homicide at all. Kissel could've shot himself."

Sid said, "Hogwash."

Cézanne glanced at Dane Kissel's police photograph. Made a silent vow to put it in a nice frame. Leave it prominently on the desk until they locked Cissy Kissel behind bars.

She said, "Why would he commit suicide? The guy lived in a mansion. He had almost five million bucks at the end of one of the most depressed economies this town's ever seen. She killed him."

Teddy handed over a textbook. "I stayed up half the night reading about this latest theory on bloodstain patterns and it talks, in-depth, about expiratory blood."

"The ME ruled it a homicide."

"Because he hadn't read this book. People with GSWs to the chest spray out a fine mist each time they exhale. The argument's compelling."

"You're both wrong," Sid said, setting aside the papers, steepling his fingers, and launching into theory. "It's true, expiratory blood spatter mimics high velocity bloodstains. When you get hit at close range, blood ejects in tiny droplets. And if you shoot yourself in the chest, a fine spray of blood bubbles out each time you exhale."

Teddy sat up rigid. "What makes your theory correct?"

Sid gave him a *That's the way it is* look that suggested age and experience entitled him.

Cézanne stiffened. "What makes you think I'm wrong?"

"I don't think you're wrong, I know you are. The Cissy Kissels of this world don't kill; they get high-dollar shysters to bleed their husbands dry in the divorce. Then they find another patsy."

"So what's your angle?"

"Somebody killed him, all right — just not her. I say we look for a boyfriend."

The pow-wow continued through the morning. At no time did Cézanne disclose information about the jaunt to Ali Baba's, nor her conversation with Reno. Around ten forty-five, Greta appeared at the door with a message.

"Your new beau phoned, Zan," she said with a hint of revenge. "I told him you left specific instructions not to disturb you but he said he was coming to town and he'd drop in around eleven. Oh, look. This must be him now."

Chapter Twelve

Bobby Noah, with his rugged good looks and ocean-colored eyes glimmering their double-dog-dare-you twinkle, stood in the entrance to Homicide dressed in a western cut suit and gray Stetson that made him appear even taller. While Greta made a fool of herself, fawning, Sid sized him up as if Bobby had wrestled control of a set of nuclear warheads and the Nation's security rested, squarely, on Sid's shoulders. Teddy, on the other hand, jumped to his feet, nodded affably, and pumped out a strong handshake.

Sid broke the ice. "So you're Sheriff of Johnson County?"

Teddy said, "That's great."

Cézanne smelled the beginnings of a Mutt-and-Jeff routine.

"So how many votes did you get?" Sid again.

"Landslide." A wry smile formed at one corner of Bobby's mouth. "Nobody much wanted the job."

"One of them *High Noon* deals, you reckon?"

"Pretty much. When it came time for the

candidates to declare, an episode occurred out in the county where a couple of girls were killed. That drew a bunch of heat."

Abruptly, Sid squinted. "You a card-playing man?"

"Poker." Bobby kept his face cautiously blank.

"Mighty fine. Never trust a man, don't play cards. You cheat?"

Everyone did a double-take. For Cézanne, the breath went out of her lungs and stayed gone several seconds.

"Any game worth playing's worth cheating at," Sid said.

"I'll remember that."

"My game's Five Card Stud."

"Western Rules Hold 'Em, for me."

Something bizarrely intense seemed to be going on between the positive and negative ions in the air — an invisible current between men Cézanne didn't understand. Didn't want to, either.

On her feet, she tried to mask the delight in her voice. "So what brings you here?"

"I was in the neighborhood to see my old buddy, Krivnek." Bobby's face lit up with reverence the way it always did when he talked about the assistant medical examiner. "Hunters discovered an old-timer in a stock tank, tangled up in pampas grass. The wife had everybody convinced he had a heart attack but Krivnek found water in his lungs and a groove in his skull when he shaved the hair and peeled back the scalp. And one of my deputies located the widow's cast iron frying pan." With a convicting nod, he added, "Blood."

Moonstruck, Greta sidled up to the sheriff. At a sleepwalker's pace, she said, "Can I get you coffee?"

He touched the brim of his Stetson. "No, thanks. I merely wandered in to find out if the lady had lunch."

Sid fixed Cézanne with a particularly evil grin, Teddy acted like his dog just drank antifreeze, and Greta remained slack-jawed enough to hook coat hangers over her bottom teeth.

Cézanne didn't have to think twice about grabbing her coat. She was too busy catching a whiff of woodsy aftershave and reliving memories of their last, lusty interlude. She wondered if Sid, with his great metaphorical fish tank, had an inkling Bobby's lips functioned as tentacles on her bare flesh not three days before. Or that she had impaled herself on him until she could barely walk.

The thought vaporized the moment she dashed out the door and ran, smack-dab, into the chief.

"Let's talk." He took her by the elbow and steered her off to one side.

She motioned Bobby to wait while she

heard out the department's head honcho.

"How're things?"

"Fine."

"I'm referring to the Great Dane. Have you made any headway?"

"I just got it two days ago. I need time to —"

"Dammit woman, time's the one thing I'm fresh out of. The Council meets in less than two weeks and you'd better get the head chopped off this fucking Medusa or I'm out the door. And if I'm out on my can, you'll be following in my footprints the second they stick Rosen in charge."

"I'm doing my best. I don't know what else I can do."

"Listen," he hissed, "do whatever you have to before that meeting. I don't give a tinker's damn if you bring in a psychic, just save my ass and you can have that job for real."

With that, he pivoted on one spit-polished boot and stalked toward the elevator, leaving her to grab Bobby's work-roughened hand and ponder her fate on the way out.

Over a burger and shake at the diner a block downwind of the PD, her apology tumbled out in a hyperventilating rush.

"I know I promised to call, but things snowballed and now my life's a Chinese curse to the third power. Rosen assigned me this unsolved homicide and sicced the press on me. My life's circling the drain."

She stopped poor-mouthing long enough to be amazed that the simple touch of Bobby sandwiching her hand between his sent a shockwave through her insides.

"Are you coming out this weekend? With Christmas right around the corner, Pop's wanting to have an open house. We thought it might be a good opportunity to invite a few friends over."

"I can't plan that far ahead. The media's practically following me into the bathroom for a statement, and I've got this kid living at my house a few days. And Roby's dog bites, so I've got to figure out a way to break him of the habit without discharging a firearm within the city limit," she said, thinking of any excuse but the real one — that, come Friday night, she planned to accompany Reno to the Dungeon of Decadence.

He let go of her hand. Rested his arm across his middle. Sat there, unblinking, with a pained expression and his oxygen supply diverted — as if she'd just gut-shot him and run off with his money.

He spoke in a low, brandy-smooth voice. "You don't want to see me?"

"Of course not. It's not that at all. It's —"

"Don't mince words. Tell me straight out."

Odd things were going on inside her head. What had formerly been cogent thoughts, seemed to reverse direction and increase in speed, as if by some miracle, rewinding the course of her speech would allow her to strike out in a more favorable direction. Something like, "When this is over, I want to spend the rest of my life with you."

What came out shocked her.

"It's over." The echo resounded between her ears. She felt her world spinning out of control and made a desperate play to salvage it. "Wait — that came out all wrong. It's not that I don't want to see you. But I'm having an organization problem and I've got to prioritize —"

"You're saying I'm not important."

"Right now, my job comes first."

"Which translates into, 'You're a scumsucking, low-rent, good-for-nothing, lowlife.' I reckon that's enough for me."

"You don't understand. Please don't go. What I said came out badly. All I meant was that I need to take a break from this relationship while I straighten out the Great Dane Murder."

"I'm sure you know what's best."

He dropped a twenty on the table, grabbed his hat off the seat, adjusted the brim low enough on his forehead so his eyes disappeared, and slid out of the booth. He didn't stick around to find out he ranked sixth in the ratings, somewhere behind Dane Kissel, the claims agent at the insurance company, Sid, Teddy, the next neck on the Homicide chopping block — and the final insult — that in two days' time, a sixteen-year-old voodoo papess had displaced him.

She felt sick at her stomach watching him command the admiring glances of every woman in sight as he walked out of the diner.

A man in a dark overcoat pushed past a group of patrons waiting at the counter for their burgers. With his head ducked, he came even with the table and slid into the bench opposite Cézanne. When he straightened against the seat back, she was staring into the cunning gray beads of Garlon Harrier. A greasy lock of hair hung over his forehead like a scythe.

Cézanne conjured up a lethal glare and leveled it at him. "You must've lost your sense of direction. The rattlesnake roundup takes place in Sweetwater, not Cowtown."

"I guess that means you're not entered this year." He leaned to one side and dug in his pocket for something to write on. "Any leads in the Great Dane Murder?"

"You know I can't release information in an ongoing investigation."

He drawled out, "Noooooooo leeeeeeads,"

while scrawling on his tablet.

"You think I'm stupid enough to fall for that?"

"What?"

"You think I'll leak information to keep you from going on the six-and-ten, assassinating my character by saying nothing's happening on the Great Dane?"

"No news is still news." Harrier grinned big, exposing a mouthful of nicotine-stained teeth. "People want to know what you're doing. So who's the black chick? A witness?"

Cézanne harkened back to the gash in Ruby's fender. "You've been following me."

"Who is she? Kissel's lover?" He poised his pen.

Cézanne slid out of her seat. She thought of a Ken doll she once had, with his little London Fog trench coat, and wondered if she might unearth it in the attic and turn it over to Duty along with the claw of hair she was straining to keep from ripping out of Harrier's head.

"Stay away from me. Unless you want a Protective Order slapped on you so fast it'll make your eyes pop." She flounced toward the door with Harrier calling out after her.

"I report the news."

"Just be sure you don't become the news," she shot back.

"Is that a threat, Captain Martin?" Loud. A real show-stopper. Disruptive enough that people with half-chewed flameburgers froze in mid-bite.

Cézanne thought fast. She had to neutralize Harrier. In a loud voice, she made an announcement. "By the way, Garlon Harrier agreed to pay for everyone's meal with his lotto winnings." Harrier wrangled his bulk out of the booth and waved his hands in a "no" motion. "Be sure to thank him before you leave."

In case the announcement didn't work, she cut across the parking lot and corralled a couple of burly bikers as they dismounted their Harleys. With FTW tattoos in prison ink on their forearms and silk-screened wings sprouting out of a chopper wheel on their T-shirts, she sauntered up, eye-level, to their raggedy beards.

"There's a guy inside called Jimmy the Weasel, wearing a gray overcoat and hair that looks like he dove into an oil spill. He's sitting in the corner booth. Apparently, he has a fifty-thousand-dollar bounty on him, but nobody inside's brave enough to take him. You boys look like you could use the cash. Call Crimestoppers when you have him in custody."

Cézanne should have counted on Greta to douse the spirit of triumph. When she sashayed into Homicide, bubbling over, the secretary didn't let her down.

"Rosen wants you in his office," she said, giddily enough to earn another mental demerit on the scorecard Cézanne kept in her head.

On the uneasy elevator ride up to The Penthouse, Cézanne rubbed her palms together until she rid them of their clammy feel. Rosen only invited people to his office to mete out discipline. She unknotted the scarf at her neck and retied it; maybe Rosen wouldn't notice the pulse throbbing in her throat.

She found herself waiting in the foyer with Rosen's secretary, a tall, slim woman with her hair pulled back in a salt-and-pepper bun; a lackey with a perpetual strain on her face who looked as if what she really needed was to be the only female with a five-gallon drum of cocoa-butter on an island inhabited by drunken, excommunicated, fraternity brothers.

Her name was Ellen and she stood tall in her severe black suit and icepick heels. Blood-red lips thinned to a thread, and a finger as long as her nose pointed at Rosen's door.

"You may go in. Try not to piss him off. Last time you left, he shattered a commemorative obelisk against the wall, which I happen to know cost over five hundred dollars because I ordered it."

Quietly, she opened the door and took a visual inventory. In that Rosen was in the corner with his back to her, staring out the north window directly overlooking the police academy, she assumed he was mentally assigning grades to the derrieres of female cadets.

Without turning around, he said, "Harrier filed a complaint. You threatened him."

"I refused to comment on an ongoing investigation. That's SOP."

"It isn't Standard Operating Procedure to sic a couple of Bandidos on the media. It's bad PR."

"PR, SOP, BFD, I don't give a R-a-t. I didn't threaten anybody; Harrier's a pantywaist."

"Turns out those bikers are wanted out of Sturgis for murder. A couple of mounted patrol officers heard Harrier screaming like a stuck pig. Thanks to you, now that those officers evacuated the café and are awaiting transport, customers are standing outside freezing while their food gets cold." Rosen seemed to lose interest in whatever he'd been staring at because he did a one-eighty and aimed his scalded eyes at her. "Unfortunately, I'll probably have the bad luck to watch you parlay this into an FBI commendation for yourself."

At least he didn't fire her. But what he

did say turned out to be just as bad.

"You've been through a lot lately, what with losing your partner and your mother's admission to the state hospital. By the way, have you heard from her since the Mental Unit carted her off in leg irons?"

That Rosen could be so cavalier referring to how a judge sentenced his sister to treatment on a ninety-day mental commitment angered her. But while she considered driving her fingers into her ears to put an end to her uncle's taunts, Rosen answered his own question.

"I guess not. Patients usually aren't able to talk right after they receive electroshock."

"Stop." Cézanne felt the lightheaded rush of someone pumped full of adrenaline. "If you want the Great Dane Murder solved, I can't have assholes like Harrier dogging me around, mucking things up."

"I made an appointment for you to see Whitelark. We can't have our new Homicide ace going ballistic, can we?"

"I don't need the police shrink. What I need is a Protective Order that keeps Harrier from coming within five hundred feet of me."

"Your appointment's in an hour. If you harbor any illusions about keeping your job, you'll be there."

Her jaw dropped open. It never ceased

to amaze her how Rosen had too much time on his hands. And for the first time since Carri Crane died, she rather hoped he'd find a top-heavy female cadet among the ambitious recruits, to keep him out of her hair. As for his secretary, Cézanne wondered if Sid might have any thoughts that might knock that halo off her head.

Around two o'clock that afternoon Cézanne found herself back on Aden Whitelark's hot seat. At first she thought the police psychiatrist was pricking with her, sitting there enveloped in the vapors of Angel for Men, Doug Driskoll's cologne of choice; then she found herself ignoring Whitelark in his navy blazer and heavily starched khakis, dismissed the single peach rose laying on the diagonal of his blotter, and concentrated on fighting off memories of their last visit.

"How's the new job?"

"I'm still a homicide investigator." She wondered if she could engage the good-looking, athletic head-shrinker in mindless chit-chat long enough to keep him from trying out a new battery of tests on her.

"I'm speaking of your promotion. How do you like being in management?"

"I'm pretty sure I doubled my enemies."

"How's the Great Dane Murder coming?"

"You know I can't talk about that."

"Sure you can. I work directly for the chief."

She wished she'd known that a year ago, when IA investigated the shoot-out in Driskoll's kitchen. When she found out the hard way that Doug Driskoll wasn't divorced, that he didn't live in a four-bedroom house all by himself, and that his wife had secretly been target practicing with his back-up revolver. That Darlene Driskoll wasn't a very good shot didn't make the event any less traumatic. There was something pretty sick about a woman streaking to the car wearing nothing but a cup towel, and Driskoll on his knees pleading for his life, with an engorged erection suddenly dangling limper than an old rubber band . . .

"How's Klevenhagen working out?"

That threw her for a loop, Whitelark taking an interest in Sid. Then she remembered what Sid said about staging public flare-ups to throw Rosen off the scent.

"I doubt Klevenhagen'll pan out. I wish I'd consulted you before I transferred him into the unit."

"Why's that?"

"Let's just say I'd like to see his MMPI."

"You think he's crazy?"

She wanted to ask who wouldn't be, after putting in time under the current administration. Instead, she said, "I should have looked at each of my detectives' files."

"Why's that?"

"I'd like to see who recruited a couple of them — so that you could give the recruiters MMPIs, and determine where some of these poor hiring decisions originated."

Whitelark let out a belly laugh. He seemed to enjoy their visit, but when he picked the rose up and handed it to her, the silence became cavernous.

Thoughts were still banking off the inside curvature of her skull when he said, "I thought it would be nice if somebody noticed your promotion."

"I haven't received a rose in a long time."

"You should be given flowers — and often."

The abrupt turn in Aden Whitelark's demeanor set off "ooga" horns in her head. She wanted to believe there were still good guys in management — including herself — but her history with Whitelark always seemed to play out badly.

"It's nice." She held it to her nose and inhaled its sweet fragrance. "Thank you."

He took a deep breath and steepled his fingers. "Actually, I'm partial to African violets and orchids but they don't travel well. You're a bit like an orchid yourself, Cézanne . . ." Hungry eyes traveled shamelessly over her body. ". . . stunning in appearance . . . fragile . . . yet, able to withstand the heat. I see I've made you blush. Would you have dinner with me?"

She was certain she misheard him.

He tried again. "You busy Friday night?"

"As a matter of fact, I am. But I'll check my schedule and give you a call when I'm free."

When there are no more men on the planet.

She got up to leave and he let her. It wasn't until she returned to her office that she realized the police shrink never dredged up one word about the episode with Garlon Harrier. And that's when she knew: Rosen placed him in her path as an obstacle. A way to occupy the lonely nights while Driskoll trolled for another gullible recruit. Someone to create a setback in the Great Dane.

A goal-snatcher.

Chapter Thirteen

Sid was locking the door to Cézanne's office when she returned from the unpleasant visit with Whitelark.

He said, "I've got reservations."

"About what?" Irritated.

"No, I have reservations tonight at Alpenhaus."

"Sorry." She unjammed her fist from her hip and let the tension drain out of her arm. "I'm a little on edge. Garlon Harrier filed a complaint on me, so Rosen made me see Whitelark. What a prick."

"Harrier or Sigmund Freud?"

"Rosen." She shook her head and moped, "He won't stop 'til we fail."

"Chin up, missy, it's just day three. It ain't over yet. C'mon, I'll walk you out."

"Captain Crane used to say a really good detective could solve a homicide in under two weeks. That leaves eleven days."

Sid mulled it over. "How long do you get if you're just average?"

"What difference does it make? If we're not good enough we might as well not even be here."

Sid's eyes narrowed into the crafty slant

of a fox. "And if you're the best?"

"Roby Tyson was the best. According to him, homicide detectives work for God. And God deserves the best." Her mood did a swan dive. When silence unhanded its grip on her throat, she rasped out a thick, miserable tribute. "I miss him."

Sid slipped a wily arm around her waist and gave her a squeeze. "Well, little missy, I'm the best there is now."

"We're not talking about sex, Klevenhagen."

"I know that. But compared to Yours Truly, these detectives couldn't hit a Brahma's balls with a kayak oar. So I'll make you a deal." His eyes glittered like he'd just won the scratch-off. "I make sure you solve the Great Dane Murder in the next ten days and you give an old man some nookie."

"How about you help me solve it on time, and I'll let everybody think I gave you some."

"Deal. But only if you pass the word to those busybodies in Records, that it's bigger than the radiator hose on a 'fifty-two Buick."

They shook on it.

When they reached the parking garage, Sid noticed Ruby's trunk. "A crying shame. How'd you get that dent?"

"For God's sake, I almost forgot to phone my insurance agent." Words took flight as she left him standing next to the Kompressor.

Back on fourth floor, she caught Greta slipping out of her office. "What's going on? How'd you get in?"

"I have a key. Captain Crane always liked his messages on the desk first thing in the morning. I figured you'd want me to do the same for you."

Her chin quivered and for a moment, Cézanne thought the menopausal woman might burst into tears.

"I'll take that now."

Greta slipped the key off its ring and handed it over. "I'm sorry, Cézanne. I didn't mean to make you angry. It's scary, breaking in a new boss."

With red streaks that resembled claw marks climbing up her neck, she waddled back to her desk to catch the bleating phone.

While dialing the insurance agent, Cézanne punctured one of Greta's trademark pink phone messages with the heel of her shoe. There was no way to prove the woman deliberately left it on the floor next to her chair, but Cézanne had her doubts it ended up there on its own.

3:30 P.M. Urgent. Reno called. Said she'd leave the fire door open.

Managing to create an empty block of time to work Reno in before dinner took some doing, but Cézanne pointed the flashy red car toward Ali Baba's, and flattened the foot-feed against the floorboard. The strip club parking lot was already filling up with pickups and Cadillacs by the time she located the willowy dancer at the rear of the building.

In a voice breathy with excitement, Reno said, "Wow, that's some ride."

"Get in. I want to avoid rush hour."

"Is this one of those dope cars y'all seize? Because I'd like to go to the next auction and get me one of those 'Vettes they confiscate from drug dealers." Reno adjusted the bucket seat to accommodate her long legs, then melted against the buttery soft leather with a look of orgasmic bliss spreading over her face. "I could live in this car."

"This is my personal vehicle. I saved forever to get her."

"Her?"

"Her name's Ruby."

"You named your car?"

"Why not? Every car has a personality. I called my old white BMW, Hope, because she shined like the Hope Diamond even though she had rust patches. But Roby Tyson said she had a cracked block so she went from Hope Diamond to Hope-We-Make-It."

"You're a riot."

"The moment I saw this car I knew her name was Ruby. I even talk to her. She listens better than any man I ever knew. I imagine that sounds quirky."

Reno seemed to fix her sights on some point in the distance. "I guess I named mine, too, come to think of it. Only I call it Motherfucker. Maybe that's part of the problem." And then, "Did you know you have a dent?"

Up the highway, Reno was getting a kick out of riding with the top down, even though signs of windburn reddened her cheeks. She used the opportunity to tease men riding too close in their pickups, by inching her skirt up her thigh. After a big Ford with loud exhaust and oversized tires rolled up beside Ruby at the red light, Cézanne admonished Reno sharply for exchanging lewd comments with the driver.

"Quit flashing before you get us curbed. If I have to empty my piece, you're taking the first round."

"You're no fun."

"I like my life. I'd like to keep it."

"Spoilsport." The light changed and Reno blew the cowboy a kiss as they sped away. "Go down this road until you reach the circle, then take a right and I'll point it out," she said, talking about the adult toy store.

"How do you know all this bizarre stuff?

Have you just made a lifetime of being kinked-out?"

Reno let go a delighted laugh. "How do you get DNA off a cigarette butt?"

"By using immuno-globulin allotyping serology to check the saliva. Why?"

"When somebody scrubs blood off a surface, how do you get it to show up in the dark?"

"Luminol it. What's your point?"

"It's my job. Here's the turn." She pointed to a nondescript rectangle of whitewashed buildings. "Isn't that great, you get a parking spot right in front?"

"Thrilling." Fortunately, Ruby's paper dealer tags had no license number, only her name in chicken scratch, with the ink still bleeding from the last rain.

The sign out front said Penelope's, lettered in swirly purple and pink neon. To conform with obscenity laws, the storefront glass had been covered with wrapping paper, and whomever selected the loud colors made sure the windows could be seen for blocks. Cézanne jerked up the emergency brake. She got out of the Kompressor and joined Reno at the entrance.

The stripper issued a stern warning. "Try not to act like a cop."

"How's that?"

"Like you've got rebar up your ass." She

gave the door a yank and the two slipped inside.

A dozen mechanical penises in various sizes and glow-in-the-dark colors jutted up from atop merchandise shelves to greet them. With articulated movements, the wicked gizmos beckoned them, come-hither, buzzing over an instrumental version of "Hotel California" piped through the speakers.

Cézanne felt herself slipping into shock. She grabbed Reno's slender wrist and jerked her to a stand-still. "Tell me again why we're here?"

"Because you can't go to a play party without toys."

"I thought I made it clear I just want to watch."

A man in the handcuff section one aisle over gave her a depraved grin. She tugged Reno in close. "That's not what I meant. I'm there to observe."

Reno's laughter carried like wind chimes. "To come to a party you must be willing to participate."

"What was I thinking? It'll never work. I'm outta here."

"We need props."

"You have plenty." She ought to know. Two weeks before, on the night she went to Reno's to talk about Hollywood's dead roommates, she barely escaped without having Reno's sex gadgets clamped to her. "Why can't you just bring yours?"

"Because you need your own." In a voice rich with command, the dancer called out to a sales clerk. "Can somebody unlock the fetish room?"

Cézanne's stomach fluttered. "Oh, for God's sake, why don't you just take out a TV ad? Announce it to the world?"

"Don't be such a prude. C'mon."

Rifling through a key ring, the sales girl stood next to a door that blended into a wall painted black. The customer on the next aisle moved around where they could see him. Reno noticed his hand on his crotch and exchanged grins.

She thumbed at Cézanne. "Forget it, dude, you're wasting your time. She's gay."

Cézanne whipped around and snarled, "I am not."

"You're right, that was cruel." Reno shifted her attention to the man with the raging libido. "She wants you bad."

Cézanne stalked off, with Reno trotting to catch up.

If the eyes got a visual assault upon entering Penelope's, the other senses were equally tested in the fetish room. While the smell of incense hung thick inside the enclosed space, a tape filled with titillating whispers of pleasure, and whimpers of pain, could be heard over the speakers in whip-crackingly decadent, sense-surround.

"That does it," Cézanne said. "I'm outta here."

"Keep your shirt on. It's fake."

"Sounds real to me."

Reno moved close enough to smell her mouthwash. "One time, this guy paid me to do the voice-over in a skin flick. I had to yell my tonsils out."

"I don't need to hear this. What are we looking for?"

"Something to wear. Something to take to the party. Here, how 'bout a nice collar?"

Cézanne eyed it warily. "It belongs on a poodle."

"Isn't it great? I like the little sparkles." Reno held it up to her neck and checked herself out in the mirror. "Gather up my hair in the back so I can try this on."

"Gather your own hair."

"If you don't," Reno sing-songed, "I won't give you the low-down."

With a huff and a snort, Cézanne bunched the fiery mass of curls into a pony tail. Reno secured the clasp and gave her reflection an admiring glance. "I like this pink one."

"It doesn't go with your hair."

"I meant for you."

"I'm not wearing that."

"Fine, we'll get it in black." Reno tossed

it back into the bin. "Here's the thing about subs: nobody can make another sub do anything at a play party without the Domme's permission. Domme's short for Dominatrix. That's me. If you go as my slave, I promise not to loan you out."

"Like I'd actually trust you."

With her fleshy lips in a pout, Reno strutted off. Realizing the stripper left her standing next to the adult diapers, Cézanne bolted in her wake. She caught up to the stripper in the five-X video section, reading the cardboard sleeve on a trans-gender film.

"Here." Reno handed it over.

The label pictured an interracial two-some of men decked out to the nines in sequins and frills. Which explained the title: *Arse and Nick in Old Lace*. Cézanne wondered, fleeting, which one was Nick.

"I wouldn't watch this if someone duct-taped me to a chair and held a gun to my head."

"That's my flick. The voice-over." With eyes downcast, Reno slinked away.

Cézanne slapped the video on the shelf. She found the exotic dancer next to the flavored Kama Sutra oils, sniffing one with the essence of waxy bubble gum.

"You asked for my help." Reno screwed the lid back on and exchanged the container for one that smelled like coconut.

"Look, it's not that I don't appreciate what you've done —"

"Then what is it? You don't like my company?"

Cézanne took a long breath and slowly exhaled. There was no easy way to say it. "We're not friends, Reno. Never will be. We run with different crowds and live separate lives. This is a business partnership. You're my business partner. What we're doing — it's strictly business."

"Have it your way." The dancer spun on one heel and headed back into the main showroom.

Cézanne found her scoping out the marital aids.

"Pick one," said Reno.

"I'm not plunking down good money for something called the Big Bopper."

"You don't have to do anything with it; just bring it with you so people think you do."

"I don't want anyone thinking that."

"Fine. Let them think you're an uptight cop with rebar —"

"Enough." Cézanne snatched a box off the shelf and forced herself to stroll, regally, to the checkout counter. Reno wandered to the exit, a sly smile forming on her lips.

Cézanne was so busy lowering her head into her bag to keep anyone from getting a good look at her face while she dug for

179

cash, she barely noticed the gum-smacking cashier with the Gothic black hair, black lipstick, and skin whiter than bird-splat. By the time she heard the sucking sound of two D-cells sliding down the plastic chute, the Big Bopper was already out of its carton, cranked up, full speed ahead, with the torque of an Evinrude. Patrons jerked their chins in Cézanne's direction.

She leaned across the counter and hissed, "For God's sake, what're you doing?"

"We test 'em. They're not returnable." The girl cut the switch. "Works good. You want on our mailing list?"

"By all means." She flicked a twenty on the counter and snatched the sack out of the cashier's hand before the girl could make change. In her flight for the exit, she yelled over her shoulder in the voice of the town crier. "Just make the receipt out to Greta Carr," she said, and gave the address of HQ.

Cézanne had barely dropped Ruby into reverse and whipped into traffic when the stripper tossed a black-studded collar into her lap.

"You didn't pay for that."

"You're right. You did." Reno pulled a glass vial out of her bag. "Here y'go."

"What's that?"

"Don't tell me you never heard of poppers?" The bottle had the word "Zap" written in lightning bolt letters, but the small block print underneath spelled AMYL NITRITE. "You sniff it. It gives you a rush during sex."

"Did you kype that, too?"

"You're mad at me," Reno said, eyes as intense as a wounded animal.

Cézanne pulled over to the curb, cut the engine, and gazed at the horizon as the last of the crimson sun all but disintegrated into a sky full of purple clots. In under an hour, she would be meeting Sid and Teddy. Since she wasn't about to let anyone in on her little caper with Reno, she didn't have jack-shit to tell them when they pooled information.

"I never should've gotten you involved," she said harshly. "This isn't a joke. It's my career. A man died, and with or without you, I'm going to make it right."

"I'm trying to help. You're acting un-grateful."

"You're right about the acting part. For me, this play party shit's a role. I don't have to do anything, I just have to act like I'm doing it. So don't try to make me feel like I owe you. If it works, I get my information. If it doesn't, I'll figure out something else. Plain and simple."

She fired up the Kompressor and zigzagged into the six o'clock stream. Reno slipped a skinny cigarette out of the pack, then slid it back in when Cézanne cast an evil glance.

It wasn't until they were flying down the open road that Reno broke the frosty silence.

"You're wrong about the acting job."

"Yeah?"

"Don't be screwing up your face like I'm not as good as you. I'm the teacher, sweet pea. If you don't learn how it works, we're done for."

"Now look who's being dramatic."

"You think this is a game?" Her eyes clouded with genuine fear. "You think if your cover's blown, you just go back to your office and activate Plan B? These people are high-rollers. Rather than get their names in the paper over shit that could cost 'em their reputations, they'd kill you. And me, too, for inviting you in."

Chapter Fourteen

With less than thirty minutes to spare, Cézanne slid her house key into the deadbolt and waited a few seconds for Butch to come skidding down the hall with his teeth bared. When he didn't, she let herself the rest of the way in.

The house came alive with the sounds and smells of cooking. Cajun seasonings filtered out from the kitchen, where they mingled with the scent of spicy candles, aging Persian rugs, lemon-polished antiques, and living room furniture upholstered in glazed leather. It was a nice welcome home, and she felt a twinge of guilt for not phoning ahead to let Duty know they wouldn't be dining together. She dropped her coat on the sofa, temporarily stashed the Penelope's sack behind the bookcase, and followed the aroma. Over the blue gas flame of an ancient porcelain stove, Duty was browning flour in a cast iron skillet. She wore her same threadbare dress from the day before, and had one of Cézanne's grandmother's scarves wrapped around her hair in gentle folds.

"What's the meaning of this? You need

to ask permission before you use my things, do you understand?"

Duty's reaction came in the form of an eye blink. She reached for the salt shaker and gave the pan a sprinkle.

"What did you do while I was at work besides borrow my eye shadow? Is that my new nail polish?"

"I cleaned out yo' ice box. Did you know there's green stuff growin' in yo' Tupperware?"

She should thank her. Should fall on her knees and beg her to attack the week's worth of laundry piled on top of the washer. Instead, she blew a gasket, "Aren't you supposed to be gone already? Did you hear from Leviticus Devilrow?"

A headshake.

"Did you put in a call to your grandmother like I told you?"

"My gramma Corinthia, her phone disconnected. There's alligators in the bayou; sometimes they snap the cable."

Lacking patience, Cézanne said, "Don't you have any people in your family with real names?"

"Whatchoo mean, real?"

"Something normal. Like John."

Duty rolled her eyes. "Everybody got a John. My cousin Colossian, she got two boys: First John, Second John."

Cézanne winced inwardly.

"Ohhhh," Duty dragged out the dawning realization. "You mean do we got anybody with White names like Tiffany or Britney or Brandy."

"Exactly."

"No. Devilrows mostly stick to God's word. My great-gramma Ruth say maybe God give us extra credit at the gates when we check in with Saint Peter, so nobody in my family got an exotic name. 'Cept maybe my Auntie Philemon's kids. Hers were the first Devilrows to get born by a real doctor, 'stead of a midwife."

"I'm almost afraid to ask."

"We got Anna —"

"Short for Pollyanna? Annabelle? Louisiana? Or just plain Anna?" Her mind started playing the name game: Anna-banana-fo-fanna. "Is it short for Anastasia?"

"Anesthesia. My Auntie Philemon, she have triplets, and the doctor, he have to knock her out. After the gas wore off and she came to, she said the names of her babies got revealed to her in a vision."

"A vision?"

"Yessum. My Auntie Philemon had a vision. Angels in white, swarmin' over her. Sayin' the names of her babies. When she woke up, the names came to her: Anesthesia, Epidural, and Episiotomy."

Cézanne stared numbly at the girl's caked-on lipstick. Duty's chatter setting straight the Devilrows' genealogy had inadvertently blurred her anger. "What about your grandmother on your father's side?"

"My other gramma, Mablene? She passed."

"Passed a kidney stone? Passed a test? Passed out from the stress of having to keep straight an entire houseful of in-laws named after Books of the Old Testament? Passed what?"

"Dead."

"Jesus." Cézanne glanced around. Nothing left to do but feign sadness.

"I was with her the night she took sick. She put her wrinkled hand on my cheek and said, 'Duty, I won't be here tomorrow. Tonight's the night I'm gwine to be with my king.' "

"That's eerie . . . poor woman. She knew she was going to see Jesus."

"Not Jesa. Elvis. My gramma Mablene loved Elvis. It was all about Elvis."

Cézanne wanted to thunk her head against the doorframe. Her eyes locked on her grandmother's silk scarf. "Don't be using my stuff. And I forgot to tell you, I'm having dinner with Sid and Teddy." She added a lukewarm, "Sorry," but the flimsy apology got no response. For no reason other than instinct, she demanded, "Where's the dog?"

The teen's eyes rolled in the direction of the guest bedroom. "Frieda be watchin' him so's I can cook."

"Frieda who? Oh, yes. Your imaginary friend."

Duty muttered, "Well she ain't that imaginary, walkin' 'round all night. Bitch kept me up wantin' to know where's her baby. Lordy, don't axe me. I wasn't even born when he took the fever."

"What in God's name are you babbling about?"

"I said Mercury's in retrograde and all yo' planets are augerin' in. And I wouldn't take that plane trip if I was you."

"I'm not taking a plane trip."

"That's whatchoo think."

"Look, I only popped in to see if you needed anything. I suppose I don't have to worry about bringing home fast food, now that I know you can cook."

A slow blink.

A mild sense of obligation made her ask, "Need anything while I'm out?"

Duty reached into the sink. She presented an empty jelly jar, with its damp, faded label still stuck to one side.

"Could you maybe bring me back some Holy Water?"

Leave it to Sid to pick out the restaurant. With strands of twinkle lights dangling

187

from the ceiling, an oompah band playing in the corner, and bad German art prominently displayed on the walls, Cézanne experienced a sensory assault unlike anything she'd seen since the District Attorney asked her to preview eight hours of porn flicks to see if they could make an obscenity case against Peter Pumpkin Eater's.

At the round-table discussion, Sid exerted his usual take-charge manner. "Where are we at?"

"Hell would be my first guess." Cézanne unfurled her napkin and placed it in her lap.

"I was referring to the Great Dane. But now you mention it, what's wrong with this joint?"

"It's loud, it's gauche, the music's giving me tinnitus, and I swear when I first walked in, I saw people on the dance floor doing the Chicken Dance."

With a child's innocence, Teddy said, "I kind of like it," and got instant demerits for good taste.

"See? Junior likes it." Sid clapped him on the back so hard the pat of butter slid off Teddy's knife and stuck to the paper placemat. To Cézanne, he said, "You don't see any cop cars here, do you?"

"No. Which to me is a dead giveaway the food's overpriced, and awful, to boot. We'll probably end up with ptomaine. If one more kid pops a birthday balloon, I can't be responsible for returning fire."

Sid was the epitome of patience. "Let's see . . ." he pulled a pair of reading glasses from his shirt pocket and scanned the menu ". . . if the food's lousy and the carnival atmosphere repels you, and beat cops wouldn't darken these doors if management had a food giveaway, I'd say the place probably isn't bugged, wouldn't you?"

"Unless silverfish comes with the salad."

Teddy pulled out his notebook and pen. "What should we talk about?"

"About five minutes." Sid grinned.

A buxom waitress dressed in an Alpine frock, with perspiration dotting her forehead, squeezed between tables and demanded their order. By the time she finished scrawling, the band launched into a polka. With the lead singer crooning, diners headed for the rough-hewn floor.

Beneath the tablecloth, Teddy touched her knee. "Dance?"

"I never learned to polka," she fibbed.

"It's easy, I'll show you. It's like waltzing in overdrive."

She dashed his hopes with, "I'm not drunk enough," but the tingle from his electric touch stayed on her skin long after he removed his hand. She wondered what Bobby was doing, and wished she could juggle a career and a social life without one or the other getting short shrift.

Sid's beer stein arrived and he took a long gulp. After returning it to its cardboard coaster, he leered past the foam on his lips as if he, alone, had the inside track on her love life.

Teddy pulled some notes out of his jacket pocket. "I finished reading the entire case file. I'm working on an angle."

"Well, Junior, I hope you're off that suicide kick."

Teddy advanced another theory. "The reports mentioned a stalker."

Cézanne said, "According to Featherston, neighbors called in a stalker but we never ID'd him. I culled through everything in that file, and I didn't find any stalker reports."

"They're there." Sid swigged his beer. "You overlooked 'em. Anyway, I don't think there was a stalker."

"It says so." Teddy.

Cézanne broke in. "I didn't overlook anything. They weren't there."

"Okay, I'll burn fresh copies."

She shook her head. She didn't like what she was thinking. "You don't understand. I caught Greta coming out of my office this afternoon."

"You think she took 'em?"

"She said she was leaving messages on

my desk but she had Crane's key. I made her surrender it."

Sid had been studying the bread, and he ran his hands over his stomach as if he were calculating whether he should butter a piece. "It's probably nothing. Maybe the copy place made a mistake. Won't be the first time them highway robbers over-charged me."

But the presence of Greta in her office alarmed her. "Do you think we should set up a video camera, Sid?"

"You act like there's some kind of de-partmental conspiracy going on. Why would Greta want some old reports when she could just make her own copies?"

"Maybe she didn't know they were copies. Maybe she thought she was swiping the originals — which are locked up."

"You're paranoid. Cases will do that."

"You sound like Whitelark. Tell me why you think there wasn't a stalker. You think somebody falsified police reports?"

"I think it's mighty convenient to have prowler calls on file right before a fellow meets his Maker."

"Unless it really happened. And that's why Crane and Featherston never solved the case."

The waitress returned, balancing three plates of wurst and kraut, and slammed them on the placemats. When they were alone again, Cézanne said, "Stranger-on-stranger murders are the hardest to solve. What you're insinuating is, somebody on the PD cooked up those reports."

"I know what I read." Sid reached for his knife and sawed into a cutlet. "They were all marked Complainant Refused."

It didn't bother her in the least that the caller wouldn't leave a name or call-back number. It would have been unusual if he had. What seemed unusual was Sid's refusal to entertain thoughts of a real stalker.

"There's no basis-in-fact to rule out a prowler if we've got reports on file."

"Why're we arguing? You're the one saying the Widow Kissel killed him. Seems like it'd be mighty convenient to throw us off the trail."

"You're confusing the issue."

"I'm not. I'm Devil's advocate."

"Or just plain Devil."

In a voice rich with indignance, Sid snapped, "Well if that's not the catfish calling the bullfrog Bigmouth, I don't know what is."

Teddy, who had faded into the decor during the lively exchange, chuckled.

Dessert arrived and, considering the oompah band broke for fifteen minutes, they ate in relative silence. By the time they topped off the meal with espresso, the bad cuisine lived up to Cézanne's expectations.

The bill came and Sid gave it a thorough scrutinizing. "Junior, you're looking a bit puny. I think you should go home and catch up on sleep. Me and the Captain can finish brainstorming at my place." He leered at Cézanne. "Or we can head for yours. Frankly, I think it should be yours."

"We can't use my house," she said quickly. "Duty's there and she might overhear us."

"See?" He cupped his hand to his mouth. "Told you she was a screamer."

Even in dim light, Teddy's face clearly reddened.

"I'm talking about Devilrow's niece listening in. That girl's downright spooky. When I left this morning, she asked if I could bring her some feathers. Awhile ago, she wanted Holy Water. Like it's something you pick up at the store."

"Long as you don't find a dead rooster on your stoop. That means you're marked for death. Oh, well," Sid said with a sigh, "guess it's my place. Can't say I didn't try. You come, too, Theodore. Just don't get so drunk you have to sleep over. I never had any —"

Cézanne cringed, expecting him to call Teddy a "meat hound."

"— men in my bed." He rattled the tab, inches from Teddy's face. "You a wagering man? Let's see who gets to pay this."

"Fine by me."

Sid's eyes found a point on the ceiling. "I'm thinking of a number between one and ten."

"Four."

"No, that's not it." Sid slapped the bill down on the placemat and reached for his sport coat. While Teddy tried to read the numbers by candlelight, Sid helped Cézanne to her feet and leaned in close. "Don't worry, Captain," he whispered, "I'll leave the tip."

She almost concluded Sid was a Class-A jerk, until he dropped a fifty on the table to cover the cost of dinner before taking her by the arm and steering her out.

Chapter Fifteen

Fort Worth police lieutenants made good salaries. And even though Cézanne suspected Sid could afford a nice place, she never expected to trail him down a cobblestone driveway to a cabana in back of a Park Hills estate.

"My daughter's," he said before she had a chance to ask which bank he robbed.

Her head tingled with a sense of *déjà vu*. They passed the ice-blistered remnants of an English garden, where the reflection of a swimming pool shimmered under the light of the moon like the turquoise waters of the Caribbean. The roar of a lion filled the night.

"The zoo's just below the cliff," Sid explained. "Sometimes they tune up something fierce. Did you know they can be heard for five miles? I don't mind the big cats so much as I do the monkeys, though."

At the hum of an engine, they glanced down the drive at the headlight beacons of Teddy's late-model truck.

Cézanne and Teddy trailed the lieutenant in out of the cold. While Teddy poured a bottle of vintage wine from Sid's collection, Cézanne made herself at home on a hairy cowhide sofa printed to look like giraffe skin. The interior of Sid's living room seemed to result from the involuntary mating of African Safari and Texas Longhorn, but she liked the rustic touches interspersed throughout the luxury, and the way the pale light from the wrought iron candelabras reflected off the textured ceiling.

They were sitting in front of a blazing fireplace, swirling wine in their glasses, when Sid started a good-natured interrogation.

"Who'd you catch the law enforcement bug from, Theodore?"

"My brother."

"I didn't know you had a brother."

"He's assigned to Crime Scene. You know him. He's the one everybody calls Slash."

Cézanne almost spewed Riesling on Sid's zebra-print rug. "You're related to Slash?"

"Guilty."

Teddy's brother had earned his nickname. One part Sherlock Holmes to two parts Zorro, the guy had no reservations about flicking open his razor-sharp buck knife and carving out sections of upholstery or carpet at crime scenes. But the real incident that earned him the wicked-sounding moniker occurred when he nicked a two-million-dollar oil-on-canvas, taking blood scrapings from a homicide at an antique dealer's estate in a posh section of Ridglea.

"What about you, little missy? You got kin who're po-lice?"

"I needed a way to finance law school and the PD happened to be hiring."

She wasn't about to tell them about the diseased limb on her family tree — that the most hated man in the PD happened to be her uncle. They'd exchanged promises when Rosen first assured her a slot in the police academy that she would never speak of the relationship because of nepotism, and he wouldn't bail her out of any jams. So far, neither breached the agreement. When the incident with Doug Driskoll put her job in limbo, Rosen remained true to his word. He never lifted one damned finger to help. "What about you, Sid?"

"My daddy was Sheriff and his daddy and his granddaddy were U.S. Marshals. I always thought my girl Betsy would make a fine cop once the PD got a big push-on for women and minorities. But she strayed into the valley of darkness, and made so much money it's embarrassing. Being a lawyer's like having a license to steal." He finished his wine and held out the goblet for Teddy to pour. "So you finally got that bar card?"

"Three weeks ago."

"How come you're not with some high-falutin' firm?"

"I asked myself that same question. I always wanted to be a prosecutor, ever since the first time I caught *Perry Mason* on our black and white TV. When Perry kicked Hamilton Burger's ass, I knew I had to fix that. Growing up, it never occurred to me I wouldn't be doing God's work. But when Roby got in trouble and I sided with him, the DA closed ranks." She stared into the bottom of an empty wine stem. "Since that shootout at Ali Baba's, there's no way. The DA expects his employees to lead uneventful lives, and I haven't mastered that yet."

"Try again next year."

But Cézanne shook her head. Her eyes drifted over the Texana decor and came to rest on a lithograph of Judge Roy Bean. A brass nameplate nailed to the frame read: The Law West of the Pecos.

"I was a Two-L before it hit me: even Hamilton Burger's name was a joke. No, my fascination with the DA's office is over."

Rheumy-eyed, Teddy cocked his head.

"Hamburger, Junior. Perry made hamburger out of him."

In the way of old friends they got to know each other, talking well into the night about anything but the Great Dane

198

Murder. And somewhere between the fraternal twig on Teddy's family tree and Sid's ancestral roots, their voices faded into a low buzz that made the end of a high octane day conducive to sleep.

It must have been after midnight when Cézanne awoke, squinting into the darkness of Sid's living room. A lightweight tartan blanket covered her. Logs were reduced to neon-orange embers, and somewhere beyond the top of the stairs, Sid was snoring like a sea lion.

She grazed her fingertips along the wall for balance, to a half-bath at the end of the hallway. Inside, she ran warm water into the pedestal sink and splashed a handful over her face.

They were good guys, Sid and Teddy. Not like Roby, but the three of them made a fine team. And in the wee, dark hours with the tick of Sid's grandfather clock filling the silence, she knew there would never be a better chance to solve the Great Dane Murder.

Chapter Sixteen

Cézanne couldn't remember the last time she started a day with a bigger headache. And although the greasy sausage from the night before caught up with her before her first mug of coffee, it was the hazy memory of picking up a tail down the street from Sid's house that opened a floodgate of acid in her stomach. If it turned out not to be a bad dream, then she'd blown Ruby's left rear tire somewhere in the getaway, and ridden her home on the rim.

She hustled to the front windows and moved aside a flounce of lace. The back wheel looked like an empty spool tangled with threads of shredded black rubber. A gunfight erupted in her head.

"When will it end?" She picked up the phone in the hall and dialed Damsel in Distress Rescue Service to change the tire.

When she staggered to the kitchen, Duty already had the coffee perking and the newspaper folded open to Ann Landers and Dear Abby.

She stood over the cast iron skillet, wielding a spatula. "Whatchoo want?"

"Nothing, thank you," Cézanne said dully.

"I make good flapjacks."

"I'm not hungry."

"I cook French toast."

"I said no. And where are the curtains?" The gauzy cotton panels over the window at the sink were missing. Duty's eyes darted over the ceiling as if reading from a list of invisible answers.

"I . . . uh . . . washed 'em? Yeah, that'll do. I washed 'em."

"Oh. Good. Because I think they probably needed it." She slumped into a chair and rubbed her temples. "I should be home in time for dinner. And I want you to try to find Leviticus Devilrow. Nothing personal. I just can't accommodate you any longer."

"Don't I clean good?"

"That's not it. I'm one of those people who happens to do better alone. And by the way, there's a thermometer on the back porch. If it stays above freezing you can put that dog outside."

Time tightened its grip, and Cézanne dressed quickly. She chose a periwinkle blue suit fashioned in tropical wool, with a brooch of multicolored stones fastened onto the lapel of a matching cashmere coat.

By nine o'clock, Sid arrived at the office with an extra copy of the stalker reports. He talked her into going for a ride before meeting Teddy at the ME's office at eleven to discuss Dane Kissel's autopsy. When she asked, "Where to?" he gazed out the windshield and said, "You'll see."

"I've been meaning to mention something. You need to call me 'Captain' when we're in the presence of our colleagues."

"I do."

"No, you don't. Missy's a dog's name. Besides, I heard you use it on Greta the other day. I think you just call women 'Missy' when you can't remember their names."

"Tell you what. I'll use 'Captain' when it counts."

"Or you could just learn my name."

"Oh, I know it," he said wryly. "Before this Great Dane deal's over, I expect you'll be a household word."

She could tell by the shift in his eyes, he meant infamous.

While Cézanne scanned paperwork, Sid ended the ride by pulling over to the curb a block shy of Worth Price's house.

"What're we doing here?"

"I say let's go have a talk."

Cézanne thought fast. She didn't want to tell him about Reno, and she couldn't very well infiltrate the Dungeon of Decadence if Cissy Kissel knew what she looked like.

"Coming?"

"I don't do well with women. I'll catch

up on these reports and you can fill me in."

She could see he didn't like going it alone, but he traipsed down the hill and up the long ascent of tiled steps. When he reached the front door, a maid let him in.

She watched through the passenger window and listened to the dispatcher assign a dog bite call. Elsewhere, a unit radioed out on a traffic stop. In minutes, Sid was hiking back up to the car.

He opened the door and slid behind the wheel. "She's at the Country Club. It's not that far."

"We should get back. Teddy's waiting and we need to hear what Krivnek has to say about the autopsy."

She sensed Sid was about to mount an argument, when the radio crackled to life. The dispatcher announced channel closed, a move to cut down on unnecessary radio traffic. Sid turned up the volume. Garbled transmissions from a screaming, first-line officer pierced their eardrums. They listened in stricken silence.

Sid's eyes took on a speculative gleam. "Officer needs assistance," he said with a terrible intensity, then fired up the engine. "What's his Ten-Twenty?"

"He's out on the Tom Landry Highway."

"We're too far away to do him any good."

"Start that direction anyway."

A second panic button went off and another shriek came over the frequency in unintelligible bursts.

The carefully-modulated voice of the dispatcher concealed her dread. The cool-witted woman advised of an ambulance en route to their location. But the frantic officer howled there wasn't time. In the background, a communications supervisor called for Air One. For close to a minute, only the yelp of a police siren came over the radio.

Sid said, "Some asshole's mike's hung."

Adrenaline sent chills coursing through Cézanne's veins. "I think his assist put him in the patrol car. He's not waiting for the ambulance; he's bringing him in."

The chilling transmission of a back-up officer filled their space. "Clear channel, clear channel. He wants this on tape, Dispatch. Go ahead, hoss, you've got their attention."

The weak plea of a young man, convinced he was about to die, left its gut wrenching impact. "Tell my wife I love her. Tell my kids . . ."

The back-up shouted, "Outta the way, fuckhead. Can't you see the goddamm lights? Aw, Jesus, hoss, don't you go and die on me."

Dead air followed.

Cézanne's heart bounced in her chest. It was as if she'd been riding in the back seat with the injured man, wanting desperately to help and being unable to. Second-guessing whether the first-line officer made the right decision, piling his fallen comrade in the car. Convinced that he had.

Seconds later, Sid's cell phone bleated. He checked the digital readout. "It's Greta."

After a series of half-sentences and grunts, he hung up and said gravely, "A routine traffic stop." His eyes misted and he turned his head toward the driver's window and shaped his anger into words. "Goddamm these assholes in the training academy. I blame them, personally. Don't they know how to teach a seven-step approach anymore? Poor kid took a round in the gut."

"Ohmygod."

Sid poked a finger into his ribs. "It entered his side, where the body armor didn't cover. Between you and me, the vest would keep it from making a clean exit. If that were to happen, it would ricochet around until it chewed up his intestines. Greta's got a contact over at County, says they just pulled in. Nobody knows if he'll make it but I'll tell you one thing — I wouldn't be surprised if Wardancer's suspect is good for this."

He jabbed his fingers into the air, ticking off reasons, one-two-three. "A small caliber bullet'll slice your insides up like a fan blade. Wardancer's shooter used a .22 with copper-jacketed stingers. Slow, but thorough." His eyes pinned her. "No reason anyone should pull a gun on a cop over a busted tail light unless he's running from the law."

"Who's the injured officer?"

"Quint Carrol. A rookie. And you were right. His back-up didn't wait for the ambulance. That's what I'd want. Junior's brother's standing by to collect the bullet, assuming there's enough lead to run through ballistics."

"Let's head that way."

Sid tromped on the gas. "You don't have to tell me twice."

The county hospital's ER burgeoned with an ungainly mixture of migrant workers, illegal aliens, and the homeless. Due to the sheer volume of patients, it had a reputation for being one of the best trauma centers around. And when Quinten Carrol arrived on his deathbed, he received four-star attention.

Outside the emergency room, down a hallway lined with winos, Cézanne and Sid buttonholed a uniformed troop for an update.

According to the street cop, Corporal

Carrol called out his location on Interstate 30 — Tom Landry Highway — four miles east of Downtown on a well-traveled but sparsely populated strip of roadway peppered with call boxes. When his panic button went off, the communications officer pinpointed him immediately and dispatched back-up units, Code-Three. The first assist found him barely conscious on the gravel shoulder with his ticket book next to him, fluttering in the wind gusts. Carrol's last citation, partially filled in, gave good information. But according to the 10-28 return, the license plates came back stolen. The best clue came from a description he smeared on the citation in his own blood.

Wht 4 dr 2BM

In an effort to get a copy of Duty's composite sketch down to the hospital, Sid stabbed out Wardancer's number on his cell phone.

A scream of tires, skidding across the circular asphalt drive, sounded just beyond the portico. Cézanne glanced out the window —

— and the cow patty hit the turbo-prop. The Channel Eighteen van screeched to a stop at the ambulance entrance and Garlon Harrier bailed out. The hospital's automatic doors slid open and the investigative reporter lumbered their way with his trench coat flapping.

"Captain Martin," he hollered out in a way that spiked her blood pressure, "will the shooting affect your Cold Case investigation? Will the Great Dane Murder take a back seat? Do you have the officer's name? Does he have any family? Give us a comment."

A cameraman caught up to Harrier and blinded her with his overhead spotlight. She turned what she believed to be her good side to the camera, and spoke into the outstretched microphone.

"Harrier, you're a world class asshole."

As soon as the words hit the air she wanted to suck them back in. She knew she'd hear them again at six-and-ten, along with the rest of the Metroplex, and didn't like to think what was coming.

She spent the remainder of the shift between Rosen's office and Aden Whitelark's, dodging their threats to send her to charm school, and discussing the subtle differences between openly hostile behavior and protecting an investigation. By the time she locked up for the day, she decided a good stress reliever might be to treat Duty to what could probably be her first meal at a swanky restaurant. She selected André's, for its table linens and napkins folded into turtle shapes, and for the French cuisine that disintegrated almost as soon as it hit the tongue.

Maybe she could teach Devilrow's niece some style. Improve her manners. The girl could be made presentable with the right clothes and haircut, and when she returned to her family in East Texas, she could make ladies and gentlemen out of the rest of them. But when Cézanne arrived home, the plot to refine Duty ended as soon as she entered a house pungent with fumes of down-home cooking.

Down-home in the swamp.

Duty had a spread of blackened catfish, dirty rice, and grilled corn steaming on an elegantly set table. She even brought out the Waterford, filled to the brim with dark, fruity liquid.

Duty apparently caught her staring, because she quickly shook her head and drawled out an explanation. "It's not wine. They wouldn't sell me wine."

"Who wouldn't?"

"Delivery people."

"What delivery people?"

Duty pulled out a chair and motioned her to sit. "Did you know you can make a list of stuff on the computer and the delivery people come out?"

"You ordered this off my computer?"

" 'Cept for the wine. They wouldn't leave it on account of it's illegal to sell me spirits. They say a person gotta be twenty-one. I don't have this kinda trouble back home. My cousin, 'Miah, he make his own."

"Who?"

"Nehemiah. He my unca Ezra's boy. He in the choc business."

"Moonshine?"

"We don't like to call it that. Nehemiah, he in the liquor trade. Only with Nehemiah, he bypass the tax."

Not to mention the Health Department. The IRS. Matter of fact, Nehemiah probably didn't worry about the stream of commerce at all, except to line the pockets of his overalls.

"Stop talking." Come hell or high water, she'd get to the bottom of the unauthorized purchases. "How did you pay for this?"

"Credit card."

Her muscles knotted. "Whose credit card?"

"While I was dustin' I ran across yo' credit card."

Cézanne saw red. "You stole my credit card?"

"Mmm-mmm. You didn't leave 'em out for me?"

"Why the hell would I do that?"

Duty shrugged. "That's what I say to myself. I say, 'Self, why she go leave her cards where somebody could swipe 'em?'

But I didn't have a answer. Did you want to sit at the table or move into the living room so we can watch *Jeopardy!*?" And then Devilrow's niece whipped out a pair of scissors. "You got a scraggly piece of hair hanging in back. Mind if I snip it?"

Hours later, while Duty sat cross-legged on the floor watching a TV sitcom, Cézanne poured over the stalker reports spread across the Duncan Phyfe dining table. She studied them under a lamp, comparing them to additional reports the Crime Analysis Unit retrieved by location. Nearby, Butch the dog walked in. He sprawled out on the hardwood looking like the canine version of Hannibal Lechter in a new leather muzzle.

Cézanne dropped the papers, enough to peer over the top. "What's on his face?"

Without turning to look, Duty said, "That's what yo' friend from Cleburne sent you."

"Bobby?" Her heart skipped. "You opened my mail?"

"Mmm-hmm. In case it mighta been important."

"You opened my mail." *Hotter'n hell.*

"Just makin' sure it wasn't a letter bomb."

"Are you nuts?" Duty made her want to rip out fistfuls of hair. "Why would anybody send me a letter bomb?"

"Don't axe me. You the one people mad at."

"Nobody's mad at me."

"Mmm-hmm. That's why yo' phone never ring, that's why nobody come to visit, that's why you drag in everyday lookin' like you could use a facial. I got a homemade paste — if you was to let me rub it on — would change yo' luck."

"I don't want anything to do with your potions. Are you aware it's a Federal offense to putz around with people's mail? You could go to prison."

Duty paused a few seconds, seemingly taking the news under advisement. "Is the Federal pen where they have tennis? 'Cause I'd like to be like those Williams sisters who play tennis. Bet if somebody was to give me a racket —"

"Don't ever touch my mail again, do you hear me?"

On TV, a black family worked out their differences and everyone got a group hug at the end of the show. Fleetingly, Cézanne wondered about Duty's life — not just about coming from a broken family — the Devilrows were downright mangled.

"Was there a note in the package?"

"He say it's a present. He say, 'Love, Bobby.' " The voodoo matchmaker had deceit written all over her face.

"He did not say, 'Love, Bobby.' I want to see the letter."

"No letter. Just a scrap of paper."

Cézanne's heart skipped. "Give it to me."

"Dog ate it."

So Bobby wanted to give her a nudge? To set it up so she'd call to thank him?

She wouldn't do it. Dane Kissel deserved her full attention. If Bobby couldn't wait, didn't respect her enough as a colleague to let her do her job, well . . .

Cézanne re-focused her attention on the reports.

The first — classified as an offense report — had been logged into the system three months before Dane Kissel died, twelve blocks south of Worth Price's estate, across the freeway. She set it aside. If there was a link between the Kissel murder and the homicide on Horne Street, she couldn't see it.

The next two reports involved barking dogs, the kind of dispute FWPD generally deferred to Animal Control to resolve. The only pattern that turned the incident reports into a curiosity was that they occurred weekly during the one-month period prior to Kissel's murder. On Thursdays. Around shift-change. And they carried the signature of the late P. J. Wehmeyer.

Coincidence? Maybe not.

With random thoughts swimming in her head, she set them aside and scanned another report.

A week before the Kissel homicide a neighbor called in a prowler. Beat officers combing the area failed to locate anyone. Although Benji Wardancer's name appeared on the paperwork, Jock Featherston wrote a supplement.

The last report prickled the hair on her neck. Three nights before Worth Price's nine-one-one call went through dispatch, another stalker report came in — signed by P. J. Wehmeyer. With a supplement from then-rookie, Doug Driskoll.

Across the room, Duty's laughter rose above the murmur of the television. Butch thumped his tail against the rug in hard, deliberate whacks, glowering through lattices of leather.

Hello, Clarice.

Cézanne straightened her papers and stuffed them back into her briefcase. Leaving Duty to keep an eye on Butch, she retired to her room and changed into blue jeans and a lilac pinpoint oxford, heavily starched. With a tobacco-colored Eisenhower jacket cut from sueded leather thrown over one arm, she returned and sat on the edge of the sofa.

"I have to leave for a bit."

Duty pushed up on her elbows and

twisted her neck until the very sight cried out for an exorcism. "You talkin' to me?"

"No, to the dog." Sarcastic.

" 'Kay." She swiveled her head back to the TV.

Cézanne took a breath and held it. "Yes, I'm talking to you. The dog doesn't understand."

"He know you don't like him."

"I like him fine." Her eyes flickered to Butch and, for a fleeting moment, the mournful look in his eyes almost convinced her he wasn't a minion of the Antichrist. Flexing her punctured ankle sent a pinch up her leg and helped her regain her senses. "I've been meaning to ask you about my Baccarat owl."

"Huh?"

"The crystal figurine that's supposed to be on the mantle."

Duty's eyes shifted to the fireplace and back.

"Do you know what happened to it?"

A headshake. "Frieda mighta took it. She don't much like you. Says you been keepin' her up, mostly dancin' 'round in yo' underpants singin' show tunes outta key."

"Frieda, huh? When do I get to meet this Frieda?" She got a one-shoulder shrug. "If you broke it, you should tell me."

Another headshake.

Cézanne got up from the couch and fished through her purse for Ruby's keys. The beehive clock lacked only moments from chiming the ninth hour.

"Stay off the computer."

In a flash, Duty bounded to her feet, her face tight with worry. "Where you runnin' off to?"

"The Auto Pound."

"What for?"

"Not that it's any of your business, but I have to ask a guy some questions."

"I'll go, too."

Cézanne wagged her finger in a no motion. "Official police business. You're not going. That's the end of it."

Duty sprinted into the guest room. She returned with what appeared to be a plastic Baggie with tea grounds in her outstretched hand. "Slip this by yo' heart. Go on, take it."

"What is it? Controlled substance? I haven't stuffed my bra since high school." Cézanne opened the plastic zipper and unleashed a powerful odor.

"Close it, quick," Duty shouted, and hopped on one foot. She snatched the Baggie from Cézanne's grasp and let out a squeal. Her fingers danced in front of her lips and she sealed her eyes so tight they wrinkled at the corners and plumped her cheeks. "Minkisi magic, warn the heart, care for her when trouble start."

"What the hell's the matter with you?"

Duty's eyes peeled back. "Loa."

"Gimme the damned thing."

Half out the door, she stuffed Duty's concoction into her purse. Inside the Kompressor, she decided to ditch the contents as soon as she hit the highway; until she caught sight of the girl's relieved expression, backlit in the halo of the porch light, with her fingers working overtime casting puppet shadows onto the bricks.

Chapter Seventeen

In an industrial area north of Downtown, condensation billowed out from the Auto Pound's heating unit. When it met the crisp night air, steam veiled rows of mangled cars. Under the eerie blue cast of mercury vapor lamps, dead vehicles took the sinister form of a foggy, bayou graveyard. Cézanne half expected a couple of snarling Dobermans to barrel out from the portable office building; instead, FWPD Auto Pound's top dog, Doug Driskoll, bounded down the steps holding an aluminum clipboard. He stopped within a few feet of the Kompressor's hood and took notice.

She hit the electric window button. As the glass slid halfway down, her breath turned to vapor. Their eyes locked in a murderous bent, and she wasn't at all certain the chills creeping up her neck were solely a result of the cold.

Amazingly, the lines in Driskoll's face softened with recognition, as if he were happy to see her and bore her no ill will for professionally neutering him.

"Oh, it's you. Sorry. I just got off the phone with some chick, bitching about her boyfriend's car, threatening to sue. Something I can do for you, Captain?"

"Eight years ago, you took a stalker call a few streets east of Dane Kissel's. I want you to tell me about it."

"Sure thing. Walk with me and we'll talk. I need to get a VIN off a car."

Something told her not to. That they could conduct business right there, beside the roadway, with the Kompressor idling and her foot poised to stomp Ruby's gas pedal. But she hungered for any information that might help break the cold case open, and Driskoll's eyes still had the same charismatic allure they always had whenever she moved within his magnetic field. She found herself following him down the middle of junk heaps and impounds, away from the well-lit protection of the front gates, aware only of the loud crunch of gravel beneath her tasseled Cole Haans.

The City crew hadn't mowed since late summer. Near the back of the lot, where knee-high grass had long since shriveled to hay, a berm-like incline rose up to obscure the view of the Trinity River.

Cézanne glanced around. "How come it's so dark back here?"

"It's blacker than midnight under a skillet, isn't it? Some asshole got bored and shot out the lights. You get used to it."

"Y'all can't get the maintenance crew

out with a ladder to change the bulbs?"

"It just happened a few days ago."

Driskoll stopped between two circa-sixties Buicks, dropped his cigarette, and ground it out with a boot tip. He tugged out a small flashlight tucked between his belt and the waistband of his jeans and switched it on. A pale wash of light illuminated his face. It made the hollows below his cheekbones and under his eyes more pronounced, and gave him the overall appearance of a jack-o-lantern. Even cars with front end damage seemed to be grinning.

He said, "Do me a favor? I need the VIN off the engine block. I hurt my knee last week and I can't bend."

"I'm not about to crawl under this car —"

"You want to talk about the prowler don't you?"

"Now I remember why we broke up. Gimme the damned light."

He handed it over and she flicked the on-switch.

His gaze drifted over the fleet of autos. "Most of these cars don't run."

"Neither do I." She propped herself against a fender and they stood, locked in each other's sights.

Driskoll opened the LeSabre's hood latch and pushed it up. "Lotta these cars have been here for years."

"Probably so." She slipped her purse

strap off her shoulder and placed the bag on the adjacent car, then bent across the front grill and aimed the beam into a mass of rubber lines, crazed with age. The smell of dead gas filled her nose. "I came here about your supplemental report, so start talking."

"I was about to. Trouble is, I took that call so long ago, it's going to take a minute. You got that number yet?"

"It's caked with grit. Do you have a rag?" He fluttered a handkerchief beside her face and she used it to wipe away the grime. "Write this down."

She rattled off the serial number and made him repeat it aloud. Satisfied, she cut off the flashlight and raised up.

Driskoll turned his face to the moon and the light played over his perfect profile. "Okay, I need a number off the trunk."

"Have fun."

"No, babe, I need you to get it for me," he said in a velvet voice. "I told you, I can't bend."

A strong pulse throbbed in her neck. "Look, Doug, I didn't come here to do your job, I came here to do mine. I want to talk about that supplement you wrote."

"Sometimes I get amnesia. Now be a good girl."

She got the drift. The old *quid pro quo*. Lazy bastard. She did right getting rid of him.

A change in breeze brought a hint of Angel for Men close enough for her to fall victim to its intoxicating fragrance. The man standing beside her, opening the trunk, bore little resemblance to the lover who once consumed her waking thoughts.

"You know the kind of information you pick up when you're sitting around with nothing to do, swapping war stories with your partners?" he said. "Some bored asshole threw a dead dog out here. He came back at the end of his watch and it was gone."

"Interesting." She depressed the switch and ran the shaft of light across a mat lining the trunk. "Junk food wrappers."

"Yeah, some bored asshole comes out here to eat. Here, babe, let me get that for you." Driskoll balanced the clipboard on the chrome bumper, raked the fast food sacks out with his hand, then yanked out the rotted carpet. The fading glow from the yellow bulb caught years of dust sifting down from the air. "Better hurry, not much life left in those batteries."

She balanced one knee on the bumper and kept her other foot grounded. Leaning in with the light, she said, "Tit for tat, Driskoll, start talking."

Her voice echoed as though it came from a crypt.

In the distance, faint chirps carried on

the breeze like a thousand squeaky bed-springs.

Driskoll said, "Let's see . . . that night, Westside was shorthanded. The Blue wanted a raise and the brass didn't want to give us one. A lot of guys called in sick — blue flu — that's how I ended up working."

"You didn't follow suit?"

"I was a new hire just out of rookie school. They pulled me off at the end of my shift and made me work a double-back. I didn't want to get canned."

Cézanne shined the beam across the metal interior. The distant chirping grew louder.

"What's that noise?"

"What noise?"

"Listen . . . don't tell me you can't hear that?"

"Dead grass. Rustles something fierce in a good wind."

"It's not dead grass. Where's the VIN on this car?"

"You may have to stretch. There should be a stamp at the very back. See anything yet?"

"Not one eff-ing thing." She lifted her foot off the ground. If she knew Driskoll, he was eyeing her tush.

"You may have to get in to read the number."

"If you think I'm climbing inside this filthy —"

"You want this information, Zan. Trust me. Now slip in, read it off, and let's get outta here. I'm cold."

She had already started wrangling out of her leather bomber when he said, "Nice jacket."

She tossed it over his face and hoisted one leg over the lip of the trunk. "Talk fast, Doug. All I've gotten so far is yammering."

"Quit bitching and try to follow along. I'm only going to tell this once. Joey Wehmeyer was first on-scene. I wasn't assigned to that beat so I had to come from five miles away. When I pulled up to the curb, I saw him thrashing his way out of some bougainvilleas behind one of the houses. They'd grown into trees, five deep, and formed a natural barrier. Wehmeyer was white as a sheet."

"How come?"

"This feels nice." He pressed a leather sleeve to his nose and filled his lungs. "You won't believe this next part."

"You have my attention."

"Wehmeyer committed suicide, you know." She was completely in, as far back as she could go when Driskoll said, "It should be right above your head. It'll be easier to read if you roll on your back."

"You're out of your mind." Cézanne froze in a crouch. "There's that sound. You'd have to be deaf not to hear that."

"Oh, that."

The doom-like quality in his voice died out with the stream of light. Vibrant colors in his shirt faded into various shades of bruises. Stars framing the outline of Driskoll's body winked as if they knew the punch line to a sick joke. Her hand grazed something slick and greasy, and when she jerked away, the putrid stench of rotted meat hit her nostrils.

"Ohmygod, what the hell's that stink? Did y'all get a dead body out of here?"

"Sewer rats," he said. "Big as possums."

She made a valiant attempt to scramble out, but the cry of a rusty hinge pierced her ears and the lid came down hard across her back. A rush of air left her mouth. She landed, face-first, on the floorboard with the wind knocked out of her. Azure dots danced before her eyes. A snap of the lock filled her with fright.

She was thinking, *Get me out,* but the words got caught in her throat. Except for thin shafts of blue light visible through the rusty pock marks, darkness surrounded her.

"Quit screwing around." Driskoll, his voice muffled.

"Open it!"

"Quit fucking with the lock."

The word lock sent a chill through her heart. "Get me outta here." She beat at the light source, chipping away at the car cancer to make a bigger airhole.

"You're not dicking with the lock?"

Her voice climbed in pitch. "Why would I do that?"

"We've got to get you out before the rats make it over the hill. Some bored asshole's been leaving burgers out here, thinking he can domesticate them." His voice was velvety and taunting. "That's what it's like to work in the middle of no-fucking-where. If you don't start out sick, you end up that way."

Steel rattled, heightening the terror. She fought a whimper and picked at the mangy metal.

"I wouldn't do that if I were you. You could cut yourself. The smell of blood sends them into a frenzy. Got that dog I was telling you about."

Driskoll moved beyond a warped section of trunk where the rubber gasket had rotted away. Even though she could no longer see him, the condemnation in his tone compounded her panic.

"Nobody ever comes this far back. No need to. We can't move the cars out because of new ones coming in every day. Eventually, the tires give out. Rubber disintegrates, and when it rains, the cars leak. Do you have any idea how long it takes metal to bio-degrade?" His demonic laugh danced between her ears. "Longer than a body, that's for sure."

A jolt of adrenaline zipped up her torso, leaving her with a lightheaded, nauseating rush. Horror heightened her senses. Silence gripped her throat.

She angled her body where she could deliver a mighty kick to the lock, and did. It held. She grappled for a tire iron, beyond her grasp.

"Sometimes I sit at my desk at night, look out at this boneyard, and wonder if anyone ever checks what's inside these cars beyond the log-in date. If someone disappeared, nobody'd ever know — except for the flies. I've seen swarms so thick they formed little tornados."

He intended to leave her. Thoughts of survival fragmented inside her head.

"Only other guys who work out here are marking time for their pensions. Rickety old flatfoots don't have the energy to get up and stretch their legs. Me, on the other hand, I pace like a panther."

Footfalls crunched against the gravel.

She imagined the oxygen depleting. The concept of smothering stripped away her last vestiges of reason.

"Let me out, you psycho son of a bitch."

"That's not nice. It doesn't do a thing to get me in the mood. I remember when you used to —"

Her mind reeled with Driskoll's graphic descriptions of their love life. As he wove the most intimate details in with seductive insults, the orange peel and chocolate scent from his cologne filled her head.

She thought she would wet herself.

Each verbal perversion Driskoll dished out seemed worse than the one before. Finally, she snapped. "I'll have you in IA so fast the mere speed will shear off your dick."

"You've obviously taken leave of your senses. This was purely accidental. Now I'm trying as hard as I can, babydoll, but the lock's stuck."

As soon as he spoke, the incongruity of his words took flight from her thoughts. He wasn't going to let her out.

"Ohmygod, what was that?" She held her breath to hear better, but the external sounds were eclipsed by her thundering heart.

"Stay put, babe, I'm going for help."

"Don't you leave me out here, you deranged sociopath," she screamed. "There's rats."

"What do you expect? Some bored asshole's been throwing out Big Macs."

She kicked out a taillight. Thrashed

around. Beat her fists against the trunk until pain shot up her arms.

"Poor Captain, you're alarmed. I don't think they can climb up the undercarriage, though. Then again, if they smell food . . ."

Limp and disoriented, she flailed her arms in a feeble attempt to gain release. She wanted the gun in her purse. She'd rather have her ears ring the rest of her life, than her bones gnawed clean. Her hand hit something solid and she knew at once she touched the tire iron. She clawed at it with her fingernails —

— and felt its grit against her palm.

The last vile thing she heard Driskoll say was, "Don't fret, babe, I know just how to deal with rats. Piss on 'em."

Followed by the sound of his zipper running along its metal track.

And the splatter of fiery hot liquid trickling in on her through the cracks.

Chapter Eighteen

Alone inside the LeSabre's trunk, Cézanne chipped away at a gangrenous fissure. What started out as a dime-sized hole ended up as big as a fist, and she widened another chip enough to poke her head through. She almost wished she hadn't. What appeared to be a dark, undulating blanket topped the berm and advanced toward the cyclone fence in a mirage-like wave.

Carnal panic filled her senses.

Desperate squeaks reached her ears. She ducked back inside and stabbed the lock with the point of the tire iron. Sweat rolled down the small of her back.

She switched on the flashlight and got a burst of candlepower, enough to glimpse the mechanism. As it snuffed itself out, a whiskered snout poked through the broken taillight. She stomped at it with her shoe and the agonizing shriek died out.

Blood whooshed between her ears. She breathed so hard, she couldn't hear beyond her own intakes of air. Then she held her breath and listened for Driskoll.

Tiny claws skittered on metal.

Something scurried along her leg. She let

out a cat-in-heat shriek. Took a swipe at it with the jack. When she breathed again, she vacuumed in the musty odor of dead vermin.

Properly motivated, she jammed the lever under the catch and delivered a mighty kick. The lock popped away and hit the floor with a clink; she threw open the trunk lid and scrambled to her feet. On the ground, rats leapfrogged over each other's backs in an attempt to ascend the LeSabre's framework. One made it to the bumper and with tire iron in hand, she knocked it into the cyclone fence like an Alex Rodriguez homer. Hoisting herself the rest of the way out, she scrambled up onto the roof.

It took an Olympian vault, but her feet hit hard on top of the adjacent Buick. She swooped down and snatched her purse up by its strap, then sprang from hood to hood until she came to a row of cars too far apart to leap. She hit the ground running, and bounded toward the portable office with homicidal thoughts rampaging through her head.

Pistol-whip him 'til he's dead.

Drag his bloody corpse out back.

Pump lead in him 'til I'm out of bullets. Reload.

Halfway across the lot, truth's harsh reality sank in.

Can't do a fucking thing, and Driskoll knows it.

Rosen wanted her gone. Harrier wanted a story. Driskoll wanted her to pay for taking his job. Fort Worth wanted its most famous crime solved. The last thing the Cold Case Squad needed was negative publicity. And the last thing she needed was to become the focus of another IA investigation.

Inside the window, Driskoll was talking on the phone. The glass-bottled Coke he raised to his lips was three-quarters gone, and a set of car keys lay on the blotter.

With her gun hand inside her purse flap and a grip on her Smith, she grabbed the doorknob with her free hand and flung herself into a spartan room with smells of coffee and cigarette smoke permanently embedded in the walls.

"Gotta go." Driskoll slammed the phone down. "Jeepers-creepers, what happened to you?"

"On your feet, you insane dement."

He didn't so much as flinch. "Sorry it took so long. I had to find the keys."

"You're sitting here, smoking, you asshole. Look at you, you deranged psychopath — your feet are propped on the desk."

With a look of practiced innocence, Driskoll pointed to the keys.

She stood with her chest heaving, watching her reflection in the window glass behind him. Hair stuck out in a rat's nest. Slobber oozed from one corner of her mouth, clamped thin and turning into a purple snarl.

"You pissed on me."

His eyes filled with puppy-dog trust. "Hey, you need to show some gratitude. I just got off the phone with the Fire Department. Which reminds me . . . I reckon I ought to call them back, tell them to disregard. No point dragging out the jaws of life if you're free, huh?"

"You tried to kill me."

"Me? No. I tried to save you. And you don't have any witnesses to the contrary."

It was all she could take, watching him lounging in his chair, mocking her. She imagined how he'd look with her .38 screwed up his left nostril, when —

— out came her Chief's Special.

That re-shaped the cockeyed grin on his face.

Yeah, cheater-pants, how about a little frontier justice?

His boots hit the floor with a thud. Green eyes darkened with fear. Two years of stock-piled rage over Driskoll's lies bubbled to the surface. She liked the feel of the Pachmeyer grips against her damp palms, and got primal satisfaction seeing an ever-widening stain soak the front of his pants. Her gaze flickered to the trashcan, where she half-expected to find her leather bomber. It wasn't there. She ground her molars so hard a trajectory of pain rifled through her head.

Common sense resurfaced.

She was plotting a strategy that began with marching him to the back of the lot to look for it, making him crawl through rat shit on all-fours until his knees were raw, degrading him the way he had done her when —

— the slam of the door rang in her ears.

Flashes of her career went up like a careening truckful of nitro.

Just when she thought it couldn't get any worse, she turned to surrender her piece to —

— Garlon Harrier? Dancing the full-bladder jig with his hand cupping his crotch?

"Go right ahead, don't mind me, I just came in to use the john."

"She tried to kill me," Driskoll shouted.

"Bullshit, you lying cretin. You tried to suffocate me."

"I came at a bad time, didn't I?"

"You're my witness, Harrier. She tried to croak me. Thank God I've got a witness."

"Whoa, dudes, I just stopped in to use the can."

"You're still following me, aren't you, you voyeuristic son of a bitch?"

"You should be happy I got here when I did." In a modified bunny hop toward the latrine, the reporter's oily hair parted under its own weight, and the bear claw lock of hair made a pendulum swing across his forehead.

And then Harrier couldn't have surprised her more if he whipped out his fireman and doused her with his hose. "Here's the deal, take it or leave it. I didn't see anybody pull a gun on anybody. Now, I might've witnessed somebody get locked in a trunk —"

"You saw that? Ohmygod, that's fantastic. This bored asshole meant to kill me."

"— but it's awful dark outside, especially way back in the corner. May I?" He tiptoed close enough to cup a hand to his mouth and pipe a suggestion into her ear. "If I don't see a gun, this guy's got no complaint for IA. That means you keep your job . . . keep looking into the Great Dane."

Driskoll flinched.

"Hup!" Cézanne tensed her grip. Without taking her eyes off Driskoll, she mumbled, "What're you driving at?"

"I want to be part of the investigation."

"Fat stinking chance."

"Captain," he hissed, "you pulled your piece."

"I don't make deals with terrorists. You saw what this rat-bastard did. I'll subpoena you to the Grand Jury. Make you testify."

"Fine. I'll be there. Only what you're doing isn't self-defense anymore."

"Screw you, and the horse you rode in on, Harrier. Even if I lose my job, at least I'll get plenty of ink as a celebrity. Only way you'll ever be on a major TV news network is if you print the letters 'CNN' on a piece of paper and sit on it."

"Your opportunity to plead insanity, or crime of passion, is long gone, Captain. Now, it's just attempted, premeditated murder." As if she didn't understand, he enunciated, "Let me in on the cold case."

"I hate you." It seemed like the right thing to say, and made her feel ever so much better. "I hate your nasty, weasel guts."

"Everyone does." Eyes the size of black olives got even bigger. "So . . . we have a deal?"

Driskoll turned surly. "What's going on over there?"

She decided to throw in with Harrier and lowered the .38.

"Sorry, bud, but I'm with her."

"We're even for now, Driskoll, but steer clear. You ever cross me again, your cell in I-Block will make Auto Pound seem like a week of R-and-R. And if you really called the Fire Department, they've got a suck-dog response time."

The last person Cézanne expected to have coffee with was the one she was sitting across the booth from. At Dottie's All-Nite Diner, Harrier's looks didn't get any better under the harsh glow of the fake Tiffany mounted overhead. But he'd gotten her out of a jam, so she agreed to listen to his take on the matter.

"Here's how I figure it." He propped his elbows on the table and leaned his squat body forward until he all but hovered over the sugar dispenser in the middle of the table. "I'll take a month off and do nothing but cover the Great Dane."

"And hound me the whole time? Forget it."

"How long do you think it'll take to solve it?"

She checked the clock mounted over the check-out register. One minute after midnight. "Nine days."

"No shit?" He pulled out his spiral notebook, but she snatched it out of his hand and held it hostage for his attention.

"Listen, and listen good. You're a civilian. You don't have any police training —"

"I cover the police beat."

"— you wouldn't know how to respond in a crisis, and I'm not gonna be liable if you get creamed. Am I making myself clear?"

Harrier nodded. The disdain she dished out seemed to leave him breathless with excitement.

"Convincing Chief Rosen to approve the ride-along will be a hurdle. What I told you back at the Auto Pound, I told you in good faith. But it won't matter if Rosen doesn't go along with it. Agreed?"

"Agreed."

"And if Rosen says 'No dice,' we're even. Ask no quarter, give no quarter. Agreed?"

"You think he won't approve it, don't you?"

"Honestly? I don't. It all comes down to money, and the PD doesn't want the liability. Not even if the exposure's minimal and the liability's capped."

Harrier practically thumbed the lapels on his trench coat. "I can make him let me ride."

She wondered if the reporter had dirt on her uncle.

But that didn't stop her from thinking, *I can make him veto it.*

When Cézanne pulled Ruby into the drive, she spotted Duty on the front porch, huddled in her blanket, shivering. Devilrow's niece stopped wringing her hands long enough to come flying across the grass, panic-stricken. She chanted a mantra of, "Thank you, Oya," to the stars.

But when Cézanne opened Ruby's door and swung out a leg, Duty cringed. "Oh, law, Miz Zan. You be fine now. Lemme help you outta yo' car."

"Go back inside, it's freezing."

"Did you know yo' headlight's broke?"

"Some bored asshole must've done it."

"Oya take care of you tonight."

"You didn't invite somebody over while I was gone, did you?"

"Miz Zan, you funnin' me now. You need me to steady you?"

"No. Who's Oya?"

"You come on in. You got some rum? 'Cause we could use some rum and some cigars — maybe some candy for Eleggua. He like that. And we need to give Oya a gift for savin' yo' life. Oya like lipstick. And good perfume. You got some toilet water you're not using? Want me to put a hex on somebody?"

The idea sounded outstanding until it occurred to her that endorsing Duty's religious practices might mean she'd lost her grip.

"Who's Oya?"

"Warrior. She guard the gates of death. You want coffee? I make you coffee. Got a nice European roast from the delivery people."

"No coffee. Just a hot shower. I'll be fine. Quit making such a fuss."

But Duty wouldn't be placated. "Miz Zan, won't do no good to ask Obatalla for peace. You need a good curse. I like curses. Only gotta be careful or the spell come around, bite you, too."

It took some doing, but she convinced Duty to hold off on mayhem for the night.

After a shower where she all but scrubbed her skin raw, Cézanne curled up on the living room sofa with the lights turned up enough to put a drain on the transformer. Duty sat cross-legged on the rug at her feet, without comment. But when the girl reached under the lampshade to dim the switch, Cézanne stopped her.

"Leave it."

"You ought to get some sleep. Forget what happened."

"Keep the lights on."

"You want I should go back to bed?"

The girl appeared genuinely rattled. It probably wasn't easy for her, staying in someone else's house, conforming to another's rules, being away from family. Since Roby died, loneliness had managed to get a claw hold on the fragile infrastructure of Cézanne's emotions. Now with Bobby out of the picture, life seemed pretty empty.

And she was ashamed of herself.

She hadn't been very nice to Devilrow's niece.

"If it's all the same, Deuteronomy, would you mind staying put until I'm asleep?"

The last thing she remembered as she drifted off was the soothing tickle from the girl's thin fingers stroking her hair.

Chapter Nineteen

Instead of meeting Garlon Harrier in Rosen's office at eight o'clock sharp, Cézanne made it a point to arrive early. Standing in the outer office, waiting for Ellen to track down their boss, she silently plotted ways to sabotage Harrier's request. The angle to use, she concluded with a certain degree of smugness, would be the department's SOP. And Standard Operating Procedure dictated no more than one ride-in per guest in a six month period.

She could control what day Harrier rode and where they went. Not a bad compromise.

A superior outcome would occur if Rosen banned Harrier from riding, period. Ever since a female news anchor rode-in with one of the supervisors, then did a scathing five-part exposé on the PD, the department adopted an unwritten, unofficial, understood policy barring reporters. If she got lucky, Rosen would see fit to enforce it.

She no sooner finished inspecting the black velvet lapels of her ice pink jacket and matching wool skirt for lint, when Harrier burst through the doorway out of breath.

He broke into a smirk and wagged his finger at her. "Clever. I figured you'd try to queer this deal."

She summoned a wounded look. "I have an appointment with Krivnek at nine and can't be late."

"You're seeing Krivnek without me?" Harrier's face reddened with anger. "We had a deal."

"I didn't welsh on our deal. You knew any deal we cut had to be blessed by the Pope."

Ellen's eyebrows arched into severe peaks. Rosen sauntered in, and Cézanne and Harrier stopped arguing long enough to follow him into the inner sanctum.

"Coffee?" Rosen pointed them to the guest cups on the credenza.

Cézanne shook her head.

"Love some." Harrier winked.

He poured enough sugar into the Styrofoam container to start a cavity, then dampened it with coffee. When he settled back into a chair, Rosen gave him the eye.

"What's so important I had to come in early?"

"I want to accompany Captain Martin on her investigation."

"Is that so?" Rosen regarded her pointedly. "What do you have to say?"

She shot the reporter a look of utter disgust. "I think it's a great idea. But I told him it's your call."

"How about it, Chief?"

"Highly irregular." Rosen stroked his chin. He stared at a point on the wall, just above their heads.

She knew her plan took a downturn when he didn't immediately send them packing. Desperate, she clapped a hand to her mouth and fluttered her eyes in mock astonishment. "I forgot about SOP."

Harrier glowered. "What's SOP?"

Rosen said, "You can't ride-in."

"Sorry, I tried." She fixed her lips in a pout.

"But I'm the media. You can't make an exception?"

Rosen was starting to waffle. Was actually rethinking his position. Looking at her as if trying to decide whether she'd just foxed him. Her heart skipped a beat. It could go either way.

Cézanne played along. "Can't we make an exception?"

"I thought you two didn't get along."

"A simple misunderstanding. Matter of fact, I think it would be great if he rode-in. He could do a feature on me every night on the six-and-ten, and when the Great Dane Murder is solved, he might even have enough footage for a documentary." She stared dreamily into thin air. "Think of the publicity. I'll be a celebrity. Harrier might even be nominated for one of those journalism awards. And think how great the PD would look. Hell —" she chuckled and tossed in a devilish thought "— this could lead to my own talk show."

"I doubt that."

"You're right, Chief Rosen. That's a wild card. But I might look so good I'd become a contender for your job."

She could almost sense the exact moment he puckered up.

Several nail-biting seconds passed before Rosen got to his feet, his usual way of terminating an interview. She kept her poker face on.

"Sorry, Harrier. Policy's policy. Maybe next time."

Traffic around the county hospital was at its worst. By the time the appointment with Krivnek rolled around, Cézanne circled the block several times before she found a parking spot near the Hebrew Rest Cemetery. She walked a half-block west on Feliks Gwozdz Place to the brown brick Tarrant County Medical Examiner's Office and Forensics building. Sid and Teddy were waiting under the portico, each looking snappy in their western cut suits.

While talking, they rarely glanced at each other. In the way of the beat cop, they looked past the other's shoulders, or side to side, scanning the area and watching each other's back, with an eye out for danger.

Sid kept his pipe burning as Teddy drew a picture in the air for him to follow. "I love my truck, don't get me wrong, but I'm ordering one of those PT Cruisers. They got one in at the dealership and I checked it out last night. It's so big you can get two-by-fours in the back seat."

"Two whores in the back seat?" Sid spoke between puffs. "Hi, little missy. Did you hear? Junior's gonna get a paddy wagon to haul whores around in. All I can say is, thank God." He winked. "You look sharp. Pink's a good color on you. Lotta women in power positions would think it made them look wimpy. Not me. Titty Pink's my favorite."

Teddy turned beet red. "Morning, Captain."

"Good morning, Teddy . . . Sidney."

Sid sneaked a few last minute puffs before emptying his pipe on the dead grass. "Ready?"

"Yes. Krivnek won't like what I have to say, so I'd appreciate it if you guys backed me up."

"You're the boss," Teddy said, but Sid was checking out her backswing, and when she reached the door, she looked back in time to catch him leering.

Beyond the lobby, they found Krivnek in his lab coat, hunched over a microscope. He was focusing the lens over a slide, right-handed, and hen-scratching notes onto a form with his left. He must have started the day early, because the strong scent of camphor and posted bodies still lingered on his smock. When he glanced up to acknowledge them, the gauze patch taped above his left eyebrow made his tortoiseshell horn rims sit crooked on his face.

Sid pointed out the obvious. "Barroom brawl? Forget to duck? No, wait — rough sex?"

"Melanoma. Skin cancer, for you lay people." He pushed away from the microscope and stood for handshakes, all around. Another patch behind the ear had them staring, and when Krivnek pulled the tape away and showed them burns the size of quarters, Sid said, "Hell, that's not skin cancer, those're crop circles."

"You have to stay out of the sun when you're young." Krivnek directed the remark at Cézanne and Teddy. "What did we know? I grew up on the beach."

"Yeah, well, they said eggs were bad for you, too," Sid chimed in, "then they said they weren't, then they said they were. You doctors can't seem to make up your minds."

"I've made up my mind on this." Krivnek had the Kissel file on the counter next to a stack of medical books. "I didn't do the autopsy and I wasn't here when the deceased took the GSW to the chest. But the report lists the cause of death as a homicide, and that's good enough for me." He stared at Teddy in a way that made Cézanne think the detective had already advanced his suicide theory. He turned, and his eyes took on a speculative gleam. "So Cézanne, what can I do for you?"

She chose the stool next to Krivnek and settled onto it with the confidence of a reigning monarch. "I want to know if exhuming the body would yield more information about distance and trajectory."

"Dig him up?" Krivnek lapsed into layspeak. "What's with this inordinately ghoulish fixation to deny the dead eternal rest, Ms. Martin? This is the second body you've wanted to disinter in a week. Did your parents not give you a shovel and sand pail when you were little?"

"I think his wife shot him while he slept. If someone stood over the victim and pulled the trigger, you could tell that, couldn't you?"

"Yes, but —"

"And you could tell how far away they were, based on gunpowder residue, couldn't you?"

"Yes, but —"

"If we got a search warrant and went in

and Luminoled the walls, and took photographs, and let you look at the bloodstain patterns, you could tell if he was lying down or standing up, right? And the approximate height of the person who shot him?" She paused for air.

"Yes to all of it. But you're forgetting something."

"What?"

"Politics."

She checked Sid's flat expression, then Teddy's with his eyebrows corkscrewed in wonder.

"Ms. Martin, the ME's office is merely a cell in the Tarrant County organism, along with other cells such as the PD, the SO, and the municipalities of satellite cities in and around this continually sprawling amoeba we affectionately call Cowtown. So let me make this easy. If one cell gets sick, they all get sick. Or, the diseased part is surgically removed for the good of the whole."

As if she didn't get it, Sid said, "He means we've gotta get along."

"I get along fine. I love the ME's office. We have a symbiotic relationship, don't we, Krivnek?" She dared to glance at the frowning man. "I'm not stepping on any toes."

"Let's discuss the players." Krivnek again. "In his heyday, Worth Price did some pretty impressive things for this city.

After a downturn in the economy, when the S-and-Ls and the oil business went belly-up, he took a financial beating. But the last decade, he's his old philanthropic self. I'm surprised they haven't dedicated a building — perhaps commissioned a bronze in his honor — overlooking the Trinity River. Now, I'm not so shallow as to think you wouldn't pull something like a court-ordered exhumation; but while you may be in charge of this investigation, someone else is in charge of you."

Her stomach knotted. She knew, without asking, he ratted her off to Rosen. Just like he did in the Lady Godiva case. A dozen thoughts took flight. But Sid's hand came down softly on one shoulder and Teddy's came down on the other and she knew, without doubt, they were a team.

Sid said, "If we get a court order, it's a done deal. Not every judge in Tarrant County got where he is on account of Worth Price."

"And come to think of it," Teddy added with only the tiniest warble, "I'd imagine Mr. Price would want to remove any cloud of suspicion from his daughter. Unless she did it."

Cézanne glanced over in time to see a smile angle up one side of his face.

"She didn't do it." Sid, again. "No motive."

"Oh, there's a motive, all right." And

Cézanne prepared to disclose it. What brought her tongue skidding to a stop was Rosen strolling in, spit polished and knife creased, with his dark blue eyes gleaming stubbornly from their cold depths.

"If this isn't a rogue's gallery. I'm glad to see my people out on such a gloomy, dismal day."

Cézanne needed an immediate change of scenery. She excused herself to the ladies' room, hoping in the time it took to return, Rosen would forget things that didn't concern him. Like motive. And how things were shaping up on the Great Dane. Old Judge Pittman would sign that order. Old Judge Pittman, a principled man, was not inclined to be bullied by Rosen, or some oil baron from the Westside.

She gave herself a long, critical look in the mirror. Dried her forehead with a paper towel and patted the sheen on her nose with a powder-puff. She was freshening her lipstick when the door to the men's room creaked open. Voices echoed off the tile and filtered through the vent.

"I just got off the phone to IA." Rosen.

"You don't say?" Sid.

"You're responsible for your conduct in this department, and what I've noticed is a continuous assault on family values unseen since the millennium-ending shenanigans of Bill Clinton."

"If I'm fixing to get days-off, do you think we could run 'em in conjunction with the holidays? I'd kinda like to get me a couple of broads and fly to Aspen."

"Don't fuck with me, Klevenhagen. You're hanging by a thread."

"Cut to the chase, Chief. I'm from the old school. Women don't belong in police work. They need to be home, runnin' the kids to soccer practice, and makin' supper for their men. And when the breadwinner gets home, they need to send the kids to the neighbor's and meet the boss in the bedroom, naked, on all fours. Now, that don't gel with some people, especially these dykes somebody in Recruiting keeps signing up. But if they're gonna spray paint their pants on and strut their stuff, I'll be the first to test the waters."

"That would be fine if it were just a toe you were dipping," Rosen said nastily. "Speaking of bosses, what's yours up to?"

"Delusions of grandeur. Thinks she can work the Great Dane, herself. Won't let anybody near it. I offered —"

"She's working it alone?"

"Nitwit." Cézanne's heart stalled and the breath rushed out of her. She watched her eyes grow large, listening to Sid run her down. "She's got everybody in the unit pissed-off so bad they're about to mutiny, and while she's out running down old leads, the damned place could go up like the burning of Atlanta; she'd never know the difference."

"Really?" Rosen sounded lost in thought. In an instant, he came alive. "I like your grit, Klevenhagen, so I'll offer you a deal."

"I'm listening."

The hair on Cézanne's arms stood up like needles in a pin cushion.

"You keep me informed on everything Zannie does, and those audiotapes your last complainant played for IA might just get stored in the property room next to a big-assed magnet."

She waited through the long pause, wondering what Sid could be thinking as he mulled it over.

Three years 'til retirement.

He could lose his pension if they fired him for misconduct.

Would he give her up? Surely not. Sid was a man of integrity. Roby Tyson once told her Sid had brass balls, and platinum character.

Air came in shallow breaths.

"If she was to quit or get fired, who'd run Homicide?"

"Why, Sidney, I'm surprised you had to ask."

She closed her eyes and willed it not to be so. But with Rosen's words, the die was cast.

"You would."

Chapter Twenty

Greta Carr was clacking furiously on the computer keyboard, with every phone line blinking, when Cézanne returned from the ME's Office. A hard-looking man with work-roughened hands scraped the first "R" from Charles Crane's name, readying the glass for CÉZANNE R. MARTIN to be stenciled on the glass pane in fresh paint. Her stomach still sloshed with battery acid from Sid's conversation with Rosen, but it was Gentle Bison's reverse Mohawk, and the padded bandage sticking up on top of his head like first base, that made her temporarily forget the betrayal.

"What's with Wardancer?"

Greta stopped typing long enough to look over the rims of her half-glasses. Circles of rouge had tear tracks through them. "Benji needs to talk to you; he won't say why."

"And what's upset you?"

"Just sentimental, I reckon." She backhanded her nostrils in time to catch a drippy nose, then reached in a drawer and pulled out a tissue. "Today's my birthday and the only one who remembered was Captain."

She meant Crane.

"Happy Birthday," Cézanne said unenthusiastically. "Have Benji come into my office." She squeezed past the man at the door. "It's almost lunch. If you want to take yours now, I won't tell."

He didn't move very fast until Wardancer lumbered over and glowered. The guy took off.

Deep hollows as dark as tea bags settled under the big Indian's eyes. A thick gauze square taped to the top of his shaved head, curled up at the corners.

"What happened?"

Wardancer stared at his boots. "Trouble at home."

"Want to talk about it?"

"No." But in the next breath he said, "Being a woman, maybe you can tell me what the hell's wrong with my wife?"

Apparently, Scalped Bison's bride didn't believe he stayed out late running down leads on the Quinten Carrol shooting. When he dragged in around dawn, rheumy-eyed and smelling of rancid whiskey, she was waiting behind the front door with a pool cue.

"I need some days off, Captain. I love my job but I can't sacrifice my family for it." He wore the miserable expression of a man whose unraveling marriage was steeped in his round, puffy face.

254

"How long have you been married?"

"Eleven months."

"Benji, I need you. We've got cases."

"I'll work Sunday, Captain, I just need to be home right now. If I know my wife, she's got a moving van and six bruisers loading up furniture. Last time we had a fight, she dismantled the faucets and peeled off the bathroom wallpaper before she left." He hung his head, and picked at a callus on his thumb. "They say the rookie's out of ICU."

That wasn't the point. Under her direction, guys in Homicide were systematically defecting.

"Let me talk to your wife. I'll reason with her. You know as well as I do, if we don't catch these guys in forty-eight hours, we'll be relying on Crimestopper calls from here on out. Nobody wants that."

"The doctor said my equilibrium's screwed up because she cracked me so hard. Besides, Jock can cover for me. He said he'd trade days off, if that'll help."

"Featherston doesn't know beans about your cases. He doesn't give a damn about solving them."

"I can catch him up in two minutes. We didn't have shit yesterday; we don't have shit today."

She heaved a weary sigh. "Twenty-four hours. Suck it up and get it together. If you can't patch things up and you leave me short-handed, don't plan on returning to this unit. Ever."

Moping Bison left in a huff. But Featherston, who was developing into a regular Eddie Haskell, poked his head in.

"How's it going, Captain? Anything you need?"

"I'm heading out." She grabbed her purse off the floor and slung the strap over her shoulder. "Check with Benji. I want you to buff up on the Quinten Carrol shooting." She rifled through her handbag and pulled out a twenty. "Next time you go out, stop at the bakery and pick up a birthday cake for Greta. She likes chocolate. And a nice card if you have time. Say it's from all of us."

She never made it past the door. As soon as Featherston backed out, Constable Jinx Porter took his place. He entered without invitation, with pep in his step and his bald head shining. A silly grin angled up the side of his asymmetrical face, and the thick lenses on his wire-rims made his gray-green eyes look like nickels. The good news was, they matched the fine wool tweed of his sport coat.

She winced inwardly.

Taking time out for Jinx Porter ranked somewhere between cleaning out the trap in the bathroom drain and scraping up doggie-do after short walks with Butch the dog. But Porter had a weird hobby of amassing his own personal database of thugs and unsolved Texas cases, and she never knew when she might need a favor. And with Sid mentally sidelined, she probably should be nice. At least see what Porter wanted.

"Got a minute?" he asked.

"Why not?" She made no effort to offer him a seat.

"I thought we might go for a bite."

"I'm on my way out."

But Porter had an interesting way of capturing her attention and hanging onto it. That morning, around five-thirty, one of his deputies arrested a convicted felon on a blue warrant, the document used by the Parole Office to command a violator's arrest. In the typical "You ride the way you hide" policy that made Porter's office a legend among Tarrant County recidivists, deputies brought the offender Downtown wearing nothing but his 'Looms.

"What does that have to do with me?"

Porter beamed. "He's a dead ringer for the composite sketch your guys put out on the convenience store shooting."

Finally, a break.

Before the afternoon was over, Drew Ingleside, the oldest, most decrepit member of the unit happened to pick the wrong day to mention that, one hundred thirty-six days away from retirement, he had finally caught up on his cases. Instead of an attaboy, Featherston buttonholed him and dragged him, carping all the way to the elevator, to the county jail to interview one Manchester LeDemien Freedman.

Cézanne didn't wheel the Kompressor into the drive until a little after four. Although she entered the house to find Duty dusting furniture, she knew something was up by the brackish smell emanating from the kitchen. Lured to the stove, she glimpsed Devilrow's niece shadowing her from behind. Whatever bubbled in Duty's cauldron had a rolling boil the consistency of tree sap, and put out a bouquet just as noxious.

"What is it?"

"Just something to fix things."

"Fix things? Like what? Stripping furniture? Asphalting a parking lot? Tarring a roof? No-no, let me guess: this is one of your East Texas solutions to conflict, am I right?"

"Miz Zan, why you always so cranky? You axe me, you need to getchoo a man and do somethin' with him."

"I don't think I need to take marching orders from a teenager. Now dump this outside, it stinks. I don't even want to know where you got the stuff to make this . . . whatever it is."

"Candles. I been making candles. And my gramma, Corinthia, she say I might only be sixteen in calendar years, but I'm wise beyond time."

"Yes? Well you don't have enough experience to be dispensing advice to me about my social life."

"That's 'cause you ain't got one."

Something repulsive bubbled to the surface.

"Ohmygod. Is that fur floating on top?"

"Dog hair."

The way Duty said it, Cézanne knew she was lying.

"Pour it out." She headed for the bedroom with enough time to catch an hour's nap before departing for Reno's. "I'm hitting the rack so keep the noise down. And you're wrong — I don't need a man."

She slammed the door but Duty still managed to fire the last verbal shot, even if it was, "Mmm-mmm-mmm."

The empty Penelope's sack lay in a crumpled ball on the nightstand, a grotesque reminder she was a single woman without a mate. As for a rendezvous with the Big Bopper, she'd draw less attention firing up an outboard motor.

Screw it. One could never be too clean.

She stripped off her clothes, grabbed her robe, retreated to the bathroom, and bolted the door, convinced it was a woman who invented the shower massage.

Chapter Twenty-One

It took Cézanne less than thirty minutes to reach Reno's run-down single-wide, in a trailer park off the Jacksboro Highway. And when she rolled up at six on the dot, Reno was visible through the bathroom window, brushing out her long, red hair. As if protesting the sharp rap on the door, a shutter broke loose from its fittings and swung, cock-eyed, across the aluminum siding. It teetered precariously as the mobile home's underpinnings creaked from the footfalls. At the crack of the deadbolt, the rickety shutter pulled free and dropped with a splat, into the mud.

Reno opened the door in a clash of perfumes, wearing full make-up, cocooned in a bath towel. With a pout, she said, "You're not dressed."

Cézanne stepped inside. She removed her coat while Reno shut out the cold.

"I'm not about to drive over in my skivvies. The way my luck's been running I'd get pulled over by some motor jock who'd frisk me, inventory my car, and call in the bomb squad when he found this." She rattled the sack from Penelope's.

"Well, hurry up. The Scene starts at eight and we've got work to do." Reno looked her over with cold scrutiny.

"You act like I'm a condemned building."

"C'mon back. Let's find you a costume."

Cézanne started to ask Reno what she meant by The Scene, but the stripper was already heading down the hall toward the bedroom, leaving only a scented wake of vapors between them.

"The main thing you need to remember is that you're going as my slave. That should cut down on the amount of talking you have to do. Mainly, don't say anything unless I give you permission."

"What if somebody talks to me?"

"Unless you stray, I'll be right beside you."

An hour later, after Reno orchestrated her make-up and hair, Cézanne could hardly believe the transition to Gothic. Her cheeks had the gaunt look of a half-dead street whore, and her eyes, the hollows of a skeleton. With Reno's jet-color hairpiece falling straight down her shoulders, she hardly recognized her mirrored reflection. But against the shockingly pale skin, blackberry-stained lips, and heavily mascaraed lashes, her periwinkle blue eyes practically jumped out of her head.

"This could be a problem," Cézanne said.

"What if somebody recognizes me from all the pictures in last week's newspapers?"

"I'm way ahead of you." Reno opened a bathroom drawer and pulled out a boxful of disposable contact lenses in a rainbow of colors. She stirred the loose packets with her finger. "They're not prescription, so just pick out a color and pop them in. I even have some black ones with yellow stars in the middle, and red ones if you dig the vampira look. Or, you could do tiger eyes. These are orange with a diamond-shaped pupil. Utterly freaky, don't you think?"

"What'd you do, date an ophthalmologist?" Cézanne sifted through the box until she found a pair of brown lenses in individually sealed packets.

"Sweet pea, in my business, men have the most amazing needs. Some want fantasy women. I have Devil horns, vampire fangs, a latex space alien mask, you name it. I even have a ukulele and can sing 'Tiptoe Through the Tulips' in a raging falsetto. But I draw the line at pretending to be Tiny Tim. Although I have been Lucy Ricardo . . . man, was that weird. Dude showed up at my door dressed like Ethel Mertz.

"Once, I tied up with a date who wanted me to act like his mother. I spanked him, belittled him, two months straight. One day I got bored. When he showed up at my door, there I was, dressed like June Cleaver with a string of faux pearls and brownies baking in the oven. Only instead of carping and paddling his ass, I hugged him and told him what a good boy he was and how much I loved him. He almost had a nervous breakdown. Never saw him after that. Too bad, he paid great."

"That's disgusting. Don't tell me anymore."

"The world's made up of sick-os." Reno blotted her lips with a tissue, then stretched her mouth and smoothed her lip line with her pinkie. "You'll meet some tonight."

They made the half-hour trip across town in Reno's car, an old clunker that looked worse inside than out. Cézanne pulled at her black lace-topped thigh-highs, thrilled that Reno kept the over-the-thigh, black patent fetish boots for herself. Billowy red curls cascaded over the dancer's shoulders and came to rest inches from the car seat. As they drove past each corner, the glow from the streetlamps glanced off Reno's shiny black bustier, trussed up at the waist.

"You look like a street whore," Cézanne said, a pronouncement that delighted Reno, "and I look like a trashy, medieval wench." She adjusted the elastic waistband of the diaphanous chiffon dress, sheared into uneven peaks at the hem and sleeves. "Want to tell me where we're going?"

"To a house in Ridglea. I visited there once, a long time ago."

"You never did say how you finagled this invitation."

"Some things, you don't need to know. Where's your collar?"

"I refuse to wear that. It's degrading."

"I figured you'd pull some shit. Here, I got you this." Reno groped her coat pocket and produced a small box. It contained a thin gold necklace chain, with an odd-looking drop that appeared to be a variation on the yin-yang symbol, mutated into thirds.

"What is it?"

"A gift. It'll make people think you're one of us. Just wear it."

"What's it mean?"

"Call it an alternative lifestyle identifier. Kind of like the olden days when Christians were persecuted. They came up with a way to identify other Christians; that way, when they came across someone they didn't know, one would make a curve in the sand with his staff. If the other one connected it, it was okay to let them know of their faith. That's where the fish symbol came from. It was all hush-hush."

"How'd you know that?"

"Brother Phillip. That's what everybody

called him. My uncle was a preacher. Whenever my heroin-addicted mother went cattin' around, her brother would drop in with food and read us four kids Scriptures."

Reno was full of surprises.

"He must be very proud of you," Cézanne deadpanned.

"Yeah," she said, completely missing the point, "that was before CPS took us away and stuck us in foster homes. I blame him for being where I am today."

"You're making it your uncle's fault you're a hooker?"

With an edge to her voice and a furtive glance, Reno corrected her. "Exotic dancer."

"Stripper," Cézanne said with disapproval, but Reno cast a rueful smile that foretold the life she got, but never asked for.

"Little kids'll do a lot of things, long as they think God wants 'em to. And according to Brother Phillip, God wanted me to learn how to be fruitful and multiply."

In the silence that followed, the words sunk in. "Ohmygod. You're saying —"

"It probably wasn't in the cards for me to grow up and get college educated, like you, but I don't think I would've ended up where I am, either. Probably would've been a manager at a fast-food place, unhappily married, cranking out dirty-faced toddlers back to back."

"That's awful. I'm sorry, I really am."

"Don't sweat it. How could you know? We never talked like this before."

Words of comfort, once spoken, seemed superficial. And what Reno probably needed — a sisterly hug — wouldn't cut it. They weren't friends. And she wouldn't do anything to mislead her into thinking they were.

"How long ago did it happen?"

"I'm twenty-two." Reno seemed to cipher in her head. "I was seven when it started. It stopped after I turned seventeen — when I left home and lied about my age to get a job in the skin industry."

Cézanne did the math on her fingers. "You could file charges. The statute of limitation isn't up yet. You've still got five years. I say put him away."

"Spoken like a lawyer." Reno heaved a great sigh. "No, I could never do that to Brother Phillip."

"He deserves to be in prison. I could help you initiate a report."

With blue eyes thinning, Reno looked over and regarded her calmly. "No."

"Why not?"

"Because I liked it."

She made a big production out of picking her lifeless beeper up off the console and consulting the digital display. In the long silence, they drove until they reached Camp Bowie Boulevard, an old Westside

266

street paved with red bricks, which eventually petered out near the upscale residential neighborhood Cézanne recognized as Ridglea.

Across the seat, Reno evaluated her through shrewd eyes.

"I don't expect you to understand but it's the truth, plain and simple. I didn't dig it at first, but later . . . by the time I was in high school, football jocks paid me to go behind the gym. Or meet under the bleachers between quarters. After that, me and the other kids never had to do without. And once, this dude in the Lebanese mafia took me to my senior prom. In a limousine. I only stayed long enough to pop out of the moon-roof so the cheerleaders could see me — made 'em pea green." Reno curbed the car across from the golf course and killed the engine. "We're here."

The house sat atop a hill, obscured by a cinderblock wall eight feet high, which sprawled in the shape of a horseshoe over a half acre, and gave privacy for the Olympic-sized pool set in the center.

Reno extended an open palm. "Gimme your driver's license."

A rush of air left Cézanne's mouth. "They look at our licenses?"

"They check ID."

"A blind man could tell we're over eighteen."

"They still check. Sometimes they take down the info."

"Are you crazy? I can't show my license." Fear set into panic. "I have an unusual name. I spent last week splashed across the front pages, for God's sake. The shooting with Hollywood got a lot of ink, or don't you read the paper? Don't roll your eyes at me, Reno. I was on TV Monday, or maybe you don't keep up with the news?" The shrill echo hurt her ears. "Jesus, I can't show my license."

"You don't have a fake one?"

"Why would I? And who do you think you are, Monty Hall? Next, you'll offer to give me a hundred if I can produce a boiled egg or pull a rubber snake out of my bag."

"Didn't you ever work Vice?"

"No." Exasperated whine.

Reno fired up the ignition and dropped the bucket of bolts-and-bailing wire into gear.

"Where're we going?"

"Ali Baba's. Hollywood's stuff's still there. You can use hers."

Cézanne went limp against the seat, ignoring the exposed spring goring her shoulder blade. "Well that's ingenious. I don't look a thing like Hollywood. She wasn't nearly as tall as me and she bleached her hair white."

"Quit bitching. Everybody plays dress-up

268

at scene parties. With all that yak-doo on your face, who'd know? Besides, Michelle Parker's a common name. If anybody says anything, play dumb. Act like you don't read the newspaper. For me," Reno said, suddenly tickled, "it's true."

They were a short dash from Ali Baba's when the dancer first came up with the idea to use Hollywood's ID, but it took fifteen minutes with Cézanne waiting inside the car before Reno returned with her bustier lopsided and her hair in a tangled mess.

"Did you get it? Let me see."

Without comment, Reno flicked Hollywood's license across the seat, and slid behind the wheel. Breaths came in short pants. She stared through the windshield, seemingly at nothing. Beneath the glow of the street lamp, her clutched fingers blued with her grip on the steering wheel. The Dominatrix from hell looked more like Reneé, the scared seven-year-old who put her faith in Uncle Phillip.

"Reno, what's wrong?"

"It's true. There's no such thing as a free ride."

"What happened?"

"Been ducking that creep since he took over the business."

"You didn't."

"Let's drop it."

"Reno, I never meant —"

"I did it for you, okay?" She floored the accelerator, bounced over the curb, out of the parking lot, and into traffic.

"Oh, no you don't. I'm not wearing your shame. It doesn't fit; it's not mine; I'm not putting it on and you can't make me. You're not blaming me."

"I don't dig men, sweet pea. What I did before, I did before I knew I should be with women." Reno fished a cigarette out of the box, pushed in the lighter, and waited for it to pop out with the coils red. "I'm not trying to pawn off guilt. But friends help each other. I helped you because I want to be your friend."

"I thought we covered the friendship issue at Penelope's."

"I'm not using the word like it's a euphe . . . euphem . . ."

"Euphemism."

"Yeah, that. You think I want you for my girlfriend, but I can scare up plenty of bed buddies. What I need's a real friend."

The last thing Cézanne wanted to do was scuttle the party. So, she didn't tell Reno being friends would never happen, not in a lifetime. Instead, she said, "Maybe that's something we can work on. I don't have many myself," and turned away.

The possibility of becoming pals seemed to revive Reno's mood. When they pulled up in front of the big house for the second time and she said, "How do I look?" Cézanne answered, "Pretty, in a decadent sort of way."

The car door creaked when Reno opened it. She slung out a leg and got out, stretched, straightened her clothes, and took in a deep breath. Crisp, clean air smelled like cold rain in search of a roaring campfire, and for a brief moment, Cézanne closed her eyes and thought of Bobby. A delicious image that Reno blasted out of her head with a volley of words.

"I probably don't need to tell you, but you can't take your gun in."

"How would they know?"

"Just don't do it. If they make us check our coats, you never know who could rifle through your pockets."

"Oh, good, because for a minute I thought you were thinking there might actually be a place I could conceal a weapon inside this see-through scarf you're trying to pawn off as a dress."

But there it was, duct-taped to her skin, digging into the small of her back, a North American Arms five-shot .22, loaded with copper-jacketed stingers. It was tiny but wicked, about the size of a pager after she modified it with collapsible grips, with the stainless steel body folded up inside; so small she could almost close her hand entirely around it. But uncoiled and fully extended, it manifested itself as a dangerous weapon with a comfortable feel and a venomous bite if properly aimed and cocked. Not that Reno needed to know. She'd have plenty of opportunity to explain, later, if she had to resort to its use.

At the massive wooden doors, a bearded man wrapped in an indigo cape that flowed down his back and grazed the floor, responded to the chime. Strains of druidic music from the distant underbelly of the house bubbled up through the hardwoods and vibrated the soles of her suede flats.

The mood was set.

With the right touch of gloom, the man extended an upward palm. "Good evening, ladies. IDs?"

Cézanne studied his wizened face, trying to memorize the arch of his brow and the way his bottom teeth seemed to disappear when he spoke.

Reno collected Hollywood's DL and handed over the licenses. Cézanne held her breath. Looked away. Checked the cross timbers bracing the vaulted ceiling. Studied the oak plank floors. Counted the wall of glass blocks next to the lanai leading out to the pool. Anything to avoid a head-on confrontation. After scrutinizing their names and birthdates, the man invited them inside.

As if Cézanne didn't exist, he addressed

Reno. "Is this her first time?"

"First time here."

"Then pick up a copy of the house rules, and go over them before you take her to the Dungeon." He gestured to a table set with an expensive arrangement of tropical flowers and linen cloth. "Sign the consent forms and bring them back to me with your entrance fee. Twenty-five, each. Anyone choosing to leave will not be allowed to return. No exceptions."

Out of earshot, Cézanne whispered, "How come he didn't ask me?"

"He knows you're my slave. You're not permitted to speak unless I say so."

Cézanne read the boiler-plate language in the consent form. "This wouldn't hold water in a court of law. What's this? 'I agree and hold harmless . . . for serious bodily injury and or death?' These people are crazy."

"Just sign the damned paper and let's get on with it. This whole thing was your idea."

"That was before I found out I had to give them permission to kill me."

"Nobody's gonna kill you."

"You've got that right," she snipped, feeling surprisingly lethal. "I'm signed in as Alana, Hollywood's middle name."

"Won't do any good. As soon as we walked away, he wrote down the information on our licenses."

After exchanging consent forms and a fifty for their DLs and two printed tickets with intertwining D's, the man asked, "Will you be needing any special effects?"

Reno jiggled a small tote and shook her head. "Just point us to the Dungeon."

"End of the hall, stairs to the right."

They passed a large industrial kitchen with long granite countertops, and industrial freezers that looked like they'd been purchased from the movie set of *The Shining*. Cézanne's police training kicked in.

"The homeowner's a caterer. Has to be."

"Naw, they just put in big slabs to perform human sacrifices."

Cézanne stopped breathing.

"I'm kidding. What's the matter with you? Are you gonna be in a crummy mood all night?"

"No. I'm sure I'll feel better once the first blow is delivered."

Near the stainless steel sink, a petite bleached blonde in a French maid's uniform filled a silver tray with hors d'oeuvres. Another tray sat off to one side, with cans of cold juice beaded in sweat.

"She's somebody's slave," Reno whispered knowingly. "That's what they do at these parties, make slaves serve the guests."

Such news was enough to get deliriously excited over. "That sounds safe. Why don't you volunteer me? I could do that."

"You'd think so — until some asshole uses you for an ashtray."

"Better than having your rump roast tenderized."

"Not if he puts a cigar out in your hand. Or makes you his urinal. Besides, spankings give you a rush."

"Speak for yourself. Do you people ever do role-reversals?"

"Lots. Why?"

"Because I think you should know in advance that if you try to inflict pain on me, I'll pistol whip you until you're a radish."

"Assuming you survive," Reno said cheerily.

At the end of a dim, mood-lit corridor, they came to the stairs. At the bottom step, an armor-clad knight stood near the door, taking tickets. While making her descent, Reno issued a critical reminder.

"If we get separated for any reason, the less said, the better. Remember to address me as 'Mistress' when I speak to you. And don't forget to say, 'Yes, ma'am' and 'No, sir.' Try not to look anyone directly in the eye. You are, after all, a submissive." She winked at Lancelot. "Hi-ya, big guy. What're you supposed to be tonight? An armadillo?"

A woman in a white wig, piled high and

styled into ringlets, holding a peacock-feathered Mardi Gras mask at eye-level, glided their way. Pink tulle petticoats peeked out under the hem of her elaborate silk ball gown, and rustled with each dainty step.

"*Bienvenue. Je m'appelle Marie Antoinette.* I'm your hostess."

"I'm Mistress Xorra and this is my loyal slave . . . Atlantis. Please excuse her manners. Sometimes I think she fails to curtsy in order to force me into administering discipline. She loves it so."

What Reno administered was a swift knee to the back of Cézanne's leg, buckling it instantly. Marie Antoinette was not amused.

"Yes, well, you may wish to introduce your naughty servant to the stocks. Most of the good paddles are taken, but there are still a few left behind the bar. And we rent riding crops and cat-o'-nine-tails for the evening if you don't have your own. All proceeds go to charity."

Sure enough, a tall man of slight build, wearing leather underwear, biker chains laced to leather straps crisscrossed over his chest, and studded cuffs and a collar, tended a fetish booth converted from Marie Antoinette's wet bar. A handful of spectators gathered around the stocks, where a man teased red welts on his com-

276

panion's buttocks with the fringed end of a satin rope.

Between clenched teeth, Cézanne mumbled, "I'm standing at the intersection of Sodom and Gomorrah."

Sometime between entering the room and gawking at the spectacles, her heart fell in tempo with the slow, drumming bass. She came to an unsettling realization. Although her mind had been unwillingly drawn into this den of iniquity, her body was responding on its own.

"I think I'm having cardiac arrhythmia. Have these people gone insane?"

But Reno didn't answer. She had wandered away, to a far corner of the room where a waif with a bob-cut the color of a Palomino's mane was lashed to a Saint Andrew's cross — a couple of two-by-fours, bolted together in the center to form an X, and mounted, upright, on a stand, to the floor. It was clear they knew each other by the way their tongues moved enthusiastically in each other's mouths.

Revolting.

Cézanne shook off the disturbing image and scanned the area.

A visual head count stood somewhere between thirty-five and fifty, and she roamed the room, taking care to move on before anyone had the chance to strike up a conversation. She waited for Reno near a homemade cage constructed with wooden dowels. Inside, a naked brunette crouched, blindfolded, in one corner. Another dark haired girl wearing a thong, and rubbing the sting from the handcuff marks on her wrists, soon joined her.

Jesus. Never gonna pull this off.

When Cézanne glanced around again, Reno was gone.

Ohmygod. What if they see through me?

She moved quietly, branding each depraved image into her memory. A tight group of spectators she tried to blend in with, dispersed. She knew she stayed too long, watching a slave do time in the pain box, when a gentle weight came down on her shoulder. With a darting glance, she glimpsed blood-red fingernails.

A seductive whisper came from behind. "I don't believe I've seen you before."

Cézanne turned to look.

A harem girl a few inches shorter than herself stood nude from the waist up, with voile pantaloons gathered at the ankles and gold bracelets running the length of her forearms. A veil stretched across her face, secured to a silk turban. Pale blue eyes, rimmed in coppery lashes, smudged with dark pencil, seemed to disappear into the whites. Richly outlined lips pouted behind the sheer fabric.

Oh, shit. I'll never fake out these whack-os.

It dawned on her to curtsy.

The lady had a whiskey voice. "I like your outfit. I love black, don't you? It's incredibly sexy."

"Yes, ma'am." Soft-spoken and subservient. She remembered to drop her gaze, but the effect lasted only a moment. Traveling back up the see-through harem pants, her eyes stalled at a huge emerald, plugging the woman's navel.

"Are you alone?" Scheherazade took her hand and caressed it.

Light from the wall sconces ignited fiery gemstones set in the rings on her fingers. The diamonds appeared to be genuine.

Should've worn the damned dog collar.

"My Mistress stepped away." She averted her eyes to avoid the intensity of the woman's stare.

"You appeal to my Master. And I do what pleases him. I know it's bad form to ask for favors without your Mistress present, but we often visit the Dungeon in search of new . . . talent."

Cézanne's face tightened in confusion.

"Don't look so surprised. You have certain — how shall we say? — qualities we're looking for. We're not interested in your Mistress, you understand. Only you. If you accept the invitation, you would come alone, of course."

Bad idea.

She didn't know how to react, and what she said, came out clumsy. "I don't think I'm what you're looking for. I don't take orders well. My Mistress stays angry at me . . ."

"It would change your life. You would give me the opportunity to please my Master, and naturally, I would find a way to repay you."

"Repay me? I don't understand."

A piercing scream penetrated the wall and stopped conversation. The pleadings of a talking cat being strangled filtered in from the next room, then abruptly fell silent. Another male voice, stern and deliberate, vibrated in Cézanne's ears. She didn't know whether to pull her gun or lay low.

The blonde took her hand. "Don't be afraid."

Cézanne's voice dissolved to a whisper. "What's happening?"

"It's a play piercing."

Wails grew louder. A man's desperate begging made her stomach clench. But when his pain turned to the mewlings of a kitten, her skin crawled.

"Play piercing?" Hair follicles stood on end. She drew strength from the .22, taped to the small of her back.

The blonde said, "Fish hooks."

Cézanne wanted to shriek. "He wants to be pierced?"

"In this case, it's punishment. We have this game called Dr. Mengele. Usually, we save it for disobedient subjects, or participants with high thresholds of pain. But on occasion, outsiders try to infiltrate the Dungeon of Decadence — you know —" she flip-flopped her hand in a casual manner "— reporters, fraternity pranks, nosey parkers, Feds . . . which we simply cannot allow. The Dr. Mengele game discourages them from returning. Especially the stun gun." She thumbed at what appeared to be a door to a closet. "Would you like to watch as the weights and pulleys are attached to the sub's little soldier? He already got his little duffle bags zapped. Once you observe a couple of these, you can tell the level of punishment they've reached by the pitch of the scream."

For a brief moment, the room went out of focus. The startle reflex in Cézanne's brain kicked in and pulled everything back into place. She clung to the blonde's hand and tried to keep from hyperventilating. The buzz of conversation heated back up, but did nothing to dull the agonizing, tortured-cat screams.

She tried to convince herself that screaming was good. That as long as he was screaming, he was alive. Her voice trembled. "What'd he do that was so bad?"

"He didn't like me." Behind the veil,

fleshy lips curled into a smile. Where the harem girl's eyes crinkled at the outer corners, fine spider-web lines appeared.

"Didn't like you? That's all it took?"

Mama told me not to come. No shit, Three Dog Night.

"That's it. As I was saying, relationships lose their magic if not properly kindled. Master finds you attractive, so, you're invited."

"Where?"

"To a private party. Tomorrow night."

Behind the wall, a spectral shriek rocked Cézanne's senses. Then only the rush of warm air could be heard through the vents.

Ohmygod. They killed him. I'm at a crime scene.

She glanced across the room to the Saint Andrew's cross, where she last saw Reno and her playmate. With her pulse thudding in her throat, the desire to inflict serious bodily injury on Reno took a distant second to saving her own skin.

Her new acquaintance pulled her, two-handed, into the corner. "Do you like me?"

Hell no.

"Yes, Mistress." Her head spooled through her reasons for being there. "If I'm not too bold, may I see your face?"

The harem girl loosened the veil. It skimmed her nose and floated off to one side. Thin wisps of strawberry blonde hair

282

stuck out from under Turkish silk. Cézanne's veins iced over.

Cissy Kissel.

The face matched the updated driver's license photo Sid picked up from the issuing office of the Texas Department of Public Safety.

"What kind of look is that?"

Cézanne's heart fluttered. She knew, at once, her expression betrayed her. "I . . . you're . . . so pretty."

Faster than the flick of a snake's tongue, Cissy Kissel raised on tiptoes and planted a soft, wet kiss on her mouth. Fighting the urge to see her lunch in reverse, Cézanne felt the lightheaded rush of someone about to black out.

The Great Dane's widow said, "Will you come? Nothing would please my Master more."

She pressed an unobtrusive business card into Cézanne's hand. It was trimmed into the shape of a flower, its texture made richer by petals embossed into the pastel paper.

Cézanne dropped her gaze.

The Wild Orchid Society.

And a phone number.

I'm in.

Her heart thundered in her chest. "Who's your Master?"

A deep, resonant voice came from behind. "I am."

Cézanne's pulse skidded. No introduction necessary for the muscular man without a shirt, and a chest so smooth it looked like it had been waxed, bare, with some ancient, Egyptian formula. She flinched at the sight of a stun-gun, then forced herself to stare past the black hood, directly into obsidian eyes, hypnotic and steady behind the slitted holes.

The Executioner.

Chapter Twenty-Two

Blood was still wooshing between Cézanne's ears when she located Reno in the kitchen, nibbling on a wedge of salami and a hunk of cheddar pinched between her fingers.

Cézanne snatched the can of apricot juice away and tossed it into the trash. "Let's get the hell outta here."

"I hope you're not mad, but Krystal and I go back a long way." Reno pointed across the room where the reed-thin girl with the wheat-colored bob was retrieving a cloth handbag from the guardian of the bar. "Look, I hate to ditch you, but you're straight and chicks like Krystal don't come along every day, and the truth is —"

Reno's sing-song, childlike voice was starting to annoy her.

"Give me a ride back to my car and we're even. All I want's a long shower, a loofa sponge, and a bottle of mouthwash — preferably one that forms a mushroom cloud." Outside, she whipped out the card. "Look."

"So?" Unimpressed. "The chick in the pain box got one, too." Reno giggled. "Get a look at your face. You act like I just slapped you."

"I thought I was unique."

"You are unique, sweet pea. Everyone is. But The Wild Orchid Society's like a fraternity, and not everybody wants to join. I hear they make you do things."

"What things?"

Reno turned evasive. "The problem with rich people is they get bored easy. They have to keep inventing new ways to get their jollies."

"They couldn't be any flakier than our hostess. 'All proceeds go to charity?' Whose charity?"

"Charity Rabinowitz. The chick bent over the portable spanking table in the corner. You remember — the one with the glass eye? Got hit in the face with a whip last month and lost her sight."

"You're screwing with me."

Reno's mouth gaped in mock astonishment. "You cracked my code." Through a sly smile, she said, "You're so cute when you're pissed."

The girl Reno referred to as Krystal waved good-bye to the bartender and joined them on the sidewalk.

She pulled out a card and flashed it at Reno. "Check it out."

The Wild Orchid Society.

Reno clapped a hand to her mouth and squelched a gasp. "You can't go."

"But he invited me."

286

"Promise me, baby. Please." Her eyes welled; she gripped her playmate's shoulders and shook hard enough to rattle her teeth. "Think what you're doing, Krys. It's The Executioner."

While Reno put some real estate between them and the house at Ridglea, Cézanne grew brass bon bons. Several blocks from The Scene, with Krystal following in her muscle car, she glanced over her shoulder. A vehicle had fallen in a few lengths behind the Camaro, but the headlights didn't come on until they pulled onto the red bricks of Camp Bowie Boulevard.

"We picked up a tail." Did she care? Hell yes.

"Want me to lose 'em?"

Thoughts of a caravan racing through town, busting red lights and causing pedestrians to dive for the curb, held about as much appeal as being pulled from the mangled wreckage dressed like Lily Munster. The last thing she needed to read was a headline in sixty-point type:

Acting Homicide Captain in Sado-Masochistic Lesbian Love Triangle.

And in smaller print, *Martin Flees Crime Scene Before Body Gets Cold.*

"Of course I want you to lose him."

"He who?"

"That reporter from Channel Eighteen. Garlon Harrier."

Reno drew in a sharp breath. "You know somebody on TV?" Clearly, the idea held some allure. "I can see the tabloids." She made a panoramic sweep across the wind-shield with her hand and announced her fantasy. "Exotic Dancer Propelled to Stardom in Chase With Newsman."

"Step on it. He's making my life a living hell."

"This is exciting."

"You only say that because he's not after you."

Gonna lose my job. Maybe my life. What was I thinking?

Harrier had to know where she lived. It wouldn't have been hard for him to find out, considering she subscribed to the newspaper. Newsmen had pals on the paper with the power to wheedle her ad-dress out of the circulation department. Treacherous bastards.

Then she got mad. "How come you were excited when I got The Wild Orchid Society card, but when you found out Krystal got one, you went into a panic?"

"You're a cop. You can handle it. Krystal's just plain stupid. I don't want her hurt."

"What about me?"

"Occupational hazard. You assumed the risk."

A mile or so from Reno's trailer, with Krystal riding their bumper, the tail car's headlights seemed to be closing in.

Cézanne hatched an idea. "Is there a back way out?"

"Yeah, but it's confusing. If you're drunk or you drive too fast, you'll go airborne, straight into Lake Worth."

"Where does the road go?"

"That Mom and Pop store we passed a half-mile back? It comes out there."

"And the entry to your drive — could two cars block it?"

Reno caught on. "You bet. I'll motion Krystal to pull up beside us. You jump out and hoof it. How much of a head-start should we spot you?"

Cézanne developed a conscience. "If somebody missed the hairpin turn, how far down is the dropoff?"

"Five, six feet. Not enough to kill anybody, if that's what you're getting at; the water's up to its banks. It's muddy, and there's lots of silt. If they went over, it'd take a tractor to pull 'em out."

"Give me thirty seconds. I want that prick to follow me. If he bottoms out, maybe he'll quit stalking me."

A few feet shy of the turnoff, Reno engaged her flashers and braked to a crawl. She rolled down the glass and stuck out an arm, waving the Camaro up beside her.

Krystal let the passenger window down.

Reno hollered, "Some shithead's following her. We gotta block the entrance."

Tires crunched to a halt.

Cézanne bailed out.

Hunkered over in a crouch, she dashed to the car and fired up the engine. Without benefit of headlights, she spun out onto the gravel road, churning up dust. Nearing the bend, she signaled Reno with a tap of the brakes. Beyond the turn, she increased her speed. At the paved, county road, she flicked on her high-beams and floored it.

In her rearview mirror, receding headlights pulled in single file. Seconds later, the light stream from the beacons of the tail car bounced over a hump in the terrain. They bore down with a vengeance. The next time Cézanne consulted her rearview mirror, she saw only darkness.

With the porch light off and Ruby's only working headlight panning the driveway, two sneering gargoyles welded atop the posts of the wrought iron gate Leviticus Devilrow fashioned three weeks before, projected an ominous aura. Cézanne avoided looking directly at the winged menaces, unable to shirk the sense that although affixed to their perch, they could still track her moves through beady stares.

Since the only lamp burning inside the

house was an ancient hurricane fixture on an end table near the front door, Cézanne assumed Deuteronomy was asleep. She tiptoed in and found Devilrow's niece in the study.

Backlit by the glare from the computer monitor, Duty hunkered over the keyboard, her skinny fingers pecking furiously.

"You'd, by God, better not be ordering anything."

Duty came up three inches off the cushion. "Miz Zan, you not s'posed to be home for a hour. And why you dressed like a witch? You been at a costume ball?"

Cézanne moved in for a closer view of the screen. "What the hell's this?"

"Chat room."

"Who're you talking to?"

"Willie."

"Who's Willie?"

"He work out at the meat plant."

"I thought you didn't know anybody here but Leviticus Devilrow."

"Hadn't met, yet. But Willie say he have a Corvette, he'll come pick me up, maybe take me somewhere nize."

Cézanne dropped her purse on the floor. With a bump of the hip, she muscled Duty out of the chair.

They call me Willie B. Dragon 'cause it's so big I have to drag it around.

A sharp intake of air, and Cézanne said,

"That's disgusting. Who's Black Beauty? Is that you?"

Duty stood, mute. A new message popped up from the man with the big ego.

I can have you back home in an hour.

Cézanne torqued her jaw. Her fingers swarmed over the keyboard until it clacked like an old man's dentures.

Bad idea. My mother walked in with a loaded gun and an extra clip. She says if you come near me, she'll stretch your surgically re-moved penis over a railroad tie and stomp it with cleats until it looks like a luminaria.

Duty read over her shoulder. "What's a luminaria?"

"A lantern with holes in it." She entered the message and awaited the response.

"Anybody ever tell you, you have a cruel streak?"

"A thread, not a streak. I'll admit a tiny thread of cruelty might run through me. A teensy, microscopic thread made by a silk-worm."

"Ain't no thread, mm-mmm. More like a cable. Maybe even a telephone pole."

"While we're exploring personality traits, anybody ever teach you the definition of 'gullible?' "

Willie B. Dragon has left the room, popped on-screen in bright red letters.

"But Willie have a nize car."

"No. Willie says he has a nice car. What

Willie probably has is a station wagon with fake wood peeling off the door panels, an expired inspection sticker, defective exhaust, bald tires, and a rape kit under the seat. What's the matter with you? Didn't your mother teach you not to talk to strangers?"

"My mama never home. What's a rape kit?"

"Duct tape and a butcher knife. Now listen to me and listen good. Until that shiftless Devilrow comes back, I'm the closest thing you have to a mother," Cézanne said harshly, "and I'd never let my child get in a chat room with a pedophile. Do you understand?"

"What's a pedophile?"

"A pervert."

"What's a pervert?"

"A deviant."

"Oh." Duty's eyes rolled upward, where they seemed to be consulting the invisible dictionary on the ceiling. "Is that like when somebody take a different direction?"

"Close enough."

"Miz Zan, why you dressed up like Elvira?" Abruptly, Duty cocked her head and listened. "And how come yo' purse is hummin'?"

Chapter Twenty-Three

The gloomy, gray skies of Saturday's dawn should have been conducive to deep sleep, but Cézanne awoke with big plans in mind. While she showered, the timer to the coffee maker went off and brewed a pot of European blend.

After dressing in jeans and a UT Longhorn sweatshirt, she filled a mug and dropped in an ice cube. Duty still hadn't stirred by the time she drank the pot down to the grounds, so she grabbed her navy pea coat and drove to the Auto-Erotica body shop to get an estimate on the Kompressor's repairs. In the mechanic's bay, a fiftyish man in a green flannel shirt and corduroy slacks who appeared to be in charge, gave her the eye-popping numbers.

"It's a car, for God's sake. I just want it fixed, I didn't plan on taking out a mortgage."

"It's a Mercedes, not a Kia. Factor that into the equation," he said with a nasty gleam.

"I'm not paying that kind of money. She's got a little scratch and a dent. That's it."

"She?"

"Ruby."

"You named your car?"

"Don't mess with me, my head's a pressure cooker."

"We can schedule you a week from Tuesday."

"A week from Tuesday? How hard can it be to fix a nick and a dimple?"

"Not hard. Expensive. And that isn't a nick. It's the Panama Canal of dents." He tilted his face to the ceiling and spoke to the exposed rafters. "I'm only bumping you up because you seem unstable."

"There're lots of body shops in this town."

"Then you shouldn't have any trouble finding one."

He had her there.

"Since I'm already here, will you at least put in a new headlight?"

"Sure . . . cost you a thousand dollars."

She sat in the waiting area, leafing through an outdated *Cosmopolitan*, until the shop foreman waved her back into the bay.

"It's ready."

She stared at the invoice. "This is a week's lunch money."

"You may want to diet."

She pressed the pen down so hard writing the check, it left an imprint on the next one in sequence. When she ripped it from the pad, it sounded like a seam splitting.

"Go ahead and schedule Ruby's appointment a week from Tuesday."

"Sure thing. It'll be ready the following Friday."

"Friday?"

"Yes, Friday. Three days after you bring it in."

"I'll need a courtesy car."

"No loaner."

"But when I bought Ruby the salesman promised —"

"Those guys'll say anything." The foreman was still guffawing when one of the mechanics sauntered up, grim-faced.

"Mrs. Kissel's here for the Benz."

"Tell her it's not ready."

But the mechanic had other ideas. "You make more than I do. *You* tell her."

Cézanne alerted like a drug dog. "Cissy Kissel gets her car serviced here?"

The foreman let out a huff. "Don't tell me you're friends? My cholesterol's too high, my arteries have so much buildup it'll take a pickaxe to chip the plaque off, and the last thing I need is another pain in the ass coming in, throwing her weight around, trying to run roughshod over me and my crew."

"I take it you don't care for Mrs. Kissel?"

"An understatement. Everybody knows she corked her husband."

"Everybody?"

"Social butterflies. Even her close friends think she did him. I've worked here fifteen years and I don't think I ever heard anybody venture a guess someone else did it." A young girl around twenty shuffled into the bay with the heels of her Justin Ropers scuffing the concrete. She handed him some paperwork. "The cops can't — or won't — put her behind bars. Those sons-of-bitches all stick together."

"Men," said the girl with disdain. "You're gossiping about Mrs. Kissel again, aren't you?"

"None other." He readied his pen to sign the triplicate forms.

To Cézanne, she said, "Her daddy's just the nicest old fella. Mr. Price never, ever raises his voice. Never gets mad. Just says, 'Fix it, li'l darlin', and call me when it's done.' But Mrs. Kissel always comes in here mad enough to swallow a horned toad backward. If that car's got so much as a fingerprint on it, she yells up a storm. One time, she brought her Benz back because she found a grease spot on the —"

"Here ya go. Get back to work."

The girl scuffed off with the foreman's eyes glued to her swing. "Reopening that case got everybody in an uproar. Anyone who walks in here's an authority. Frankly, my hat's off to that gal the PD's got working Mr. Kissel's case, but I still don't think it'll pan out. Money talks."

"You don't have much confidence in the PD."

"I don't have much faith in people, period. For one thing, I've been around rich people nigh-on fifteen years. And if there's one thing I know about millionaires, they tend to close ranks, even if most of them don't have much use for her since she did her husband in."

"You said, 'Those sons-of-bitches stick together.' Who sticks together?"

"Cops."

"Why would the police try to bury an unsolved murder when it's their job to solve it?"

"Lady, don't you know anything? It's common knowledge around here, back when her husband died, she was having a steamy affair with —"

"Gotta go. Sorry we got off on the wrong foot. I'm not a friend of Mrs. Kissel, and I'll deliver Ruby a week from Tuesday."

Cissy Kissel was stomping through the showroom with her strawberry blonde hair flying. The contours of her face hardened, and she stabbed a finger at the Series 500, platinum Mercedes parked on the lot. Nothing about her resembled the harem girl from the previous night.

"And you're wrong about the police. They have top-notch officers." With goosebumps peaking beneath her sleeves, Cézanne beat a hasty retreat. "They're doing all they can to put the right person behind bars. And next time you start a pool, you can put money on the lady running the show."

A few car lengths from Charles Crane's two-and-a-half-story Victorian on Grand Avenue, Cézanne pulled over to the curb and took in the view. Icicles overhung the slate roof like jagged teeth. Through frost-coated windows, backlit in the glow of hurricane lamps, the former captain of Homicide read the morning paper with his bald spot to the cold outdoors.

She wheeled Ruby onto the old brick pavers, behind a dark blue, late model Cadillac and cut the engine. On the walk to the stained glass door, she rehearsed her words, not totally convinced it was the cold making her shudder. She pressed the buzzer and Crane's house came alive with the sound of footsteps straining the hardwoods.

The throw-bolt to the front door cracked like the report of a rifle. Through the open sliver, one steely eye peered out.

"Morning, Captain. Mind if I come in?"

Color drained from his face. "Sue-zanne." Whiskey breath, strong enough to draw blood blisters on a rawhide boot, soured their shared space.

"Who is it, Chuck?" Crane's wife, Agnetha, the epitome of refinement. "Shall I dress?"

Crane yelled not to bother. He opened the door in pajamas and robe, unkempt and unshaven, with a week's growth of whiskers sprouting across his face.

"May as well come in before we all freeze." He pointed fiercely to a sofa next to the fireplace.

The scent of mesquite filled the room. As she shed her pea coat and dropped it over the brocade arm of the settee, the faint odor of flowers caught her attention. Agnetha Crane, radiant in peach silk pajamas and matching kimono, stood in the hallway. Though only a week had passed since their last contact, no amount of make-up could hide the dark circles beneath the grieving woman's eyes, nor their sadness. But the hair — long, thick hair the color of fine champagne — was done up in an elegant poof, with every strand lacquered in place. As if she had received an invitation to the Trail Drivers Ball, and had only to dress before the limousine pulled up in front of the house.

"Oh, it's you," Crane's wife said in a voice weary with resignation. "I remember you take cream. I'll get coffee."

"Don't make any on my account."

"Nonsense. It's my job."

300

"I apologize for barging in so early."

"Chuck's been up half the night," she called over her shoulder. "He's so excited. Got his first deer of the season."

"Hit my first deer, you mean. Damned doe jumped out in front of me, coming back from the deer lease. Scared the dickens out of me, springing up out of the ditch." He returned to his easy chair and to the newspaper folded open to the obituaries. "What brings you out into the elements?"

"I'm here about the Great Dane."

The pulse throbbed in his throat. "You solved it?"

"Fat chance."

"You should have everything you need in the file."

"Teddy Vaughn dug up a whole lot of dirt on Worth Price's finances that nobody ever delved into, and Sid . . . God only knows what Klevenhagen's doing. But we're each working an angle. I'm here because you're the best," she said, and meant it. "But you couldn't solve it."

His arms rested on the chair with hands hanging limp over lace doilies, safety-pinned in place. Leather house slippers were buffed to a high gloss. He stared, without expression, through dead eyes. When she gazed at the walls, she noticed that photos of Carri Crane, so proudly displayed the week before, had disappeared.

Even the oil on canvas of Carri as a child had been replaced with a daguerreotype of a Civil War hero, and she knew without asking that the picture of Crane's ancestor had been brought from the attic, where his daughter's now collected dust in its place.

It was the only way he knew how to cope.

Mrs. Crane glided in with a tray, rattling with dainty bone china. "I don't have any cream."

"It's okay. I didn't mean to put you out."

"Nonsense. Chuck, do you want a refill?"

Only Crane wasn't answering. His watery eyes were fixed on some distant point beyond the archway leading into the dining room, to the black wallpaper with enormous pink flowers and exaggerated green leaves.

"Chuck?" Louder. "More coffee?"

"No." The big man's skin looked like old parchment, thin and translucent, and sallow in color; as if at any moment, a change in expression would make for an instant rip in his fragile shell. "I don't know why we couldn't solve it. We should've solved it. Then Joey Wehmeyer died and took what he knew to his grave."

Without invitation, she reached for the sugar bowl. "Wait a minute. I thought Jock Featherston was your partner."

"After Joey hung himself."

"What went wrong?"

"What always goes wrong — lack of co-operation, new cases piling on, witnesses clam up — a botched crime scene."

Cézanne tensed. "Somebody botched the crime scene?"

"No. There just wasn't much to work with."

Surely he didn't believe that. The captain was the first to berate a detective with Crane-isms: a suspect always brings evidence to a crime; and he always takes evidence away with him.

"Who do you think did it?"

"I have no idea."

But Agnetha Crane did, and she said so. "That's not true, Chuck. We always thought —"

He silenced her with a glare.

"I'm afraid I must dress now," she said with an air, and floated out of the room with her shoulders squared, and her silk pull-ons skimming the floor.

"I think Cissy Kissel killed her husband and I aim to prove it," Cézanne said.

"The only way you'll do that is by finding something in that house. First, you have to get inside."

"I intend to."

Crane uncrossed his legs. Scooted to the edge of his seat. Propped his forearms on his knees, clasped his hands together and settled his chin into the grooves of his fingers. Clearly, she had his attention. Even better, he seemed to view her as an equal.

"What do you think you'll find after eight years?"

"I don't know." Then she ventured the truth. "A bloody wall."

"They checked the walls."

Undaunted, she said, "I know, Captain. But y'all assumed Dane Kissel was murdered in his bedroom. What if he was murdered in another location? That would account for the odd bloodstain pattern."

He stared into the dining room, glassy-eyed. "You'll never get a search warrant for that house."

"I won't need one. I'll get in with the owner's consent."

"The only room that was totally theirs was the bedroom."

"They used common areas, though, and I intend to have a look around."

"What about the not-so-common areas? Mr. Price lives there, too. You'll have a devil of a time invading his privacy."

"I was thinking I'd just ask."

Instantly, Crane's eyes lit up. They swept the room like lighthouse beacons. Pain seemed to slide down his face, past his shoulders, and disintegrate. Color flooded his cheeks. "What's today?"

"Saturday."

"No, what day is it? A really good detective can solve a case in two weeks."

"Day six."

"That leaves eight to go."

"What do you think I should do, Captain?"

"Whatever you were planning to do before you came over this morning. And one more thing. I'd like you to run everything by me as you get it. I'd like to help."

Her visit seemed to give him a new lease on life, and she felt it in his grip when he shook her hand at the door and sent her on her way. But the longer she drove, listening to the purr of Ruby's engine, the more her thoughts nagged.

Why's he all of a sudden being so nice?

Chapter Twenty-Four

Roaring down Main Street under the power of Ruby's accelerating engine, Cézanne punched out the phone number for The Wild Orchid Society. On the second ring, she heard a click, followed by a distorted recording.

"The Wild Orchid blooms Saturday, half past seven. Number One Madrid Lane. After-Five dress. Members, thirty-five; fifty per couple. Admission free with invitation. Dare to sample the nectar of The Wild Orchid Society. Positively no uninvited guests. Latecomers will be fined one hundred dollars. All proceeds go to the National Registry for Exploited Children. Mum's the word."

The line went dead in her ear.

The skin on her thighs was still crawling when she dialed Reno's for an explanation of After-Five attire in the world of sado-masochism and bondage. On the fourth ring, a recording came on and she ended the call without leaving a message.

As for Captain Crane, it didn't bother her that he didn't believe she'd get into the Price house. And she didn't need his wife to spill the beans that he thought Cissy

Kissel killed the Great Dane. She'd left the Victorian with confidence buoyed — so buoyed, in fact, she decided to take Duty to the mall to shop for new clothes.

By lunch, Cézanne carried three bags full of Duty's purchases. When the girl stared in awe at the mall's food pavilion, she stuffed the sacks under the small Formica table and sent Duty to buy lunch. Devilrow's niece returned with two loaded baked potatoes.

"I never been in a mall before. Back home, we got a Dollar Store and the Sears catalogue."

"Where, exactly, do you live?"

"Weeping Mary."

"Never heard of it."

"It's not on the map. But there's Indian mounds close by and those are on the map."

Cézanne's mind shifted into overdrive with thoughts of a road trip, to a spot in "Eeze" Texas where Indian mounds made the map, but a colony of blacks couldn't. If Devilrow didn't come for his niece within the week, she'd buckle the girl in the car and strike out for Duty's home. Get to the bottom of this nonsense.

"So what do you think of this place?"

Duty's head bobbed. "It's nize. Miz Zan, you know I got no money for this." She scooped the plastic fork into melted cheddar and lifted it to her mouth.

"I told you I'd pay you at the end of the week. This," she thumbed at the sacks, "is coming out of your check."

"Do I get sick leave?"

"No."

Duty ran the tines along her tongue until she'd licked the cheese off. "Vacation?"

"No."

"Then what I get?"

"A roof over your head until I find that shiftless con-man, Leviticus Devilrow."

"If I want the day off?"

"You're fired."

Duty reached across the table and gave her hand a playful swat. "Miz Zan, I know you just funnin' me."

"What would you do if I gave you a day to yourself?"

She'll say Six Flags. And if she does, when this mess is over, I'm taking her.

Duty sat, pensive, sipping through a straw until the last of her drink gurgled. With a straight face, she said, "I'd come to work with you."

"You were bored the other day."

"You need somebody lookin' after you, Miz Zan." Her jaw had a stubborn tilt, while her eyes took on a serious glint. "You got a thrill-seeking gene something powerful."

Duty made her laugh. But inwardly, she grimaced.

Don't start liking her. She can't stay.

They finished lunch and angled over to a trash receptacle. A blouse in a nearby store window caught Duty's eye. She hopped up and down until Cézanne agreed to go inside. When Duty came out of the dressing room modeling it, the unusual shade of blue lit up her face to the point of radiance.

"Miz Zan, I would work extra hard around the house if I was to be able to get this."

"How much?" Cézanne reached for the tag and scowled.

"It's more than the other stuff, but if I was to be able to have it, I'd be extra nize."

She made a big production thinking it over but her protests lost effect. Duty got to her. "You can have it."

"Can I have two?"

"You'll have to clean the windows inside and out."

Devilrow's niece couldn't seem to take her eyes off the shirt. "I would do that."

Cézanne gave her the go-ahead, but when Duty met her at the checkout counter, she brought two identical blouses.

"You already picked blue. Why don't you get a pink one? Purple would look nice, too."

"You said yourself, Miz Zan, the blue one complicated my skin."

"Complemented."

"Whatever. You said it made my skin beautiful. So, I'll be needin' a extra, in case of emergency."

"It's a waste of money to duplicate this shirt. You'll probably grow out of it before you get enough wear out of it."

"I may never find this color again, and I would need a spare if somethin' was to happen to it. Like if I spilled."

The air thinned. Chills raced across Cézanne's shoulders.

"Oh, no, Miz Zan, you not gonna cry, are you? I don't hafta have it if you say no. It was just one of my bright ideas. I was hopin' maybe you would approve if I explained, but I don't hafta have it if it makes you sad. Are you havin' a heart attack?"

"No."

"Miz Zan, maybe you should sit. Say, miss, you got a chair? She might be gonna have a seizure. It happened before when somebody hit her car. I know 'cause I saw it."

The flash of intuition that began when Duty wheedled for a back-up shirt, jogged her memory and startled Cézanne into generosity.

"I'm fine. You can get an extra blue one. And you can have the pink and purple, too. Whatever you want."

But Duty acted bridle-wise. "This a trick? Tell you what I'll do — I'll do the

310

windows inside and out but you can't make me clean under yo' sink. Did you take a good look at what's under there? I'm scared to stick my hand in, maybe I'd draw back a nub."

"You don't have to do extra chores. Let's just call it a reward for giving me a brainstorm."

"Is that like a busted blood vessel where you fall in a coma and die?"

To the sales clerk, Cézanne said, "Wrap them up," with an air of authority in her voice. But all the way to the Kompressor, a kind of giddy excitement that could only come with great sex or a good night's sleep left her walking on air.

The picture she had shown Special Agent Longley of Cissy Kissel at the Trail Drivers Ball left a residue in her brain that germinated when Duty requested a back-up shirt. Maybe the Great Dane's wife had done the same. Maybe she bought the real Emmannuel and had an exact copy made. If she wanted to kill her husband, she could have worn one of the gowns to the Trail Drivers Ball, dashed off long enough to kill her husband, changed out of her bloody clothes and into the spare, and re-appeared at the Country Club.

The police confiscated her evening gown. Forensics checked it for bloodstains and didn't find any. Eventually, she got the dress back — probably the Emmannuel as opposed to the knock-off — and either destroyed the copy or had it cleaned. Nothing in the analysis of the dress suggested the presence of a wine stain. Come Monday, she'd check into it a little closer. Call that sweat shop in La Jitas. See if anybody out there ever heard of Worth Price or his daughter.

"You look extra happy, Miz Zan. Did I cause that?"

"I'd say so."

"You makin' fun of me?"

"Definitely not. I was just thinking what an enigma you are."

Duty stopped in her tracks. With a pout of defensiveness, her voice faded to a whisper. "That's not nize, Miz Zan. I don't go 'round callin' you names. Why you wanna call me somethin' ugly? Makes me wanna cry when you say mean stuff." Duty bowed her head. "Friends don't call each other bad names."

She wanted to hug her. To undo the mistakes inflicted by others. On one hand, Duty frustrated her. On the other, she took her mind off the bad things happening all around her. Lamely, she moved closer and lowered her voice.

"E-n-i-g-m-a. En-íg-ma. An enigma is a mystery. You're like a thousand-piece puzzle of a Kansas wheat field and I don't know which piece to start with. It's not a bad word, it's a compliment."

"Mmm-hmm." Grunted as if she didn't believe it. "So I'm a 'nigma?"

"Enigma."

"That's what I said." And then Duty seemed to hatch an idea of her own. She broke into a grin. "I can't wait to call Nehemiah that."

Sleep gnawed the afternoon away, but Cézanne was up and running again by four-thirty. After phoning the dispatcher and asking for a Crime Scene detective to meet her at the station, she almost sneaked out of the house, undetected. But Duty pulled a fast one — she stood on the porch, raring to go, in her new wool slacks and cardigan.

"What're you doing? Get inside where it's warm. I'm not running up a doctor bill if you get sick."

"I'm riding shotgun."

"Where'd you learn that word?"

"Mista Sid taught me."

"You don't even know where I'm going."

"Don't much care."

Duty's flat, unblinking stare unnerved her.

"If I let you tag along, you have to promise to keep a low profile."

"What's low profile mean?"

"Stay out of the way."

"I can do that. I do good, blending in. Like I bet you don't know, sometimes I stand in your bedroom doorway, watch you sleep, you don't even know I'm there."

What she needed was a lock. And until she could install one, a chair jammed under the knob would do just fine. Maybe booby trap the door by stacking empty Dr Pepper cans against it.

Fifteen minutes later, they pulled into Crane's reserved space at the police station. Cézanne keyed her way into the Crime Scene office and found Slash in his midnight blue FWPD polo shirt and acid-washed denims, sitting on a desk with his legs crossed at the ankles. He glanced up from a copy of *Guns and Ammo* folded open to a feature on assault weapons, then tossed it aside. Without Teddy's boyish freckles, he looked like the kind of guy who could inspire a girl to turn out the lights and do bad things.

Duty slid into a chair and stared, wide-eyed, at the tall, striking man with Teddy's rust-tinged hair and piercing turquoise eyes. "You tall enough to hunt geese with a grass rake."

Cézanne felt a fire in her cheeks and realized she was staring.

"They didn't tell me it was you," he said.

"They didn't tell me it was you, either."

"What do you need?"

She caught a glimpse of Duty making an obscene gesture with her fist and index finger, and shot her a wicked glare. "I need to fingerprint something."

"I believe they teach that in the academy. Is there some reason you can't do it with a brush and some powder?"

"Actually, there is. I figured a Crime Scene detective would be my best bet since it's embossed paper." She pulled out a plastic Baggie with The Wild Orchid Society card and thrust it in front of her.

"Chemical development works on latent prints." His head bobbed. "Spray ninhydrin on it."

"It'll leave a stain. I don't want anyone to know I printed it."

"Then you shouldn't have told me."

"You're safe. I'm talking about the people who gave it to me. I don't want them to know because eventually I may have to give it back."

He gave it the visual once-over through the clear plastic. "It's a small enough specimen. We could try iodine."

"Won't that turn it red?"

Slash's lip curled up at one corner. "Iodine crystals subjected to a small amount of heat aren't permanent. Matter of fact, the latents begin to fade once fuming stops. Somebody would have to be standing by to photograph the prints, right then."

"Just point me to a camera."

She followed him into an ante-room. Duty brought up the rear and watched, spellbound, while Slash completed the process in under thirty minutes.

He unloaded the camera and dropped the finished roll into her palm. "That about does it."

"One more thing — a favor. Please keep this to yourself?"

He had the same Vaughn charm as Teddy. The kind of grin that made her want to peel off her clothes and crush the smile off his face with a hot body, sheened in sweat —

Duty's squinty-eyed glare stopped her runaway imagination. She knew by the crease forming between Slash's brow that he'd said something that called for a response.

"Pardon?"

"I was saying, once you get the film developed, I can send those through AFIS for you."

"Sure."

It was a lie. Now that she didn't know who to trust in the department, she'd ask Jinx Porter to help. Porter could do it; he was a fingerprint expert. He could classify them — hell, if the constable maintained his own database of thugs, he might even have a classification bank like the Automated Fingerprint Index System. Cissy Kissel's would be among the exemplars, of that she was certain. But would The Executioner's?

Slash locked the door behind them. In the hall, he said, "I knew you didn't plug that stripper at Ali Baba's. I could tell as soon as I saw the bloodstains on the wall. Close contact wound. All your shots came from across the room. I put in so much overtime I was eating out of vending machines and doing without sleep. When I finally got a chance to have a real Thanksgiving dinner at my parents', I dropped off, face-first, in the broccoli."

Bet it looked great on you.

Chewing the inside of her lip kept her from blurting out compliments. Like how she'd like to lick his face. Maybe more. Being sexually frustrated sucked. Dating the Big Bopper sucked worse.

He stuck out his hand. "Good to formally meet you."

She liked his firm grip, and the way he didn't look away. "It occurred to me, I don't even know your real name."

"Slash'll do. 'Til we know each other better."

With the film dropped off at the photo

processor, and nothing to do but wait, Cézanne took a break from scanning documents from the Kissel case into the computer. By early evening, she changed into a short black dress with a matching Chanel jacket and called out to Duty.

"Living room." Her voice lilting.

"Have you seen the dog?"

Duty, sitting on a rug in front of the TV, threw back a flap of blanket. The Scottie was in her lap, glaring. Through the lattice work of the leather muzzle, bared teeth caught the light like two rows of marquis-cut diamonds.

"I was thinking I'd take him to this vet I know." Bobby Noah had a veterinary degree from Texas A&M University. Maybe he'd know if Butch was depressed. Perhaps she could wheedle a prescription for doggie Prozac.

"Um-hmm. I got you figured out, Miz Zan. You striking out for where that Bobby-fella stays."

"Wrong, smarty-pants."

"Uh-huh, I can tell. You all gussied up. You got that look. Saw it in yo' eye when you was talkin' to that po-lice detective — that man named Shred."

"Slash."

"Slash, Rip, Shred . . . what's the difference? I know how you think. I know that look. I watched you, and I know you want

318

to get yo' hands on that vegetarian."

"Veterinarian. And what look is that?"

"Tiger look. If you see the vet, he better have a whip and a chair, maybe some tranquilizer darts, Lordy mercy." Duty was laughing, evidently scratching a good place behind the dog's ear, considering his back leg started drumming the floor.

But Cézanne had something else on her mind, and fear darkened the mood. "If something were to happen to me —"

"Like what?"

"If something happened where I didn't come home —"

"Why you not come back?"

"I'm just saying if worked out that way . . . say, if you woke up in the morning and I wasn't here, what would you do?"

"You mean besides get on yo' computer and buy me some nize threads with yo' credit card? Or find me somebody to bring me over a nize Kahlua for my chicory coffee?" Cézanne figured she must have looked stricken because Duty quit clowning and regarded her gravely. "Call nine-one-one."

"Before that."

"Make a spell. And gris-gris, for protection."

"No."

"Phone Mista Sid?"

"Not Mister Sid." Not since he neglected to tell her about his conversation with Rosen in the men's room. "We're not bothering Mister Sid. I'd want you to call a man named Jinx Porter."

Duty shrugged. "You wrote down his number?"

"In the kitchen, on the cork message board by the wall phone."

Unexpectedly, Duty sprang to her feet. Butch spilled out of her lap and sprawled across the floor. Under the new, sleek pajamas, the only ones she would probably ever own made of duppioni silk, Devilrow's niece was shaking.

"Where you goin' whatchoo can't say?"

Chapter Twenty-Five

Number One Madrid Lane took on the look of any other multi-million dollar estate in Fort Worth at dusk — lights out, except for the fixture overhanging the porch and a couple of Tuscany sconces mounted on the gate pillars. Well-heeled folks the caliber of Worth Price didn't get rich and stay that way by giving money to the utility company. They drove old cars and cut corners, hired migrant workers or poor blacks for yard work, housed them in servants' quarters when they were young and cared for them well after retirement, often until death. Subscribers of the can't-take-it-with-you theory, they found creative ways to thwart the inheritance tax laws of the bloodsucking IRS by hiring big-gun lawyers like Lucky McElwell to stash money in trust for their kids, or draft living wills that ensured the plug to the life support equipment didn't get pulled until the last dime had been spent.

Cézanne leaned forward and paid the taxi driver. "There's an extra twenty if you come back at ten and wait for me."

"Sure thing."

She watched him pull away, not totally convinced he would return. If he didn't, she could always hike up the hill, retrieve her things, and walk a mile to the nearest convenience store.

For the next few minutes, she concealed herself in a stand of pecan trees on a neighboring estate and inventoried the contents of her handbag. The digital camera had the capability to take night photos, and she would use the binoculars, field notebook, and pen to record license numbers. Her house keys, she left at home. But Hollywood's ID would be available in the event The Wild Orchid Society's calling card wasn't sufficient. The twenty dollars for cab fare, she'd already rolled up and threaded into the hem of her dress.

The few cars traveling down Madrid turned at the corner and came back up the hill on the Majorca side of the house. No one entered through the massive front doors. Shivering in the shadows, Cézanne grew uneasy.

With her gut knotting, she returned the camera to her purse, stuffed the bag into the crotch of a giant pecan, and started the walk downhill to the Mediterranean villa. With each step, she wished she'd defied instructions to come alone.

Should've brought Reno.

Reno would know what to do.

Reno would've been the canary in her coal mine.

Worth Price's grand ballroom turned out to be bigger than Cézanne's three-bedroom house. If sheer size wasn't enough to command respect from the purest of critics, the Prices decorated as if they had the budget of a Greek tycoon. The room came alive with the musical tones of an ebony grand piano. Velvet drapes hung in splendor. Persian carpets and Baccarat chandeliers added a richness unlike any she'd ever seen. Gilded moldings framed the swirl of mythological characters looking down upon the Prices' guests through a ceiling of painted clouds.

Awed, Cézanne stood at the entrance. She could've been at a gathering of Fortune Five Hundred; everyone in the room — all thirty or so — reeked of wealth in their tuxedos and bugle-beaded gowns, and carried themselves with the confidence of corporate wheeler-dealers. And judging by their collective, unspoken appraisal, showing up wearing nothing but the rhinestone barrette fastening Reno's hairpiece wouldn't have made her feel more out of place. After-Five for the filthy rich obviously translated into more than a black velvet cocktail dress cut on the bias.

"I'm sorry." She dropped her gaze in an

effort to avoid their stares. "I'm afraid I'm underdressed."

"Don't be silly." Her hostess seemed to delight in her discomfort, since, at best guess, the Great Dane's widow wore an original Versace similar to one recently featured in *Vogue*. Cissy Kissel shoved a consent form under her nose. "Fill this out. We use first names here. Tonight, I'm Sicily. And you are?"

What had Reno called her? Elena? Atlanta?

"Atlantis."

Alana. She winced inwardly. Too late.

"When you finish looking over the release, I'll explain the rules. What kind of wine would you like?"

"Nothing. I'm not a big drinker."

"Try the champagne. It's so smooth it slides down your throat."

"Club soda would be nice."

Cissy Kissel had only to glance at the man tending bar to get a club soda brought over. "Tonight's our business meeting, and phase one of the induction service. You'll have an opportunity to meet many of our members. A few are under the weather and sent their regrets."

Cézanne mustered up a doe-eyed, ain't-it-sad look and raised the crystal flute to her lips.

"Tonight's discussion concerns the prac-

tice of Tantra as it relates to sexuality —
not a topic the group's particularly interested in — but Royce's friend is a practi-
tioner, and we've agreed to let her
enlighten us." She pointed to a man about
sixty, and caught the attention of the
young Asian lady, with hair hanging to the
waist, clinging to his arm. They fluttered
their fingers in an affected wave. "We have
a video presentation and, of course, we
can't wait to see the devices she brought."

The phony smile faded from her lips.

"Anyway, after our program, you'll be
voted in, or blackballed. It's very brutal
and you mustn't take offense if you don't
make the cut. If you do, you'll obtain pro-
visional status and an invitation to a play
party. Depending on the outcome at the
end of the evening, you may be asked to
provide your true name. After a thorough
background check, you'll pay annual dues
and receive a regular membership. If at any
time you feel uncomfortable and wish to
leave, you may." She flashed a mouthful of
perfect teeth, all filed to the same length.
"Just don't bother ever coming back."

"I'll stay."

"Let me finish . . ." A middle-aged
couple entered the room. Cissy Kissel took
notice and motioned them over. "You're
late. That's a hundred-dollar fine each.
Drop the money in the Gallé cameo vase

on top of the piano or make a check payable to the National Registry of Exploited Children."

She refocused her attention on Cézanne. "As I started to explain, if you desire to leave, you may never rejoin. We expect anonymity, so it wouldn't be in your best interest to blab about our socials. Our members are connected to the most unlikely people. I'm not saying this would happen to you, darling, but people have been known to lose jobs, go bankrupt, fall ill for no apparent reason . . . but look at you. Your skin's all blotchy." Her voice turned unexpectedly soothing, and she grazed a finger across the base of Cézanne's neck. "You're frightened when there's no need to be. In the entire history of The Wild Orchid Society, only one member was excommunicated. Believe me when I say, once it's done, it's permanent. Just don't talk to me if we stumble onto each other in public. Questions?"

Cézanne assessed the members through darting glances. Scanning the room, she wondered which fashionably dressed man would turn out to be The Executioner. None looked tough enough to be the paradigm of debauchery.

She didn't glimpse Krystal among them. "Last night you gave someone else I know a card. I don't see her."

"Several invitees already left. Not their cup of tea, I suppose. A couple sent their regrets. One didn't bother to respond to the invitation." She snorted in contempt. "They won't be invited back. I can't abide bad manners. So what do you think? Are you game? And it is a game, Atlantis. A wonderful game when it works as designed." Fleshy lips played out in a sphinx-like smile.

Oh, God, they'll see through me.

Her heart drummed so hard she wondered if Cissy Kissel could hear it over the tinkling of piano keys. She made a decision — then regretted it as soon as the words left her lips.

"I'm game." Cézanne raised the crystal flute in a mock toast.

"Come. I'll introduce you around." Kissel's widow linked arms. "You're not one of those bored housewives like Jasmine, are you?" She pointed to a lady draping herself across the baby grand. "Or, do you actually work for a living?"

Look at 'em, staring with their x-ray vision.

"I do . . . social work. I work with . . . the emotionally disturbed."

"How delightful. I volunteered at the children's hospital once. It was quite rewarding. One of our maids had a sick child and we took cookies down for a party."

"How unselfish."

Cissy whisked the perceived compliment away with her hand. "I didn't actually go inside. Too depressing, all those little kids with their heads shaved, but my driver carried in the food and we got a nice thank-you note from the director. That reminds me, I need to have Blanca call to find out when their next event is scheduled."

Midway across the wood parquet, Cézanne got cold feet.

"Could you point me to the ladies' room?"

"Certainly. Through those doors and to the right. Shall I come with you?" She winked.

"Thanks, I'll find it."

"I once did naughty things in a public restroom." Spoken in a conspiratorial whisper. "The acoustics are divine — all those moans and groans echoing off those teensy-tiny little tiles. Don't tell."

Cézanne wanted to poke her fingers into the hollows of her ears, clear down to the drums. To flutter her tongue between her teeth and make choking calf noises to block out the noise.

Way too much information.

And if she doesn't stop accidentally grazing my breast, I'm gonna knock the fire out of her.

She walked past the bar with the carriage of a runway model, past the concert pianist playing "Stardust," beyond the disconcerting stares of The Wild Orchid Society boring holes in her back.

They know I'm a fraud.

Outside the massive doors, she took the unguided tour: left, away from the powder room, and down a long corridor matted in oriental runners. She tried the first door handle and opened a closet filled with furs. With a feather touch, she closed it and checked the next one.

Locked.

She ventured down the hallway, heart beating time-and-a-half, rehearsing an explanation in case someone caught her snooping. Her hands trembled.

They'll come looking. It's like I want to get caught. Death wish.

She hurried past a set of glass doors leading outside to a veranda. His-and-hers swimming pools rippled beneath a waxing moon. An inflatable shark drifted in the shadows beneath the diving board.

She tried the next door. Locked. But the double doors at the end of the corridor gave way when she turned the handle.

Worth Price's part of the house.

Had to be.

She slipped inside, easing the catch back in place until she heard the faint click.

At the first room on her left, she tested the brass knob.

Bingo.

She could have just as easily entered an alpine ski lodge overlooking powder-coated slopes. Gas logs blazed in the stone fireplace, while the glassy-eyed stares of wild game hung high upon the walls. With their mounted heads casting long shadows through the room, they followed her steps. A zebra skin with its taxidermied head still attached rested atop a hassock where it appeared to await the fall of a swordsman's blade; the hide from its body, legs, and tail eased onto the floor, interrupting a direct path to the wet-bar. Unnerved by its accusing glare, she lengthened her stride to side-step it. A leather-topped library table with deeply carved legs had an open ledger on display, but when she moved in for a peek, the snap of a lock jolted her into the fixed pose of a statue.

Off to one side, a section of mahogany wall paneling swung open.

Out of the black, a small-framed white-haired man ascended a set of hidden stairs. He stepped into the room with a book in one hand, and a cane in the other. She stood perfectly still, childishly hoping he wouldn't notice her framed between a matched pair of leather wingbacks. He nudged the door with the cane's rubber tip. The wall clicked shut.

For a fleeting instant, she wondered if the safari animals experienced the same sense of doom right before the hammer fell. The little man wore pajama bottoms and a red silk smoking jacket richly embroidered with gold fleur-de-lis. And when the surprise wore off his face, he squinted through rimless spectacles, and raised a gnarled finger browned by nicotine.

He spoke in the raspy whisper of a three-pack-a-day smoker. "State your business, young woman."

"I'm a guest. I was searching for the powder room and must've taken a wrong turn." An apology gushed out before she could come up with another way to conceal her guilt.

"You a friend of Cissy's?"

"She invited me." Words spilled out in a hyperventilating rush. "You have a beautiful home, but I don't know how you navigate your way around. I never met anyone with two swimming pools." She paused for breath. "Well, if it's all the same to you, I'll get out of your hair —"

"Take a seat." Worry-lines in his forehead relaxed.

It didn't take any energy to drop into the nearest chair, since she was quite certain her kneecaps just went sideways. By now, they would have started to look for her. How stupid to have taken such a chance.

Not to mention Worth Price hobbling over on his bird's-eye maple stick, giving her a crooked grin. The thread of smoke from a lit cigar coiling up from a malachite ashtray made her head go dizzy.

"You a member of that botanical society?"

"Excuse me?"

"That club Cissy belongs to, the one that grows flowers? They specialize in tropical plants."

She blinked. "Plants?"

"Orchids. Least, that's what they tell me." He sank onto a cowhide sofa cushion and balanced his cane against the over-stuffed curve of the arm. He reached for the cigar and sucked in a couple of puffs. "You raise those persnickety hothouse flowers, too?"

"Me? No. Now and then, if I'm lucky, I get roses. That's about the extent of my horticulture experience."

The decrepit little elf didn't have a clue what was going on down the hall.

"Mr. Price, I have to go. They'll be worried."

"Feel free to visit anytime, young lady. You remind me of Evangeline, my lovely wife, God rest her soul. It's been lonely all these years. She had black hair, like you. Dark eyes, too. Your voice is deeper, but I enjoy a filly who sounds like she means business. You're easy on the eyes, and you're welcome back."

Another engaging grin flashed behind thin, blue lips. Beyond his thick lenses, wiry hairs poked up from his eyebrows. She wanted to dart out of the room before he could rise and come over, but she steeled her raw nerves and willed herself to present her hand so he could buss it.

Her knees trembled. She forced her most bewitching voice. "I'd love to visit again, Mr. Price. And with your personal consent, I'd enjoy the opportunity to see the rest of this beautiful place."

She made it as far as the veranda when the bolt slid back and the rifle-action clatter from the ballroom doors echoed through the corridor. Given the choice, she scampered outside and waited on the pebblestone walk. Better to stand by the pools, looking ethereal or confused, than to have them think she nosed around.

Besides, she'd probably get the boot when they found her.

Her mind went through a series of mental gymnastics.

Nothing ventured, nothing gained.

Curiosity killed the cat.

Dead men tell no tales. Dead women, either.

Cissy Kissel burst through the doors. Her pale eyes flashed like bottle rockets from hell. She descended a short group of flagstone steps like a bad bride with her train fluttering on the breeze. Each high heel struck the pebblestone with the crack of a starter pistol. Her manner was anything but hospitable.

"We're about to start the program," she said archly. "You're holding things up. You're familiar with our system of fines?"

"Forgive me." Cézanne ducked the glare. "I came outside to smoke before I realized I left my cigarettes in the car. I'm trying to quit."

Oy vey.

Almost made her roll her own eyes at the feeble whopper.

But Cissy Kissel launched into a diatribe about being bullish on punctuality and bearish on lally-gaggers that finally ended with, "Don't ever do that again."

Words swirled inside Cézanne's head. "Beg your pardon?"

"Wander away like that. I'm beginning to see what you meant last night when you said you didn't take orders well."

"I certainly didn't mean to offend you, it's just . . . I'm unfamiliar with protocol. That and the fact that I got lost. I apologize."

"For the life of me, I don't know why Master wants to fool with you, but as long as he does I'll indulge him. However, if you continue to be willful, you'll be harshly disciplined. Do you understand?"

The conversation seemed as scripted as

the interplay between the Dommes and subs at the Dungeon of Decadence, but the angry voice chilled Cézanne to the bone. Made the flesh creep on her arms. Dane Kissel heard that tone just before he died — of that, she was certain.

She played a hunch. "If I didn't know better, I'd think you were jealous. You have no reason to be."

With a disdainful sniff, the widow said, "Don't be silly. Master and I are irrevocably tied. You can't come between us. You're an amusement. A trifle. I'll be with Master long after he tires of you."

"Why's that?"

"We have a history." The lady of the house flashed a smile loaded with lust. She smoothed the tiny pearls beading her sleeves, and held her head aloof. "It binds us."

"I admire your confidence. So what can he possibly want with me?"

"Why don't you ask him?"

"Maybe I will. Where is . . . Master?"

"Where he always is when we induct new members. Watching us on the security monitors. Master likes to watch."

Instinct betrayed her. She avoided the widow's odd, pale eyes and glanced under the eaves, looking for a pinhole camera mounted where the mitered corners met. The black cylinder honed in on them like a tiny sentinel.

She must've tripped a laser-eyed beam.

A furtive glance at the woodwork framing the double doors confirmed it. The Executioner caught her red-handed. Mapping directions inside her head, she hatched a plot to return with a can of Luminol and a UV-light, even as Dane Kissel's killer stood not two feet away from her. The prime suspect hardened her already-irritated expression.

"What would you have me do, Mistress?"

"Much better." Her tone turned sensual. "You're a bad girl." Closing in until her lips were inches from Cézanne's jaw, she dropped her voice to a sultry whisper. "We'll have to work on that, won't we?"

The question was purely rhetorical but Cézanne couldn't have answered if she wanted to. The woman's tongue darted out and flicked her neck, slimed a trail up to her earlobe, then snaked its way into the curves and hollows. She pulled back until her lips hovered near the shell of Cézanne's ear, then whispered into her hair with breathy seduction.

"He's watching us, you know. It angers Master if I strike out on my own. He likes to orchestrate these things himself. I'm afraid your insolent streak's rubbing off on me." She traced a fingernail down the back of Cézanne's neck. "I imagine once my guests leave, I'm in store for a bit of behavior modification. I'll tell him it's your fault, if you like."

She threaded her fingers through Reno's borrowed hairpiece and closed her fist, securing Cézanne snugly in her grip. The pull of the pins fastening the dark wig in place smarted like a dozen tiny icepicks.

Murmuring, "It won't make any difference, of course; he knows it's my way," the mistress of ceremonies tugged her so close her delicate fragrance glutted Cézanne's senses. "But you have every right to worry. He's very possessive. I'm sure he'll discuss the matter with you, fully, once you meet."

Suspended in time and place, Cézanne floated inside herself, unable and unwilling to extract herself from the euphoria of Cissy Kissel's clutches. Hair follicles in her ear canal stood on end. Blood seemed to crystallize in her veins. To crumble into millions of tiny granules. To fall through the tubes in her body like hourglass sand, settling in her lead feet until her arches collapsed. Her tongue felt thick and swollen, as if at any moment, it would close off her throat and suffocate her.

And then it was over.

Release came, and the moment evaporated in the same way Cissy Kissel's hot breath turned to vapor in the chilly night air.

"No harm, no foul. Let's go watch a movie, shall we? Tomorrow night, you'll be invited back for the real party."

"How do you know? You said I could be blackballed."

"Who in their right mind would say no to me?"

The demented widow raised a manicured hand. She slid an acrylic nail under the thin gold chain around Cézanne's neck, and pulled until Reno's amulet came out. Upon seeing the charm, she cracked what seemed to be a genuine smile. When she let go, her hand grazed Cézanne's breast. As if snuffing a candle wick between her thumb and forefinger, Cissy Kissel reached under the Chanel jacket and pinched her nipple until she blinked back tears.

Abruptly, she let go. In a sensuous, clawlike motion, her hand fell away. "You're going to love being one of us."

She threaded her fingers between Cézanne's, and squired her back inside, down the hall to the grand ballroom. When they entered, everyone remained seated in folding chairs draped in white slipcovers. Eyes moved in a collective shift, and the low buzz of conversation faltered.

Ohgod. Like trying to sneak a sunbeam past a rooster.

A movie screen descended from the ceiling. The Asian woman left her chair and walked to a podium with a microphone.

Guided through the dimly lit room by

the soft touch of her hostess, Cézanne reached her seat and settled in. The lights went out. In the pitch black, Cissy leaned over and slid her hand a few inches up the inside of Cézanne's leg, stopping short of the lace tops on her thigh-highs.

"Tell me, dear," she whispered huskily, "how do you feel about body piercings?"

Chapter Twenty-Six

Cézanne didn't know a whole lot more about the members of The Wild Orchid Society when she left than she did when she first arrived, but the poolside rendezvous with Worth Price's morally bankrupt daughter seemed to make inroads. The widow's endorsement led to an invitation to return Sunday night for phase two.

Around ten o'clock, when the group turned out, she'd absorbed about all of the Tantric sexuality instruction someone whose only bed buddy came with D-cell batteries could stand. While she waited for her cab in front of the Price mansion, she concentrated on memorizing a couple of license plates on high-end autos parked in the shadows.

She sensed a presence watching her.

A man behind a second-story window peered out through binoculars as the Great Dane's widow closed the door behind departing guests.

The Executioner, unmasked —

— yet, too far away to make out his features.

During the cab ride, a foreboding

thought occurred: she'd been the only guest. And whomever lurked in the shadows, did so for the sole purpose of taking down the number of her taxi.

The Wild Orchid Society's background check had begun.

The Pakistani cab driver started to curb the taxi at the neighboring estate, but Cézanne urged him on. She could return for her personal items later. As soon as he turned onto Camp Bowie Boulevard, she took a backward look and ordered him to pull over. In the parking lot of an all-night donut shop, she slipped the twenty out of her hem, paid the fare, and hurried inside.

A teenaged cashier with a bad case of acne loaned her a pen. She stood at the register under the bright fluorescents and printed the LP numbers she memorized onto a paper napkin. At a flash of her smile, the boy let her borrow the house phone.

She caught Teddy fresh out of the shower.

Close to eleven, the detective bounced his pickup over the curb and into the parking lot. From the look of his starched jeans and crisp shirt, he was ready for two-stepping. When she hiked up her dress enough to climb into the cab, he gave her a wolf whistle.

"What's up, Captain? Date run out on you?"

"I'm working."

He grinned. "If I'd known this was your corner, I'd have come along sooner."

"Sid's rubbing off on you. Stay away from him before you end up in IA."

They rolled down the incline, onto the street.

Teddy said, "Where to?"

"Trinity Park?"

"Closes at ten. Besides, Vice is out trolling for gays. You know that."

"Why would I know that?" Insulted. "You think I'm a lesbian just because I can't keep a steady boyfriend?"

He eyed her warily, as if he overturned a rock and something with scales slithered out. His voice stayed even and metered. "You should know. You're a cop. That's what we do. Enforce laws. All of them."

"Sorry." Clearly, the time spent with Reno and Dane Kissel's wife had eroded her confidence. "Working in a male-dominated field, I guess I'm starting to question my femininity. I've had strange women hitting on me all week."

They were thick into the oak-covered countryside by the time they passed Whiskey Flats, a suburban nude-bar-and-beer-joint-laden blot on the landscape. Teddy turned down a dirt road and didn't brake until he came to a mailbox. A dilapidated house with a sagging porch and a roof full of holes sat off in the distance. He cut the engine and moved the seat back as far as it would go.

"Want to tell me about it?"

"I'm running out of people I can trust."

"We're on your side."

She figured he meant Sid, too, and shook her head. "Promise you won't discuss this."

"That goes without saying."

"Sid's not one of us. I overheard him talking to Rosen. It's just me and you, now."

But Teddy wasn't convinced. She had to lay it out for him, then wait for it to sink in. His mouth opened, finally seeing where it was heading.

"Sid wouldn't undercut you."

"He already did. If I use up my last transfer booting him back to the jail, I slice my own jugular."

"Put him in charge of Wardancer's investigation."

"I'll have to bring somebody else in on the Great Dane or we won't crack the case in time."

"In time for what?"

"To save the chief's job — and my skin."

The light of a full moon paled his face. Boyish freckles disappeared from his nose and hands and when he reached over and patted her knee, soft-core porn disguised as Tantric teachings swirled in her head. She placed the napkin with the license numbers on the dashboard.

Her heart fluttered. She knew she shouldn't, but she'd torpedoed the relationship with Bobby, and Teddy's innocence lured her past the divided seat. When he shifted his knee, she draped herself across him and found his lips. At first, he did nothing. Just sat there, unresponsive to her kiss, with his hot breath exhaling, rhythmically, against her cheek. But she ran her palms over his chest and threaded her fingers through the hair barely touching his ears, until he shifted beneath her weight.

Slowly, he parted his lips. The tip of her tongue was already tracing the boundaries of soft flesh when he gripped her shoulders. But instead of drawing her closer, he lifted her until their mouths disengaged like a couple of suction cups. With her nose inches away, she whiffed his minty breath and grazed a fingernail down one side of his emotionless face.

"I need this, Teddy."

Ohgod. I'm turning into Klevenhagen.

After he returned the kiss, after she discovered the magic of his mouth devouring her like a rich dessert, after his strong, gentle hands electrified her skin until she thought her hair would stand on end and snap off at the roots, something went terribly wrong. He held her immobilized, as if he'd pressed a stun-gun to her neck.

About the time she noticed the tiny stud piercing Teddy's ear, he came clean.

"We can't, Captain. I've got somebody."

Of course. Just because she was sex-starved didn't mean everybody else was.

"I apologize if I made you uncomfortable. Oh, Jeez. What was I thinking? Let me borrow your gun."

"No harm, no foul. Blame it on the moon."

Her muscles went rigid. She smoothed her hands over the skirt of her dress and wiggled across to her side of the seat, as if the image in her head could be rewound by simply reversing her movements.

No harm, no foul?

She studied his profile in the moonlight. The Wild Orchid Society specialized in cat and mouse games. Could Teddy be The Executioner? Or was his word choice merely a coincidence?

I've finally entered the fifth circle of hell.

On the drive back into town, sleet pinged off Teddy's windshield. He touched the steering column and engaged the wipers. At slow intervals, they squeegeed the glass, and thumped back into place. He slid a Chris Isaacks CD into the player and adjusted the volume. Cézanne sat in

345

stricken silence, listening to Chris's voice shoot up like his gonads were caught in a fox trap; lamenting his woman's wicked game-playing ways, explaining to the listener why he didn't want to fall in love. Sorry, sorry.

She spied a Garth Brooks CD and changed discs, along with her mood. Garth, she could understand. She and Garth were connected by sorry, rotten luck. Garth knew the score. He had friends in low places. Well, so did she. She leaned a shoulder into the door and tried to shrink in size, while pondering whether the Limón brothers were coming up for parole. Maybe she'd put in a call.

Hi. Remember me? I'm the one who locked you up. How'd you like to do me a favor? There's this guy called The Executioner. I don't want you to kill him, just bust his knee-caps so I can yank off his hood.

Before long, Teddy wheeled the extended-cab truck in front of her house and cut the motor.

"I have news about Worth Price that'll interest you," he said, all starched and businesslike, and oblivious to that fact that a half hour ago, she had wild thoughts of stripping the teeth off his zipper. "Price owns oil derricks out in West Texas. A few months before his daughter married the Great Dane, Mexican nationals sabotaged

Price's oilfield. They had to bring in one of those specialized firefighters to put out the blasts. Price almost had to declare bankruptcy.

"But that's not all. Six months later, the guy had more money than Saudi Arabia. How does that happen, Captain?"

"Where'd you get your information?"

"I've got a CI."

Confidential informants were hard to come by. She knew by the set in his jaw, sneaking gold out of Fort Knox would be easier than getting her detective to reveal his source. Besides, after that slip of the tongue, she wasn't even sure about Teddy anymore. He might've made the whole thing up to throw her off.

She said, "Why Mexicans? It doesn't make sense."

"I keep asking myself the same thing — why would Mexicans be interested in Worth Price?"

"Maybe you got it backwards. Maybe Worth Price got interested in them."

For such a cavalier remark, she figured they were on the right track when Teddy did a double-take. They exchanged astonished glances and piped up in unison.

"Narcotics?"

As soon as Cézanne cracked open the door to the guest room and saw the blankets plumped with pillows, she knew Duty tried to put one over on her. The ruse might have worked if the mop of wiry blonde hair on the pillow hadn't belonged to the dog. And she might not have noticed Butch at all, had he not lifted his head and acknowledged her with a low growl.

"There's a thing called euthanasia," she grumbled, backing out. "I hear it's painless." If not for her great love for Roby Tyson, son of Cujo would already be at the Humane Society, up for adoption — or walking the green mile.

Pecking noises came from the study.

She gritted her teeth until it smarted. Deuteronomy commandeered her computer again. She tiptoed down the hall, listening to the frantic click of fingernails against the keyboard. In one fluid motion, she grasped the knob and stormed through the door. Duty snapped her head around. Her eyes widened into huge, garnet-colored spheres.

"Didn't I tell you to stay off that computer?"

Text on the monitor crumbled away, like small tiles in a disintegrating mosaic. The page went white and a skull and crossbones appeared. A demonic laugh filtered out from the speakers as the skull's teeth clacked together, yukking it up.

Duty lapsed into the throes of panic. She heaved great sobs, babbled unintelligible phrases, wrung her hands and shifted from one foot to the other like she'd just perfected her audition for River Dance.

"Yo' computer got VD. I had yo' computer messing with Willie and he gave it the clap."

"What?"

The bleating telephone pierced Duty's real life cries, eclipsing the computer-generated chuckles coming from the speakers.

"Yo' computer got AIDS. I tried to stop it — didn't do no good."

Taunting messages in a barbed wire font appeared on-screen.

GOTCHA.

Remnants of each shrill ring hung in the hallway.

The computer's next message went beyond taunting. It was pure-dee filth. As if a person could really contort themselves into the suggested position and —

"Ohmygod. Quick, turn it off."

"Won't do no good. I tried already. It told itself to ignore the command."

"Cut it off at the wall."

"Already did. You need to buy you some computer rubbers, inoculate yo' computer so it don't get the clap. Ain't you never heard of safe sex?" Duty's arms snaked around her chest. "I tried to fix it, Miz

Zan, but everything I did made the picture disappear. You got a back-up generator on this thing?"

The skull and crossbones crumbled away to form new letters: I KNOW WHAT YOU DID AND . . .

Cézanne flew at the computer.

. . . YOU'LL NEVER GET AWAY WITH IT.

She jerked the connector to the battery pack, but it had fused so tight she needed a pry-tool to create a fulcrum.

"Ohgod."

The Kissel file.

"Duty, for God's sake, answer the damned phone."

The girl fled the room and put an end to the pealing chime. She crept back inside with the receiver pressed to her chest. "It's for you."

"Of course it's for me. Who else knows you're here? Gimme the damned thing. Hello?"

A woman with an engaging voice spoke. "Ms. Martin, this is Citibank —"

"Not interested. Take me off your call list."

"Don't hang up. I'm with Security."

The computer posted another X-rated suggestion and Cézanne shot it the finger. The message crumbled into a blank screen. Orgiastic sounds of whore-and-donkey copulation brayed over the speakers.

"I'm calling from our twenty-four-hour hotline. You aren't buying a mink in California with your Platinum Card, are you?"

"What?"

"Your credit card. When the amounts are this high, we verify. We started seeing some strange activity coming in earlier this evening. You didn't fly to San Diego from Botswana, did you?"

"What?"

"We're trained to keep an eye on suspicious purchases. Even though it's no one else's business whether you put a six-carat diamond and tanzanite solitaire on your credit card, it didn't seem possible to be in Africa the same time you were charging a pair of Peruvian llamas to your account."

"What?"

"Simultaneous purchases, Ms. Martin — if this really is Cézanne Martin." After a few seconds of dead air, the caller said, "I think we need to verify your identity. What's your mother's maiden name?"

"Rosen."

"No, that's not it."

"Of course that's it. What else could your records show?"

"We can't disclose that. It's a privacy issue."

"It's *my* card. *You* called *me*."

"We don't really know that, do we?

Please verify your address."

She did.

"Date of birth?"

She gave it.

"Please hold."

"Don't put me on hold."

Click-click.

Duty balled up a fist and forced it against one teary eye. "Miz Zan, you want I should bring you a chair? You shakin' all over, and yo' face look like my gramma Mablene, when she gnashed her teeth during that fatal heart attack."

"Get my purse. Somebody stole my credit card."

"Wasn't me." Duty hurried off mumbling a string of denials under her breath. "Don't be thinkin' it was me 'cause it wasn't. Maybe I story now and then, but I don't steal."

Cézanne was treated to an instrumental version of "Puttin' on the Ritz." At first, she thought it was Muzak piped through the telephone until she realized it was coming from the computer.

Duty returned as the caller came back on the line.

"You live in Fort Worth, right?" Long pause. "I don't get it. What on Earth would make you buy a set of snow tires in Minnesota?"

Duty dragged up a chair. As soon as the

wooden edge touched the back of Cézanne's leg, her knees melted.

"You don't mind if I put you on speaker-phone, do you? I need my hands free." Without waiting for permission, Cézanne punched the enhancement feature and thumbed through her badge case. She located the platinum card sandwiched between her police ID and permanent peace officer's license, and pulled it from her wallet. "There must be a mistake. My card's right here."

Then it hit her.

"Ohmygod. It's the computer virus. It found my credit card and passed it around the country. You've got to stop it."

"Do you speak Chinese?"

"What?" But she was thinking, *Sum ting wong. Ai so dum.*

"Chinese. The bill that just came in appears to be Chinese. Hang on a sec." Covering the mouthpiece. Muffled voices in the background. "Mr. Wong, is this Chinese? What's it say? I don't think she'd buy a full length fox when she just purchased a mink." Then loud and clear and full of doom, "Oh. A Volkswagen Fox. Uh-oh, I'm afraid your card's being used in the Orient."

Duty tuned up crying.

With her eyes bulging in their sockets, Cézanne yelled at the mike to the speaker phone. "For God's sake, do something."

"We could cancel your account?"

"Do it right now."

"Of course you'll be responsible for these purchases in that you don't have protection."

"What?"

"Credit card protection. Costs fifty bucks a year and it's worth it. Only you don't have it."

"See, Miz Zan, didn't I tell you to use protection?"

"Deuteronomy, bring my gun. I'm going to kill you now."

Duty squeezed her cornrows through her fingers, and hopped from one foot to the other. When she let go to dry her eyes, a couple of braids stuck up like antennae. "Miz Zan, you can't mean it. I didn't do it on purpose. I'd never hurt you."

The woman was talking again. "It sounds like the work of John Holmes."

"If you know who he is, why don't you arrest him? I'll press charges."

"John Holmes is the name of the virus. Actually, it's the ICUB4UC-Me virus, but here at the hotline, we call it John Holmes. It's awful big and reams you out really bad, and does a lot of damage. People are really getting screwed by it. The way it works is it replicates itself and attaches to every file you have until it detects a credit card number."

"What?"

A male with an Oriental accent yelled in the background. "Tell lady better get rid of before John Holmes go down on hard drive."

"Zip it, Wong. Anyway, we've been seeing a lot of this lately. It looks like somebody infected your computer. Personally, I'd take it into the shop before it ate all my files, if I were you."

The first thing Cézanne realized when she hung up was that she'd lost the data input from the Kissel case. But the thing that plagued her, long after Duty went to sleep, was something the girl said that got lost in the credit card melee.

I'd never hurt you, Miz Zan, Lord no. I come here to protect you.

Chapter Twenty-Seven

Sunday morning barely yawned when Cézanne struck out for Cleburne. Bobby Noah didn't answer his phone, but she suspected she could catch him at the Johnson County Sheriff's Office. In the SO parking lot, several brawny deputies clutching coffee mugs stepped out from under the awning to admire the Mercedes.

"Pop the hood," the biggest one said with such bluster she figured she'd just met the school bully. "Let's see that engine."

Anxious to find Bobby, she let them fawn over Ruby far longer than she planned, but it made them happy, and she never knew when she'd need a favor from a brother officer.

Bobby's father was having his coffee on the porch swing when Cézanne arrived at the home place. The old man whiffed her perfume and said, "I remember you."

Funny, a blind man bringing out her shy side.

"Hi, Mr. Noah. We've never been formally introduced. I'm Cézanne."

"My son calls you City Slicker."

"Is Bobby around?"

"Out back, tending a lame horse. Refuses to put her down, only I don't see any way around it. He's got some new-fangled idea, but what do I know? I only spent a lifetime on a farm. You ask me, he's got a mind set. Do me a favor?" He stuck out the empty mug. "Set this in the sink on your way in?"

She caught herself nodding as she took it, and wondered how much the man could actually see.

While she rinsed Pop's cup, Bobby walked in covered in mud and threw a pair of leather work gloves on the oak dining table. Discovering her in the kitchen arrested his breath.

"I couldn't get you on the phone." No response. "I'm sorry about last week." Her heart climbed into her throat, where it seemed to be stuck. Something about the way he looked at her made her want to confess the near-miss with Teddy. But she said, "Last night, I almost made a terrible mistake," and left it at that.

"Coffee?" He moved toward the cabinet, removed two Minton china cups, and caught her staring. "Mom's dishes, made in England. When it's just me and Pop, it seems sacrilegious to touch them. But Maggi Noah always made a fuss over company. You'd have liked her. She could spot a shallow person a mile away. You would've stacked up, though."

He missed his mama. She wished she could do something spontaneous, maybe give him a hug. She couldn't.

"When I was a squirt, she taught me to set a table. Showed me which side of the plate to put the forks on. Which way to face the knives." The crease in his forehead softened. He smiled as if he had suddenly been transported to a distant time where moms baked cookies, kissed skinned knees, and tucked little boys in after their prayers.

"How long has it been?"

"Twelve years. But it's something you never get over despite your age. It's different for Pop. Not that he doesn't miss her, but he's got lady friends who make a big to-do over him at church. It comes down to this: you can replace a husband or wife; you can't replace a parent." The hurt left his eyes and he turned back into the gallant host. "Hot chocolate? Spiced tea?"

"No."

He filled his cup with coffee and lightened it with cream, then set it on the counter without drinking it. "You here about that case?"

"Yes."

No. Not sure what I want. Please don't abandon me while I'm acting all crazy.

"I'm going for a shower." He strode across the living room. "You're welcome to

358

turn on the TV. We actually have cable here in Gnawbone."

She couldn't let him get away, not even for a few minutes. In an unsteady world, he kept her on an even keel. She crossed the room and crushed herself against him.

"Wait for me." And she wasn't just referring to the shower.

A few minutes before one, the old man rapped on the bedroom door. "Want some chow?"

Cézanne lifted her head from the crook of Bobby's arm, chagrined to see drool on his chest. He put a finger to his lips to quiet her. "Later."

"Can we get more wood in for the fire?"

"I'll take care of it."

The shuffle of house slippers receded. Bobby lifted a lock of her hair and pulled it through his fingers. She nuzzled closer and sensed him inhaling the fragrance of her shampoo.

"Why'd you come here, darlin'?"

"You're the only one I trust to tell me the truth."

"Truth's hard."

Beyond the window, snow flurries settled on fence posts and she knew, before long, she'd have to leave. She liked the rough hewn floors, vaulted ceilings, and three generations worth of antique furniture. The simple life these men led. And the way Bobby loved animals, and cared about doing right.

She took a deep breath and slowly released it. "How much should you compromise yourself in an undercover investigation?"

"As much as you need to without breaking the law — or sacrificing your integrity."

Chapter Twenty-Eight

Anyone living on the Westside of Cowtown knew it was only a matter of time before an SUV up-ended itself on the Lancaster Street Bridge. When Cézanne looked past the wrought iron railing, overheads from emergency vehicles flashed along the banks of the Trinity. Red, white, and blue strobes accentuated the black ribbon of water while the dive team prepared to go in.

She navigated her way over the ice-glazed asphalt, silently hoping there were no fatalities. In less than a month, the brass would tally the year-end totals for the first news issue of the new year. And anyone interested could check where Fort Worth ranked among the nation's most dangerous cities.

A few minutes before six, Cézanne zipped into the drive with an hour to spare. In that The Wild Orchid Society was bullish on punctuality, she hurried inside to ransack her closet for a suitable outfit. Instead, she encountered Duty midway down the hall with a towel wrapped around her head, carrying a basket of clothes.

"Did you do laundry?"

The girl's eyes strayed to the ceiling where she seemed to find so many of her answers. A pillowcase on top of the pile moved. The tip of Butch's docked tail caught Cézanne's rolling eye.

"Is that dog in the basket? Because if he is, you can turn around and do the wash over again."

"Butch don't feel so good. I'll be tending him in my room.."

"What's the matter with him?"

"I dunno."

Cézanne let loose an exasperated sigh. Fifty-five minutes and counting down. Whatever idiotic shenanigans Devilrow's niece had going on would have to wait. By the time she finished duct-taping the .22 to the small of her back and wrangling into a blue velvet skirt, she had less than thirty minutes. By the time she made up her face and slid into the black silk top with rose appliqués on organza sleeves, less than fifteen.

A few feet from Duty's room, she raised her voice. "I'm leaving." No response. She rapped on the door molding. "Duty, I'm leaving."

A shuffle of footsteps, and the door opened a sliver. A maroon orb peered out. "You talkin' to me?"

Cézanne relied on silence, coupled with a long stare, to convey her irritation. "I'm going out. If I'm not back by midnight, and

I don't check in so you know I'm okay —"

"I know. Call that constable. Jinx Porter." Duty slammed the door and toggled the lock.

Whatever was going on in that room would have to wait. With trepidation, Cézanne hurried to the cab, waiting in the drive.

Ten minutes to go.

The Wild Orchid Society welcomed their newest member in the same stand-offish manner they displayed the previous night. Cissy Kissel, dressed in a Camelot-inspired, cone-shaped headpiece with metallic streamers playing off the light like an explosion of bottle rockets, chatted in the corner with the Asian lady. The Executioner, if among the thirty or so people giving her blank stares, did not reveal himself.

A girl wearing a French maid costume handed her a crystal stem from a drink tray. "Club soda, right? Mistress Sicily makes me learn the drinks of choice of all her guests."

"Thanks, I'm not thirsty."

Her lip protruded. She cast a furtive glance in the widow's direction. "If Mistress Sicily thinks you're displeased, she'll take it out on me. Could you pretend to like it?"

"Nasty temper, huh?" Cézanne got an

ugly visual of the Great Dane's last moments. She took the glass and raised it.

Unexpectedly, the lights dimmed to pitch black.

The tinkle of piano keys faded out. For a brief moment, the room came to a standstill. Only the clatter of a deadbolt being thrown echoed through the room like the clang of a Death Row cell. The grand home's central heating unit shuddered, sending a rush of warm air through the vents. Heavy footsteps from some distant part of the ballroom put Cézanne even more on edge. High ceilings and poor acoustics made it impossible to tell the direction of their approach.

She caught a hint of Cissy's perfume. Sensed her closing in. Whispered, "Anybody there?" into the darkness.

"I'm so glad you made it." The Great Dane's widow found her hand. Cézanne flinched and her mouth went dry. "Darling, you're so uptight. Drink up. Lizette will bring you anything you like."

"I'm just nervous." And fidgety about Cissy's roaming fingers finding the .22. To appease her hostess, she drained the glass. "So what happens now?"

"The induction ceremony. Shhhh."

Across the room, a match hissed and a taper flared. Soon, the peach-colored flicker from thirty candles licked at their skin. Cézanne's hair prickled at the sight of their ghostly faces.

Her head seemed to swell as if someone aired it up with a bicycle pump. They were grinning. Shadows playing across their disembodied pumpkin heads, floating in the darkness, accentuated their jack-o-lantern teeth.

Behind them, a match hissed. Cézanne whipped around, unsteady on her feet. The odor of sulfur hung in her nostrils. The empty flute slipped from her fingers, pinging against the floor. A few feet away, above the flicker of the match, two onyx beads, perfectly balanced, floated in mid-air.

The startling chill of pure evil snared her in its grip.

The Executioner.

"Good evening. We've been waiting for you."

At first, Cézanne thought she had died.

Died and resurrected, flat on a marble slab like the one in Krivnek's morgue. Skull-like faces hovered over her. Celtic strains echoed through the room. Disembodied heads faded into the abyss.

She lay inert, unable to move. Closing her eyes helped her concentrate.

Number One Madrid Lane.

Club soda.

The Wild Orchid Society.

They're onto me.

Someone pried her eyelids open.

Cissy Kissel bent over her, her face distorted and sagging from gravity's pull, her hair billowing in long, loose curls.

Cézanne's lids fell to half-mast.

Near her ear, a twig-like snap, then something foul shoved under her nose. Her eyes opened wide as the room spun out of control.

"She's ready."

Reflections of creamy candlelight lapped at the ceiling like a hundred ravenous tongues. Collective voices droned, unintelligible and hypnotic, invading her mind and dulling her wit. A cardinal rule of police work took shape in her head.

Don't come home with more holes than you left with.

For a second, she imagined claws shredding her skin. A tongue darted out and flicked her neck, then her ear, while someone whispered seductive insults into her hair.

The last thing she remembered, before shutting her lids tight, was The Executioner, his eyes icy and piercing through the hood, his naked body oiled to a fine luster, climbing up beside her to the mystical chant of The Wild Orchid Society.

"Blindfold her."

Cézanne detected something familiar in his voice.

"And when you finish blindfolding her, pull this friggin' tow sack off my head so I can see what I'm doing."

"No blindfold." Cissy. "Let her watch."

"Why?"

"Because it'll make it worse."

She closed her eyes and saw black, then felt excruciating pain that hurt so bad it made her eyelids snap open. And then . . .

. . . thunderous applause.

Chapter Twenty-Nine

Cézanne knew exactly where she was as soon as she opened her eyes.

"Feel better?"

She lifted her head up off the filth-encrusted seat and blinked the cab driver into focus. Mid-fifties, five o'clock shadow, with a watch cap covering his ears and a drab down-filled vest layered over a plaid flannel shirt.

"They said you tied one on, but you seem okay now. The guy only gave me a hundred bucks to drive around 'til you sobered up. You ready to head home? The meter's nearly tapped out."

"Home?" Every muscle ached. Her joints begged for mercy. As soon as she pushed herself to an upright position, her left breast throbbed. And when she gingerly touched the skin at the base of her neck, her touch stung with a jalapeño burn.

They passed the Union Gospel Mission — a bad sign — in a rough part of town.

Her heart rattled in its cage. "How'd I get here?"

"They didn't want you arrested for DWI."

Her head pulsed. She tried looking out the window and quickly found that the slightest movement left her dizzy. "Who didn't want me to get a DWI?"

"The couple that found you outside the homeless shelter."

"Homeless shelter?"

"Yep. I didn't think you belonged there either, but that's where they found you. Passed out on a bus bench."

Her belly button itched and she lowered her velvet skirt enough to scratch. Her fingers came away dark and sticky. The sensory overload was too much. She collapsed against the seat back, melting into the smelly vinyl. "Bus bench?"

"Yep. Buses stopped running at ten. Don't start up again 'til daylight. If you don't mind my saying, you shouldn't be out in this part of town after midnight without a gun."

She had one. She slapped the small of her back.

God Almighty.

They'd swiped her pistol. Panic set in.

"My wife and I, we got a youngster about your age. Goes to Texas Christian. Majors in radio, TV, and film. You ready to go home? Meter's coming up on an even hundred. Where do you live? They said when you sobered up to ask you where you lived."

"I live at —"

Instinct kept her from telling.

His eyes cut to the rearview mirror. "I'm a nice guy so I'm gonna see you get home even though the fare's gone over. No charge. But you've gotta tell me."

She scanned the streets in an effort to get her visual bearings. The sign read Main and the cross street, Fourth. They were Downtown, a couple of blocks from the PD.

"Take me to The Worthington." She could change cabs there. Make it harder for The Wild Orchid Society to track her.

"Nice place, The Worthington." He rounded the corner and her head spun out of control.

"Stop the cab."

"But you said —"

"Stop." Her vision blurred.

It didn't really matter that he put on the brakes. She was already grappling for the door handle.

The taxi screeched to a halt. She threw open the door in time to vomit on the curb. When she regained her equilibrium, she sat up in the seat, watery-eyed, with her surroundings pulsing like a zoom lens moving in and out of focus.

"You want I should take you to the hospital? My daughter who goes to TCU? Every year kids die in hazing accidents, drinking. I'd want somebody to

370

drive her to the hospital —"

"Lemme out."

He must have realized he couldn't talk her out of it because he shrugged and dropped the car into gear. By the time he pulled away, she propped herself, wobbly-legged, against the window ledge of a storefront. When his taillights dwindled to the size of Red Hots, she sat on the narrow sill. She tried to get her bearings, but her nose wrinkled at the stench of rotted produce tossed into an alley Dumpster by a popular restaurant. For the next few minutes, she tasted sour bile and gulped in great intakes of air. When her stomach calmed, she covered her nose in self-defense.

By the time she reached the hotel, her shoes had rubbed blisters on her heels. As she made her way up to the counter, she glanced through the glass and quickly turned her back. The cab driver who picked her up on the Eastside rolled by at turtle speed with his neck stretched out like a giraffe.

After a brief exchange with the concierge, who suggested her presence might be more suited to the lobby of the No-Tell motel, she revealed she was a police captain on decoy assignment and suggested he might be more comfortable seeking employment in the telemarketing field. When he didn't believe the decoy story, she agreed to ply her trade elsewhere in exchange for a phone call.

Duty picked up on the first ring. "Lordy mercy, Miz Zan, I thought you died. And that Mista Porter, he don't answer."

"Listen carefully." She turned her back to the hotel staff and cupped a hand to the mouthpiece. "Do you have a driver's license?"

"You want me to drive Ruby? I can do it."

"Can you handle a stick shift?"

"Stick shift?"

"It's like an 'H.' Start at the top of the 'H' — that's first gear — and push the clutch in each time you shift."

"What's a clutch?"

Duty's question cleared her head like a face dashed with ice water. It was crazy — turning Ruby over to the girl — and she as much as said so. "Never mind, forget it. In the bookcase, there's a book, Tom Sawyer. Only it's not really a book."

"I found it, dusting. You had a lotta money in that box."

"You went into my petty cash?"

"Had to tip the delivery man for the groceries."

"We'll discuss it later. Is there anything left?"

"Thirty-seven dollars and four cents.

Whatchoo need with four cents, Miz Zan? You can't buy nothin' with four cents."

"Get it. Call a cab and have them drive you down to The Worthington Hotel. We'll ride back together."

"Don't hotels have taxi cabs? You can't catch no taxi cab where yo' at?"

She didn't like to think she'd become like the rest of The Blue, guys from the old school who ended up paranoid as all get-out by the time they retired. But if The Wild Orchid Society dropped her off in the scummiest part of town and hired a hack to drive her home, they could find out where she lived. And even if the cabbie let her off near The Worthington, he could have colleagues who'd spill their guts for cigarette money.

No, it was Ruby or nothing.

"Miz Zan? You there?"

"Just mind me, and do exactly what I say. I'll meet you outside. And Duty —" her voice caught in her throat "— hurry."

Under the portico of Fort Worth's toniest hotel, Cézanne shivered in the early morning chill. While uniformed bellhops unloaded luggage and valets parked luxury cars, she ducked behind a cement column and watched her cab driver, with his eyes in a squint, make the block again.

Drive me home, my ass.

373

Fifteen minutes after Duty should've arrived, Cézanne began to pick at her cuticles. Another fifteen minutes, and she gnawed three fingernails down to the quick.

Down the street, tires squealed against the blacktop. Ruby lurched into view and bucked up the crescent-shaped drive. Ugly noises came from under the hood. Duty, wrapped in her best cashmere coat, scrambled out of the car and waited by the driver's door.

Cézanne sprinted to the car. "What've you done to Ruby? And what took so long?"

"I had to get on the Internet. I was talkin' to this trucker — he say lotta people don't even have to know what a clutch is. He say I can shift without it if I listen to the engine whine. First couple of miles, Ruby didn't much care for my drivin'. I'm pretty good now."

"Ohmygod, you stripped the gears."

"I didn't peel nothin' off."

"Grind. Grind the gears."

"So that's what's makin' that growlin' noise — gears?"

Cézanne didn't remember most of the rest of what she said, except that it wasn't nice and probably would be considered abusive by Child Protective Services.

It dawned on her she must have gotten

loud. A security guard raised a two-way radio to his lips while trotting their way.

"Quick, get in."

"Can I drive?"

"No." It wasn't until they were well on their way, that Cézanne noticed Duty still had on her pajamas. "You're not dressed."

"You said hurry. When I ran outside, a car motored by so I went back inside."

"What car?"

"The one waitin' down the street. The man with the spyglass."

Garlon Harrier. Son of a bitch should've bottomed out at the hairpin turn. With any luck, the dropoff would've bent the frame.

"What kind of car?"

"I dunno. I was almost in the house."

On the drive home, the pit in Cézanne's stomach widened into a canyon full of battery acid. She swallowed hard, but not hard enough to dull the feeling.

Duty kept quiet, but once inside the bungalow, she tore through each room, closing blinds and pulling drapes. When she came back into the living room, she gasped.

"Lordy, what happened? Whatchoo not sayin'?" She moved close enough for her skinny fingers to glance off the silk voile sleeve.

Wincing, Cézanne stretched to look.

"Miz Zan, they's ugly, just plain ugly.

What kind of dudes you know, would do such evil? And you got cuts on yo' chest —" she shuddered "— I seen the same thing on my brother 'Zekial's baby after his girlfriend abandoned that child in the Dumpster. They's rat bites."

Cézanne's blood pressure spiked.

Doug Driskoll.

Doug had a thing for rodents. Was he The Executioner? She dismissed the idea immediately, convinced she would've recognized his voice.

"Deuteronomy, stop staring. I'll be fine." But the girl's eyes misted, and she appeared unconvinced. Cézanne put on her game face. "Can you help with this zipper? I want to get out of these clothes."

What she really wanted was to shower until the hot water ran out.

Seeing Duty visibly shaken, she tried a different approach in an effort to lighten the mood. As the teenager unfastened the hook and eye at the back of her blouse and ran the zipper down its track, Cézanne injected cheer into her voice.

"Tell me more about your family. Are you the youngest?"

"I have a little brother. He's five."

"What's his name?" As soon as she spoke, she wished she'd bitten her tongue.

"Two Peter. It's nize to see you smile, Miz Zan, even though you laugh at me."

After wrangling into a bathrobe, Cézanne returned to find Duty sitting erect on the couch, protectively hugging the Scottie.

"Miz Zan, why you not trust me? I live here now. How come you don't say whatchoo doin'? Me and Butch, we're scared." She ended the word with a "T."

"I can't tell you about my job. But you shouldn't worry. As long as I'm here, you're safe."

A tear bubbled over and rolled down Duty's cheek. The dog strained to break free.

"And that mutt — don't worry about him, either."

"It's got nothin' to do with Butch, Miz Zan. It's about you. I got a bad feelin'. Frieda says so, too." She broke into sobs.

Cézanne stood helpless in the hallway, wanting some way to dry the poor girl's eyes without physical contact. A lump rose in her throat. Sometimes compassion did that — made her say stupid stuff like she was about to say. "I'm not calling CPS on you, if that's what you're bawling about. You can stay until that shiftless con-man, Leviticus Devilrow, comes back."

But Duty was inconsolable. "I don't care about that no more. I'm scared of the man in the yard. The one who came tonight with a package. Only Miz Zan, I swear to the Lord —" her cries crescendoed into a coyote howl "— I didn't order nothin' off the Internet. I thought it was you buyin' me something nize for Christmas. I let him in, Miz Zan. I didn't know no better."

The announcement took her wind. "You let a stranger into my house?"

Obviously overcome, Duty barely nodded. Cézanne glanced around in a frantic attempt to discern anything out of place.

"Was he by himself? Did he take anything?"

"Wore a delivery uniform but he didn't have no van. He didn't take nothin', just come in, looked around. That marble statue you got by the fireplace, he say that's nize, you got good taste. I went in my room to get me a stick — he was leavin' when I come out."

Wild thoughts rampaged through her head. The concept of an intruder left a pit in her stomach. "This package . . . did you open it?"

"No, ma'am." Round-eyed and emphatic.

"How big is it?" In her mind, she measured the size of three sticks of dynamite and an egg timer, but what Duty said made her blood pressure drop into the danger zone.

" 'Bout like a videotape."

By the time Cézanne got the distraught

teenager in bed for the night, she screwed up her courage and hoped for a bomb. At least, that way, EOD could detonate it. Blow it to smithereens. Or bring in one of their high tech gadgets. That squatty little seeing-eye, hearing-ear robot. What was its name? Edgar?

Endless possibilities collided like meteors inside the galaxy of her head. She un-hooked the VCR from the TV set in the den, carried it to the bedroom, and recon-nected it. Rifling through the bathroom cabinet, she ran across a pair of latex gloves left over from an aborted attempt to highlight her hair. Working her fingers into each sleeve, she took great care not to con-taminate the brown paper wrap.

This was evidence.

Slash could ninhydrin it for prints.

With any luck, he might find a good la-tent on the Scotch tape. Hell — the guy was probably good enough to lift a tented arch off the smooth skin of somebody's inner thigh.

She slipped the videotape into the slot, then bolted the door. With the remote clutched in her hand, she sank against the edge of the bed and hit the play button. Her heart thudded so hard it almost eclipsed the pain in her throbbing joints.

The tape scraped against the VCR heads; a hiss filtered through the speakers. Flecks of white danced across a black screen. Then deep breaths fell into rhythm with her pounding chest.

And there it was.

The whole sordid evening caught on film, complete with close-ups of her slack-jawed face and tight shots of places that should've stayed covered. She convinced herself she'd seen the worst when the camera cut away to a human shape, heating the tip of what appeared to be a skewer, in the flame of a candle. Muted voices buzzed in the background. The lens traveled over her gleaming torso. Her image writhed against the marble until the eye of the camera closed-in on her open mouth, to the sweat glistening above her upper lip.

Her body responded with a series of shockwaves. On some level, she liked whatever was happening beyond range of the camera. The profile of a hatchet-faced man entered her film debut long enough to bite her, and his cameo appearance got two thumbs up from the spectators. A dainty hand, sporting a huge diamond, smoothed back her hair, and held it.

Then came the madness.

The sizzle of searing flesh, followed by the skewer's red hot tip disappearing from the screen. At once, the desire for a shower took a distant second.

She wanted to vomit.

Cézanne hit the stop button. Dropped the remote. Broke for the door. In the bathroom, she grabbed a hand mirror to check her reflection against the mirror on the medicine cabinet. No wonder her neck burned. Sweeping her hair back exposed angry, raw skin. Unmistakable lines plumped up in the shape of flower petals.

By scarring her, they tried to make her one of them.

The acting Captain of Fort Worth's Homicide Unit wore the brand of The Wild Orchid Society.

Chapter Thirty

In an enclave called Berkeley, where brick bungalows built in the twenties and thirties lined the streets a few miles south of Downtown, one impressive two-story Tudor stood out from the rest. Barely able to keep warm in her sweat pants and Longhorn pullover, Cézanne paced along the sidewalk out front until a series of lights came on inside. They started in the upstairs corner, and illuminated three leaded glass windows staggered along the curvature of the stairs. The front porch fixture flickered on and the door opened wide.

Marvin Krivnek, in striped pajamas, with his hair sticking up like he survived electrocution, stood barefoot on the tiled floor of the foyer.

His expression was uninvitingly blank. "This better be good."

"I need you to draw my blood."

"I go to work in three hours." Pissed. "The ER's open all night."

Without pausing for air, she caught him up to speed with a breathless, run-on sentence. "You're the only one I trust to do it; if I went there, they'd make a report; I can't tell you what's happened but I can tell you I don't have a lot of time — you're it — please, you have to help me."

Starting at his forehead, Krivnek rubbed his hands down his face and worked his eyes over until she thought he'd formed a deliberate plan to gouge them out to keep from dealing with her. His broad, Silly Putty nose rebounded from a quick swipe and sprang back into place.

"Explain yourself."

"Please don't ask."

"You've got a screw loose."

"When this is all over, I'm going into therapy." A lie. She pulled at her sleeve until it rode up over the elbow.

Krivnek shook his head. "We'll do it at my office."

"We can take my car."

She had already turned her back on him when he said, "Good night." The door clicked shut. She whipped around, grabbed the handle, and flung herself back inside before he could throw the deadbolt. His eyebrows peaked like a bald-face lie on a polygraph printout.

"We have to go now." Her hand closed firmly on his wrist and she tightened her fingers in vise grip until she saw a flicker of pain.

"I'm in my night clothes." Incredulous.

"Time is of the essence." Her voice

pierced the air with such urgency Krivnek reared back his head. But he did follow without her having to put him in a come-along by jamming a ballpoint pen behind his earlobe.

Halfway down the sidewalk, he planted his feet against the bricks and cinched his robe. "I hope you brought your gun."

"The only time I don't have one with me is when I shower."

"Good." He seemed genuinely relieved. "If anybody sees me dressed this way, I'll tell them you held it to my head."

Krivnek didn't ask questions, just sat her down on a metal stool in the lab, and located a syringe. He set it on a tray long enough to stretch a rubber tourniquet tight around her arm.

"Make a fist. Now hold it." He positioned her arm where he could probe the crook until a vein plumped up like a garden hose. "That's good. You'll feel a little pinch. Try not to move."

"You get one shot, Krivnek." She found a spot on the wall and tried not to think about him, poised to puncture. "If you don't hit it the first time, don't dig."

"I never got any complaints."

"You work with dead people."

She took a quick breath and held it. By the time she scrunched her eyes and felt the sting, it was over. He capped the glass vial with a rubber stopper, labeled it with a stick-on tag, and thrust it toward her. Merely glancing at the crimson tube gave her a dizzy rush.

"Keep it."

"What shall I do with it?"

"Test it."

"For what?"

"Whatever."

Stoop-shouldered, Krivnek backed his haunches up to the edge of the counter and delivered his words in carefully measured sound bytes. "Captain Martin, if you expect me to run this through the gas chromatograph, mass spectrometer, you're in for a big disappointment."

"Why?"

"It's not like making a selection from a soda machine. You don't just plug in a sample and have it spit out the answer; the machine's not that refined. If you believe you've been drugged or poisoned, I need to know what elements to test for. The possibilities are —"

"GHB."

"— endless."

"I want you to test for traces of GHB." Gamma hydroxybutyrate. Heap bad shit.

"The date rape drug," Krivnek said flatly.

They kept their places, locked in the energy of each other's unwavering stares. The irritation that had creased his face since her arrival on his stoop evaporated.

"You should go to the ER for further testing," he said gently, but she was already shaking her head. "I could take some swabs if you like, but it might create evidence problems when it comes time to prosecute."

"No, but thanks. Just do the blood test and give me the results."

"You know who did this, don't you?"

She kept her face carefully blank. After several uncomfortable seconds, Krivnek padded off down the hall.

She trotted after him. "I need another favor." He shot her a wicked glare and kept walking. Cézanne said, "You have a camera here, right?"

Krivnek blinked. "In there." He stopped at the double doors and jerked his chin in the direction of the autopsy room.

"I need a picture."

"Of what?"

He was pissed now, and not afraid to show it. Without going into a play by play, Cézanne edged over and twisted the lock on the door. Without fanfare, she crossed the room and stopped a few feet in front of the Assistant ME, peeled the sweatshirt off overhead and stood bare breasted.

Krivnek's reaction came in the form of a

low whistle. "Jeepers creepers."

She understood his reluctance to take a closer look. If he hadn't been a medical doctor, if he'd peered out through those watery, myopic blue eyes in any other way than to view her as a case study, it would have mortified her to feel his touch. But he cupped her breast in his hand and gently skimmed the angry indigo bruise with his thumb.

"Stay put. I'll get the camera."

"No, I'll get it. You start the test. I don't want any breaks in the chain of custody." His breath warmed her skin and she directed his attention to a series of marks along her collarbone. "Are they rat bites?"

"If you're asking whether you need rabies shots, the answer's no." She was almost relieved until the ME said, "Somebody used a stun gun on you."

She let Doug Driskoll off the mental meat hook.

A ringing phone from a distant office pierced the quiet. Krivnek checked the time on the wall clock. Three-thirty. He excused himself and exited a side door, but not before the answering machine picked up. Over the hiss of the pneumatic hinge, she heard the message loud and clear.

"Letting you know, Marv, Quinten Carrol made the list. Died about an hour ago. Call us back when you get this message."

The loss of a brother officer sickened her as much as the horrific images her mind conjured up the moment she shut off the unfinished videotape. But that didn't keep Cézanne from thinking straight.

Now, she had a way to get Harrier off her back. A good-faith gesture of cooperation.

Let Harrier scoop the competition.

Get that syndicated TV show he had a hard-on for.

After the uneventful ride back to Krivnek's house, she read off the phone number she copied onto her palm at the ME's, and punched it out on the keypad of her cellular. The phone purred in her ear.

A lilting voice answered, "Newsroom," but when Cézanne asked for Harrier, the chipper inflection went flat. "Who's calling?"

"Captain Cézanne Martin, Fort Worth Homicide. Is Harrier there, or not?"

A long pause, and then the ominous reply, "I'll put you through to the station manager."

The phone clicked and bad music came through. For a few brief moments, she found herself orbiting in the ether of tele-communications. Another click, and a hostile male baritone spoke.

"You the one calling about Harrier?"

"Yes."

"Where'd you find him?"

"I didn't find him. I'm looking for him."

"You mean he's not dead?"

"My sentiments exactly." But the man on the other end of the line didn't chuckle. She said, "I called to give him a lead."

"So he's not dead?"

"Not that I know of. You mean he isn't there?"

"If he was, would I be asking if he was dead?"

"You might if you killed him."

She pegged him as a hard-drinking, meaty man with a thousand broken capillaries beneath his crimson cheeks and bulbous nose. The type whose extracurricular activities in high school included playing the tuba and receiving an occasional blue ribbon from the bowling club.

He said, "What do you want with Harrier? For that matter, what does anyone want with Harrier?"

"I've got a story."

"Give it to me." As if Harrier wasn't coming back.

"Does Mr. Harrier still work there?"

"Not when I get through with him. He'll wish he was dead. Hey, I got an idea; why don't I call you then?" Sarcastic.

"I don't understand."

With a terrible intensity, Harrier's boss said, "Don't you flatfoots ever communicate with each other? We filed a report with Missing Persons Saturday morning when the jerk didn't show up for work. I sent a man to the house, but he didn't answer the knock and the car's gone. I thought you called to say you found him. I've got a business to run, and if that asshole's not here by tomorrow, he'd better be dead or held for ransom."

Her thoughts skipped to Friday night, to the car chase at Reno's.

Reno must've been mistaken about the depth of that dropoff. Especially when it had rained off and on for three weeks.

She knew where to find the pesky reporter.

And his car.

Garlon Harrier was at the bottom of Lake Worth.

Chapter Thirty-One

Cézanne stood on the short expanse of gravel in front of Reno's single-wide and studied the pale yellow glow through the window sheers for signs of movement. The stripper didn't answer the knock at the door. And Cézanne didn't get a response from the wireless call she placed, either. But the Yugo was parked in the drive like an incurable skin lesion, so it didn't take long to deduce the exotic dancer didn't want company if she was home. And why should she? Cézanne checked her watch.

Five-thirty.

She returned to the Kompressor and drove to the end of the J-curve. Soon, dawn would break.

She imagined the grimaces that would appear on the faces of the dive team when they got the call to come out in freezing weather. The ghoulish sight of Harrier, still seat-belted behind the wheel of his auto, his skin a pale gray and in an advanced state of decomposition, played out in her mind's eye. A violent shudder went up her arms, and she turned Ruby's heater up as high as it would go.

Experience had taught her the worst bodies were floaters. If a corpse stayed in the water too long, its removal became an art form. Once, she watched alongside Roby Tyson while a member of the Swift Water Rescue Team disentangled what used to be the high school halfback from a mass of submerged tree limbs at Eagle Mountain Lake. Half back, half an arm, half a leg. Each time the diver exerted too many foot-pounds per square inch, a body part came off in his hand.

Remembering turned her stomach.

The tip of her nose finally thawed and she lowered the heat. She reached for the wireless and tapped out nine-one-one.

In her heart, she knew they were in danger — herself, Duty, and anyone else she might come in close contact with. With the icy chill whipping across the lake, she came to a decision.

From now on, if they couldn't locate that con-wise reprobate Leviticus Devilrow, Duty would be safer out of the house. Bottom line: wherever she went, Duty would have to tag along.

Dear God, keep me from having to commit a felony watching over this kid.

Chapter Thirty-Two

Bright and early Monday morning, while everybody else straggled in sleepy-eyed, Greta Carr bustled around her desk. Decked out in a hot pink poodle skirt and saddle oxfords, she could have been waiting on her date to take her to the hop. Red rhinestone glasses hung around her neck by a chain and rested against the angora sweater stretched tight across her oversized bosom. She hooked her short, gray-brown hair back over her pixy ears until they looked like a head vase with calla lilies sprouting out of the side. Enveloped in the vapors of yesterday's perfume, her very presence constituted an assault on three of the five senses.

"It's for a fifties party," she said, as if anyone actually expected her to come up with an excuse for the freakish getup.

They did not. But Duty couldn't keep her eyes off the tufted yarn making up the shock of pink poodle hair and she ventured forth in order to graze her fingers over it.

"The secretaries are having a luncheon today and it's a fifties theme," Greta sing-songed.

With the slur of a drunken barfly, Duty

said, "You mean like Elvis?"

"Yes, except we're not celebrating Elvis. Not many of us got flowers on Secretary's Day and this is our way of doing something nice for ourselves."

"Did you make yo' skirt? How you make that dog look like that? Izzat real dog hair? You got a dog? I got one. His real name's Butch but I call him Buttercup when nobody's home 'cause his hair's real light. Can I have yo' skirt when you get done with it?"

Cézanne interrupted. "Duty, wait inside my office. Greta, get on the phone and order a nice spray of flowers. Have them sign the sympathy card and send it to Quinten Carrol's widow." That took the flounce out of her poodle skirt. "And I need some electrician's tape."

The secretary fished a spool of black tape out of her top drawer. She tore off a piece long enough for Cézanne to wrap, horizontally, around her gold badge, in the traditional sign of mourning.

"When the guys come in, see that they get some."

Greta's jaw dropped.

"Tape, Greta, not sex. Black tape. Are you hanging out with Sid now?"

"I didn't hear anything on the radio," Greta whined, as if the absence of news made it proof positive that the tragic event hadn't occurred.

"It hasn't been released."

Cézanne created a space on the credenza where Duty could draw. Without offering to catch the bleating telephone lines, she hung her cashmere coat on Crane's coat tree, then peeled off her driving gloves and popped them into a drawer. Flopping into her chair, she thumbed through six pink message slips she'd picked up off Greta's desk. The one of greatest interest regarded Gentle Bison.

"Miz Zan, you think I could get me a skirt like that girl?"

"That so-called girl as you call her, was old when the first redwood was nothing but a twig. She probably kept that as a souvenir from high school."

"If you was to buy me some fabric, I could cut Butch's hair, maybe make me a skirt with Butch on it. My gramma Mablene, she showed me how to sew once."

"Listen carefully. If you don't want me to call CPS, you'll sit quietly while I try to think."

Duty's face split into a grin so big her eyes crinkled into dashes. "You don't mean it. You a lotta big talk."

Cézanne craned her neck for a peek into the outer office. "Greta, come in here. What's this?"

The self-ordained office manager bebopped in with a handheld police radio balanced against one breast while she swapped out the battery pack.

"What's what?"

"This message from IA about Benji Wardancer."

"Oh, that." She feigned distress but deep down, Cézanne knew she could hardly contain her excitement. "Well, Friday, you told Benji if he didn't come in —"

"Yeah?"

"— you'd transfer him; okay, so he tried to work on things with his wife, but this time she stabbed him in the crotch with a pair of scissors —"

When will it all end?

Cézanne propped her elbows on the desk and rested her forehead against her palms.

"— and the first time, she missed his neck, and got him in the head —"

Jeez.

"— but the second time, she got him in the crotch —"

Duty chimed in. "She chopped off his stones?"

Cézanne held up a hand to stop the run-on madness. "Hit the high spots. Is he alive?"

"Oh, sure. You know how Benji is. Tough as a cob. He just can't reproduce."

"Lordy Mercy."

Cézanne glared Duty into submission.

"So what does IA want me to do?"

"They opened an investigation and said not to expect him back until further notice."

Great. And she couldn't do a cotton-picking thing about it since it wasn't his fault.

Apparently Greta wanted some time off, too. She started in about her mother needing dialysis when Sid walked in.

"Dallas? I hate Dallas." He let his brief-case drop onto the chair. "Howdy, Duty."

"Mista Sid." She batted her lashes and coyly averted her eyes.

"You're excused, Greta. Come in, Sid, and close the door."

He was already talking, dragging a chair over by the window, his hair slicked back and still drying from his shower, his face full of color and his eyes twinkling. Looking natty in a dark olive silk suit and lighter shade shirt. On this day he wore a tie silk-screened with fingerprints.

Cool.

Too bad she hated him.

"Duty, why don't you go help Miss Carr?"

"Who that?"

"Poodle Woman."

With a giddy skip, the teenager was gone.

Nestled into his chair, Sid grinned big. "You ain't gonna believe what I found, combing through the newspaper archives. And by the way, may I say it takes a special kind of woman to wear a fitted red suit, knowing I'm around? Who put the snap in your garter? You play a little strip poker this weekend?" He gave her a look that needed suspenders.

"We've got a crisis. Wardancer's out. You can get the particulars from Greta. She'll derive great pleasure relating every gory detail until you're writhing in your seat. But the bottom line is, I'm putting you on the Quinten Carrol shooting."

That he didn't flinch, disappointed her.

"Well, little missy, I'll get right on it. I stopped by the hospital, and it looks like the boy's gonna get out of ICU today."

"Out of intensive care and straight into the morgue."

Sid's eyebrow corkscrewed into a question mark. "What?"

"Quinten Carrol died early this morning."

"When?"

"Does it matter?" But she could see from his reaction that it did. "In the wee hours."

"Who told you that?"

"A reliable source."

"Well, I wouldn't rely too heavy on this reliable source of yours. I just left Quinten Carrol a half hour ago, sitting up, drooling oatmeal out of the side of his mouth. So unless he died since I left, I'd say your reliable source ain't so reliable."

The last time Cézanne found herself in IA, the lieutenant had stripped her of her badge and gun. What made the memory even creepier was that their punishment left her with nothing but her wits to fend off a killer fifteen minutes later.

This time, she appeared on Wardancer's behalf. And the chair they offered wasn't the traditional hot seat, but a nice leather armchair with nail head trim. Even though the videotape confession the lieutenant slipped into the VCR starred the Apache's wife, leftover images of Cézanne's induction into The Wild Orchid Society nagged her conscience.

Shouldn't have left the house without finishing that tape. Freaked out when they branded the orchid into my neck.

She eased her hand up to her hairline and touched the Band-Aid. The lieutenant pressed the on button and sat on the edge of his desk with his arms folded across his chest. Snow popped up on the TV screen and quickly disappeared.

Sheila O'Riorden Wardancer sat at the gunmetal grey table across from a family violence detective, still wearing the red and black negligée she had on when the uniforms took her into custody. Dabbing her eyes with a tissue, she recounted a variety of practical jokes Benji played on her during their one-year marriage. It started, she said, with a rubber snake Jock Featherston loaned him. He coiled it to tumble from the refrigerator the moment the door opened. She lifted one satin slippered foot to show the detective the scar left by the wine bottle that fell out with it.

Then she showed him the scar from the third-degree burn on her shin, the one she got unhanding a dishful of King Ranch casserole, straight from the oven, when Benji sneaked up from behind and goosed her.

She asked for a cigarette and the detective denied her. "Non-smoking ordinance," he said, grimly sympathetic.

Sheila Wardancer had more to tell.

A few weeks before, around the time Carri Crane bought the farm, Benji left instructions that she make doubly sure she locked the doors whenever he left for work. The PD had a black suspect in the Lady Godiva Murder, he'd said. A rapist, and real bad dude — and the uniforms last sighted him on the fringe of the Wardancers' neighborhood.

Cézanne paused the remote control and turned to the lieutenant. "We never had a black suspect in that case. From the get-go, everyone thought Roby Tyson did it. Except for me."

"You're quite the walking lie detector, aren't you?" the lieutenant deadpanned. "Keep watching."

The stink of IA came back to haunt her.

She engaged the remote, and Benji's wife gave a mind-numbing recollection of life with the Apache.

"Last night, he said he had to work. I'm a bingo caller, so I work evenings. When I got home, I was real tired, so I took a Trazadone and went to bed. Benji came in and kissed me goodbye. I didn't even hear the door shut, I was so out of it."

"You were asleep?" The detective.

"Pretty much. I don't remember anything else, until the black man broke in." She stopped talking long enough to sob into the tissue. When it disintegrated in her hand, she asked for another, and the detective shoved the entire box her way. "Next thing I remember, he pulled my hair. My head came up off the pillow so hard it closed my throat. My eyes snapped open, but the room was so dark I couldn't make anything out. Everything happened real fast. He put his lips against my ear and growled, 'Gimme some, bitch.'"

She doubled over with her face in her hands and wailed. The detective studied her, stone-faced.

For a few anxious moments, she writhed against the table, then sat bolt upright.

401

"You don't know how scared I was. When Benji first told me a rapist was loose, I hid a pair of Fiskars under my pillow."

"Fiskars?"

"Scissors. Real sharp ones." Wardancer's wife sniffled. "I grabbed the Fiskars and stabbed him. He screamed and let go and that's when I sat up and stabbed him again."

"Your husband."

Sheila Wardancer wailed. "I didn't know it was him. Don't you see? He said it like a black man. 'Gimme some, bitch.' All I did was protect myself."

Her arms thrashed about in a wild gesture of explanation, until her left breast escaped the slinky fabric. Without telling the distraught woman her headlights were flashing, the investigator stared, mesmerized, while Sheila Wardancer gave graphic details of her husband's near-vasectomy and possible scalping.

Cézanne stopped the tape. "I've seen enough. Don't charge her until I've had a chance to talk to my detective."

But the lieutenant made no promises. "He's in interrogation as we speak. Rosen's considering filing charges against Wardancer, too."

"Why charge Benji? If stupidity was a crime, the department would have less than five people running it."

The lieutenant didn't appreciate the sarcasm and it showed in his face. "Look, Captain, it's enough that you know Rosen doesn't want you talking to the guy unless you read him his Garrity rights."

Paranoia struck. The sweet scent of pipe tobacco from the lieutenant's bulging pocket filled her nostrils and made her stomach somersault. The walls of IA seemed to close in, the way they always did whenever she stopped by.

Rosen would get to Benji Wardancer. Would make him a deal like Sid's. Rosen would strongarm the Apache into spying.

She said, "I won't foul up your investigation. But I have an office to run and this guy has cases to solve."

With her sleeves ringed in sweat, she left IA with the lieutenant scrambling for the telephone. He was phoning Rosen, of that she was sure.

Back in Homicide, she took a visual inventory. Nothing had improved. Teddy hadn't checked in and Greta was trying to raise him by radio. Drew Ingleside's desk had paperwork oozing out like molten lava. Wardancer's in-basket sat empty, and Jock Featherston was leaning against a north window with the phone growing out of his ear, checking the sky with the dedication of an air traffic controller.

She searched her desk for the Garrity

warning and found one, laminated, in Crane's folder of disciplinary material. In law enforcement, reading a cop his Miranda rights was no longer enough. Garrity provided for an administrative warning as well.

Sid sat quietly while she retrieved it.

Cézanne said, "I don't know what's in store for Wardancer. Take Featherston and see if you can get a statement from Quinten Carrol. Matter of fact, take the video camera with you. That way whenever we get to court, the jury can see his condition for themselves. And see if you can find out why someone from the hospital would make a call saying he was dead."

Instead of hopping to it, Sid pulled out his pipe and a pocket knife. He began to empty scrapings into a sickly pot plant left over from Crane's administration. When he cleaned it just so, he brought out a foil of tobacco and began to tamp the bowl.

"Something bothering you?"

She looked him dead in the eye. "No."

"Want to talk about it?"

"No. Tell me what you found out about the Great Dane."

"I think one of us should start talking to the boys out in West Texas. We could put Junior on it. Seems Price had a couple of oil derricks somebody set fire to. Never did catch 'em, but at the time, they blamed it

404

on Mexican Nationals."

"I already heard this from Teddy."

"Junior told you?"

"Saturday night. And I think you should be the one to go. Teddy and I can get along fine."

That put a hitch in his get-along.

Sid bowed up with a look on his face that suggested he could hold a grudge for three generations. "When I said we should talk to them, I meant on the phone."

"It's better in person."

She half expected him to put up a fuss, when Jock Featherston rapped on the door.

"Hey, you two, people are beginning to talk." He flashed a mouthful of great teeth. His eyes thinned into slits. He seemed to focus on her throat, and when he moved in for a closer inspection, she caught wind of his leather jacket and smiled inwardly. Featherston smelled like a new car.

He said, "Cool necklace. What's it mean?" She realized she still wore Reno's drop, and that it worked its way out from beneath her collar. "Is it Chinese?"

"This? A cheap piece of jewelry. You know how it is; somebody gives you something, you feel obligated to wear it before passing it on to Goodwill." She covered the medallion with her hand. Tucked it back inside the black wool shell, where it snaked between her cleavage like a snowflake. "While you're here, maybe you can tell me something."

"You want me on the Great Dane. I accept."

"Nice try. Name all the detectives who worked on the case. Even guys who never wrote a report. Anybody who ever so much as looked over your shoulder."

Featherston thought a moment. "Besides me and Crane? Ingleside did gopher work. Driskoll wrote a few supplements, and Vaughn's brother worked the crime scene."

"Nobody else?"

"The ME's Office. And, now, you guys." His eyes shifted to Sid, sucking on the unlit pipe.

She took a deep breath and slowly let it out. "Okay, Jock, you're taking over the Quinten Carrol case, you and Sid."

"What about Benji?"

"Out for an unspecified term." She didn't want to discuss Bison-In-Need-of-Marriage-Counseling; Greta could cover that to everyone's satisfaction.

"Lieutenant could handle it all by himself. That would free me up to help you, Captain."

"Teddy and I have it under control." Big fat lie. "Besides, it's looking like that Arab convenience store shooting's tied into the Carrol shooting." She pulled out her ace and appealed to his ego. "Who knows?

Catch the perp and you might just trampoline yourself into a promotion."

It wasn't until he left that she began to wonder.

How come he didn't mention Joey Wehmeyer?

Cézanne parked near the Hebrew Rest Cemetery, locked the patrol car, and walked the half block to the ME's Office. Two big trees in front of the brownstone dropped the last of their foliage in big orange piles, and what remained resembled a couple of withered hands with upraised fingers. Pausing inside the foyer long enough to remove her driving gloves and stuff them into the pocket of her coat, Cézanne noticed Krivnek heading out a side door. When she called out, he waved and lengthened his stride without so much as a backward glance. She took long steps that strained the kick-pleat in her skirt, and finally intercepted him near a set of double doors marked EMPLOYEES ONLY.

"I have to talk to you."

"Not now."

"Can't I have a couple of minutes?" Uncowed.

"You haven't heard? We're running a two-for-one special. I have bodies that need posting. People are dying to get in."

"What is that? Autopsy humor? What

difference can fifteen minutes make? It's not like they need to be somewhere."

"Your compassion overwhelms me." He practically broke into a trot. "The answer's no. Had I known you were coming, I would not have slathered hot sauce all over my breakfast tacos. You have a way of giving me indigestion."

"Did Quinten Carrol die, or not?"

"Junior? No. Senior? Yes. He was spending the night in his son's hospital room and had a heart attack early this morning. Ironic, isn't it?"

"Slow down, Krivnek. You're making it hard to keep up." Her winded request brought out a heavy eye-roll on the ME's part. "Gimme ten minutes. Please."

He stopped abruptly and she shot past by a couple of steps. When she whipped around, he held up his hand to prevent interruption. "Did you get checked out at the hospital?"

Krivnek's way of saying she should have an AIDS test.

"I'm going as soon as I leave here." *A lie.*

"No, you're not. And if you don't, I'm not getting sucked into this any further, so you've got some decisions to make." He rocked his head from side to side while consulting his watch. "Five minutes. You're on the clock. What do you want?"

"Joey Wehmeyer. I need a look at the file."

"Wehmeyer's file is hands-off to you."

"Just me? Or to anybody on the PD?"

Krivnek stroked his chin. "How shall I put this? Your deputy chief left instructions you're not to touch that file. He used those words specifically — not to touch — since you managed to circumvent his wishes on the Carri Crane homicide. In that case, I believe he said you were not to have copies. You understand these latest orders prevent me from letting you go through our file at all."

"Strictly speaking, you could pull the file and someone could, say, turn the pages while I read it."

He snorted. "Why would anyone in their right mind put themselves in such a position?"

She leveled with him. "Admit it Krivnek, you like me." His eyebrows arched into severe peaks and she took it as a sign. "You don't always approve of the way I do things, but you like that I get them done in spite of the roadblocks assholes put in my path." His eyes drooped. She lowered her voice to a hiss. "You work for assholes, too. People who undermine your authority. Face it — if the PD was a corporation, the shareholders would fire the board of directors. Deep down, you want to help."

It was as if she had reached behind his ear and scratched the right spot. Any minute, he'd be thumping the floor with the ball of his foot. She put him on a first-name basis. What the hell? He'd seen her naked from the waist up.

"I'm fast, Marvin. I even brought along a micro-cassette recorder. Just open the file and spread it out. I'll do the rest. And I promise not to touch a thing. You can even watch."

"Let me check your head for bumps. Nostradamus predicted the reappearance of the Antichrist. If I find horns, I'm calling in the Catholic Church."

"Call the tabloids. They'll pay you enough to live like a sheik." She knew by the fierce squint behind thick glasses that he'd pull Wehmeyer's case.

And he did.

When he brought it to his office and laid out each page, she rolled up a chair and pulled out her tape recorder. Under his watchful eye, she activated the button and cleared her throat.

"Case number 9596097, Preston Josef Wehmeyer, white male, forty-two, six-one, one hundred ninety-one . . ."

She wheeled her chair along the edge of the table, expecting to see a suicide ruling on the last page under Cause of Death.

Only it didn't.

"Accidental death?" She swiveled around, open-mouthed. "He didn't hang himself?"

The assistant ME went into a panto-mime, pointing to the tape recorder with an exaggerated wag, then sliced a finger across his throat.

She disengaged the play-record button. Krivnek took a few steps closer and squinted at the tape. He brought himself up rigid, with his arms braced across his chest.

"Oh, he hanged himself, all right. Just not the way you think."

"I don't get it."

"There are many ways to kill yourself, not all of them on purpose."

She conjured up her best *Are you nuts?* expression. "He had a rope around his neck."

"Quite true. But he didn't slip it over his head with the intent to kill himself. He did it to — how shall we say — induce eu-phoria during a masturbatory act."

She gave him a slow stare. "How do you know?"

"Because if you read the section where we inventoried the articles of clothing, you'll see they found him in the closet wearing women's panties, with dried semen on his leg and the rope looped over the clothes rod."

The little hairs on her arms stood straight out. Krivnek had just described auto-erotic asphyxia.

"Poor bastard must've had a high threshold of pain. He applied a stun-gun to his testicles."

She felt her face muscles wringing themselves into a gross caricature of her former self.

"You can cringe until the world looks flat but it won't change the truth. The late Mr. Wehmeyer had a secret, m'dear. And the head honchos in your department expect it to stay that way."

"Is that it?" Her skin was still crawling.

"Not quite." He closed in and leaned over her shoulder. Let his eyes drift over the pages until he found what he was looking for, then mashed a finger down in mid-text. "They found him with a racquet-ball stuffed in his mouth. He'd taken fishing line — ten-pound test — and threaded it through the rubber. Then he tied fish hooks to both ends —"

She clapped a hand to her mouth.

"— I thought I'd seen it all. I've had them brought in with garter snakes, White-Out, firecrackers, Wesson Oil bottles, and hundred-watt bulbs coated with Astro-Glide shoved up their rectums, but this was about the most decadent thing I'd ever run across. How sick do you have to be to run fish hooks through your nipples, and jam a rubber ball in your mouth? You'd think he would have known as soon as he climaxed that any jerk of the head would have filleted his skin."

But Cézanne had stopped listening to Krivnek. She heard only the scurling bag-pipe cry of a tortured man, piercing the walls of the Dungeon of Decadence.

Dr. Mengele.

Chapter Thirty-Three

So the lead investigator on the Great Dane Murder had a fetish.

Or not.

Cézanne waited until the light changed, then turned onto the cross street and headed the Kompressor for the Auto-Erotica service center. As planned, Jinx Porter waited on a side street near the mechanic's bay. Behind the wheel of his unmarked patrol car, he lowered the *Wall Street Journal* enough to peer over the top. While he powered-down the window, she pulled up even with his driver's side window and made the handoff.

"Here are photos of the fingerprints I asked you to run. I'm not that hopeful we'll get a match through AFIS. These people aren't the type to have police records."

"You're kidding, right? This is Texas. You've got a spectacular chance for a hit."

"These are Westsiders, Porter. Money talks, but their money shouts. Even if they were to get in trouble, they'd have the means to fix it."

He took the envelope and used his thumbnail to slit the clear tape sealing it. "Don't look so worried. If your suspect

414

does have a record, we'll find out soon enough." Porter reached into the passenger seat for a Styrofoam cup stuffed with tissue. He put it to his mouth and she glanced away, unwilling to look back until she heard the telltale *pfttt* into the makeshift spittoon.

"Even if he's clean, I'll bet he has prints on file with the Department of Public Safety. If he's a law abiding citizen, he probably has a permit to carry."

Porter was right. The odds favored her. In Texas, only babies didn't carry guns. She suspected that was only because they hadn't developed the upper body strength necessary to lift them.

He agreed to give her a ride back to the PD, so she aimed Ruby into the nearest bay. The foreman burst forth through the showroom door with a souring smile.

"Your appointment's not today."

"Growling noises are coming from under the hood."

"What do you expect me to do about it?"

"Fix it."

"We're booked solid."

"Like hell. I'm standing here looking at three empty bays."

"Don't swear. I'm a born-again Christian. Are you?"

Cézanne's eyes went into auto-squint. "Will answering 'yes' influence the speed in which my car's repaired?"

Her tormentor ignored her. "Pop the latch." He strolled to the front of the Mercedes and lifted the hood. "I'm what they call a radical save."

"I get to hear this whether I want to or not, don't I?"

But he was staring skyward, seemingly reliving the moment of his conversion. A rapt smile formed on his lips.

"It happened in my office last weekend after you ended your unpleasant visit, and I had to deal with Mrs. Kissel. I'm not ashamed to say I was having a few unkind thoughts about the both of you — mostly about cutting the brake lines to your cars. Mysteriously, I found myself compelled to flip through a Bible my estranged wife sent me. All of a sudden, I dropped onto my knees and asked God to come into my life. That precise instant, He knocked a demon out of me."

"Good. Since you've figured out how it's done, how about knocking the demon out from under my hood?"

"You're mocking my beliefs."

"Look, I'm sure your conversion to Christianity was nothing short of miraculous. But I want my Kompressor put back like new, and I don't care how you do it as long as when you're through, that engine hums like a whore on East Lancaster."

He reached for an oil rag and wiped a grease spot from his hand. "All right, leave it. I'll get to it when I can." He slammed the hood.

"When will that be?"

"Couple of weeks."

"A couple of weeks?" Her voice climbed in volume and pitch. "My life's in the toilet. My job's a pressure cooker."

"Look, lady, I don't make the rules. If it's got tits or tires, it's gonna have problems."

She clamped her jaw so tight a lance of pain shot from a molar. "Listen carefully. The last time I was feeling this puny the doctor said I could use a little iron. Right now, I'm thinking he's right, I could use a little iron — a tire iron. So let's try this one more time. Exactly when can you get to it?"

"Check back after five." He fixed her with a hard stare. "You're not a very nice person."

"Thank you for the spiritual uplift. Feel free to pray for me. And speaking of lifts, how about putting Ruby on that one?"

She gave Jinx Porter the thumbs-up. He folded the *Journal* and started the patrol car. Before leaving, she remembered to ask the foreman about the remark he made when Worth Price's daughter stormed in complaining about her car.

"You said there was a rumor Mrs. Kissel

was having an affair when her husband died."

"The guy was a jerk."

"Dane Kissel?"

"Mr. Kissel was a swell guy. Very polite. I meant the cop."

Cézanne blinked. "She was seeing a policeman?"

"As a born-again Christian, I shouldn't monger the rumor. Besides, I don't remember. What's it to you?"

Across the street, the constable was giving her the evil eye. To emphasize his impatience, he revved the engine and twirled his finger in the universal *wrap it up* sign. She pulled out her badge case and flashed the gold panther shield.

"I'm investigating the death of Mr. Kissel."

The toughness left the set of his jaw and the pleats in his forehead relaxed. "You're that chick from TV." He let out an unamused chuckle. "I'd hate to be you. That guy threw you to the wolves."

"What'd the boyfriend look like?"

"Six-two, two hundred. Bulky guy. Worked out at the gym. Either that, or he took steroids."

"It would help if you could remember his name."

"Well I can't. But I might be able to find out —" glittery eyes told her he was willing to barter "— assuming we could work out an exchange."

Here it came. The part where she was expected to compromise her integrity and fix a ticket. If a motor jock wrote it, no dice. Those guys had reputations for citing their own grandmothers. The shop foreman disappeared several minutes; he returned leafing through a stack of cards.

"Here's the jig . . . if I find what you're looking for, you promise you'll never bring this car back in here as long as you own it?"

"Give me the name and fix what's wrong with her, and you've got a deal."

Jinx Porter was leaning on the horn. The foreman ran a finger down the entries for Cissy Kissel. He flipped the card and checked the back.

"Here it is," he said without letting her peek. "He picked up her Benz twice. The first time was the day after Mr. Kissel died. He came back two weeks later for some touch-up paint. Never saw him again. By that time, rumors were flying how Mrs. Spoiled Brat offed her old man."

"Who's the guy?"

"Says here his name's Preston Wehmeyer. You all right? You look like you just saw the embalmer."

Chapter Thirty-Four

By the time Cézanne left the service center, Sid should have been halfway to West Texas with a subpoena *duces tecum* for the business records of Herschel Escamilla, the tailor for D'Emanuel designs. On the ride back to the PD she coaxed another favor out of Jinx Porter. "You can get prints off Scotch tape, right?"

"If you fume it."

The videotape wrapper was sealed in an evidence bag, and she removed it from her purse and placed it on the seat between them. "I want you to take custody of this. Fume it for prints, and compare them to the ones on the photos."

"Anything else?"

"Tag it as evidence and lock it in your office safe. I'll let you know when I'm ready for them."

By the time Jinx curbed the constable car in front of HQ, the Chief of Police was trotting down the front steps ashen-faced, looking as if he could use a couple of pints of blood. As soon as Cézanne stepped from the vehicle, he buttonholed her.

"What's the latest on the Great Dane?"

"We're making progress."

"See here, Martin. At this point, I don't care if you bring in a freaking psychic to solve this thing. Just make it quick. My ass is on the line."

She didn't tell him one might already be waiting upstairs.

The first marked police units converged on Garlon Harrier's apartment.

When they kicked in his front door, they found him proned-out, belly-up in his easy chair, with his doughy paunch oozing over the elastic waistband of his jockey shorts, and a beer can draining onto his furry chest. And Drew Ingleside couldn't wait to waltz through Cézanne's door and tell her about it.

"Shoulda seen him, Capt'n. Bloodshot eyes, breath worse than a thousand buttholes. Said he didn't hear 'em knock but I think he was blacked out cold. Seems the station manager gave him a coupla days off, if you know what I mean, and Harrier got so depressed he went on a bender. Sombitch was drunker'n Hogan's goat."

"Where's he now?"

"Probably at the offices of Moses, Lonstein, Cohen, McElwell, and Kidd, filing suit. Coupla uniforms splintered his door to a fare-thee-well. God, what I'd give to be twenty years younger and back on the street."

He said it like he meant it.

It occurred to her as she sat looking at the white hair, rosy cheeks, and eyes that caught the light like a pair of six-carat sapphires, he must have been quite a pistol in his heyday. She shook her head ruefully and offered Ingleside a seat. "But first, close the door."

When he eased into a chair and whispered confidentially, "Hemorrhoids," she got the idea. "Thirty years ago, I used to be a motor jock. Little did I know about hemorrhoids. Doctors cut enough out to make into a sling shot."

"Tell me about Joey Wehmeyer."

"Nice guy." Ingleside relaxed. Draped his hands over the chair arms. "Didn't talk much. Kept to himself. Guess it's no wonder nobody knew he was depressed. Everybody has girl problems. Heck-fire, my old lady left me for the next-door neighbor, and I got over it. Fellow used to call me up, ask me did I want him to trim my grass since he already had the mower out of the garage. Who would've thought that was some kind of sex code? I just figured, hey, I won Yard-of-the-Month ten times this year. Miserable bastard." Ingleside rocked the chair onto its back legs.

"Things have a way of evening out,

though." A canine tooth glinted through a lopsided grin. "Let's just say I inadvertently passed on a nasty case of poison ivy I got brushing up against a little cocktail waitress down at the Torch Club. By the time I realized bartering with the Lord wouldn't make the itch go away, the sombitch next door's pecker nearly rotted off. That's how I found out. My old lady 'fessed up about Mister Rogers — they never did figure out it was me, gave it to them. That winter, I got rid of her. Never trust a broad who cheats. But you asked about Joey . . ."

His eyes drifted lazily over the room. "It's hard to imagine somebody you sat next to every day for five years taking his own life. Especially a brother officer. Statistics show cops have a high suicide rate, but most of the guys I know wouldn't off themselves on account of some chippie — they'd kill the one making them miserable instead. I can't honestly say that didn't cross my mind with my old lady."

She made a tentative suggestion. "Maybe he didn't kill himself."

"Sure he did. The funeral director even pulled his shirt practically up under his chin so the rope burns wouldn't show."

"Did you attend the service?"

He nodded. "Along with most of the department."

"What about the family?"

"Joey didn't have any family to speak of except the old folks, and they were well into their eighties. Senile, the both of 'em, and living in a nursing home. Hell, I don't know if they even knew. If they did, they probably forgot. No," he added wistfully, "Joey didn't have anybody I know of besides the girl."

"Tell me about her."

"Drugstore blonde. Real short hair. Bleached white as the driven snow. Store-bought tits." He cupped his hands in front of his chest to illustrate cup size. He broke into a wide grin, and she saw an empty space where a molar should have been. His eyes danced.

"Who was she?"

"I have no idea. She didn't stay long, I can tell you that much. Walked straight down the aisle to the front, stared a few seconds, and made a beeline for the exit. It was almost like she just came to make sure the poor guy was really dead."

"No one thought that was strange?"

"The only thing strange about her was that hat. She had on one of those hats like were popular with women in the early sixties. My wife wore one like it to church. You know, the kind with the fishnet hanging down in front like a little veil? Pillboxes, they call 'em. Like Jackie wore. She had on one of those. Black. Like she wanted to hide her face, but lemme tell ya — there was no way to hide those eyes."

"What about her eyes?"

"They could drill you a half-mile away. Even through the netting. Pale blue. So light they almost blended with the whites."

Chills shot up Cézanne's arms. "Are you sure you can't think of her name?"

"Some Greek name. Maybe Italian. I wouldn't know, it's been so long."

But Cézanne knew.

Sicily.

The afternoon was quickly drawing to a close when Jinx Porter phoned Cézanne's office.

"I've got your prints."

"You know whose they are?"

"Not yet, but I developed a nice big latent. Probably a thumbprint. It came from the tape, just like you said. And you'll like this even better."

She knew by the silence he was stringing her along.

"It's a triple whorl. And there's also a little bitty print. Probably belongs to a juvenile."

"Or a woman with small hands."

"Maybe. In any event, you hit the jackpot."

"How's that?"

"A triple whorl's almost a deformity. If he's in the databank — or she — we could know in a matter of hours."

"You're kidding."

"Not in the least." He chuckled through the phone line. "So what came in the wrapper? Porn?"

"What makes you say that?"

"I just re-folded it along the creases. You ordering videos in brown paper bags?"

She would have laughed it off, but she'd made no effort to hide the tape from Duty. Nor had she locked her room that morning when they left the house. Now Devilrow's niece was supposed to be with Teddy Vaughn, out for frozen custard on a dismal winter day. And since they had ended up on the Westside of town, Cézanne had radioed him to give him the go-ahead to drop Duty off at the house early.

It surprised her when Sid's voice came over the air, telling her Teddy had already left for the day.

That Sid had Duty riding around with him.

That conversation took place, what — a half hour ago? "Gotta go."

"Wait. How 'bout that dinner? I know a little place —"

"Call if you get a hit out of AFIS." Five minutes later she was out the door in a footrace across the parking lot, headed for the unmarked patrol car.

When Cézanne opened the front door to

the bungalow on Western, she smelled a vile odor coming from the kitchen. Duty had changed into sweats and was standing at the stove, downcast, with a wooden spoon in her hand and a string of fresh garlic pods hanging from her neck.

Cézanne demanded answers. "What in God's name is that?"

"A present from me to you and Obatalla."

"I'm not eating that. It smells like dead skunk."

"It's not for eatin'. It's for soaking."

"It's not gonna happen." She looped the strap of her purse over a kitchen chair and began to disrobe on her way to the bedroom. Once she shed her clothes and climbed into fresh garments, she would finish watching the tape. See what else happened at The Wild Orchid Society.

Except when she opened her bedroom door, the TV was already on and the picture had turned to snow.

Duty knew.

She stomped into the kitchen and confronted her.

"What have you done?"

Duty stopped stirring. "I went in to watch Jerry —"

"Jerry?"

"— Springer, but it didn't start for ten minutes. I remembered I hadn't finished that movie about that yellow dog. I went to turn it on, only it wasn't no movie about no dog." She started to cry. "Miz Zan, you in worse trouble than I thought. Bad stuff gonna happen, I just know it." She slipped the garlic lei over her head, held it out, and came toward her with arms outstretched.

"Stop right there."

The girl backed off.

"Deuteronomy," her eyes fluttered and she took a deep breath. "Whatever you saw, I want you to forget. Somebody played a cruel joke on me. Nothing more. Everything'll be fine."

"How can you say that, Miz Zan?" the teen wailed. "You on the Internet."

"*What?*"

"You got a site on the Net. At the end of the tape there's a website, and I looked it up on the computer. Miz Zan —" Duty's words came out in short, staccato bursts "— yo' in a snuff film."

Chapter Thirty-Five

Making hot chocolate gave Cézanne something to do while she mulled over whether or not to permit Duty a second viewing of the video. She decided she had nothing to lose. While they watched the tape, Duty rubbed the odious camphor oil pâté over Cézanne's bare shoulders until it absorbed into her skin with a burn.

"Stop torturing me."

"This gonna take out the bruises. Gonna make 'em disappear faster than a brother with a court-ordered paternity test."

"It reeks."

"Why you have to be so cross? You always act —"

"Shush."

With the slow, deliberate trudge of a zombie, a woman roughly the same height, with the same haircut, made up to look like her, stepped through underbrush, the back of her naked form to the camera.

"Miz Zan, you ain't got a stitch on."

"That's not me."

"She got yo' hair."

"I'm telling you it's not me. Now hush."

Duty said, "Looks like Blair Witch

without a stitch. Hey, that rhymes."

A clearing came into view and a gravel road opened up in front of the body double. The next frames of film had been shot as if the surroundings were seen through her eyes.

The eye of the camera panned to a trailer, a single-wide with a cockeyed shutter.

The doorknob turned under the actress's grip.

The camera cut away.

A quick splice, and Cézanne witnessed herself out cold on the marble slab with the flames of a dozen candles silhouetting The Wild Orchid Society. Dancing shadows distorted their faces. Intense, druidic strains from an Enya album provided dubbed-in background music.

Cézanne tried to shield Duty's eyes, but the girl avoided her with a series of fake-out moves. "Turn your head."

"I already seen it." Duty mashed her shoulder muscles hard. "It's awful. You killed 'em."

"Somebody dies?"

Duty nodded grimly.

"Ohmygod. That's not me."

"Sho 'nuff looks like you."

"It's not."

But Duty was right. When the camera cut away and the door to the trailer gaped open, even the grainy film didn't undermine the uncanny resemblance of the ghostly apparition running out, dotted in blood.

Pagan forms danced in the shadows. The Executioner walked into the shot with his trademark hood cowling at the shoulders. Although he kept his back to the camera, Cézanne glimpsed a medallion hanging from a gold chain around his neck. She paused the remote control, then rewound several seconds of tape.

With The Executioner angled just-so, she freeze framed the shot. It looked like —

It looked like —

It looked like a yin-yang symbol, mutated into thirds.

Reflexively, her hand clutched at Reno's amulet. With a curious mixture of dread and anticipation, she engaged the play button.

Duty moved in, inches from her ear. "You know that man?"

"It's possible. I'm not certain. What happens next?"

"Sinful stuff."

What Duty referred to, appeared in a flash.

The Executioner forced the understudy to her knees, where her face disappeared into his hips. With one hand, he grasped her hair and tightened his grip enough to elicit a whimper. With the other, he produced a North American Arms .22 with collapsible grips. It hardly mattered that the zoom lens brought it close-up. Cézanne recognized it on sight.

Her skin crawled. They'd taken her piece.

In an electronically altered voice from the Underground, The Executioner said, "Have you satisfied your blood lust, Cézanne?"

The film faded to black.

Duty came unglued. "Who'd you kill, Miz Zan? And what was you doin' to that man? My gramma Corinthia that lives in the bayou, she served turnips with nutria once and I thought I'd never get the taste outta my mouth, but you —" Unexpectedly, she wagged her finger at the TV. "There it is, just like I said. Yo' website on the Net."

Reeling, Cézanne gave the address at the bottom corner of the screen a hard stare. Her throat felt as dry as a Sahara sunrise. The tape spooled to the end of the cartridge, engaging the VCR's automatic rewind.

She said, "I need a drink," and returned to the kitchen with her untouched cocoa.

Duty hollered, "I could use a rum and Coke, myself. And while you up, I would kinda like to have some crushed ice with that. You can take a big ol' knife and bust the cubes into little chunks." Followed by, "Or not. I see by the way the vein in yo' neck's plumpin' — just fix it anyway you want. Or I could drink straight from the bottle."

Cézanne gave her a hard look. She started to ignore the outrageous request, then took a fresh highball glass from the cabinet and poured. Contributing to the delinquency of a minor was the least of her worries.

She returned with two well-watered drinks, and she and Duty started the nightmare all over again — this time on the worldwide web. Based on the number of hits on the site, over a thousand sexual sick-os had already viewed *Femme Fatale*, starring Cézanne Renoir.

Her blood pressure dropped. She watched her name scroll through the credits. Whoever set her up for whatever they set her up for, knew exactly what they were doing. And they were close enough to her social and professional circles to know her middle name.

Not even Doug Driskoll would take such measures to get even. Besides, for a wham-bam-thank-you-ma'am kind of guy, he lacked the wattage to pull off something so intricate. Driskoll's *modus operandi* was to mind-fuck women into thinking they had a future with him. Once the relationship dead-ended, he moved on to the next victim. Come to think of it, the Four-F's Driskoll learned in high school might be the only information he retained from youthful years spent in the back seat of a 'sixty-seven Mustang convertible.

No, she ruled Driskoll out.

It had to be someone who harbored an intense hatred for her. Not Rosen. Oh, he hated her all right. But they shared a birthright. Among Jews, blood was thicker than axle grease.

It would take someone like —

"Whatchoo thinkin' Miz Zan? I can see yo' wheels spinnin' like a gerbil on a treadmill. Whatchoo got goin' on up there?"

Softly, numbly, Cézanne whispered, "I think I know who killed the Great Dane. Now I just have to prove it."

Chapter Thirty-Six

More than ever, Cézanne needed Reno. But the trip through the cedar-covered countryside brought anything but comfort. For one thing, she expected to use the drive time to think, but Duty refused to let the silence between them work its magic. For another, she found it difficult to come up with answers to pacify her houseguest, once the floodgate of questions opened wide.

"I like this car. This a nize car. I am sittin' in a patrol car and I'm not even goin' to jail. Do you tell 'em they can beat the rap, but they can't beat the ride?"

Cézanne refused to humor her with anything more than a glance.

"Yeah, I see a little smile startin'. That's whatchoo say to folks you lockin' up. Mmm-mmm. What's this button do?"

"Don't touch the siren."

"Got lights on this car? Red and blue ones?"

She nodded.

"How come I never saw lights?"

"They're recessed behind the front grill. Don't touch that either. That's the PA system."

"Whatchoo do with a PA? Yell stuff at people? Can you say, 'Getcho black ass outta here'?"

"Without ever leaving the car."

"Mmmm-mmm. Can I say my name on it? Can I say, 'Hey everybody, it's me, Deuteronomy Devilrow'? Can I say that?"

"No. Stop picking with stuff. This is for life-or-death emergencies only."

"Know what I'd really like, Miz Zan? I'd like to ride in a parade in this car. In Weeping Mary, we have a parade every summer. I would sincerely like to drive this car and yell hidee to my kin. I would get on that PA and say, 'Hey everybody, it's me, Deuteronomy Devilrow.' Know what else I'd say?"

Not wanting to encourage the fantasy, Cézanne let the silence speak for her.

"I'd call 'em enigmas. I'd say, 'Whatcoo enigmas doin' this fine, sunny day?' " She nestled her shoulders into the seat. "That I would do," she said softly. She turned her face to the window where Cézanne was certain she was imagining the reaction of her people.

They caught the traffic light. Cézanne studied her during the wait, certain Duty was plotting ways to circumvent departmental SOP. When they pulled away on a green signal, the teen perked up.

"Where we goin' this time of night? We

goin' to see friends?"

Reluctantly, Cézanne answered. "In a manner of speaking."

A few hundred feet from the exotic dancer's trailer park, Ruby's headlight beacons swept across the entrance. Cézanne's plans came unraveled. The sheen of yellow tape caught the beam of light, and she knew without reading the words repeated across the long strip of plastic ribbon; they spelled trouble.

CRIME SCENE — DO NOT CROSS.

Sheriff deputies had cordoned off the area fronting Reno's trailer.

She knew better than to alight from the car, but she left the engine running so Duty would have enough heat, and got out anyway. Inside her head, she made excuses to explain why Day-Glo tape would link the trees surrounding the house.

Reno probably got busted in a dope raid. All the strippers at Ali Baba's did drugs. Hollywood snorted coke. Did it right in front of her, not two days before that terrible shootout. The other girls smoked pot, Reno'd said so. And Reno herself? Ecstasy seemed to be the willowy redhead's drug of choice.

Bad stuff, those X-tabs. MDMA was its chemical name, and the synthetic drug combined the effects of a psychedelic and an amphetamine. A user had better odds loading five out of six chambers and playing Russian Roulette.

Reno's car was missing. Which meant the SO could be inventorying it. Or maybe Krystal took it.

But Cézanne knew better. Something terrible happened.

The strong desire to see Bobby, and the thought of sprinting back in the patrol car and heading Code-Three for the comfort of the sheriff's arms, held more than a degree of interest. Bobby had become the brightest light in her otherwise dark world.

At once, it struck her. Her feelings for him ran deep — the kind of love that caused the sensation of animated birds swirling overhead, and swelled her chest until her lungs stretched so tight, a slice of pain traveled through her heart.

She never saw the lawmen bailing out of their cars, secreted in the brush. But the thunder of boots against the gravel sounded like a volley straight out of hell.

Images of men in riot gear flashed in her mind.

When she spun around, her heart jumped. Three sheriff's deputies with guns drawn and pointed at the kill zone shouted simultaneous commands.

"Hands on your head."

"Hit the ground."

"Don't move . . . so much as twitch, you're dead."

Paralyzed with terror, she froze.

Voices blended like demons from hell.

"Hands on your head, dammit."

"Are you fucking deaf? I said eat the dirt."

"Freeze."

They looked pretty much the same in their black uniforms and body armor — big and brutish — with four-and-three-quarter's worth of pressure on a five-pound trigger pull.

She dropped her shoulder bag and raised her hands above her head. Her tongue trembled with the effort of speech. "I'm a cop."

"BFD. Where's your piece?"

"In my purse." Her voice rang tinny and distant. Both eyes pulsed. She nudged the Coach bag with her toe. One of the trio yanked it away from her lunge, and began rifling through it. The others rushed her, each grabbing an arm. When she heard the ratcheting of handcuffs, her legs buckled. They caught her as one knee scraped the ground.

"There's been a mistake." Her tongue felt thick and numb.

"You Cézanne Martin?"

How did they know? The deputy hadn't opened her badge case. Her voice dissolved to a whisper. "Yes."

"You're under arrest."

"Hey, motherfuckers, whatchoo doin'?"

Duty, on the PA.

"You motherfuckers getcho hands offa her . . . motherfuckers got no idea who yo' dealin' with. I'll put a curse, make yo' dick rot."

She tried to shape her fear into words. "I know I should have called child welfare but I thought she was an emancipated minor —"

"What?"

"Deuteronomy. Her uncle dumped her on me. He left her in the cold and I tried to get rid of her, but she kept coming back, so I had no choice."

"Let me guess." His voice dripped sarcasm. "You're gonna claim you were in the bathroom when things went down, right?"

Behind her, the PA crackled to life. "I mean it, motherfucker, don'tchoo come any closer, I'll kick yo' ass."

Damned Reno and the criminal element she ran with. Well, they weren't going to suck her into their nefarious lifestyle. She didn't need to give Rosen another reason to can her.

"I don't understand. What went down?"

"That's right, play dumb."

She was certain she would faint dead away but she was wrong. Every blade of dead grass came into sharp focus. Every wave on the lake rippled into view. An icy tingle covered her skin, and blood seemed to back up in her veins.

Behind her, an unearthly shriek erupted

from the bowels of her patrol car.

Duty.

Screaming.

Not the ordinary shrill, but a howl so terrifying that it played to the night skies, and frightened open every pore.

A deputy cried, "Don't do it."

She twisted to see over her shoulder. "Ohmygod, somebody tell me what's happening."

The answer came in the form of an elbow upside the head. The deputy standing guard over her squinted fiercely. Without warning, he let go of the handcuffs and defensively shielded his face.

A mind-numbing explosion almost stopped her blood flow. The echoing report of a shotgun did more than create a timeless moment in infamy. It liquidated her bones and melted her knees.

Unexpectedly, the officer released his grip on the handcuffs. The ground rose up to meet her dead weight. Tasting dirt and a trickle of liquid iron from her nose, she desperately denied the last ten seconds — as if by doing a simple chant in her head, she could stop the damage caused by an instant of poor judgment.

Not Duty.

God, no.

Please, not Duty.

Chapter Thirty-Seven

Before the deputies could lift Cézanne, still stricken, to her feet, tires screamed against the pavement, scattershooting pea gravel and vanishing into the abyss.

The fall had taken her wind. She labored to breathe; her lungs burned from oxygen deprivation. In eight short days, she'd been urinated on, drugged, stripped naked, physically violated to a fare-thee-well, splashed across the Internet like the Queen of the Bs, and betrayed by her colleagues. But this took the cake. Now, proned-out, face-down in the dirt, the biggest case of her career had drop-kicked her into the perfect metaphor.

She lay powerless to suck in great gulps of air, aware of the clarity of the deputies' voices, as if each word were being piped directly into her exposed ear.

"She got away."

The smallest of the bruisers pointed to the inky horizon. "She hissed like a radiator when me and Luke started over, Sergeant. Brandished a gun, too —"

"— That's right, Sarge, we had no choice but to open fire."

Just when she thought she would black out, Cézanne pulled in her first breath. The huge intake of oxygen reinflated her lungs and left her greedy for more.

Panting, she rallied to Duty's defense. "Wasn't . . . a gun."

"Then what the hell was it?"

She said, "Chicken bones," between gasps.

Her last act of courage, before they caged her in the squad car, was to demand an explanation. "What am I under arrest for?"

The deputy began reciting Miranda. When he finished, he glanced in his rear-view mirror and viewed her through slitted eyes. "Do you understand your rights as I've read them?"

"Yes. What's the charge?"

Instead of a straight answer, he asked if she wanted a lawyer and offered an opportunity to give a statement.

"That depends on what I'm being accused of."

"You'll find out Downtown."

Her mind raced with possibilities. Getting shanghaied by the SO could be part of Rosen's three-pronged approach to do her in. Or this could bear the hallmark of Doug Driskoll — a sneak-attack he thought up one night while fattening rodents at the Auto Pound.

God only knew where Duty would end

up. No DL. Unauthorized use of a motor vehicle. Driving without headlights. If she totaled the unmarked unit — or even got pulled over in it — there'd be hell to pay. In her head, she ticked off violations under the Juvenile Code until there were too many to keep straight.

An uneventful life with Bobby looked better than ever.

The back seat of the patrol car stank of drunks and urine. She thought of the sheer volume of suspects she'd interrogated during her stint as a detective, and tried to recall whether exercising their right to remain silent influenced her opinion regarding their guilt. In the end, she decided it did.

Near the city limit, she broke her silence. "I don't do drugs."

"You think that's what this is about?"

"Isn't it?"

"Five miles to go. Let's have some music." He tuned the radio to an FM station, where LeAnn Rimes belted out a suggestion for the girl who stole her beau. The singer was onto something.

Instead of driving into the sally port and marching her directly to the booking desk, the deputy parked the patrol car into a space behind the SO and killed the engine. Other squad cars pulled in, too.

Except for a small section of building

dedicated to the probation department and the constable, the Tarrant County Sheriff's Office took most of the space in the multistory Criminal Courts Building. The structure's west wall connected to the PD's east wall like a conjoined twin. And no matter how the janitorial staff cleaned, they couldn't mask the perennial odor from the downstairs bathrooms, or the permanent decay hidden behind the grime of the elevators. No amount of paint could freshen the walls in a place so old and depressing, and being led past a warehouse of desks in the Criminal Investigation Division to a cramped interrogation room didn't alter her opinion about the upstairs, either.

An odd thought occurred.

The cheese stands alone. Just like the children's song.

They were gonna make limburger out of her.

The sergeant tapped two Kools out of a pack. "Smoke?"

She shook her head. The gimlet-eyed stare, wheat colored hair, broad nose, and lips with plenty of color did little to alter the impression she formed at the scene: that her protests never lost effect, because they never had any to begin with.

He pulled a chair away from the gunmetal gray table and straddled it. "Drink?"

"Piña colada, frozen."

Sparse eyebrows above close-set eyes

445

sharpened into inverted V's. "I meant a sody-water."

Something about the way he murdered the King's English struck her funny. She realized her mistake as soon as the first chuckle left her lips. The smallest of the three slipped up behind and uncuffed her cold, bloodless hands. While she massaged the bruised indentations on her wrists to speed along the circulation, Heckle and Jeckle left the room.

Another player entered with a small tape recorder. She recognized the gold captain's bars on the points of his collar and didn't like to think what was coming. She hadn't given much thought to the blond sergeant, but did so now. The captain motioned him over and whispered out of her earshot.

He seemed to be in a filthy mood. Reaching down by his side, he turned on his handheld radio and fumbled with the channel selector. She couldn't be certain, but it appeared that he switched to an intercity frequency capable of picking up FWPD transmissions.

His processed dark, slicked-back pompadour and thick sideburns reminded her of Elvis in decline, and she didn't much care for the way his deep-set eyes refused to blink, or the hard-as-nails gleam that radiated from his pupils. But it was the ears that bothered her most. She couldn't understand why

446

someone with a captain's salary and two satellite dishes mounted on either side of his head didn't consult a plastic surgeon for help.

He dismissed the sergeant with a glance. After an audible click from the door knob, he towered over her chair and set the intimidating machine on the table.

"I'm Captain Vanderhoven. You can call me Van."

"Thanks, Van. You can call me a cab."

"It's no joke."

"No, it isn't." But she was thinking, Getting the boxers sued off you for a civil rights violation is never funny. God help them if they hurt Duty.

The captain pushed the play-record button, gave the date and time, identified her by name, and made his own brief introduction.

"So're you ready to discuss what happened?" Vanderhoven slung his leg over a chair and scooted it so close their knees grazed. He leaned in and lowered his voice. "Where were you Friday night?"

"Out with a female acquaintance."

"What's her name?"

"Reno. That's her street name."

"Where'd you go?"

"Driving. We dropped by her workplace. Had a few laughs. I went home." The truth. Just not the whole truth and nothing but the truth. Abruptly, she went silent. Volunteering information would only dig a deeper hole.

He wasn't taking notes, and it bothered her. It was an old investigator's trick she'd used herself when she wanted a suspect to think she knew more than he did. Only in this case, Vanderhoven did have the upper hand and it scared the bejesus out of her. It was as if the percussion section of the Fort Worth Symphony Orchestra had taken up residence behind her ribcage.

Her eyes cut to the two-way mirror and back. She had no illusions the deputies and their sergeant were anywhere but behind the glass, watching her prop her elbow on the government issue table, and analyzing everything she said. Air came in short, shallow breaths. They thought she'd committed a crime or she wouldn't be here. Hyperventilating would cement their opinion of her guilt.

She forced her arms against the chair rails, let her hands hang, limp, over the ends, and locked gazes with Vanderhoven.

"I haven't been told why I'm here. Is this the way you people do business?"

"I'm asking the questions," he said firmly. "What time did you get home?"

"Around eleven, maybe. Definitely before midnight."

"Can you prove it?"

She wondered why she should have to. Did they know about The Wild Orchid Society? Instinctively, she pulled at her hair to ensure the Band-Aid stayed covered.

"I have a house guest. She was awake. I caught her using my computer and we had a lively discussion about it. Yes, I can prove it."

"Name?"

"Deuteronomy Devilrow."

Vanderhoven didn't bat an eyelid. Unexpectedly, he stood tall and stretched as if his shoulder pained him. He asked about her promotion. Wanted to know about the Great Dane Murder, and how it was coming. After a polite, noncommittal exchange, she fixed him with a wounded look and tried to pin him down.

"Why am I here?"

"Did you spend Friday night at your house?"

"Yes."

"Gonna use your house guest to alibi you on that, too?"

"I'm not using anybody for anything. I was where I said I was. If you want to verify it, fine by me."

"Were you with Miss Devereaux Saturday morning?"

"Devilrow. No. I took my Kompressor in for service around seven-thirty. I went by Charles and Agnetha Crane's — my former captain's house — then picked Duty up just before lunch."

"You own a Kompressor?" His eyes convicted her. "I didn't know the PD paid that good. Besides oilmen and dopers, there aren't many people who can afford wheels like that," he said villainously.

So Reno got busted for drugs and dragged her name into the equation. Probably figured if she couldn't help work a deal with the prosecutors, she'd suck her in for more muscle.

"I don't do drugs," she said with a pout of defensiveness.

But the captain didn't seem to be listening. And in the awkward silence, while he peered thoughtfully at the lock of hair strategically placed over the raw spot on her neck, she knew he was setting a trap in his head, and buying time to spring it.

"How long did you stay at the mechanic's?"

"Long enough to get clipped. An hour, maybe."

He eased back into his chair and shook out a Chesterfield like he'd just had the greatest sex in his life. She wanted to tell him smoke gave her a headache, but something about the way he smacked the butt against the table stopped her.

"You said you didn't pick up Miss

Devereaux until noon. When's the last time you saw them?"

"Devilrow. Saw whom?"

"The lucky couple. Were they together when you saw them?"

Startled, she fell silent. This was about the Cranes? He leaned to one side and his eyes locked on her throat. Her pulse jumped against the neckline of her pullover.

Her runaway tongue took off. "I went by Crane's before I took Duty to the mall. I asked him about the case. He led the investigation eight years ago —" Her eyelids fluttered in astonishment. Her mind danced with multiple scenarios, all bad. Crane's grief finally got the better of him. She told him she would solve the Great Dane and his jealousy ignited. He'd been out hunting; his wife said so. Crazy son of a bitch probably killed her, then turned the gun on himself. But that didn't explain why the deputies were out at Reno's. Coincidence?

Vanderhoven must have said something.

Her fingertips whitened against the edge of the table. "I demand to know why I'm here."

"We lifted your prints. They were all over the place."

"She offered me coffee. We had a nice visit."

"Who offered you coffee?"

451

"Agnetha Crane. When I stopped by to talk to Captain Crane Saturday morning." Her voice crescendoed. Words rushed from her mouth. "I can't help it if Crane twisted-off. Everybody knows he's been half out of his mind since his daughter's murder. He could've snapped at any minute." She started to grab Vanderhoven's hand while making her appeal, and stopped short. "My God, ask Dr. Whitelark if you don't believe me. Crane was so unstable Rosen forced him into emergency medical leave."

"What does that have to do with what we're talking about?"

She found herself gasping for breath.

She should ask for a lawyer.

Invoke her Fifth Amendment right to silence. "Can I stand?"

"Long as you realize there's nowhere to run."

She rose on unsteady legs and walked toward the mirror. Putting both palms flat against the glass, she spoke directly to the men on the other side. "Would somebody please tell me what's going on? Did something happen to the Cranes?"

She caught sight of her interrogator's reflection. He blew a stream of smoke off to one side, then balanced the smoldering butt in the groove of a plastic ashtray with a beer logo on it.

"It's about Ms. Lively, who, by the way, isn't." He pulled a Polaroid from his pocket and got to his feet. "Neither is Ms. Warren," he said coming her way. "The one you call Reno."

Chapter Thirty-Eight

One look at the snapshot of Reno and Krystal, their naked bodies marred by maroon clots, made Cézanne eager to account for every minute of her time since leaving the Dungeon of Decadence. And if Captain Vanderhoven hadn't been monitoring the PD's Northside channel on his police radio, she couldn't have unloaded on him fast enough. He fiddled with the volume enough for her to comprehend that a Sugarland Express of blue-and-whites were in hot pursuit of an unmarked patrol unit.

"Are you willing to go on the box?"

He wanted her to take a lie detector. She almost jumped at the chance — after all, she had nothing to hide. Well, almost nothing. Long as he didn't know about the Dungeon of Decadence and The Wild Orchid Society, she'd be fine.

They returned to their seats, where Vanderhoven set the handie-talkie in the middle of the table. The way he cocked his head reminded her of the RCA Victor dog.

Nipper. That was its name.

A crazy time to remember trivia. Probably teetering on an emotional collapse.

Before she could give him the green light on the polygraph exam, a shrieking, black soprano that could only be Deuteronomy Devilrow, came over the air with the intensity of a Pentecostal preacher on snake handler Sunday.

"Where'n God's name you at, Mista Sid? They got Miz Zan in the pokey, and we gotta save her."

"Take it easy, little missy, don't do anything stupid." Sid.

She should've been happy. But Duty made a terrible mistake. Klevenhagen was a traitor. Her stomach knotted and she sensed the air thinning inside the cramped quarters.

Officers in hot pursuit keyed over each other's transmissions. A low-pitched rumble exploded through the speaker and obliterated their voices. Then Sid was back, shouting over the hi-lo scream of his siren.

"Clear channel, clear channel. Lieutenant Klevenhagen, here. I'm ordering you knuckleheads to break off pursuit."

But a sergeant with other ideas broke in. "That car's stolen, Lieutenant." The yelp of his siren switched to wail-mode.

"I don't care if it's Publisher's Clearinghouse with a million-dollar check, I said knock it off."

Cézanne's anxiety turned to dread.

Without witnesses, what lengths would Sid go to, to silence Duty? Impulsively, she made a grab for the handheld but Vanderhoven wrestled it away.

"Let me talk to them," she cried. "I can get her to pull over. She'll listen to me."

"Nothing doing. We're not interfering. So how about it? You want the lie detector or not?"

She locked him in her gaze. "Who's the polygraph operator?"

"I am."

The radio sat inert. Unearthly silence cast a pall over the room. Vanderhoven seemed to be siphoning off more than his fair share of oxygen, and the dizzy rush brought on by thinning air left her light-headed. If she didn't take it, he'd find a reason to hold her. If she passed it — and she would — he'd let her go. Cops loved polygraphs. Ate the results up like cotton candy. Worst case scenario, she'd flunk and post her own bail.

"If you want to put me on the box, do it now."

Grinning big, Vanderhoven used the table to push himself out of his seat. "Let's go."

The radio crackled to life.

Someone screamed, "She's left the roadway. Airborne. She's in the Trinity. Get the Fire Department."

"Aw, Jesus." Sid.

The sickening moan of a drowning siren died out. But wails and whoops of pursuing patrol cars continued to transmit over a stuck mike like hounds yelping into a foxhole.

In her mind, Cézanne saw two scenarios, each vivid and frightening. The first left a startling impression — the strained hope that Duty escaped her murky prison and swam to shore where she concealed herself in pampas grass, and cast hexes on The Blue using her chicken bones.

But the second visual sent a chill zipping across her shoulders and a high-voltage spasm to her stomach. She imagined the patrol car filling with icy, inky water. Shorting out the electrical system. And Deuteronomy Devilrow with the doors locked, beating on the window in a desperate fight to break free, as the car slipped below the waterline.

Cézanne clutched her throat. Breathed in shallow, useless breaths.

She saw Duty thrashing.

Gulping air.

Kicking the safety glass.

Heard the sucking sound of the car settling to the bottom of the Trinity. And nothing but deathly silence, followed by a sudden, final explosion of bubbles gurgling to the surface.

Chapter Thirty-Nine

By the time Vanderhoven led her into an office no bigger than a walk-in closet, Cézanne's skin was practically crawling. A hard-shell suitcase about the size of two VCRs lay, open, on the desk. On the left, a spool of paper with needles balanced on top took up one half; on the right were control knobs. Vanderhoven turned on the machine and the needles jumped at the first jolt of electricity. While it settled into a quiet hum, he picked up a plastic-coated line resembling a coil of telephone cord, and had her raise her arms. He wrapped it around her ribcage and fastened it in back. After he seated her in a chair across the desk and away from the polygraph, he reached for her hand. Making unnerving small talk, he attached the leads to her fingertips with Velcro.

"The box measures perspiration, respiration, heartbeat — involuntary reflexes you can't control. Lotta people try to beat it. If you do, I'll catch you. Just thought you oughta know." He pulled a pen from his pocket and pushed a piece of paper in front of her. "Before we start, you'll need to sign this release stating you're taking the polygraph voluntarily."

She observed him through keen eyes, letting the ballpoint hover over the signature line. Of course it wasn't voluntary. Nothing about the whole evening had been voluntary except for her asinine decision to dash out to Reno's.

Reno.

Sadness numbed her spirit. In some small way, her mind still denied the stripper's death. She hadn't completely ruled out the possibility she was on TV and her eyes darted furtively around the room for signs of pin cameras hidden in the room, but what kept her from shrieking was her faith in Marvin Krivnek's almost rabid willingness to test beyond the scope of a routine autopsy. If he'd let her visually examine the wounds —

Her stomach sank. Maybe she wouldn't just be looking at Reno and her friend. Maybe she'd have to ID Duty, too. She exhaled a deep sigh of grief, so audible and filled with internal pain that Vanderhoven quit tinkering with the dials and stared.

"Change your mind?"

If she didn't sign, he wouldn't administer the test. Without it, she didn't stand a chance of leaving without posting bail. If she had enough money in her account, she could post her own and be released on a walk-through in a matter of hours. "Can I make a phone call?"

"Who to?" he said nastily. "Your lawyer?"

"The one–eight hundred number for my bank."

She recited the phone number. He dialed out and handed her the receiver. Soon, the automated teller came online. One by one, she coached Vanderhoven which numbers to punch out on the keypad. An unexpected response from computerized sound bytes introduced a new level of terror.

Your account is closed.

Chills ripped across her skin and climbed into cavities.

The Wild Orchid Society.

Rich people. Influential people. People in high places — bank presidents. In retrospect, it didn't surprise her they pricked with her account. She handed over the receiver and scrawled her name on the voluntary release.

"Admit it," he said, and she could see that her act of hesitation pleased him. "You were fixing to change your mind, weren't you?"

She regained some of her dignity and kept her voice low and even. "I was merely wondering how good you are. The polygraph's only as good as its operator."

"If you're innocent, you don't need to worry. I'm the best there is."

She tried charm. "That's exactly the way I see it — a smart man like you. I knew the moment we met, if anyone could sort out the confusion, you could."

He asked if she was ready, and when she took a deep breath and nodded, the needles bucked.

"Ever taken a lie detector before?"

"Long time ago."

"Pass?"

"You know I did."

"False sense of security."

Vanderhoven made her nervous. Even if she passed, he could still hold her awhile longer. Before he asked the first question, she needed to set some groundrules of her own.

"Have you figured out what you'll ask me?"

"What we talked about back in Interrogation . . . where you were Friday night, Saturday morning. What you did. Who you saw. Whether you shot Ms. Lively and Ms. Warren in the back and chest, respectively, while they were engaged in a — how shall I put this? A deviate sex act."

For the first time that night, Cézanne laughed with abandon. The sudden movement sent red and blue ink scrawling across the paper in severe, jagged peaks. Vanderhoven fixed her with a harsh look and set his jaw. Cold eyes worked their sobering effect.

461

Incredulous, she gasped. "Ohmygod. You think you're dealing with a lovers' triangle?"

"Do I?" A short pause. "I'll be asking you about the murder weapon and what you did with it."

"That's it?" Waiting, she gnawed the inside of her mouth.

"That's it. Except for the control questions."

He scribbled out ten questions, four of them suggesting answers he knew she'd answer truthfully, and calibrated the machine to her reactions. Then he slipped in the zinger.

"Have you ever done anything immoral?"

"Yes."

She sensed him fighting back a smile. The entire artificial environment was intentional, right down to the arrangement of the room and the psychology associated with springing loaded questions. The vertical pencil mark Vanderhoven made on the graph told her the exam was underway.

"Is your name Cézanne Martin?"

"Yes." Her ears picked up at the scratch of metal against paper. She shuddered inwardly. The polygraph rolled along. It was real. And in Vanderhoven's mind, its results were conclusive.

"Are you a captain with the Fort Worth Police Department?"

"Acting Captain. Yes."

He stopped fiddling with the dial long enough to cut his eyes in her direction and glare. "Do you own a Kompressor?"

"Yes."

He looked back at the graph and allowed his gaze to settle on the ink patterns. He seemed to have made a calculated decision to pace his questions at ten-second intervals. "Do you live on Western?"

"Yes."

"Did you know Ms. Warren?"

"Yes."

"Did you see Ms. Warren Friday night?"

"Yes."

"Are you a captain with FWPD?"

"Yes."

"Were you and Ms. Warren lovers?"

"No."

He shot her a look that suggested he didn't believe her, but her glance flickered to the needles moving steadily across the rolling paper and she satisfied herself the machine was in working order. Red, black, green, and blue ink marks registered onto the paper in steady peaks and waves.

"Did you kill Ms. Warren?"

"No."

"Did you shoot Ms. Warren with a gun?"

"No."

"Do you drive a Kompressor?"

Time on the box seemed to suspend. In a sick way, it brought a modicum of comfort in that it kept her mind off Duty. She caught herself smiling at her own joke — Sid's joke, really, when he first met the girl and made bad puns out of her name.

"Captain Martin, listen up," Vanderhoven snapped.

She cleared her throat and he penciled a mark on the graph. "I'm sorry. Repeat the question."

"Did you kill Ms. Lively?"

"No."

"Do you use illegal narcotics?"

Cézanne grinned big. "Absolutely not."

"Are you a captain at the PD?"

Jutting her chin, she answered with pride. "Yes."

"Were you and Ms. Lively lovers?"

"No."

All in all, he ran three separate tests with a small break in between each of them. He seemed to be winding down, and from where she sat, she could almost interpret the results herself. She wanted her freedom. To browbeat Vanderhoven into letting her use his handie-talkie. To contact Sid and find out about Duty. Blood coursed through her veins and she noticed the needles fluttering with each breath. She almost felt victorious as he posed the last two questions.

"Have you been truthful in this examination?"

"Yes."

"Did you shoot Ms. Lively and Ms. Warren with a rifle?"

Beyond the glass double-doors of the Criminal Courts Building, seated on a breezeway park bench downstairs, Sid Klevenhagen puffed on his pipe. Mud caked the soles of his boots and a damp spot ringed his Wranglers up to the knees.

Seeing him alone, Cézanne's breath caught in her throat.

She quickened her step and burst through the exit with an eye set on vengeance.

"What the fuck did you do to her?" Within three feet of him, she balled up her fist, reared back, and took a swing. She moved the air in front of his chin. For an old geezer, Sid had great reflexes.

"Whoa, missy. You've got a beef with the wrong person."

"Where's Duty, you lying bastard?" She clenched her fist and drew back again. Sid clamped onto her wrist and pulled her to him. Off-balance, they fell onto the bench. Cézanne came out on top.

"Really, Captain. I suggest we get a motel."

"You killed her. Devilrow left her with me. I was supposed to watch out for her. She tried to help me, and you fucked us over." She got in a couple of good licks pummeling his chest before he grabbed her

465

wrists and neutralized her. Inches from his face she hissed, "Swear to God, if it's the last thing I do, I'll —"

"Miz Zan, whatchoo doin' on top of Mista Sid?"

The sweet sound sucked the air out of her lungs and depleted her energy. With drool slobbering down to her chin, she turned to see a drenched Deuteronomy Devilrow, peeling cellophane off a tri-pack of coconut-raspberry Twinkies.

"Duty?" Tears sprang to her eyes. On rare occasions, friendship choked her up.

"Miz Zan, don'tchoo think Mista Sid's a bit old for you?"

"Now wait a damned minute, little missy —"

"Ohmygod, Duty, it's really you." She used Sid to push herself upright, stumbled over to the irritating black girl that had made her life a living hell, and flung her arms around her. "You smell like a dirty dog."

"I got baptized in the Trinity. You shoulda seen Mista Sid —" She laughed the laugh of an old lady. "I was hidin' in the weeds — hee-hee-hee — and Mista Sid was tellin' the firemen where to drag for my body. The Swift Water Rescue Team come out with the Zodiac boat, and he sent 'em far away while I sneaked to his car. Then we came here, Code-Three, to bust you outta jail. Hee-hee-hee."

Cézanne studied the sponge cake with cold scrutiny.

"Well, okay, maybe the man upstairs told Mista Sid you were on your way down, so there wasn't no need for a breakout. But we was here just the same and that oughta count."

With her mouth agape, Cézanne marveled at Deuteronomy Devilrow. Then reality set in.

"What about my car?"

Maroon eyes, ringed in white, looked like Saturn orbiting in her head. "That car's got a powerful engine. Did you know you can corner on two wheels? One day I want a car just like that. Well —" she grinned sheepishly "— not exactly like that, 'cause I wouldn't wanna be drivin' on the river bottom."

Cézanne faced facts. "I'm going to lose my job," she said dully.

"No you're not. Me and Mista Sid, we divined a plan."

Her eyes cut to Duty's partner in crime.

"Yep." Sid brushed off his sleeves and straightened his bolo tie. "Somebody stole your car. Hopped right in and drove off. Couldn't be helped."

Duty did a little tap dance while he fabricated the story.

"Ditched the car in the Trinity and got

clean away. Nobody's seen 'em since." He folded his arms across his chest, the same way she knew he'd do if anyone dared to contradict him.

"But the SO guys know the truth." She glanced at Duty, afraid for them both.

"That tow-headed sergeant you were so disrespectful to? He's in that job on account of me. And those other two fellows? I recommended one for an off-duty job. And the other boy? Well, that's your old buddy Roby Tyson's nephew. I believe if they're asked, they were in the bathroom at the time."

"What about the hole in my windshield?"

"I wouldn't know how that got there. I wasn't present. Neither were they. Problem solved."

But it wasn't and she as much as said so. "What about fingerprints?"

Sid's eyes glimmered in the moonlight. "What fingerprints?"

"The latents on the steering wheel."

"Oh, those? There aren't any."

Of course there were. Little tiny Deuteronomy Devilrow prints, left by wrapping bony fingers around the steering wheel. She continued the protest while Duty let off energy dancing an Irish jig.

"Sid, you know good and well when they pull that car out, they'll turn it over to Slash for processing. That guy could pick out a green speck on a cedar tree six miles away."

"Already taken care of." He slung his arm over her shoulder and began moving her toward the parking lot in back of the SO. "Junior's on his way over to pay his brother a visit, as we speak." He grinned big. Almost as big as Duty's big white teeth under the light of the silvery moon. "I know what you're thinking. You're thinking Slash'd never monkey with evidence. That Theodore can't make him do anything wrong, and you're right. Both of those Vaughn boys're honest to a fault. But sometimes there's a thin line between what's honest and what's right. Slash'll do what's honest. Now, Junior?" He looked up at the sky and back. "Junior's doing what's right."

She no longer hated him for conspiring with Rosen to get her job. She'd gotten Deuteronomy back safe and sound and she thought she knew, beyond a certainty, who killed the Great Dane. And when Jinx Porter got the prints back from AFIS, she'd know if she was right. What she didn't know was why, all of a sudden, Sid wanted to help.

So she asked.

He opened the back door of the low-slung unit and put Duty in the cage. Then he pinned Cézanne's shoulder to the passenger door and brushed the wild hair out of her face with his free hand.

"If you thought I was against you, you should've confronted me about my conversation with Rosen that day in Krivnek's office. Nothing to it. I told him what he wanted to hear, and it kept him off your back, didn't it?" He leaned down and gave her forehead a gentle peck. "I never gave a thought to stealing your job, missy. You'll kick Rosen's ass in a way I never could, and besides —"

With the slightest touch, his hand grazed her breast enough to make her wonder if it happened by accident; knowing, full well, it did not. He consulted the stars, as if by doing so, he would find the exact words to convey his feelings.

"— I probably shouldn't admit it, me being an old fart and you, a pretty gal. But sometime over the last ten days —" he unpinned her shoulder "— you stole my heart. There. I said it. I'm in love with ya."

Sid drove the ladies to the house on Western and stood guard at the front door while they hurried inside for a change of clothes.

"What about Butch?" Duty asked.

"What about him?"

"Can we take him with us?"

"No."

But in the end, stubborn insistence won out, and Duty put the Scottie in the back seat with her where he growled all the way to Sid's.

While Cézanne stretched fresh sheets over the guest bed, Duty sat in the corner and played with the neurotic beast.

The girl spoke directly to the carpet. "You oughta lemme have him."

"He belonged to my friend, honey. It would be like slapping a dead man in the face." She smoothed away the last of the wrinkles with the flat of her hand.

"But I love him."

Sid stepped into the doorway looking tired and haggard. "Let the girl sleep and come on downstairs."

"Can Butch get in bed?" Duty looked up expectantly.

Simultaneously, Cézanne said, "No," while Sid overruled her. Duty scampered across the room and jumped onto the mattress. She gave the dog the go-ahead, and he bounded across the room and joined her. Sid turned off the light, and pulled the door to.

They sat outside near the pool, each wrapped in a plaid wool blanket, sipping coffee from mugs. Jumbled thoughts of Marvin Krivnek tumbled through her mind. If anyone could pinpoint the time of Reno's death and the trajectory of the bullet, he could. When she had almost sorted out a plan, Sid spoke.

"Do you trust me?"

She found the question laughable. "I don't trust anybody."

"You're gonna have to."

"Why's that?"

"I got the low-down from Vanderhoven while you were on the way downstairs. Even a fool could see you got yourself mired in something big. I've called every night for the last four days and never once did you pick up."

She wasn't ready to tell him about The Wild Orchid Society. "Maybe I was in Cleburne with Bobby."

"Only you weren't. Level with me."

She gave him a hard look.

"Maybe I called Sheriff Noah, looking for you." The very thought made her sick to her stomach, especially when Sid's eyes drilled her. "Maybe a lady answered and it wasn't you. Maybe the sheriff thinks y'all called it quits."

She wanted him to stop talking. To quit saying things she didn't want to hear. But Sid wasn't through.

"You need to come clean, Captain." She tried to perfect a look of innocence, but Sid sipped his coffee, seemingly unfazed. "Maybe you're in a lot deeper than you think, so I staked out your place and followed you."

Her jaw went slack.

"Before you light into me, I knew you intended to freeze us out. That you pegged me and Junior as the enemy."

They were looking out for her and it touched her. At the same time, she wanted to pop him one.

"Be glad I trailed you. The Eastside's no place for a lady, especially once the sun goes down." His eyes drilled her.

She handed him an empty cup and got to her feet. They still had time to catch a few hours' sleep before they went in to work. "I'll tell you about it over breakfast."

But she was thinking, *Once I'm sure —* after *I talk to Jinx Porter.*

In Sid's living room, Cézanne's eyes adjusted to the dark. For a long time, she lay snuggled against Sid's couch listening to the clock tick. She'd peeked in on Duty, and it relieved her to see the girl clutching the dog. Poor animal, Duty braided his tan fur into cornrows. Amazingly, it suited him.

The rhythm of the clock's pendulum worked its hypnotic effect. Her lids grew heavy, and tension evaporated from her body. Westminster chimes sounded three strikes. The lingering scent of Sid's pipe tobacco on the furniture left her peacefully reassured. No one would harm them tonight, not with Sid around.

She had almost drifted into a fitful slumber when a floorboard creaked. Her eyes snapped open, and she sat bolt upright and made a grab for her pillow.

Duty stood in the shadows, facing the fireplace, dressed only in cotton panties and one of Sid's undershirts.

Wistfully, she addressed the dying embers. "I wouldn't accept that ride, if I was you. That's not yo' friend."

With the lethargic pace of a sleepwalker, she glided back to the stairs. Cézanne called out her name, but the girl ascended the steps without acknowledgment.

Devilrow's niece gave her quite a scare. Wide awake, with her heart pounding, Cézanne fluffed the goosedown pillow and settled back onto the sofa. Everyone in her social circle, even members of The Blue, were suspects — everyone but Duty, people under the age of ten, and herself.

She hadn't trusted Sid and Teddy.

But she trusted Smith & Wesson.

And she trusted her Chief's Special.

Under the pillowcase, she grazed the cold steel and squeezed her hand around the Pachmeyer grips. And that comforting act, alone, made closing her eyes easy.

Chapter Forty

By early dawn, a light snow blanketed the city. At HQ, the foyer turned into a carpet of transients.

Duty's eyes got wide and she pinched Sid's sleeve. "None of 'em have homes?" Her clutch tightened around Butch until he yelped.

"The chief lets 'em sleep on the floor when it ices over." Sid took a closer look at the dog. "What the hell's wrong with his fur?"

Duty shot Cézanne a squinty-eyed glare. "I fixed his hair like mine, but Miz Zan made me unbraid the cornrows. I told her his hair would look like rick-rack but she forced me. Don't laugh at him, Mista Sid. He gets embarrassed. It's not nize to make fun of the dog."

A few steps short of the elevator, she came to a standstill next to a bedroll. A raggedy man with a scraggly white beard looked up. "Stay off the railroad tracks today if you know what's good for you." She stepped aboard.

Cézanne heard her name called out behind her. When she turned to look, Aden

Whitelark was headed her way.

Aw, hell. Now what?

Sid held the elevator. "Want us to wait?"

"I'll meet you upstairs. Don't let Duty out of your sight. And Deuteronomy — hide that dog unless you plan to stumble around all day pretending you're blind."

The doors slid shut, sealing them off from view.

Her pager vibrated against the waistband of her camel hair slacks. She recognized Jinx Porter's extension on the digital readout.

Whitelark sidled up with a big smile on his face. He touched her elbow. "How's everything? I saw you smiling across the room like your ship just came in."

"I'm not saying my ship's safely docked, but it's certainly in the 'No Wake' zone."

"How's the Great Dane coming along?"

"I'll be announcing that soon."

The happy grin dropped off his face. Veins throbbed in his neck and the skin between his eyebrows pleated into a deep frown. He tightened his grip. "You know who did it?"

"I'm saving it for the press conference." She eased her arm from his grasp and took a step back. "Was there something you wanted?"

His eyes darted over the transients. "I'd like to talk to you. Let me take you to breakfast. My car's out back."

I wouldn't accept that ride, if I was you. That's not yo' friend.

Her wireless went off. Jock Featherston's excited voice vibrated in her ear.

She said, "Hold on a minute," and left Whitelark standing in a sea of stinking bodies with a simple, "Sorry, I have to go."

Rosen would arrive at nine, which gave her less than an hour before IA would be demanding an explanation for the stolen patrol unit. The Deputy Chief would be wanting her rump roast on a butler's tray.

She started for Jinx Porter's office next door. "What is it, Jock?"

"Captain, we've got trouble. No time to explain. You need to come right away. Meet me at Trinity Park. Whatever you do, don't broadcast over the radio. The last thing we need is Garlon Harrier on our asses. Just get a car and come. I'll catch you up in person."

"What's it about?"

"Benji. Hurry, Captain."

The connection went dead.

She dialed the constable and got a busy signal.

Porter's office was right around the corner, through a connecting door, not thirty steps away. But she headed for the parking lot, to Sid's patrol unit. She had no problem getting into the car. The locks to the vehicles assigned to Homicide were all keyed the same.

The traffic signals along Belknap Street were unsynchronized. To make better time, she ran Code-Two using only the emergency strobes, and rolled to a California stop at the red lights.

Two miles from the station, Trinity Park attracted an interesting cross-section of people. Vice officers hung out near restrooms, waiting for gays to hit on them. Even in the snow, joggers and bicyclists burned up the hike-and-bike trail. An odd assortment of feral cats roamed the area, accepting food left by picnickers and the homeless. They seemed, instinctively, to know the difference between regular park-goers and Animal Control. Each spring, their population doubled.

Cézanne checked her watch. She could hook up with Featherston in under five minutes. And when she returned to the office, she planned to buttonhole one of the guys to distract Duty while she told Sid everything.

Sid would know what to do about Charles Crane. And he'd know what to do about The Wild Orchid Society.

Cézanne had already left to meet Featherston when Teddy Vaughn escorted Herschel Escamilla into Homicide. Escamilla, the tailor from La Jitas, showed his reluctance to turn over a brown envelope by clutching it tightly to his chest. It contained the requisition for Cissy Kissel's knock-off D'Emanuel ball gown and a photograph of the original Emmannuel. He even brought fabric swatches and a detailed sketch that provided for exact measurements, French seams, and bound buttonholes the same size as the couture version.

Escamilla easily remembered Worth Price's daughter. For one thing, her unusually pale eyes distinguished her. For another, he never met another client who insisted on retrieving every scrap of information concerning an order. And he never had a patron warn him, "Forget you ever heard of me and lose my number," when she paid cash for the dress and gathered her receipts.

But thirty years in the business left Escamilla with a fair share of street smarts. On the office photocopier in the back of his sweat shop, he made copies of the documents Cissy Kissel insisted on recovering when she came to make payment.

Now, as Sid and Teddy ordered-in breakfast tacos and reviewed Escamilla's paperwork, they saw why their captain suspected the Great Dane's widow. The backup dress for the Trail Drivers Ball had been copied a full three months before Kissel's death.

Which shored up the captain's premeditated murder theory.

While Duty captivated detectives with her spellbinding psychic readings, Sid and Teddy agreed.

Cissy Kissel looked guilty as hell.

Near Greta Carr's desk, the facsimile machine abruptly came alive, spitting out copy at a rate of two sheets per minute. When it didn't cut off after a reasonable period, the secretary hoisted herself out of the chair and waddled over to identify the culprit responsible for tying up the machine.

A never-ending offense report originating from a police department in West Texas filled up the tray. It identified Worth Price as the complainant in an oil rig explosion. But it was one of the witness statements that sent her scurrying into Cézanne's office, breathless with excitement. The fact Sid and Teddy were preoccupied didn't daunt her in the least. Or that she had obviously interrupted their animated conversation with a Mexican man wearing a mustard-colored shirt in duppioni silk under an impeccably tailored, raw silk suit in bright turquoise. And it didn't matter that she was at the top of the captain's shit list without a shred of hope of getting off — short of an untimely death. The latest development was too big to ignore.

"Lieutenant, I think you better take a look at this."

At the Medical Examiner's office, Marvin Krivnek proofread the autopsy reports on Renée Warren and Krystal Lively. He shook his head in sympathy. Two attractive young ladies, robbed of life by a single gunshot. What a waste.

The ME had charge of the bodies; the SO had charge of the crime scene. Any minute, the deputies would call. They could share the ballistics results before he signed off on the reports.

He slid his glasses up over his thinning hair and ground his fingers into tired eyes. Through the sudden burst of blue spots, he wondered whether Captain Martin ever went to the ER.

She was right about having GHB in her system.

God help the schmuck who slipped it to her.

Uneasily, he considered the possibilities if she took the law into her own hands.

It wouldn't surprise him at all, one day, to learn he'd posted the perp's body and didn't have enough evidence for the DA to be able to prosecute the killer.

The lady was smart, even smarter than he was. She knew how to exact retribution — and God help him — he might have

481

even played a part by constantly satisfying her thirst for forensic knowledge.

If anyone could figure out how to get away with murder, the new acting Captain of Homicide could.

Having an office full of policemen staring, open-mouthed, while she turned Tarot cards, gave Duty a sense of importance she hadn't previously experienced. Sure, some of them yawned like she bored them; a few rolled their eyes like they didn't believe she had the gift. But she relayed personal details about a couple of fellows in the semi-circle, and those were the ones she zeroed in on to prove her gramma Corinthia was right — that she did, indeed, have second sight. And for the skeptics, she had a little consolation prize: a vicious little hex that would have them up at midnight, over the toilet, screaming to high Heaven with the sensation they were peeing razor blades.

She gathered the Tarot cards and waved her hand inches from Drew Ingleside.

"I'm gettin' something over here. There's a man who passed. Could be somebody's father. Is yo' daddy dead?"

"He's in a nursing home."

"No, it ain't yo' daddy, it's yo' unca. Or cousin. Did yo' unca pass?"

"Yes." Ingleside punctuated his answer with a nod.

"Yessir, that's who's with us. He a big man?"

"No."

"Good. I was just makin' sure 'cause this man, he a little fellow." She made another broad sweep of the hand, moving it over her torso in a circular motion. "He died of something in this area, didn't he?"

"Lung cancer." The old detective lounged against his chair back with his legs outstretched and his feet crossed at the ankles.

"Yessir, that's yo' unca 'cause he's showing me he had a problem breathin'. You got a sister?"

Ingleside shook his head, no. "Brother."

"Good. Because yo' unca, he say tell yo' brother he owes you money."

"My brother's dead."

"I know that. Yo' unca say yo' brother with him and he owes you money. He say you not gonna get it. You play cards with yo' brother?"

Ingleside nodded. "Pinochle."

"Did yo' unca have a lot of money? 'Cause he's showing me a gold watch."

Ingleside's head bobbed. "His retirement watch. He got it from the UAW."

Duty made her move. "Yo' unca say he wanted to give money to charity before he passed. He say the angel of death swooped down and got him in a clutch before he could make a donation. He say —" If she

483

played her Tarot cards right, she could fleece Ingleside out of some pocket money for school supplies for the children of Weeping Mary, or at least get enough to pay for a Coke and a package of raspberry Twinkies. "Yo' unca say you still have a chance to help him make that donation —"

Abruptly, she experienced a harpoon of pain behind her left eye. It came so suddenly it derailed her train of thought. The only time her eyeball smarted was if someone close to her was in trouble. She tried to shake it off — to hook the lure into Ingleside's wallet — but the electrical jolt that followed, momentarily blinded her. She massaged her temple and grabbed the nearest chair back for support. Even the dog glanced up from his spot at her feet and whined.

It played out like it always did — she couldn't alter the course once it started. First, the fog; then the human shape coming toward her. Once the haze lifted, she'd know whoever was standing there needed help — bad.

The shadow closed in. With Duty's eyes scrunched tight, the figure seemed only as far away as the tip of her nose. The mist left a cool, damp sensation around her eyes. Then it got cold as a glacier. So frigid the tiny drops turned to ice and cascaded to her mouth like glittery shards from a broken window, leaving only the taste of hot pickle juice on her tongue. Suddenly it was over.

Leaving the hair against Duty's neck wet, and her forehead, sweating.

And the razor-sharp image of Miz Zan centered between both eyes.

Evaporating.

Across town, in an old clapboard house with intricate crown molding and a wrap-around porch, Benji Wardancer sat at his mother's breakfast table, where he'd taken refuge after Sheila went off the deep end and tried to scalp him with Fiskars. Across the vintage Formica, his bride sat, rosy-cheeked and sexually sated. In a bedroom down the hall, his mother slept soundly, with her teeth in a glass of Polident and her hearing aid on a night table beside the bed. There would be hell to pay if the old lady woke up to find her troublesome daughter-in-law in the kitchen, but Benji no longer cared.

Sheila's home pregnancy test turned out positive, and she still loved him.

Whatever he had to do to make things right, he would do.

Even if it meant quitting the PD.

In the men's room of the old Criminal Courts Building, Jinx Porter emptied a pinch of snuff and bent low enough to pull in a mouthful of water from the lavatory faucet. After he swished it around and spit it out, he decided to forget about treating Cézanne Martin to breakfast. He hadn't expected her to stand him up. After all, he'd done her a favor dropping everything to run those damned fingerprints through AFIS.

But on the way back to that cubbyhole the Tarrant County Commissioners Court referred to as his office, he reconsidered —

— Even though he knew good and well she probably wouldn't fill him in on why in the world she'd need latents confirmed on someone from her own department.

Back in his office, with the fingerprint results on his blotter, he picked up the receiver and dialed.

Chapter Forty-One

Cézanne was already seat-belted in the passenger side of Jock Featherston's car when her cell phone trilled and Jinx Porter's number came up on the lighted display. Her detective double-locked the doors, pulled into the stream of traffic, and floored the accelerator like a scalded cat.

She started to caution him about beating the yellow light, but he seemed preoccupied, with his eyes fixed on some distant point in space. He hadn't even started the story about Wardancer except to say he'd gotten a lead on the Great Dane Murder.

The second ring pierced the silence.

Featherston gripped the steering wheel. "Don't answer it. I need to tell you what happened."

"Sorry, but this is one I have to take."

Featherston's jaw tightened noticeably. She suspected he found the interruption irritating but activated the talk-button anyway. "Cézanne Martin, speaking."

"Jinx Porter." Pissed. "I thought you were on your way."

"Change of plans. Couldn't be helped. Whatcha got?"

"An ID on your prints, for one thing."

Reflexively, she wet her lips, and sucked in a breath. Her heartbeat quickened, as if Porter had pulled out a starter pistol and fired it.

"Don't keep me in suspense. Let's have it."

"Not until you agree to have dinner with me."

"I already agreed."

"No," he said irritably. "I mean tonight."

If Featherston barely nicked the amber light, he flat-out busted the red one. Cézanne shot him a wicked look but he didn't so much as favor her with a sideward glance.

"Fine." But she was already thinking of a way to cancel. "What time?"

"Seven. I'll pick you up at your place."

"As you wish." She didn't appreciate Porter backing her into a corner. "So what's the verdict?"

"Are you sitting down?"

"Look, I don't have a lot of time. Give it to me straight."

"What I can't figure out, is why you asked for a rush on a set of prints that belongs to one of your colleagues."

Her heart misfired. Reflexively, she stuck a finger in her other ear to cut out the road noise. "What did you say?"

"I said AFIS got a make on your latents. They come back to your detective, Joe-Brock Featherston."

Chapter Forty-Two

Featherston peeled off Interstate 30 and took a series of side roads into the upscale residential section that bordered Westover Hills. She knew they were headed for the Price mansion, and she wondered if Featherston had glanced over and noticed her shaking. She prayed Jinx Porter could decipher her code, and that he wouldn't waste valuable time second-guessing her once she disconnected.

Tell that to Klevenhagen. Make sure the black girl knows, too.

Why's your voice so strident? Is something wrong?

Oh yes. Absolutely. Do you ever think about that night in my office?

When I saved you from taking a bullet?

Exactly. I'm having déjà vu.

And in case he didn't pick up on her distress . . .

You can do that for me again. Right now.

They were a block from Majorca Street when the contours of Featherston's face hardened. "I don't like that black chick. She practices voodoo."

"How do you know?"

"I know a lot of weird stuff."

She thought of the chicken bones Duty carried around. The way she opened Sid's guest room door a sliver and noticed them strategically laid out into a halo of crosses around the girl's pillow. And how she caught Butch gnawing on one and he snarled when she stuck her hand in far enough to flick off the light switch.

Featherston reached up and touched his sun visor. As they rounded the final corner, Price's garage door peeled back like a yawning host.

She should go for her gun, but she wasn't sure she'd make it before he karate-chopped her neck.

With Featherston distracted, she slid a hand into her pocket and mashed the cell phone's automatic redial, hoping someone would answer and listen carefully. The rest was in the hands of fate.

She heard a soft click, and knew someone picked up on the other end.

"What are we doing at Worth Price's home? Why did you bring me to Cissy Kissel's?"

"I think you know."

"You lied to me, Featherston. You said we were checking on Benji."

She made a desperate grab for the wheel. His forearm came down on her hands like a sledgehammer. She never saw him hit

490

her, but the crack of his fist hummed in her ear long after she yelped in pain. Slumped against the passenger door, she blinked back tears, and tried to keep her wits.

She cried, "Somebody help me," then realized it sounded much louder inside her head, than a mere whimper at the other end of the line.

The garage door closed behind them. She wondered if the signal was strong enough to reach the satellite. Inside the garage, a light came on. Featherston pulled an automatic from the waistband of his Dockers and pointed it. Her first impulse was to disappear; her second, to defensively shield her face with her hands.

"Oh, Jesus, Featherston, don't shoot me."

With his free hand, he reached through the steering wheel and killed the engine. "Hand over your bag. I'm not taking a bullet."

She had no choice but to comply. He could cap her from where he sat. It would ruin the inside of the car and leave him deaf for a week. But she had no doubt Worth Price's connections would step in for clean-up, or that Price's money could get Featherston fitted for an invisible hearing aid. The detective removed her Chief's Special and tucked it under his belt.

Hope sank.

She ran a hand through her hair and pulled so hard she heard the hairs rip out. With the loosened strands firmly in her grasp, she flicked her fingers until she was sure they had fallen to the floorboard. Knowing Featherston would have sense to vacuum out the car, she repeated the procedure, wedging a second handful between the seat.

Featherston rummaged through her handbag.

Desperate, she tore a fingernail down to the quick. It was the only way she knew of to draw blood without him catching on. As he tossed her badge case onto the floorboard, she wedged the piece of nail into a crevice where two upholstery seams met. If Featherston killed her, she'd give Slash plenty of evidence to work with. Finally, she instigated a coughing jag, spitting into her hand and sliming the door panel.

He tooted the horn. She noticed him casting furtive glances at a side door leading into the house, and suspected he had no key and needed someone to let them in. With no warmth from the heater, Cézanne shivered through the wait. Her adrenaline high had worn off — now her head ached.

Out of covert ways to leave traces of DNA, she plucked at the camel hair fabric with her bloody finger, intending to transfer fiber evidence. Then she picked at her shirt until she felt a loose thread. It ended up on the floorboard and she went after another.

Featherston glanced over. "Stop fidgeting."

"You're The Executioner."

He laughed, then wormed a finger underneath his collar and pulled at the gold chain around his neck. A medallion popped out and dropped onto the oxford shirt. It resembled the one Reno had given her. She almost hyperventilated.

He removed a couple of pens and a metal nail file, and tossed her purse onto the floorboard. She had no way of knowing whether she still had contact with the outside world, but she reviewed the situation, aloud, as if she did.

"No wonder the Great Dane couldn't be solved. Anytime Crane and Wehmeyer made headway, you had the opportunity to muck it up."

The side door flew open. White-faced, Cissy Kissel appeared in blue jeans and a pink cashmere sweater.

Featherston flicked the gun. "Exit the car. Slowly. Don't pull any shit." She knew by the flash in his eyes he wouldn't hesitate to kill her. He disengaged the door lock. "Did you do what I told you?" Featherston asked their hostess.

Cissy nodded and stepped aside, enough

to let them pass. She said, "Everyone's out of the house."

The detective grabbed Cézanne's arm and yanked her up on tiptoes. He pressed the gun barrel into her ribcage. "Move it."

"Where're you taking me?"

The widow Kissel kept several steps ahead. "Hurry, Jock, I don't like this."

"It's your own damned fault. If you'd paid off that cretin like I told you, Teddy Vaughn would've never found him."

Cézanne swallowed hard. "Found who?"

"Shut up, bitch."

At an intersecting hallway, Cissy Kissel took a left. She rushed ahead and grasped a gold-plated door handle. Featherston forced Cézanne inside.

She recognized her surroundings immediately. She'd stumbled upon the room, snooping, the night the wall moved and Worth Price ascended a set of stairs that led to his secret passageway.

Suddenly, everything made sense.

Why blood spatters in Dane Kissel's bedroom were inconsistent with a homicide. The Great Dane wasn't shot in his bedroom. And the police didn't know about Price's basement.

She thought of the person at the other end of the line, listening in on her murder-in-progress.

Or maybe not.

Maybe no one answered.

With strained hope, she relayed as much information as possible. "Why'd you bring me to Worth Price's study?"

"Well, Captain, it's simple. You're gonna die. And she gets to watch." His gaze shifted to Cissy.

Her pale eyes were rimmed red, and the natural flush of her cheeks had turned splotchy. "Jock, this isn't the way things were supposed to happen. You just said she'd be disciplined."

Cézanne's heart drummed. She directed her rage at Featherston. "You killed Dane Kissel, didn't you?"

"Not that you'll believe me, but the answer's no."

"I see." Facetious. "You just covered up for her."

Cissy sank to the sofa. She drew her feet up off the floor and tucked them under her legs. "I'm sorry, Atlantis, or whatever your name is. I really liked you. I thought we'd make good play partners." Her lips turned down in a pout. "You never should have tricked us. You never should have tried to deceive The Wild Orchid Society. Our group is based on trust, and you violated it."

Featherston snapped, "Get the door."

Cissy's eyes widened. She came out of her slump and sat bolt upright, then rose and crossed the room.

He wasn't referring to the door they came in through.

He was talking about the basement.

Cissy ran her hand along the molding's underside. A soft, audible click sounded. The wall swung open like a hungry mouth ready to swallow her whole. Beyond the top step, a faint light glimmered inside Price's hideaway.

Cézanne felt the jabs of unmitigated fear.

"You killed your husband in the basement, didn't you? I know about the dress. You had a copy made so the police wouldn't detect blood stains on the one you wore to the Trail Drivers Ball." Downy hairs pierced her sleeves. Her heart thudded wildly. Frantic, her eyes darted around the room for a weapon. A fireplace tool seemed to be the closest thing but the poker was too far away to outrun a speeding bullet.

"We're going to visit the pit."

"You'll have to kill me where I stand, Jock."

"I won't let you fuck up my life — or hers. We worked too hard to be together."

A letter opener on the desk glinted in the light.

"You murdered Joey Wehmeyer. You tried to make it look like an accidental death."

"Get downstairs, or I'll throw you."

The hatred in his voice sucked her breath out. Her ears pricked up. The adrenaline rush made her imagine things.

Sirens.

Cissy whimpered. "What do you mean he murdered Joey? Jock, is that true?"

"Don't listen to her. She's making it up."

Cézanne had to convince her. "Did your boyfriend have a women's clothing fetish? Jock killed Joey, and made it look like an accident."

Cissy's eyes fluttered in confusion. "That's not true. Joey committed suicide." She tuned up crying.

Although Cissy seemed in the throes of denial, intuition and desperation told Cézanne otherwise. The detective shot her a look of censure.

"Believe me, Joey didn't kill himself. I pulled the autopsy report."

"Shut up." Featherston, wild-eyed and frothing. Outside, sirens screamed. His finger whitened against the trigger. "Downstairs, now."

The glassy-eyed stares of safari trophies peered at her from high upon the walls. Laboring to breathe, she knew, without a doubt, the last thing she would see was as dead as she was about to be.

A bell chimed. Someone pounded the

door. Her heartbeat fluttered with the sound of helicopter rotor blades pulsing overhead.

"Ask Jock about the Dr. Mengele game."

"Shut up." He took two steps and planted a kick that sent Cézanne sprawling.

She hit the floor with a bounce, and immediately tasted hot copper in her mouth. Drooling blood on Price's oriental rug, she pushed herself up on one elbow. "Make him tell you about the fish hooks they found in Joey's chest."

Featherston's eyes darted to his companion.

And Cézanne lunged for the letter opener.

Chapter Forty-Three

Cézanne knew exactly where she was as soon as she cracked open her eyelids. Featherston sat cross-legged on the floor with his head cocked in the direction of the stairs and a tight grip around the frame of his .45. He seemed intent on the muffled voices coming from above — so captivated he didn't appear to notice her focusing on her surroundings. A faint glow from a night light plugged into a socket near the stairs kept the room from complete darkness. Its soft glimmer ricocheted off the railing's shellac like gold highlights on the wood's surface.

Blood hardened on her lips. Her cheek felt cold against the concrete. The left side of her face throbbed, but the fuzziness in her head quickly lifted. She remembered Featherston cold-cocking her with the gun butt and ran her tongue along the inside of her molars to make sure her teeth were still intact. Without a doubt, they'd ended up in Price's secret room.

Featherston glanced over and she closed her eyes.

Overhead, voices buzzed. Unable to

make sense of them, she lay still and listened, her quiet breaths drawing in the stale air left behind by Worth Price's pipe.

Cissy Kissel was talking.

Cézanne heard Sid Klevenhagen speak up, and the resonance from his words brought comfort. It seemed like she'd been there for hours. But when she peeked at her watch, less than fifteen minutes had elapsed.

She had no idea when the officers arrived, or whether they were on the way out. What she knew was, eventually, she'd have to choose — scream bloody murder and hope Featherston didn't blow her to smithereens, or keep quiet and have it a certainty. To buy time, she pretended to be out cold.

Until she heard rats.

The skittering claws of vermin, scratching at the wall.

Rodents, gnawing the baseboard —

Squeaking —

Not squeaking. Whimpering.

Her eyes popped open like roller shades.

Featherston caught her staring up at the door. A cell phone slid off his lap, onto the floor — her wireless. Anger pinched the corners of his mouth. He raised the gun, poised it inches from her head.

He rasped, "Utter one peep, and I'll bludgeon you into a pink stain. Understand?"

She tried to answer but her mouth wouldn't cooperate. He must have broken her jaw when he clubbed her. She fluttered her lids and rolled her eyes up into her head, pretending to slip into unconsciousness. A drop of sweat rolled out from under her armpit and splashed against her breast.

She couldn't let them leave.

She needed enough strength to create a commotion.

Voices faded noticeably. Her heart pounded so hard she could no longer hear them. If they left, she would die. Tears of pain blistered behind her eyelids. Each breath became precious. Each heartbeat, borrowed. Each second, stolen.

And then a high-pitched shriek that could only have come from Deuteronomy Devilrow cut through the silence.

"Come see, Mista Sid, Butch tracked her. That he did. Miz Zan's behind the wall."

Cissy Kissel whined, "Don't be silly."

Sid said, "It's your imagination."

"Only one thing can make Butch go crazy, and that's Miz Zan. Butch been tryin' to tear off her leg ever since she got him. I'm tellin' you, we need to get us a axe and bust down the wall." And then, "Lady, the reason you can't get that stain outta yo' rug is 'cause somebody died here and this spot's haunted."

Followed by the frenzied snarl of the hellhound that hated her so much he may've just saved her life.

On the other side of the wall, somebody let out a blood-clotting scream that timed perfectly with the splintering of mahogany paneling. Another heave-ho and an axe blade chipped out a wedge. A shaft of light cut through the dark room like a stainless steel blade and impaled itself on the opposite wall.

Featherston grabbed a fistful of Cézanne's hair and savagely jerked her to him. White spots danced before her eyes. He rammed the cold hard steel of the gun barrel beneath her injured jaw. A whimper popped out before she could squelch it. What had been a potential hostage situation became a reality.

"Tell them to back off."

She must not have moved fast enough. He ripped out a handful of hair and fisted another. This time, he pulled so hard he snapped her upright. Pain blurred her vision, but when the axe fell a third time, the wood splintered in sharp focus. It demolished a portion of paneling big enough to stick a head through.

And Duty did. Her black face filled the hole. The whites of her eyes picked up the night light's glow.

"Get back," Cézanne cried. Only she sounded like a bleating lamb.

The bluish light reappeared and she knew Duty had been yanked from harm's way.

"You down there, missy?"

Her brain commanded her to yell, "He's got a gun." But her swollen tongue betrayed her, and the spoken words turned to gibberish.

Another drop of sweat from her armpit splattered to her waist.

"Stay back, Lieutenant." Featherston, taking over now, his voice bordering on maniacal. "No reason for anyone else to get hurt."

The axe shattered the wall, knocking a huge section of wood onto the stairs. It clattered down the steps and came to rest near the night light.

Cissy Kissel screamed bloody murder.

Featherston cupped his hand to his mouth and yelled out. "I mean it, Lieutenant. Get these sons-a-bitches outta here."

Beyond Cézanne's view, police radios squawked. The dispatcher gave an order, calm and professional. "Channel closed. Channel closed. All units clear channel. Go ahead, Lieutenant."

Klevenhagen's voice filled the basement in stereo. "Start me an ambulance. And notify the ME."

Cézanne twisted enough to see Featherston's eyes change color. Her skin creeped against the cold floor. Without warning, she laughed.

"What's so funny, bitch?"

"Sid knows I'm a goner. The ambulance is for me. But the ME's for you, asshole."

Featherston came unglued. "I'll kill her. I'll blow her brains out right in front of you sons-a-bitches, you don't call off the dogs."

Oppressive silence filled the room.

Then Duty let out an unearthly scream of the damned. "No, Mista Sid. He's mine."

"Come on up, boy." Worth Price. "It's over. Come on up."

"No way. I want a car with a full tank of gas. And no Lojack or GPS, you hear me? Follow us, and I'll cap her."

Duty tuned up crying. "Please, Mista Sid, don't do it."

"Missy, can you hear me?"

Featherston locked his arm around her neck. The gun bit into her skin, and she hunched involuntarily. Black circles floated several feet in front of her.

Well hell, maybe she'd be out cold when he pulled the trigger.

"Get up. And don't pull any shit."

She figured she'd have a better chance on the floor but it turned out not to

504

matter. Events happened lightning fast. They were so inextricably linked as to make it unlikely for IA to get two stories alike.

Price poked his head into the jagged hole. "We'll hire you the best lawyer in town, son," without getting the chance to disclose a name. Featherston's bullet came within a hair of shearing off the tip of his nose.

The door to Price's secret basement swung open. Harsh light blinded her.

Duty let out a shriek capable of tilting the Earth's axis.

And a mop of tan cornrows, gnashing its teeth and spewing high-velocity froth, flew down the stairs headed straight at them.

Butch died before he ever hit the floor.

But the time it took Featherston to plug him gave Cézanne the opportunity to break his grip and roll out of harm's way. At the top of the stairs, Sid clotheslined Duty and cranked off a round. Featherston grabbed his shoulder. The gun clattered to the floor behind him and zipped beneath Price's desk.

Cézanne snaked out her arm and grabbed it like a tryout for the Stars goalie. It was the first time she noticed he carried a Jericho pistol, and the heft felt good when she pointed it at his head.

Without a preliminary, Featherston said, "I want my lawyer."

"All clear." Cézanne's jaw seemed to unlock on its own. It surprised her to hear her words make sense. "It's safe to come down. Not Duty, though. Not Duty."

She sat in the corner with her sights on Featherston, listening to boots thundering against the wooden steps. Then she realized her shoes were missing.

Sid stepped into view with his revolver stiff-armed at Featherston's chest. Cézanne rolled to her knees and used Price's chair to steady herself as she rose. Teddy Vaughn put Featherston against the wall and clamped the handcuffs on tight. The sound of ratcheting metal played like a sonata between Cézanne's ears.

She yelled, "Code-Four, Code-Four," to anyone upstairs thinking about coming down and tainting the crime scene. She glanced over at Sid, holstering his gun. "We need Slash. I want the video camera, the digital camera, and he needs to Luminol this entire room."

Sid's eyebrows arched into peaks.

"I think Dane Kissel was murdered in this room."

"Want to wait for a warrant?"

"Screw the warrant. This is a crime scene. Let the man do his job."

Duty was curled in a fetal position, rocking against one corner of Price's leather sofa, sobbing loudly into her hands, when Cézanne ascended the stairs. At the top, she squeezed her swollen feet back into her shoes. Members of the special weapons team shifted uncomfortably, impotent to soothe the distraught child.

Cézanne slid onto the sofa and wrapped her arms around Devilrow's niece. The poor girl was inconsolable.

"Is he dead?"

"I'm sorry, Duty." It seemed almost surreal to hear herself say, "But he's in Heaven now, with Roby Tyson. And I think that's maybe where he needs to be."

She didn't mention the number of times she'd considered speeding their reunion along. After all, the mutt saved her life.

Witnessing the girl in the full throes of grief, she patted her knee and made a flimsy promise. "I'll buy you another dog, Deuteronomy. Any kind you want. Just say the word when you're ready, and we'll get a new puppy."

The girl came up for air. Pushed a fist into each eye. Gave Cézanne that infamous, squinty-eyed glare. "Any kinda dog?"

"Sure, honey. Whatever you want. Maybe something small?"

Duty fixed her eyes on Cézanne's slacks. She traced her finger along the side seam. "You got blood on your shirt. Is it Butch's?"

"It's mine."

"Oh. 'Cause if it was Butch's I'd have to get me some scissors and cut it out."

Cézanne wanted to ask what the hell for, but Teddy led Featherston past with his hands cuffed behind him, and activity came to a standstill. Duty hunched her shoulders. Her fingers gnarled into grotesque shapes. She hissed at him, then let out a screech to rival tires screaming against the asphalt. Featherston mouthed, *Fuck you,* and kept walking.

But Duty had some parting advice. "I wouldn't get in a cell with that hairy dude, if I was you."

This time, Featherston said, "Screw you," loud enough for everyone in the room to hear. Teddy popped him in the back of the head, and warned him to shut up or start spitting out Chicklets.

Duty picked up Price's cowhide pillow and scrunched it to her abdomen. For a long time, she hugged it, staring at the floor. "I get to pick it?"

"Sure. Whatever you like."

"I can pick him out, and you pay for him, but he still be mine?" she said, as if somehow restating the offer would make it more binding.

"Sure."

"Uh-huh." As if pronouncing sentence. "So, if I was to find a dog I liked, and said, 'That's him, that's my dog,' you'd

pull out yo' credit card and buy him?"
Duty sniffled, then pulled her sleeve over
her fist and ran the cuff underneath her
nose.

"Yes. Whenever you're ready."

"If I'm ready today?"

Definitely not part of the plan.

The girl wasn't supposed to accept. She
was supposed to fully experience her grief.
And she needed to get permission.
Cézanne counted on Thessalonia Devilrow
to refuse her daughter a pet. Hell, the
woman couldn't even provide for her kids,
much less a dog. But Duty's fathomless
maroon eyes demanded nothing less.

"We'll be at the station all night, honey.
Even you. They'll want to take our statements."

With some urgency, Duty said, "After
that? We can get a new dog after that?"

The girl drove a hard bargain.

"Maybe you should get on the Internet
and look at different breeds — be sure
you're getting a puppy that's right for you."

But Duty was staunch in her resolve. "I
already know what to get." Her smile lit up
the room.

Cézanne held her breath.

"I'm gonna get me a black one. With a
tail like a whip. And I already got him a
name. He's gonna be Enigma. And he's
gonna be a Great Dane."

Chapter Forty-Four

Upon returning to work the following morning, Cézanne's first priority was to make sure Teddy took Herschel Escamilla in to testify before the Grand Jury. Since the PD had a case to cement against Cissy Kissel, Cézanne opted for a professional image and dressed in a like-new, lilac Chanel suit she found at the Junior League thrift shop — in case the Grand Jury wanted to hear from her.

Today, nothing would stand in the way of justice.

In the meantime, Jock Featherston had a court date with the magistrate at nine o'clock. She snatched her cashmere coat off the wall hook and grabbed her purse. The extra weight in the bag snapped her wrist and sent a jolt up her arm. She forgot she was carrying her Glock. Slash wasn't through fingerprinting the Chief's Special. He thought subjecting it to cyanoacrylate fumes overnight would raise latents belonging to Featherston.

She checked her watch, then called over to the Justice Center and found deputies had already arrived with the prisoners. The bailiff described standing room only. The press would be there, of course; especially Garlon Harrier, muscling his way in to claim a seat. But the judge made arrangements for her to sit at the prosecutor's table and she intended to be there, looking Jock Featherston dead in the eye when he entered his plea.

Activity faltered the moment Lucky McElwell strolled into the courtroom. Wearing a dark gray, worsted wool suit, with a charcoal beret cocked jauntily on his head, he pretended he didn't see her when he pitched his overcoat across one of the chairs at defense counsel's table, several feet away. He placed his briefcase on the chair next to him, opened it as if he had the formula to convert dirt into gold, and removed a squeeze bottle of nose drops. Three good sniffs, and he pitched it back inside, and snapped the locks shut.

They waited without speaking as the judge called prisoners up to the bench in groups of three. Then it was Jock Featherston's turn. He looked past her, refusing to meet her glare.

The judge regarded Featherston through keen eyes.

Did he understand he'd been charged with attempted murder?

He did.

Did he have enough money to retain his own counsel?

About the time Featherston pointed to Lucky McElwell, the spit hit the fan.

Cézanne had been so intent watching the detective she never noticed Sid enter the courtroom with the department's K-9 handler and his new drug dog, Snowball. Several members of the press, seated on the outside pews, involuntarily flinched at the sight of the passing German Shepherd. Unexpectedly, the animal went airborne —

— leaped over the bar —

— and alerted on Lucky McElwell's briefcase.

All eyes moved in a collective shift. Sid and the K-9 handler took opposite saloon doors and flanked the attorney.

The judge halted the proceedings. His eyes hardened. "What's the meaning of this, Lieutenant?"

"Well, Judge, we seem to have a problem."

Lucky wasn't about to open his briefcase, but that didn't stop four deputy sheriffs from wrestling him to the floor, and wrenching it from his grasp.

A furry mass that looked like a Frisbee with hair flew through the air. McElwell's toupee landed on the floor next to the court reporter. Snowball barked until his handler pulled a rubber ball out of his pocket and let him gum it.

The judge gaveled down the ruckus.

"Wouldja look at this?" Sid plucked a small cellophane packet from between the pages of a current copy of the Texas Penal Code, and waved it for all to see.

The sheriff's men jerked the best criminal lawyer in Cowtown up on his wingtips, and hauled him out, staining his underwear.

Jock Featherston asked the judge for a week's extension to hire a new counsel.

Worth Price left the courtroom with the assistance of an aluminum walker, shaking his head and muttering something unintelligible. Cameramen — who had started the record buttons on their videocams the moment Snowball entered — caught it all on tape and processed it in time for the six o'clock news. In an exclusive with Sid, Garlon Harrier learned the PD had gotten a break in the Great Dane Murder.

But the biggest shock of all came when Cézanne returned to find Cissy Kissel waiting in her office, looking soft and benign in an ice pink angora sweater dress, hiked seductively up her thigh.

"Nice shade of purple," Cissy said. "Matches your jaw."

"Come to turn yourself in?"

"I didn't kill my husband." Something in her pack-and-a-half voice didn't ring true.

Cézanne hooked her coat over the peg and closed the door. She moved past her desk and slid into the chair. "Why should I believe you?"

"Because I had no reason to. I loved him."

"You were having an affair with Preston Josef Wehmeyer."

"Joey was my friend. He helped me after Dane killed himself."

"Don't think so. People saw you together before you killed your husband."

Cissy crossed her legs without pulling down her hemline. It rode up over a tiny mauve orchid tattooed on her hip, and Cézanne could see she'd neglected to wear panties.

"Your husband had a hefty life insurance policy."

"I didn't get one red cent."

"Maybe you didn't find out he changed beneficiaries until after you whacked him."

Cissy's glacial exterior never cracked. A wily smile played across her lips. "You liked it, Atlantis."

"This interview's over."

"We want you to come back to us."

Cézanne rose quickly, opened the door wide, and flattened herself against it — her way of letting Cissy Kissel know she'd worn out her welcome. "We'll make a case against you."

"You liked it." The widow got to her feet and traced her tongue over her lips until they glistened. "If you don't believe me, watch the video again."

"You're gonna fry. Jock'll cut a deal with prosecutors. You're as good as on Death Row."

"Circumstantial evidence, that's all you have."

"I don't think so. When we exhume Mr. Kissel's body and the ME takes a second look, we'll have all we need."

The woman went white, except for pinched lips that seemed to turn ghoulishly gray. It made her feel sadistically superior, right up until the Great Dane's widow grazed her breast on the way out.

"Like I said, Atlantis, you liked it. If you're still in denial, come to our next meeting. We've planned a special program — we're previewing your second video."

Cézanne's stomach fluttered.

In a pronouncement filled with sensuality, Cissy drove home her point. "You're one of us now. You may not want to be, but you are." Her eyes glinted. "In order to fully appreciate power, you must be willing to relinquish it." She lowered her voice to a whisper. "Now that you've experienced The Wild Orchid Society, you'll never be satisfied with the plain existence you knew before."

"All part of the job."

But it didn't take Cissy long to piece it

together. "You'll be back. You like power, Atlantis, but power corrupts. When properly controlled, power is beautiful. Sensual. Invigorating. You need us."

Cézanne took a cue from — of all people — Jock Featherston.

"Fuck you."

Price's daughter didn't let go easily. "We're your family. We're the only ones who truly understand you. You will be back."

The grande dame of The Wild Orchid Society gave a little finger wave and breezed out of the room.

I'll be back, all right. With a warrant for your arrest.

Sid returned looking like the dog that ate the cat's food. Years of tension vanished from his face, and he walked with the narrow-hipped swagger of a young man.

"C'mon," he said, pinching her sleeve and smelling of peanut butter crackers. "We've got a surprise."

By "we" he meant to include Duty. He escorted her to the parking lot where Deuteronomy Devilrow sat in the front seat of his cruiser. Not until Cézanne reached the passenger side did she see into the vehicle.

A gangly, spotted puppy, with ears in cone-shaped bandages, sprawled his lanky

516

frame, spindly legs, and huge front paws across Duty's lap and most of the front seat. Although he appeared comatose, Cézanne knew better. She was treated to a close encounter of Armageddon with fur.

Duty stared up in rapt adoration.

"Mista Sid took me to get him, Miz Zan. He said you was busy, and all, butchoo gave him the money. I found a black one, but this'un took a shine to me. I'm still callin' him 'Nigma, just like I planned. Do you like him, Miz Zan?"

"May I see you a moment?" she said sweetly, and pinched Sid's arm. She steered him out of earshot. "What have you done? That animal's at least sixty pounds —"

"I'm thinking closer to a hundred and fifty pounds if you're converting to pounds sterling."

"You spent three hundred dollars on a damned dog? Jesus, Sid, I expected you to get her a pound puppy, not a show dog."

"I'll go in half," he said. "It's the least I can do since I'm the one who tossed Butch down the stairs."

"He's huge."

"It's what she wanted."

"He's an end table with feet."

"Serve coffee on him."

Cézanne's protests lost effect. She had a housemate she didn't want, with a dog she wanted even less. And, although she had plenty to complain about, she had more to be thankful for.

"Well, do you, Miz Zan? Do you like whatchoo bought me?"

"Very much." Cézanne reached in and tousled the girl's cornrows. "Only, I think you should name him Revelation."

"Revelation Devilrow?" Deuteronomy scrunched her nose. "Why, Miz Zan, that's just about the stupidest name I ever heard."

Chapter Forty-Five

With Lucky McElwell scratched from the lineup, a funny thing happened. Jock Featherston sent a kite — jail vernacular for a printed request — up to the cell block supervisor, asking for a word with his captain. If his request was designed to sound encouraging, it had the opposite effect. Cézanne strode purposefully down the sidewalk, muttering curses to herself as she walked. Deep down, she wanted him to confess to the murders of Dane Kissel and Preston Josef Wehmeyer. To have it over with and in the bag.

Intuition and desperation told her otherwise.

The SO locked Featherston up on I-Block. As in isolation. In I-Block, Featherston only had permission to wander around in a common foyer for one hour a day while the rest of the pod remained in individual cells. During that time, he could watch TV, peer into the tiny windows of his block mates, find the Messiah, or do cartwheels.

When Cézanne arrived, Featherston was doing military pushups in front of the TV. The commander put her in an attorney booth with a two-way telephone receiver on either side of a Plexiglas divider. She expected the space to be charged with hostility. But when the door from I-Block swung open and her detective stepped inside wearing jail khakis and flip-flops, he made a gun sign with his hand, stuck the make-believe barrel in his mouth, and pulled the trigger.

Too bad it didn't go off for real.

Cézanne picked up the receiver. Featherston mashed down a spring-loaded metal seat and gingerly eased onto the tiny circle. Whoever designed the seats didn't craft them for comfort — it was, after all, a penal institution — but Featherston seemed to have trouble sitting.

He said, "That black chick's scary as shit."

She locked him in her gaze, whipped out her Miranda card, and started reading the small type.

Halfway through, Featherston interrupted. "You wired?"

She ignored him and finished reading him his rights. Only after he acknowledged them, did she say, "You asked to see me, not the other way around."

"Let's deal."

The words made her heart race. But it wasn't her call. Only the DA could cut the kind of deal Featherston wanted.

"Maybe I don't need to deal. Maybe I've got everything I need, with locks on it."

In a voice laced with impatience, Featherston turned aggressive. "You don't have what you need. But I do. Tell the prosecutor to drop the charge to simple assault, give me credit for time served, and I'll give you Dane Kissel's killer."

"Why would I do that? I know who killed Dane Kissel. And I know who killed Preston Josef Wehmeyer." Reflexively, she caressed her jaw.

He stood abruptly and the metal seat banged against the wall like a sprung trap. "You'll never prove it without my help."

She'd heard enough and started to hang up the phone, but Featherston motioned her to wait.

"I'll sweeten the pot," he said. "Two-for-one."

"Talk."

Eyes flashed like onyx. "I'll give you Quinten Carrol's shooter."

"Go on."

"Manchester LeDemien Freedman. He's in the cell next to mine. Give me a wire and immunity from prosecution, and I'll get you a confession."

She thought of the time they'd spent in Price's basement. The way he pulled the Jericho from his waistband and threatened to pulverize her. And the videotape —

when he told Cissy to remove his hood. Instinctively, she touched the scab on her neck. She didn't need to watch the second videotape to know what else he'd done to degrade her.

"Go fish. I'll get 'em myself." She returned the receiver to its hook.

Chapter Forty-Six

The sun started out as a pale gold thumbprint on the horizon, but by noon, a steady rain sluiced down the windows at HQ, and the sky darkened so fast the streetlights blinked on.

By late afternoon, Featherston was singing like a diva. Another kite went up for a word with his former captain. This time, she took a prosecutor along.

The DA's latest golden boy didn't look much older than thirty. Rumor had it the assistant DA played one season for the Cincinnati Bengals before throwing in the towel to do God's work. Brown eyes twinkled behind smooth, olive skin, and he dressed to the nines in a suit that slimmed his stocky frame. They stood across from Featherston, wedged in the cramped space with Cézanne holding the phone away from her ear so the lawyer could hear.

The State's attorney scribbled furiously while Featherston talked.

"After the oil derrick blew, Price fell in with the Mexicans. He was in a financial bind, so he did a little drug running. You'll never make a case on that — the statute of limitations has run — but you can make one on him for money laundering."

"Money laundering?"

"What do you think those ledgers are? You get a search warrant for those ledgers, you'll see what I mean. He runs millions through those accounts. There's everything you need for an indictment."

Cézanne pressed the mouthpiece to her chest. "I don't give a hoot about busting Price for money laundering. I want to solve a homicide."

The new lawyer said, "I'll take whatever I can get."

Cézanne's eyes narrowed. "You're not from around here, are you?"

"I'm from Ohio."

"Well, I'm home grown. And I'm telling you — even if you get an indictment on Worth Price for money laundering, you'll never get a conviction."

Featherston was getting antsy and it showed in the stress lining his face.

Cézanne put the phone to her ear. "Deliver Cissy Kissel to me and we'll deal."

The prosecutor agreed to construct the immunity agreement.

Cézanne went back to her office feeling like a million in singles.

By six o'clock, she looked forward to crossing the threshold and whiffing Duty's bayou cuisine. With Featherston in lock-down, she no longer worried about leaving the girl home alone. But the moment she rounded the last block, her stomach went hollow. Gargoyle figurines on the wrought iron gate loomed in the shadows.

Something was out of whack.

She wheeled the Kompressor into a dark driveway and let herself inside an even darker house. Tossing her purse onto the sofa, she called out for Duty. No answer.

She flipped the light switch. Still dark.

Tried the lamp. Nothing.

Okay, so the breakers flipped. Electrical surges were common to old neighborhoods; over the years, hers had its fair share of transformers blow. But that didn't keep her from making out muddy dog tracks spaced across the hardwoods. They ended at Duty's closed door.

"Duty? What did I tell you about letting that dog —"

She flung open the door. A scream died in her throat.

In the shadows, an eighteenth century bookcase had been converted into an altar. As she moved closer, she saw where black candles imbedded with dog hair had long burned down into waxy circles. What looked like a giant spider web draped the area and she knew without benefit of light that the kitchen curtains had returned. On the top shelf, Tarot cards and chicken bones were laid out in bizarre, geometric shapes. Twigs and leaves surrounded the missing Baccarat owl, and a honeymoon snapshot from her soured marriage lay in the midst. Chalk marks circled a Neiman Marcus catalogue, creased open to a page with his-and-hers kangaroos. A dish of undeterminable contents fouled the air.

She backed into the unlit hall with the skin-creeping feeling she wasn't alone.

Behind her, came the unmistakable ratchet of a pump shotgun.

Good God.

Worth Price stepped out of the shadows, his face creased into a broad smile.

She did a panicky review of her options, none of them good. "Where's Duty?"

Not, *What the hell are you doing in my house?* She was about to become an unwilling participant in the organ donor program, and here she was, quizzing him about Duty.

Price said, "Don't know what you mean."

"The girl who cooks for me." No, that wasn't it. "The black girl." Wrong, again. "My friend."

Price shrugged. "You live alone."

Frantic, her eyes darted to her purse. She took a backward step.

Price pulled the trigger. A chunk of baseboard exploded inches from her toe.

Our Father who art in Heaven . . .

Blood thundered in her ears. "What do you want?"

"You snooped."

"Okay, we're even. You can go now."

"I think we should talk." He jerked the Mossberg in the direction of the sofa. "Nice and easy. I'd hate to cut you in half."

They were definitely thinking alike.

She eased through the shadows with Price behind her. If she went for her gun, she'd be nothing but a red smear on the wall. Kind of like Dane Kissel. She swallowed the lump in her throat. Stopped short of asking about Duty again. If the girl heard him coming in, she might have hidden. Bringing it to his attention might start him looking for her.

Imagination shifted into high gear.

She pictured Duty in a closet, her lifeless body in a crumpled heap, and the sixty-pound puppy with her. Thoughts of escape geysered through her mind. Unless Price took the unguided tour, he didn't know the layout of the house. If she made a break for the dining room — through the kitchen — into the back bedroom . . .

If she could get to the Colt Cobra wedged between the mattress and box springs —

Price nudged the barrel into her back

and she willingly slumped onto the sofa. He seated himself in a leather wingback, not ten feet away, and slid a cigar from his pocket. As he bit off the tip and spit it into the fireplace, she caught him evaluating her with the offhand intensity of a tiger. At the hiss of a match, his cigar lit up red.

"Where's Duty?"

"Young lady, I was in WWII. Kill or be killed. I've done many a thing I'm not proud of, but you do what you have to." He took a long draw on the cigar. The end glowed neon orange against the dark. "I cared a great deal about my son-in-law. But he had suspicions about my girl — where she was, who she was with. He invited a fellow home once — Joey Wehmeyer — actually paid the boy to spy on her. Then accused her of stepping out."

Smoke hung in Price's corner like a gauzy drape.

"My son-in-law threatened to ruin my business. I couldn't let that happen. You're smart. And I'm a man with clout."

Go on.

"So I'm thinking on the way over, maybe there's something this gal wants. Maybe she wants to be a big shot attorney. I know Lonstein would give you work down at his firm. Only now that McElwell's in trouble, you might not want to be affiliated with them. Then I thought, Maybe she's looking for one of those Anna Nicole Smith deals."

Cézanne felt her face stiffen.

"Or maybe she'd like her house paid off."

He was getting precariously close to a bribe.

"Then I got to thinking, No, this gal can make her own way. She's ambitious. Then it hit me — how much you're like my ex-son-in-law. He wanted to be Governor, did you know that?"

Cézanne's heart bounced in her chest.

"Could've been, too." Price lifted his leg enough to stub out his cigar against the sole of his boot. "Should've left well enough alone. We had the money to make him whatever he wanted."

Price leveled the shotgun. "Let's get down to business. What'll it take to get you off Cissy's back?"

He wouldn't kill her in her own house. He'd hire it done two, three months down the road. One day she'd pick up a tail, maybe notice a car pull up even with her at the mall. A couple of guys would jump out, bludgeon her into the blacktop, and roll her bloody corpse into a ditch. Happened all the time.

But Price wouldn't be there. He'd be down in his basement, doctoring his ledgers. Laundering more than his shorts. As he'd done the night his daughter went to the Trail Drivers Ball, when his son-in-law opted out and stayed home.

"You killed Dane Kissel. Your daughter was involved, too." Fear clawed at her stomach. "I know about the money laundering. And the fire in West Texas, and about you losing your capital. What I don't understand is, why?"

"It wasn't enough my ex-son-in-law wanted to leave her. He vowed to bring me down, too. Imagine — a criminal defense attorney — wanting to turn me in for a crime."

Price wouldn't let his daughter take the rap for him, of that she was sure. The question was — an old man like that — would he live to see a trial? Even with Lucky McElwell sidelined, he could stall it a couple of years. Would the townspeople convict one of their philanthropists? Probably not.

She said, "What do you want from me?"

"Let Cissy go."

"Not without your confession."

"Can't we do it another way?"

She narrowed her eyes. "What'd you have in mind?"

"Ever want to be Governor of the Great State of Texas?"

Chapter Forty-Seven

Worth Price never saw the inside of a jail cell.

As soon as he signed his name with a flourish, he tapped out a number on his cell phone and lines started jingling all over town. At the Tarrant County Jail, Abe Lonstein showed up in a white limo and posted bond on a walk-through. By eight-thirty that evening, Price was dining at the Petroleum Club.

At HQ, Cézanne gazed out her window. The City Council met the night before, and for now, the chief had locks on his job. He'd even called a press conference for eight o'clock that morning and asked her to be there. Declining hadn't worked in her favor.

Sorry, I'm trying to cut back.

Are you refusing a direct order, Captain?

You mean it isn't an invitation? In that case . . .

She'd wanted to tell him she'd sooner climb on top of her zipper-roof and swan-dive onto the spikes of her wrought iron gate than attend another press conference. But she did the next best thing — ordered

Sid and Teddy to accompany her to share in the glory.

And Duty?

Sadness gnawed at the pit of her stomach. Duty should've been there, too. They couldn't have done it without her. But after Price gave his confession and trundled out to the car with a couple of uniformed escorts, Cézanne found a note written in childish scrawl.

Miz Zan,
 Leviticus Devilrow came here. Me and Enigma went home to Weeping Mary.
  Your friend, Deuteronomy Devilrow.
P.S. I love you.

A few minutes after seven, Sid strolled into her office. She did a double-take. He looked downright handsome in his black suit, Pierre Cardin tie, and lizardskin boots. Like a Texas Ranger with that hat dipped low over his forehead and the Klevenhagen squint peering out.

"Howya doin', missy? Where's your side-kick?"

"Duty left. I had to condemn her room. Thank goodness I have my house back." It took all the resolve she had to keep from looking like she'd spent the morning peeling onions.

"Got plans for Christmas?" he said.

"Not really. Maybe I'll go see Bobby."

"Or take a trip to Crying Sally?"

"Weeping Mary."

It wasn't a bad idea. Tit-for-tat. Maybe just show up at the Devilrow compound swaddled in a blanket, demanding a place to stay. Take over the kitchen, and drive them all crazy making matzo balls. But she knew it wouldn't happen. Maternal instincts were suspect in the Martin women, and besides, she'd almost gotten Duty killed. Plus the girl had a new friend.

No, some things were better left alone.

Cissy Kissel, for instance. Worth Price might've confessed, but his daughter was guilty as sin. Given enough time, Cézanne intended to prove it.

Sid seemed to sense her melancholy and walked around the desk.

He slung an arm over her shoulder, pulled her in close, and chucked her chin. "You're a discus in a tankful of guppies. You don't school well with others."

"Thanks for the reminder."

The phone chirped and Sid picked it up. He mouthed "Rosen" and told the Deputy Chief they'd be down in fifteen. Cézanne rolled her eyes. This time, if Garlon Harrier was spoiling for a fight, she'd set him straight. When he asked how long it would take to solve the Trailer Park Murders, she'd refer him to the SO since they had jurisdiction.

But she'd tell Harrier she had a lead.

Because after the press conference, she planned to arrest Reno's killer.

The Wild Orchid Society had produced that phony videotape and put it on the Internet to cow her into submission and hush her up. They'd planned to lord it over her head, and if that didn't work, she had every reason to believe they would've used it to take the heat off Cissy Kissel by implicating her in the murder of Reno and Krystal.

Only one problem — they couldn't have reproduced those uncanny surroundings without help.

Poor Krystal. She had nothing to do with the Lady Godiva Murder. But her killer didn't know that. Behind the sheers, he only saw the silhouettes of two women he blamed for forever changing his life: Reno, a participant in the decadent lifestyle that snuffed out the light of his life, and herself — in what turned out to be a case of mistaken identity — for exposing the lurid details.

She'd take Sid along as backup. Teddy could impound Captain Charles Crane's truck. Slash should find plenty of dirt and brush on the undercarriage of the vehicle to be able to place Crane at the scene. No doubt that deer rifle would match ballistics.

The phone lit up and she suspected it

was Rosen again. Once she recognized Jinx Porter's soft Southern drawl at the other end of the line — asking what time to pick her up for dinner — she caught herself smiling. Still unconvinced as to whether Porter might be her guardian angel, or the Devil in a cowboy hat, she found herself chomping at the bit and raring to go. The constable didn't know it yet, but the chief had a medal with Porter's name on it and she couldn't wait to be the one to tell him. Having Jinx Porter save her bacon twice in a month might be the closest she'd ever come to getting Roby Tyson back.

Teddy stuck his head in the door and grinned big. He'd been aching to make sergeant and the Great Dane Murder was the boost he needed to get the chief to pull his name from the list. While she had the chief's ear, she might even convince him to pin a set of captain's bars on Sid's collar.

As for her? She wanted what she'd always wanted.

True, Dane Kissel's cold case still had a couple of loose ends.

Nobody knew exactly where to find Crane. They couldn't touch Cissy Kissel without Featherston's cooperation, and Featherston wasn't about to play ball now that the Cold Case Squad had reopened Joey Wehmeyer's suicide as a murder investigation.

Cézanne took a deep breath and willed her future.

Time to be a lawyer.

Another button on the phone's keypad brightened and stayed lit. Momentarily, Greta slunk in with a pained expression and bad news.

An early morning homicide on the Southside of Fort Worth put the media into a frenzy. Garlon Harrier, calling as a professional courtesy, got the word from a uniform at the crime scene and demanded an official statement from the Captain.

The Seminary Student Stalker had just turned into the Seminary Student Slayer.

Epilogue

A thin layer of frost covered the ground at the bungalow on Western. Christmas Eve morning found Cézanne in flannel jammies and robe, sipping spiced tea and reading the society page by the fireplace. A rustle outside the front door telegraphed a visitor. She checked the peephole and saw a blue-green eye staring back at her.

Bobby Noah.

He moved away from the glass and grinned, holding up a robust little cedar tree by the throat.

She cinched her robe tight and opened the door.

"Hello, darlin'." He pecked her cheek, strolled on in, and glanced around. "Where do you want it?" When he locked her in a lusty gaze, she wasn't at all certain he meant the tree.

"I hate holidays."

"You're just saying that because you never got what you asked for." The twinkle in his eyes told her this might be the year.

He handed her a plastic sack full of chili pepper lights and frosted glass balls in primary colors.

"What's that?" She stared at the box in his other hand.

"A present for the girl. You said she always borrowed your scarves. And chew bones for the new dog."

"Duty's gone."

"I expect you'll see her soon enough."

"God, I hope not." But it was a lie. Duty had gotten under her skin. "Know what I found when I took back the guest room?"

"Krivnek provided a few details. I figured you'd fill in the blanks."

She told him about Duty's shrine, complete with the Neiman Marcus catalog. The story left Bobby mildly amused.

Cézanne shuffled to the fireplace. She removed a poker and jabbed at the logs. A shower of orange glitter rained down on the pile. "Guess you know I took a leave of absence from the PD."

"I heard. Did they ever find Crane?"

"Still missing. His wife thinks he's dead. I'm not so sure."

She didn't own a tree stand, but Bobby came prepared. He was outside nailing a couple of one-by-fours into an X, when a delivery van pulled up to the curb.

The driver hopped out, pimply-faced and shivering. "Where ya want 'em?"

Cézanne stepped onto the porch. "Want what?"

"The crates."

She looked over expectantly, but Bobby shook his head and gave her a look that said, *Oh, yeah, well, good luck.* Her eyes narrowed. "How many crates?"

"Two."

The Wild Orchid Society struck terror in her heart. "Don't take another step. Who sent them?"

The delivery boy scoured his paperwork. "Neiman Marcus."

Bobby cocked his head, impressed.

"No, I mean is there a person's name?"

"Deuteronomy Devilrow."

Good God.

"What is it?"

"Hey, lady, I just drive the truck." He shoved an automated box with a pen at her. "Sign on the line."

She glanced over at Bobby. "Where would Duty get money to buy from Neiman's?" But she knew. Her jaw muscles tightened.

The driver started back to the truck. It perturbed her to see him fetching a dolly. But it was the airholes bored into the plywood boxes that flat-out petrified her. Whatever was inside woke up and wanted out.

Bobby stopped wiring the tree to the boards. He stiffened to his full height. "Get a hammer."

"You're right. We may have to kill it."

He narrowed his eyes. "To pry the lids open."

Good thinking. She dashed into the house as the truck pulled away in a cone of blue exhaust. When she returned, Bobby was removing a rope from the bed of his pickup.

"Oh, Jesus. What the hell is it?"

"Not it. Them."

She held the claw-hammer aloft.

Bobby gave her one of his *you're not gonna like this* looks and headed for the crates. Whatever it was thrashed violently.

"This makes my little ring look downright puny."

"What?" Her head swam. Chill bumps prickled her arms like tiny icicles. An image of herself at five years, singing "Here Comes the Bride," with a towel draped over her head and a fistful of Mrs. Olsen's geraniums, complete with dirt clumps, came back in Technicolor.

Suddenly, it didn't matter that he'd freed a pair of his-and-hers wallabies. Or that the marsupials were springing across her yard, headed for Mrs. Pietrowski's poinsettias. Or that Deuteronomy Devilrow had a photographic memory for credit card numbers.

Bobby wanted to marry her.

Distant strains of "Deck the Halls" grew louder. Down the block, Leviticus Devilrow's old truck chugged toward the house with Duty and Enigma posed on the hood, and three generations of Devilrows caroling from the pickup bed. The Great Dane had grown as leggy as a giraffe, but Duty, it seemed, was filling out nicely.

She slid down the front fender and broke into a sprint long before Devilrow's truck stalled out and coasted to a stop.

Duty flung out her arms. "Miz Zan, you a spectacle — still dressed in bedclothes in broad daylight."

Cézanne returned the embrace.

Devilrow stuck his big hand out the window. "I come for the other half o' my money."

Duty hopped from one foot to the other, grinning like she swallowed a baby grand piano and the ivories lodged in her throat. She did a couple of cartwheels, then used her arms to spell out words like a back-up singer for the Village People.

"It's Christmas Eve, Devilrow. I don't have your money. I'll write a check —"

"Wouldn't do no good to get a check." He slung a leg out the driver's door. "Devilrows don't trust banks."

She suspected it was the other way around.

Huge feet hit the ground. Dust settled over Devilrow's tattered shoes. He shoved his hands deep into his coveralls. Maroon eyes narrowed into a squint. "Of course, if

we was to strike a deal, I might could excuse the debt."

With her fists planted on her hips, she
assessed him through shrewd eyes. "What
kind of deal?"

Duty seemed to be auditioning for a position as a Mavericks cheerleader. Across
the lawn, Enigma honed his herding skills,
while Bobby lassoed one of the wallabies.

"If you maybe was to watch Duty 'til
summer . . ."

About the Author

LAURIE MOORE was born and reared in the Great State of Texas, where she developed a flair for foreign languages. She's traveled to forty-nine U.S. states, most of the Canadian provinces, Mexico, and Spain.

She majored in Spanish at the University of Texas at Austin, where she received her Bachelor of Arts degree in Spanish, English, and Elementary and Secondary Education. Instead of using her teaching certificate, she entered into a career in law enforcement in 1979. After six years of patrol work and a year of criminal investigation, she made Sergeant, and worked as a District Attorney investigator for several DAs in the Central Texas area over the next seven years.

In 1992, she moved to Fort Worth and graduated from Texas Wesleyan University School of Law, where she received her Juris Doctor in 1995. She is currently in private practice in "Cowtown," and has a daughter at Rhodes, a destructive Siamese cat, and a sneaky Welsh Corgi. She is still a licensed, commissioned peace officer.

Laurie has been a member of the DFW Writers Workshop since 1992, and currently serves on the Board of Directors. She is the author of *Constable's Run*, *Constable's Apprehension*, and *The Lady Godiva Murder*. Writing is her passion.

Contact Laurie through her website at www.LaurieMooreMysteries.com.